Peony in Love

Peony in Love

Lisa See

BLOOMSBURY

First published in Great Britain 2007
This paperback edition published 2008

Peony in Love is a work of historical fiction. Apart from some actual people, events, and locales that figure in the narrative, all names, characters, places, and incidents are the products of the author's imagination or are used fictitiously.

Indiana University Press: Excerpts from *The Peony Pavilion (Mudan ting)* by Tang Xianzu, translated by Cyril Birch (Bloomington: Indiana University Press, 1980), copyright © 1980 by Cyril Birch. Reprinted by permission of Indiana University Press.

Stanford University Press: Excerpts from *Teachers of the Inner Chambers: Women and Culture in Seventeenth-Century China* by Dorothy Ko, copyright © 1994 by the Board of Trustees of the Leland Stanford Jr. University. All rights reserved. Reprinted by permission of Stanford University Press, www.sup.org.

Conversation and reading group guide reprinted courtesy of the Random House Readers Circle, The Random House Publishing Group, www.thereaderscircle.com

Book design by Victoria Wong

Bloomsbury Publishing Plc, 36 Soho Square, London W1D 3QY
www.bloomsbury.com

Bloomsbury Publishing, London, New York and Berlin

A CIP catalogue record for this book is available from the British Library

ISBN 9780747592730
10 9 8 7 6 5 4 3 2 1

Printed in Great Britain by Clays Limited, St Ives plc

All papers used by Bloomsbury Publishing are natural, recyclable products made from wood grown in well-managed forests. The manufacturing processes conform to the environmental regulations of the country of origin

FOR BOB LOOMIS

THE MING DYNASTY FELL IN 1644 AND THE QING DYNASTY, LED BY the Manchus, began. For about thirty years, the country was in turmoil. Some women were forced from their homes; others went out by choice. Literally thousands of women became published poets and writers. The lovesick maidens were a part of this phenomenon. The works of more than twenty of them have survived to today.

I have followed the traditional Chinese style for rendering dates. Emperor Kangxi reigned from 1662 to 1722. Tang Xianzu's opera *The Peony Pavilion* was first produced and then published in 1598. Chen Tong (Peony in this novel) was born ca. 1649, Tan Ze ca. 1656, and Qian Yi ca. 1671. In 1694, *The Three Wives' Commentary* became the first book of its kind to be written and published by women anywhere in the world.

Love is of source unknown, yet it grows ever deeper. The living may die of it, by its power the dead live again. Love is not love at its fullest if one who lives is unwilling to die for it, or if it cannot restore to life one who has died. And must love that comes in dream necessarily be unreal? For there is no lack of dream lovers in this world. Only for those whose love must be fulfilled on the pillow, and for whom affection deepens only after retirement from office, is it an entirely corporeal matter.

—Preface to *The Peony Pavilion*
TANG XIANZU, 1598

PART I

In the Garden

Riding the Wind

TWO DAYS BEFORE MY SIXTEENTH BIRTHDAY, I WOKE UP so early that my maid was still asleep on the floor at the foot of my bed. I should have scolded Willow, but I didn't because I wanted a few moments alone to savor my excitement. Beginning tonight, I would attend a production of *The Peony Pavilion* mounted in our garden. I loved this opera and had collected eleven of the thirteen printed versions available. I liked to lie in bed and read of the maiden Liniang and her dream lover, their adventures, and their ultimate triumph. But for three nights, culminating on Double Seven—the seventh day of the seventh month, the day of the lovers' festival, and my birthday—I would actually *see* the opera, which was normally forbidden to girls and women. My father had invited other families for the festivities. We'd have contests and banquets. It was going to be amazing.

Willow sat up and rubbed her eyes. When she saw me staring at her, she scrambled to her feet and offered good wishes. I felt another flutter of anticipation, so I was particular when Willow bathed me, helped me into a gown of lavender silk, and brushed my hair. I wanted to look perfect; I wanted to act perfectly.

A girl on the edge of sixteen knows how pretty she is, and as I looked in the mirror I burned with the knowledge. My hair was black and silky. When Willow brushed it, I felt the strokes from the top of my head all the way down my back. My eyes were shaped like bamboo leaves; my brows were like gentle brushstrokes limned by a calligrapher. My cheeks glowed the pale pink of a peony petal. My father and mother liked to comment on how appropriate this was, because my name was Peony. I tried, as only a young girl can, to live up to the delicateness of my name. My lips were full and soft. My waist was small and my breasts were ready for a husband's touch. I wouldn't say I was vain. I was just a typical fifteen-year-old girl. I was secure in my beauty but had enough wisdom to know it was only fleeting.

My parents adored me and made sure I was educated—highly educated. I lived a rarefied and precious existence, in which I arranged flowers, looked pretty, and sang for my parents' entertainment. I was so privileged that even my maid had bound feet. As a small girl, I believed that all the gatherings we held and all the treats we ate during Double Seven were a celebration for me. No one corrected my mistake, because I was loved and very, very spoiled. I took a breath and let it out slowly—*happy*. This would be my last birthday at home before I married out, and I was going to enjoy every minute.

I left my room in the Unmarried Girls' Hall and headed in the direction of our ancestral hall to make offerings to my grandmother. I'd spent so much time getting ready that I made a quick obeisance. I didn't want to be late for breakfast. My feet couldn't take me as fast as I wanted to go, but when I saw my parents sitting together in a pavilion overlooking the garden, I slowed. If Mama was late, I could be late too.

"Unmarried girls should not be seen in public," I heard my mother say. "I'm even concerned for my sisters-in-law. You know I don't encourage private excursions. Now to bring outsiders in for this performance . . ."

She let her voice trail off. I should have hurried on, but the opera meant so much to me that I stayed, lingering out of sight behind the twisted trunks of a wisteria vine.

"There is no *public* here," Baba said. "This will not be some open affair where women disgrace themselves by sitting among men. You will be hidden behind screens."

"But outside men will be within our walls. They may see our stockings and shoes beneath the screen. They may smell our hair and powder. And of all the operas, you have chosen one about a love affair that no unmarried girl should hear!"

My mother was old-fashioned in her beliefs and her behavior. In the social disorder that followed the Cataclysm, when the Ming dynasty fell and the Manchu invaders took power, many elite women enjoyed leaving their villas to travel the waterways in pleasure boats, write about what they saw, and publish their observations. Mama was completely against things like that. She was a loyalist—still dedicated to the over-thrown Ming emperor—but she was excessively traditional in other ways. When many women in the Yangzi delta were reinterpreting the Four Virtues—virtue, demeanor, speech, and work—my mother constantly chided me to remember their original meaning and intent. "Hold your tongue at all times," she liked to say. "But if you must speak, wait until there is a good moment. Do not offend anyone."

My mother could get very emotional about these things

because she was governed by *qing:* sentiment, passion, and love. These forces tie together the universe and stem from the heart, the seat of consciousness. My father, on the other hand, was ruled by *li*—cold reason and mastered emotions— and he snorted indifferently at her concern that strangers were coming.

"You don't complain when the members of my poetry club visit."

"But my daughter and my nieces aren't in the garden when they're here! There's no opportunity for impropriety. And what about the other families you've invited?"

"You know why I invited them," he spat out sharply, his patience gone. "Commissioner Tan is important to me right now. Do not argue further with me on this!"

I couldn't see their faces, but I imagined Mama paling under his sudden severity; she didn't speak.

Mama managed the inner realm, and she always kept fish-shaped locks of beaten metal hidden in the folds of her skirts in case she needed to secure a door to punish a concubine, preserve bolts of silk that had arrived from one of our factories for home use, or protect the pantry, the curtain-weaving quarters, or the room set aside for our servants to pawn their belongings when they needed extra money. That she never used a lock unjustly had earned her added respect and gratitude from those who resided in the women's chambers, but when she was upset, as she was at this moment, she fingered the locks nervously.

Baba's flash of anger was replaced by a conciliatory tone he often took with my mother. "No one will see our daughter or our nieces. All the proprieties will be maintained. This is a special occasion. I must be gracious in my dealings. If we open our doors this one time, other doors may soon open."

"You must do what you think best for the family," Mama conceded.

I took that moment to scurry past the pavilion. I hadn't understood all that had been said, but I really didn't care. What mattered was that the opera would still be performed in our garden, and my cousins and I would be the first girls in all Hangzhou to see it. Of course we would not be out among the men. We would sit behind screens so no one could see us, as my father said.

By the time Mama entered the Spring Pavilion for breakfast, she had regained her usual composure.

"It doesn't show good breeding for girls to eat too quickly," she cautioned my cousins and me as she passed our table. "Your mothers-in-law will not want to see you eat like hungry carp in a pond—mouths open with yearning—when you move to your husbands' homes. That said, we should be ready when our guests arrive."

So we ate as hurriedly as we could and still appear to be proper young ladies.

As soon as the servants cleared the dishes, I approached my mother. "May I go to the front gate?" I asked, hoping to greet our guests.

"Yes, on your wedding day," she responded, smiling fondly as she always did when I asked a stupid question.

I waited patiently, knowing that palanquins were now being brought over our main threshold and into the Sitting-Down Hall, where our visitors would get out and drink tea before entering the main part of the compound. From there, the men would go to the Hall of Abundant Elegance, where my father would receive them. The women would come to our quarters, which lay at the back of the compound, protected from the eyes of all men.

Eventually, I heard the lilting voices of women as they

neared. When my mother's two sisters and their daughters arrived, I reminded myself to be modest in appearance, behavior, and movement. A couple of my aunts' sisters came next, followed by several of my father's friends' wives. The most important of these was Madame Tan, the wife of the man my father had mentioned in his argument with my mother. (The Manchus had recently given her husband a high appointment as Commissioner of Imperial Rites.) She was tall and very thin. Her young daughter, Tan Ze, looked around eagerly. A wave of jealousy washed over me. I had never been outside the Chen Family Villa. Did Commissioner Tan let his daughter pass through their family's front gate very often?

Kisses. Hugs. The exchange of gifts of fresh figs, jars of Shaoxing rice wine, and tea made from jasmine flowers. Showing the women and their daughters to their rooms. Unpacking. Changing from traveling costumes to fresh gowns. More kisses. More hugs. A few tears and lots of laughter. Then we moved to the Lotus-Blooming Hall, our main women's gathering place, where the ceiling was high, shaped like a fish tail, and supported by round posts painted black. Windows and carved doors looked out into a private garden on one side and a pond filled with lotus on the other. On an altar table in the center of the room stood a small screen and a vase. When spoken together, the words for *screen* and *vase* sounded like *safe,* and we women and girls all felt safe here in the hall as we took chairs.

Once settled, my bound feet just barely floating on the surface of the cool stone floor, I looked around the room. I was glad I'd taken such care with my appearance, because the other women and girls were dressed in their finest gauze silk, embroidered with patterns of seasonal flowers. As I compared myself to the others, I had to admit that my cousin

Lotus looked exceptionally beautiful, but then she always did. Truthfully, we all sparkled in anticipation of the festivities that were about to descend on our home. Even my chubby cousin Broom looked more pleasing than usual.

The servants set out little dishes of sweetmeats, and then my mother announced an embroidery contest, the first of several activities she'd planned for these three days. We laid our embroidery projects on a table and my mother examined them, looking for the most intricate designs and skillful stitches. When she came to the piece I'd made, she spoke with the honesty of her position.

"My daughter's needlework improves. See how she tried to embroider chrysanthemums?" She paused. "They are chrysanthemums, aren't they?" When I nodded, she said, "You've done well." She kissed me lightly on the forehead, but anyone could see I would not win the embroidery contest, on this day or ever.

By late afternoon—between the tea, the contests, and our anticipation about tonight—we were all fidgety. Mama's eyes swept through the room, taking in the wiggling little girls, the darting eyes of their mothers, Fourth Aunt's swinging foot, and pudgy Broom pulling repeatedly at her tight collar. I clasped my hands together in my lap and sat as still as possible when Mama's eyes found me, but inside I wanted to jump up, wave my arms, and scream my exhilaration.

Mama cleared her throat. A few women looked in her direction, but otherwise the tittering agitation continued. She cleared her throat again, tapped her fingernail on a table, and began to speak in a melodious voice. "One day the Kitchen God's seven daughters were bathing in a pond when a Cowherd and his water buffalo came upon them."

At the recognition of the opening lines to every girl and woman's favorite story, quiet fell over the room. I nodded at my mother, acknowledging how clever she was to use this story to relax us, and we listened to her recount how the impudent Cowherd stole the clothes of the loveliest daughter, the Weaving Maid, leaving her to languish naked in the pond.

"As the chill of night settled in the forest," Mama explained, "she had no choice but to go in nature's full embarrassment to the Cowherd's home to retrieve her clothes. The Weaving Maid knew she could save her reputation only one way. She decided to marry the Cowherd. What do you suppose happened next?"

"They fell in love," Tan Ze, Madame Tan's daughter, piped up in a shrill voice.

This was the unforeseen part of the story, since no one expected an immortal to love an ordinary man when even here in the mortal world husbands and wives in arranged marriages often did not find love.

"They had many children," Ze went on. "Everyone was happy."

"Until?" my mother asked, this time looking for a response from another girl.

"Until the gods and goddesses grew weary," Ze answered again, ignoring my mother's obvious wishes. "They missed the girl who spun cloud silk into cloth for their clothes and they wanted her back."

My mother frowned. This Tan Ze had forgotten herself entirely! I guessed her to be about nine years old. I glanced at her feet, remembering that she'd walked in unassisted today. Her two-year footbinding was behind her. Maybe her enthusiasm had to do with being able to walk again. But her manners!

"Go on," Ze said. "Tell us more!"

Mama winced and then continued as though yet another breach of the Four Virtues had not occurred. "The Queen of Heaven brought the Weaving Maid and the Cowherd back to the celestial skies, and then she took a hairpin and drew the Milky Way to separate them. In this way, the Weaving Maid would not be diverted from her work, and the Queen of Heaven would be beautifully robed. On Double Seven, the goddess allows all the magpies on earth to form a celestial bridge with their wings so the two lovers can meet. Three nights from now, if you girls are still awake between the hours of midnight and dawn and find yourselves sitting beneath a grape arbor under the quarter moon, you will hear the lovers weep at their parting."

It was a romantic thought—and it coated us in warm feelings—but none of us would be alone under a grape arbor at that time of night, even if we were within the safety of this compound. And at least for me, it did little to still my quivering excitement about *The Peony Pavilion*. How much longer would I have to wait?

When it came time for dinner back in the Spring Pavilion, the women gathered in little groups—sisters with sisters, cousins with cousins—but Madame Tan and her daughter were strangers here. Ze plopped down beside me at the unmarried girls' table as though she were soon to be married and not still a little girl. I knew it would make Mama happy if I gave my attention to our guest, but I was sorry I did.

"My father can buy me anything I want," Ze crowed, telling me and everyone else who could hear that her family had more wealth than the Chen clan.

WE HAD BARELY finished our meal when from outside came the sound of a drum and cymbals, calling us to the garden. I wanted to show my refinement and leave the room slowly, but I was first out the door. Lanterns flickered as I followed the corridor from the Spring Pavilion, along the edge of the central pond, to just past our Always-Pleasant Pavilion. I stepped through moon gates, which borrowed views of stands of bamboo, potted cymbidiums, and artfully trimmed branches on the other side. As the music grew louder, I forced myself to slow down. I needed to proceed cautiously, fully aware that men who were not family members stood within our walls tonight. If one of them should chance to see me, I would be blamed and a bad mark set against my character. But being careful and not rushing took more self-control than I thought possible. The opera would begin shortly, and I wanted to experience every second of it.

I reached the area that had been set aside for women and sat down on a cushion positioned near one of the screen's folds so I could peek through the crack. I wouldn't be able to see much of the opera, but it was more than I'd hoped for. The other women and girls came in behind me and took places on other cushions. I was so excited I didn't even mind when Tan Ze sat beside me.

For weeks, my father—as director of the performance—had been tucked away in a side hall with the cast. He had hired a traveling all-male theatrical troupe of eight members, which had upset my mother terribly, because these were people of the lowest and basest class. He'd also coerced others from our household staff—including Willow and several other servants—into taking various roles.

"Your opera has fifty-five scenes and four hundred and three arias!" Willow had said to me in awe one day, as if I didn't already know that. It would have taken more than twenty hours to perform the whole opera, but no matter how many times I asked, she wouldn't tell me which scenes Baba had cut. "Your father wants it to be a surprise," Willow said, enjoying the opportunity to disobey me. As the rehearsals became more demanding, consternation had rippled through-out the household when an uncle had called for a pipe and found no one to fill it, or an aunt had asked for hot water for her bath and no one had brought it. Even I had been inconvenienced, since Willow was busy now, having been given the important role of Spring Fragrance, the main character's servant.

The music began. The narrator stepped out and gave a quick synopsis of the play, emphasizing how longing had lasted through three incarnations before Liu Mengmei and Du Liniang realized their love. Then we met the young hero, an impoverished scholar who had to leave his ancestral home to take the imperial exams. His family name was Liu, which means *willow*. He recalled how he dreamed of a beautiful maiden standing under a plum tree. When he woke up, he took the given name Mengmei, Dream of Plum. The plum tree, with its lush foliage and ripening fruit, brought to mind the forces of nature, so this name was suggestive even to me of Mengmei's passionate nature. I listened attentively, but my heart had always been with Liniang and I could hardly wait to see her.

She arrived onstage for the scene called Admonishing the Daughter. She wore a robe of golden silk with red embroidery. From her headdress rose fluffy balls of spun silk, beaded butterflies, and flowers that quivered when she moved.

"We treasure our daughter like a pearl," Madame Du sang to her husband, but she chastised her daughter. *"You don't want to be ignorant, do you?"*

And Prefect Du, Liniang's father, added, *"No virtuous and eligible young lady should fail to be educated. Take time from your embroidery and read the books on the shelves."*

But admonitions alone couldn't change Liniang's behavior, so soon enough she and Spring Fragrance were being tutored by a strict teacher. The lessons were tedious, full of the kind of memorization of rules that I knew only too well. *"It is proper for a daughter at first cockcrow to wash her hands, to rinse her mouth, to dress her hair, to pin the same, and to pay respects to her mother and father."*

I heard things like this every day, along with Don't show your teeth when you smile, Walk steadily and slowly, Look pure and pretty, Be respectful to your aunties, and Use scissors to trim any frayed or loose threads on your gowns.

Poor Spring Fragrance couldn't stand the lessons and begged to be dismissed so she could pee. The men on the other side of the screen chortled when Willow bent over at the waist, squirmed, and held in her pee with both hands. It embarrassed me to see her behaving so, but she was only doing what my father had instructed (which shocked me, because how could he know about such things?).

In my discomfort, I let my eyes drift from the stage, and I saw men. Most of them had their backs to me, but some were angled so I could see their profiles. I was a maiden, but I *looked*. It was naughty, but I had lived fifteen years without having committed a single act that anyone in my family could call unfilial.

My eyes caught sight of a man as he turned his head to look at the gentleman sitting in the chair next to him. His cheekbones were high, his eyes wide and kind, and his hair black as a cave. He wore a long dark-blue gown of simple design. His forehead was shaved in deference to the Manchu emperor, and his long queue draped languidly over a shoulder. He brought his hand up to his mouth to make an aside, and I imagined in that simple gesture so much: gentleness, refinement, and a love of poetry. He smiled, revealing perfect white teeth and eyes that shone with merriment. His elegance and somnolence reminded me of a cat: long, slim, perfectly groomed, knowledgeable, and very contained. He was man-beautiful. When he turned his face back to the stage to watch the opera, I realized I'd been holding my breath. I let it out slowly and tried to concentrate as Spring Fragrance returned—relieved—with news of a garden she'd found.

When I read this part of the story, I felt great sympathy for Liniang, who was so cloistered she didn't even know her family owned a garden. She had spent her entire life indoors. Now Spring Fragrance tempted her mistress to go outside to see the flowers, willows, and pavilions. Liniang was curious, but she artfully hid her interest from her maid.

The quiet and subtlety was broken by a great fanfare announcing the Speed the Plough scene. Prefect Du arrived in the countryside to exhort the farmers, herders, mulberry girls, and tea pickers to work hard in the coming season. Acrobats tumbled, clowns drank from flasks of wine, men in gaily decorated costumes tottered about the garden on stilts, and our maids and other servants performed country harvest songs and dances. It was such a *li* scene, filled with what I imagined the outside world of men to be: wild gestures, exaggerated facial expressions, and the dissonance of gongs, clackers, and drums. I closed my eyes against the cacophony and tried to draw more deeply into myself to find my interior reading quiet. My heart calmed. When I opened my eyes, I again saw through the slit in the screen the man I'd spotted earlier. His eyes were closed. Could he be feeling what I was feeling?

Someone pulled my sleeve. I glanced to my right and saw Tan Ze's pinched little face looking up at me intently. "Are you staring at that boy out there?" she whispered.

I blinked a few times and tried to regain my composure by taking several shallow breaths.

"I was looking at him too," she confided, acting much

too bold for her years. "You must be betrothed already. But my father"—she brought her chin down while looking up at me with clever eyes—"has not yet arranged *my* marriage. He says that with so much turmoil still in the land, no one should agree to these things too early. You don't know which family will go up and which will go down. My father says it's terrible to marry a daughter to a mediocre man."

Was there a way to make this girl close her mouth? I wondered, and not in a nice way.

Ze turned back to face the screen and squinted through the crack. "I will ask my father to make inquiries about that boy's family."

As though she would actually have a choice in her marriage! I don't know how it could have happened so quickly, but I was jealous and angry that she would try to steal him for herself. Of course, there was no hope for the young man and me. As Ze said, I was already betrothed. But for these three nights of the opera I wanted to dream romantic thoughts and imagine that my life too might have a happy love-filled ending like Liniang's.

I blocked Ze from my mind and let myself be transported back to the opera for The Interrupted Dream. At last Liniang ventured out into her—our—garden. Such a lovely moment when she sees it all for the first time. Liniang lamented that the beauty of the flowers was hidden in a place no one visited, but she also saw the garden as a version of herself: in full bloom but neglected. I understood how she felt. The emotions that stirred in her were stirred in me every time I read the lines.

Liniang returned to her room, changed into a robe embroidered with peony blossoms, and sat before a mirror, wondering at the fleeting nature of her beauty much as I had this morning. *"Pity one whose beauty is a bright flower, when life endures no longer than a leaf on a tree,"* she sang, expressing how disturbing spring's splendor can be, and how temporary. *"I finally understand what the poets have written. In spring, moved to passion; in autumn, only regret. Oh, will I ever see a man? How will love find me? Where can I reveal my true desires?"*

Overcome by all she'd experienced, she fell asleep. In her dreams, she traveled to the Peony Pavilion, where the spirit of Liu Mengmei appeared, wearing a robe with a willow pattern and carrying a willow sprig. He touched Liniang gently with the leaves. They exchanged soft words, and he asked her to compose a poem about the willow. Then they danced together. Liniang was so delicate and touching in her movements that it was like watching a silkworm's death— tender and subtle.

Mengmei led her into our garden's rocky grotto. With the two of them gone from view, all I heard was Mengmei's seductive voice. *"Open the fastening at your neck, untie the sash around your waist, and cover your eyes with your sleeve. You may need to bite the fabric. . . ."*

Alone in my bed I had tried in vain to imagine what might be going on in the rockery of the Peony Pavilion. I still couldn't see what was happening and had to rely on the appearance of the Flower Spirit to explain their actions. *"Ah, how the male force surges and leaps. . . ."* But this didn't help me either. As an unmarried girl, I'd been told about clouds and rain, but no one had yet explained what it really was.

At consummation, a shower of peony petals came floating over the top of the rockery. Liniang sang of the joys she and her scholar had found.

When Liniang woke from her dream, she realized she'd found true love. Spring Fragrance, on orders from Madame Du, instructed Liniang to eat. But how could she? Three meals a day held no promise, no love. Liniang sneaked away from her servant and went back to the garden to pursue her dream. She saw the ground carpeted in petals. Hawthorn branches caught her skirt, pulling at her, keeping her in the garden. Memories of her dream came back to her: *"Against the withered rock he leaned my wilting body."* She remembered how he laid her down and how she spread the folds of her skirt as *"a covering for earth for the fear of the eyes of Heaven,"* until eventually she'd experienced her sweet melting.

She lingered under a plum tree thick with clusters of fruit. But this was no ordinary plum tree. It represented Liniang's mysterious dream lover, vital and procreative. *"I should count it a great good fortune to be buried here beside it when I die,"* Liniang sang.

My mother had trained me never to show my feelings, but when I read *The Peony Pavilion,* I felt certain things: love, sadness, happiness. Now, watching the story played out before me, imagining what happened in our rockery between the scholar and Liniang, and seeing a young man not of my own family for the first time brought out too many emotions in me. I had to get away for a few moments; Liniang's restlessness was my own.

I slowly rose and gingerly stepped between the cushions. I walked along one of our garden paths, Liniang's words filling my heart with longing. I tried to rest my mind by letting my eyes find quiet in the greenery. There were no flowers in our main garden. Everything was green to create a feeling of tranquility like a cup of tea—the taste light but remaining a long time. I crossed the zigzag bridge that spanned one of our lesser lily ponds and stepped into the Riding-the-Wind Pavilion, which had been designed so that gentle breezes on a sultry summer evening would cool a hot face or burning heart. I sat down and tried to calm myself in the way the pavilion intended. I had so wanted to experience every second of the opera, but I'd been unprepared for how overwhelmed I would feel.

Arias and music wafted to me through the night, carrying with them Madame Du's concern over her daughter's listlessness. Madame Du didn't recognize it yet, but her daughter was lovesick. I closed my eyes, took a deep breath, and let that knowledge seep into me.

Then I heard a disquieting echo of my breath near me. I opened my eyes and saw standing before me the young man I'd seen through the slit in the screen.

A tiny *yip* of surprise escaped from my lips before I could even begin to compose myself. I was alone with a man who was not a relative. Worse, he was a total stranger.

"I'm sorry." He folded his hands together and bowed several times in apology.

My heart pounded—from fear, from excitement, from the sheer extraordinariness of the situation. This man had to be one of my father's friends. I had to be gracious, yet maintain decorum. "I shouldn't have left the performance," I said hesitantly. "It's my fault."

"I shouldn't have left either." He took a step forward, and my body leaned away in automatic response. "But the love of those two . . ." He shook his head. "Imagine finding true love."

"I've imagined it many times."

I was sorry as soon as the words left my mouth. This was not the way to speak to a man, whether a stranger or a husband. I knew that, and yet the words had flown from my tongue. I put three fingers to my lips, hoping they would keep more thoughts from escaping.

"So have I," he said. He took another step forward. "But Liniang and Mengmei find each other in the dream, and then they fall in love."

"Perhaps you don't know the opera," I said. "They meet, true, but Liniang pursues Mengmei only after she becomes a ghost."

"I know the story, but I disagree. The scholar must overcome his fear of her ghost—"

"A fear that arises only after *she* seduces *him*."

How could that sentence have come out of my mouth?

"You must forgive me," I said. "I'm just an ignorant girl, and I should get back to the performance."

"No, wait. Please don't go."

I looked through the darkness back toward the stage. I'd waited my entire life to see this opera. I could hear Liniang sing, *"In my thin gown I tremble, wrapped against the morning chill only by regrets to see red tears of petals shake from the bough."* In her lovesickness, she'd become so thin and frail—haggard, really—that she decided to paint her self-portrait on silk. If she left the world, she would be remembered as she'd been in her dream, ripe with beauty and unfulfilled desire. This act—as it was, even for a living girl—was a tangible symptom of Liniang's lovesickness, since it acknowledged and antici-pated her death. With the fine lines of her brush, she painted a plum sprig in the figure's hand to recall her dream lover, hoping that if he ever chanced upon the portrait he would recognize her. Finally, she added a poem expressing her wish to marry someone named Liu.

How could I be tempted to stay away from the opera so easily? And by a man? If I had been thinking at all, I would have realized right then why some people believed *The Peony Pavilion* lured young women into behaving improperly.

He must have sensed my indecision—how could he not?—for he said, "I won't speak of this to anyone so please stay. I've never had a chance to hear what a woman thinks of the opera."

A woman? The situation was getting worse. I stepped around him, making sure that no part of my clothes brushed against him. As I walked past, he spoke again.

"The author meant to stir female feelings of *qing*—of love and emotion—in us. I *feel* this story, but I don't know if what I experience is true."

We were just inches apart. I turned and looked up into his face. His features were even more refined than I'd thought. In the dim light of the soon-to-be quarter moon, I saw the high planes of his cheekbones, the gentleness in his eyes, and the fullness of his mouth.

"I . . ." My voice closed in on itself as he gazed down at me. I cleared my throat and began again. "How could a girl—cloistered and from an elite family—"

"A girl like you."

"—choose her own husband? This is not possible for me, and it would have been impossible for her too."

"Do you think you understand Liniang better than her creator?"

"I'm a girl. I'm the same age. I believe in filial duty," I said, "and I will follow the course my father has set for me, but all girls have dreams, even if our destinies are set."

"So you have the same kinds of dreams as Liniang?" he asked.

"I'm not a pleasure girl on one of the painted boats on the lake, if that's what you're asking!"

Suddenly I burned with embarrassment. I had said too much. I stared at the ground. My bound-foot shoes looked tiny and delicate next to his embroidered slippers. I felt his eyes on me and longed to look up, but I couldn't. I wouldn't. I tipped my head and, without another word, left the pavilion.

He called softly after me. "Meet me tomorrow?" A question,

followed a heartbeat later by a stronger statement: "Meet me tomorrow night. Meet me here."

I didn't answer. I didn't look back. Instead I walked straight to our main garden and once again threaded my way through the seated women to the pillow positioned in front of the screen's fold. I glanced around, hoping no one had noticed my absence. I sat down and forced myself to look through the crack out to the performance, but I found it hard to pay attention. When I saw the young man return to his seat, I closed my eyes. I would not allow myself to look at him. Sitting there, my eyes shut tight, the music and the words penetrated me.

Liniang was dying from her lovesickness. A diviner was brought in to prescribe charms, to no avail. By the Autumn Moon Festival, Liniang was very weak, feeling a floating numbness. Her bones dreaded the autumn chill. Cold rain battered the windows and melancholy geese crossed the sky. When her mother came to see her, Liniang apologized that she would not serve her parents until the end of their days. She tried to kowtow in respect and then collapsed. Knowing she was going to die, she begged her family to bury her in the garden under the plum tree. Secretly she asked Spring Fragrance to hide her portrait in the garden's grotto where she and her dream lover had consummated their love.

I thought of the young man I'd met. He hadn't touched me, but sitting there on the women's side of the screen I could admit that I'd wanted him to. Out onstage, Liniang died. Mourners gathered to sing of their grief, while her parents keened with unhappiness. And then, in a sudden twist, a messenger arrived with a letter from the emperor. I didn't like this part of the story very much. Prefect Du was promoted. A huge celebration began, which now, as I saw it, was a great spectacle and a wonderful way to end the evening. But how could the Dus forget their grief so easily if they loved their daughter as much as they said they did? Her father even forgot to dot her ancestor tablet, which would cause her much trouble in the afterworld.

Later, lying in bed, I found myself filled with a longing so deep I could barely breathe.

Bamboo-and-Lacquer Cage

MY GRANDMOTHER WAS VERY MUCH ON MY MIND THE next morning. I felt torn between the desire to meet my stranger again tonight and the lessons that had been drilled into me since childhood about how I should behave. I dressed and set out for the ancestral hall. It was a long walk, but I took in everything as though I hadn't seen it all ten thousand times before. The Chen Family Villa had great halls, vast courtyards, and lovely pavilions that spread down to the shore of West Lake. The wild ruggedness of our rockeries reminded me of what was enduring and strong in life. I saw the expansiveness of lakes and meandering rivers in our artificial ponds and streams. I experienced forests in our carefully planted stands of bamboo. I passed our Gathering-Beauty Pavilion, an upstairs viewing perch that allowed the unmarried girls in our household to watch for visitors in the garden without being detected. From there, I'd heard sounds from the outside world, the trill of a flute floating across the lake, *pushed* across the water, and insidiously sneaking over our garden wall and onto our property. I'd even heard outside voices: a vendor calling out cooking utensils for sale, an argument between boatmen, the soft laughter of women on a pleasure boat. But I had not seen them.

I entered the hall where we kept my family's ancestor tablets. The tablets—slips of wood inscribed with the names of my ancestors written in gilded characters—hung on the walls. Here were my grandparents, great-uncles and great-aunts, and countless cousins, many times removed, who had been born, lived, and died in the Chen Family Villa. At death, their souls had separated into three parts and gone to new homes in the afterworld, the grave, and their ancestor tablets. Looking at the tablets, I could not only trace my family back more than nine generations, I could prevail upon the bit of soul that resided in each one to help me.

I lit incense, knelt on a pillow, and looked up at the two large ancestor portrait scrolls that hung on the wall above the altar table. On the left was my grandfather, an imperial scholar who had brought great dignity, security, and wealth to our family. In the painting, he sat in his robes, his legs spread, a fan open in one hand. His face was stern, and the skin around his eyes was wrinkled from wisdom and worry. He died when I was four, and my memory of him was of a man who preferred silence from me and had little tolerance for my mother or for the other women in our household.

To the right of the altar table in another long scroll was my father's mother. She also wore a severe expression. She had a position of great honor, in our family and in the country, as a martyr who'd died in the Cataclysm. In the years leading up to her sacrifice, my grandfather had served as the Minister of Works in Yangzhou. My grandmother left the Chen Family Villa here in Hangzhou and traveled two days by boat and by palanquin to live with him in Yangzhou. Not realizing disaster was coming, my parents went to Yangzhou for a visit. Soon after they arrived, the Manchu marauders invaded.

Whenever I tried to talk to Mama about that period, she would say, "You don't need to know about it." Once, as a five-year-old, I'd been impudent enough to ask if she'd seen Grandmother Chen die. Mama slapped me so hard I fell to the ground. "Don't ever speak to me about that day." She never hit me again, not even during my footbinding, and I never again asked her about my grandmother.

Others, however, invoked her almost daily. The highest goal a woman could achieve in life was to be a chaste widow who would not accept a second marriage, not even if it meant taking her own life. But my grandmother had done something even more extraordinary. She elected to kill herself rather than give herself to the Manchu soldiers. She was such an exemplary example of Confucian chastity that, once the Manchus established the Qing court, they selected her to be venerated in stories and books for women to read, if they hoped to reach perfection themselves as wives and mothers, and to promote the universal ideals of loyalty and filial piety. The Manchus were still our enemy, but they used my grand-mother, and the other women who had sacrificed themselves during the disaster, to win our respect and bring back order to the women's chambers.

I placed offerings of flawless white peaches on her altar.

"Do I meet him or not?" I whispered, hoping she would guide me. "Help me, Grandmother, help me." I dropped my forehead to the floor in obeisance, looked up at the portrait to let her see my sincerity, and dropped my head again. I rose, smoothed my skirt, and left the room, my wishes floating to my grandmother on trails of incense smoke. But I felt no surer of what I should do than when I'd entered.

Willow waited for me outside the door.

"Your mother says you're late for breakfast in the Spring Pavilion," she said. "Give me your arm, Little Miss, and I will take you there."

She was my servant, but I was the one who obeyed.

By now the corridors bustled with activity. The Chen Family Villa was home to 940 fingers: 210 fingers belonged to my direct blood relatives, 330 fingers to the concubines and their children—all girls—and another 400 fingers to our cooks, gardeners, wet nurses, amahs, maids, and the like. Now, with the Double Seven festival, we had many more visiting fingers. With so many people in the household, our compound was designed to keep each of those fingers in its appropriate place. So this morning, as every morning, our household's ten concubines—and their twenty-three daughters—ate in their own hall. Three cousins, who were at critical points in their footbinding, were confined to their rooms. Otherwise, the women in the Spring Pavilion sat according to rank. My mother, as the wife of the eldest brother, had the position of honor in the room. She and her four sisters-in-law sat at one table, five little cousins sat at another table with their amahs, while the three cousins my age and I had a table to ourselves. Our guests were also grouped by age and station. In the corner, amahs and wet nurses cared for the babies and girls under five years old.

I swayed with a flawless lily gait, moving gently across the floor, careful with my steps, my body shivering from side to side like a flower in the breeze. When I sat down, my cousins didn't acknowledge me, conspicuously leaving me out. Ordinarily I didn't mind too much. I was already engaged to be married, I would tell myself, and had only five more months of their company. But after my encounter in the Riding-the-Wind Pavilion last night, I questioned what lay ahead of me.

My father and my future husband's father had been boyhood friends. When they were matched to their wives, they vowed that one day the two families would be united through their children. The Wu family had two sons right away, I took longer to arrive, and before long my Eight Characters were matched to the younger son. My parents were happy, but it was hard for me to be excited, especially now. I had never met Wu Ren. I didn't know if he was two years or ten years older than I was. He could be pockmarked, short, cruel, and fat, but I would receive no warnings from my mother or father. Marriage to a stranger was my fate, and it wasn't necessarily a happy one.

"Today the jade maiden wears the color of jade," Broom, the daughter of my father's second brother, said to me. She had a flower name like the rest of us, but no one used it. She had the misfortune of having been born on an unlucky day when the Broom Star was most prominent, which meant that whatever family she married into would have its home swept of its luck. Second Aunt was softhearted, and as a result Broom already had the roundness of a woman past child-bearing years. The other aunts, my mother included, all campaigned to keep her from eating too much, hoping that once she married out her bad luck would be removed from our compound.

"I don't know that this color is good for your skin," Lotus, Third Aunt's eldest daughter, added sweetly. "I'm sure this is a sorry thing for our jade maiden to hear."

I kept a smile on my face, but their words hurt. My father always said I was a jade maiden and my future husband was a golden boy, which implied that the families were of comparable wealth and status. I shouldn't have, but I found myself wondering about the young man I'd met last night and if my father would have found him satisfactory.

"But then," Lotus went on sympathetically, "I hear the golden boy is a bit tarnished. Is this not so, Peony?"

Whenever she said things like this, I fought back, and I had to do it now or appear weak. I pushed my stranger from my mind.

"If my husband had been born in a different time, he would have become an imperial scholar like his father, but this is not a good course to sail these days. Still, Baba says Ren was precocious from the time he was a boy," I boasted, trying to sound convincing. "He will make a wonderful husband."

"Our cousin should hope for a strong husband," Broom confided to Lotus. "Her father-in-law is dead and the Wu boy is only a second son, so her mother-in-law will have great power over her."

This was too mean.

"My husband's father died in the Cataclysm," I objected. "My mother-in-law has been an honorable widow."

I waited for what the girls would say next, since they seemed very informed. With the Wu patriarch dead, had the family fallen on hard times? My father had provided a sizable dowry for me that included fields, silk-weaving enterprises, stock animals, and more than the usual amount of *cash,* silk, and food, but a marriage where the wife had too much money was never happy. Too often the husbands became henpecked and the subject of much banter, while the wives were known for their cruel ways, biting tongues, and heartless jealousy. Was this the future my father intended for me? Why couldn't I fall in love like Liniang?

"Just don't go braying to the heavens about your perfect

match," Broom concluded smugly, "when the whole compound knows otherwise."

I sighed. "Please, have another dumpling," I said, pushing the platter toward her.

Broom sneaked a peek toward the mothers' table and then with her chopsticks lifted a dumpling and popped it whole into her mouth. My other two cousins stared at me with evil in their eyes, but I couldn't do much about it. They embroidered together, ate lunch together, and talked behind my back together. But I had little ways of fighting back, even if they were petty. I was known to do wicked things, like show off my pretty clothes, hairpins, and jewelry. I was immature, but I only acted mischievously to protect myself and my feelings. I didn't understand that my cousins and I were trapped like good-luck crickets in bamboo-and-lacquer cages.

I spent the rest of breakfast in silence, with the others ignoring me with all the conviction that only unmarried girls can muster and with me believing I was immune to their wicked thoughts. But of course I wasn't, and I was suddenly overcome by my inadequacies. In some ways I was even more of a disappointment than Broom. I was born in the seventh month four years after the Cataclysm, when all four weeks are set aside for the Festival of Hungry Ghosts—not a propitious time. I was a girl, a calamity for any family but particularly for one like ours, which had sustained great losses during the Cataclysm. As the eldest brother, my father was expected to have a son who one day would become the head of our family, perform rites in the ancestral hall, and make offerings to our long-dead relatives so they would continue to bring us good luck and fortune; instead, he was burdened by a single useless daughter. Maybe my cousins were right and he'd matched me to someone insignificant as punishment.

I looked across the table and saw Broom whisper in Lotus's ear. They glanced at me and then covered their mouths to hide their smirks. Instantly my doubts evaporated, and I inwardly thanked my cousins. I had a secret so big they would fly apart from jealousy and envy if they knew.

After breakfast, we moved to the Lotus-Blooming Hall, where my mother announced a zither contest for the unmarried girls. When my turn came, I sat on the raised dais in front of the group just as the others had done, but I was a terrible zither player and I kept losing my fingers on the strings as I thought of the young man I'd met last night. As soon as I finished, my mother dismissed me, suggesting I take a stroll in the garden.

Released from the women's chambers! I hurried along the corridor to my father's library. Baba was the Chen family's ninth generation of imperial scholars of the *jinshi* level, the highest attainable. He had been a Vice Commissioner of Silk during Ming times, but with the chaos—and disenchanted with the thought of serving the new emperor—he'd come home. He'd taken up gentlemanly pursuits: writing poetry, playing chess, tasting tea, burning incense, and now producing and directing operas. In many ways, he—like so many men these days—had adopted our women's philosophy of turning inward. Nothing made him happier than to unroll a scroll while being enveloped in a cloud of incense or sip tea while playing a game of chess with his favorite concubine.

Baba was still a Ming loyalist, yet he was bound by the rules of humanity; he refused to work in the new government, but he still had to shave his forehead and wear a queue to show his subservience to the Qing emperor. He explained his capitulation this way: "Men are not like women. We go into the outer realm where we are seen. I had to do as the

Manchus ordered or risk decapitation. If I had died, how would our family, our home, our land, and all the people who work for us have survived? We've suffered so much already."

I stepped into my father's library. A servant stood by the door, ready to attend to Baba's needs. On the walls to my left and right were marble "paintings"—slices of marble that revealed hidden landscapes of cloud-covered mountains against a murky sky. The room, even with the windows open, was redolent of the four jewels of the scholar's study: paper, ink, brushes, and the earthiness of the inkstone. Nine generations of scholars had built this library, and printed books were everywhere—on the desk, the floor, the shelves. My father had added his mark to the collection by amassing hundreds of works written by women during the Ming dynasty and well over a thousand books written by women since the Cataclysm. He said that these days men had to find talent in unusual places.

This morning Baba was not at his desk. Instead, he lounged on a wooden bed with a rattan bottom, watching mist rise off the lake. Beneath the bed I saw twin trays, each with large blocks of ice on them. He indulged his sensitivity to heat by having our servants dig up preserved ice from underground and use it to cool his daybed. On the wall above him hung a couplet, which read:

Do not care about fame. Be modest.
In this way you will be found by others to be special.

"Peony," he said, and waved me over to him. "Come and sit."

I crossed the room, swinging close to the windows so I could look out over the lake to Solitary Island and beyond.

I wasn't supposed to see outside our walls, but today my father wordlessly permitted me this treat. I sat down in one of the chairs that had been placed before his desk for those who came to ask favors.

"Have you come to escape your teacher again today?" he asked.

Over the years, my family had provided me with wonderful teachers—all women—but from the time I was four, my father had let me sit in his lap so he could personally teach me to read, understand, and criticize. He taught me that life imitates art. Through reading, he told me, I could enter worlds different from my own. In picking up the brush to write, I could exercise my intellect and imagination. I considered him my best teacher.

"I have no lessons today," I reminded him shyly.

Had he forgotten my birthday was tomorrow? Usually birthdays were not celebrated until someone reached the age of fifty, but hadn't he mounted the opera for me because he loved me and I was precious to him?

He smiled indulgently. "Of course, of course." Then he turned serious. "Too much female gossip in the women's chambers?"

I shook my head.

"Then you have come to tell me that you won one of those contests your mother has organized."

"Oh, Ba." I sighed in resignation. He knew I didn't excel at those things.

"You are so old now I can't even tease you anymore." He slapped his thigh and laughed. "Sixteen tomorrow. Have you failed to remember this special day?"

I smiled back at him. "You've given me the best present."

He cocked his head in question. He had to be teasing me again and I played along.

"I suppose you staged the opera for someone else," I suggested.

Baba had encouraged my impertinence over the years, but today he didn't respond with something swift and clever. Instead, he said, "Yes, yes, *yes*," as if with each word he considered his answer anew. "Of course. That was it."

He pulled himself up and threw his legs over the side of the bed. After he stood, he took a moment to adjust his clothes, which were modeled on Manchu riding gear— trousers and a fitted tunic that buttoned at the neck. "But I have another present for you. One I think you'll like even more."

He went to a camphor-wood chest, opened it, and pulled out something wrapped in purple silk woven in a pattern of willows. When he handed it to me, I knew it was a book. I hoped it was the volume of *The Peony Pavilion* that the great author Tang Xianzu had published himself. I slowly untied and then unfolded the silk. It was an edition of *The Peony Pavilion* I did not yet have, but not the one I wished for. Still, I clutched it to my chest, relishing how special it was. Without my father's help, I would not have been able to pursue my passion, no matter how resourceful I was.

"Ba, you're too good to me."

"Open it," he urged.

I loved books. I loved the weight of them in my hands. I loved the smell of the ink and the feel of the rice paper.

"Don't fold over the edges of the page to mark your place," my father reminded me. "Don't scratch at the written characters with your fingernails. Don't wet your finger with your tongue before turning the pages. And never use a book as a pillow."

How many times had he warned me of these things?

"I won't, Baba," I promised.

My eyes rested on the narrator's opening lines. Last night I had heard the actor who played him speak of how three incarnations had led Liniang and Mengmei to the Peony Pavilion.

I took the volume to my father, pointed to the passage, and asked, "Baba, where does this come from? Was it something Tang Xianzu invented or is it one of the things he borrowed from another poem or story?"

My father smiled, pleased as usual with my curiosity. "Look on the third shelf on that wall. Find the oldest book and you'll get your answer."

I put my new copy of *The Peony Pavilion* on the daybed and did as my father suggested. I took the book back to the bed and leafed through the pages until I found the original source for the three incarnations. It seemed that in the Tang dynasty a girl loved a monk. It took three separate lifetimes for them to attain perfect circumstances and perfect love. I pondered that. Could love be strong enough to outlast death not once but three times?

I picked up *The Peony Pavilion* again and slowly turned the pages. I wanted to find Mengmei and relive meeting my stranger last night. I came to Mengmei's entrance:

I have inherited fragrance of classic books. Drilling the wall for light, hair tied to a beam in fear of drowsing, I wrest from nature excellence in letters. . . .

"What are you reading now?" Baba asked.
Caught! Blood rushed to my cheeks.
"I . . . I . . ."
"There are things in the story a girl like you might not understand. You could discuss them with your mother—"
I blushed an even deeper red. "It's nothing like that," I

stammered, and then I read him the lines, which on their own seemed perfectly innocent.

"Ah, so you want to know the source for this too." When I nodded, he got up, went to one of the shelves, pulled down a book, and brought it to the bed. "This records the deeds of famous scholars. Do you want me to help you?"

"I can do it, Baba."

"I know you can," he said, and handed me the volume.

Aware of my father's eyes watching me, I leafed through the book until I came to an entry about Kuang Heng, a scholar so poor he couldn't afford oil for his lamp. He drilled a hole in the wall so he might borrow his neighbor's light.

"In a few more pages"—Baba urged me on—"you'll find the reference to Sun Jing, who tied his hair to a beam, so fearful was he of falling asleep at his studies."

I nodded soberly, wondering if the young man I'd met was as diligent as those men of antiquity.

"If you'd been a son," Baba went on, "you would have made an excellent imperial scholar, perhaps the best our family has ever seen."

He meant it as a compliment and I took it that way, but I heard regret in his voice too. I was not a son and never would be.

"If you're going to be here," he added hurriedly, perhaps aware of his lapse, "then you should help me."

We went back to his desk and sat down. He carefully arranged his clothes around him and then adjusted his queue so that it hung straight down his back. He ran his fingers over his shaved forehead—a habit, like wearing Manchu styles, that reminded him of his choice to protect our family—and then he opened a drawer and pulled out several strings of silver *cash* pieces.

He pushed a string across the desk and said, "I need to send funds to the countryside. Help me count them out."

We owned thousands of *mou* planted with mulberry trees. In the Gudang area, not far from here, whole villages relied on our family for their livelihood. Baba cared for the people who raised the trees, harvested the leaves, fed and nurtured the silkworms, pulled the floss from the cocoons, spun thread, and, of course, made cloth. He told me what was required for each enterprise, and I began putting together the proper amounts.

"You don't seem like yourself today," my father said. "What troubles you?"

I couldn't tell him about the young man I'd met or that I was worrying about whether or not I should meet him again in the Riding-the-Wind Pavilion, but if Baba could help me understand my grandmother and the choices she'd made, then maybe I'd know what to do tonight.

"I've been thinking about Grandmother Chen. Was she so very brave? Did she have any moments when she was unsure?"

"We've studied this history—"

"The history, yes, but not about Grandmother. What was she like?"

My father knew me very well, and unlike most daughters I knew him very well too. Over the years I'd learned to recognize certain expressions: the way he raised his eyebrows in surprise when I asked about this or that woman poet, the grimace he made when he quizzed me on history and I answered incorrectly, the thoughtful way he pulled on his chin when I asked him a question about *The Peony Pavilion* for which he didn't know the answer. Now he looked at me as though he were weighing my worth.

"The Manchus had seen city after city fall," he said at

last, "but they knew that when they got to the Yangzi delta they'd find strong loyalist resistance. They could have chosen Hangzhou, where we live, but instead they decided to make Yangzhou, where my father served as a minister, a lesson to other cities in the region."

I'd heard this many times and wondered if he'd tell me anything I didn't already know.

"The generals, who until then had kept the soldiers under strict control, gave the order for their men to let loose their desires and take whatever riches they wanted—in the form of women, silver, silk, antiques, and animals—as reward for their service." My father paused and regarded me in that same appraising way. "Do you understand what I'm saying . . . about the women?"

In all honesty I didn't, but I nodded.

"For five days, the city ran with blood," he continued wearily. "Fires destroyed homes, halls, temples. Thousands and thousands of people died."

"Weren't you afraid?"

"Everyone was scared, but my mother taught us how to be brave. And we had to be brave in so many ways." Again he scrutinized me as though considering whether or not to continue. He must have found me lacking, because he picked up a string of *cash* and went back to his counting. Without taking his eyes from the pieces of silver, he concluded, "Now you know why I prefer to look only at beauty—to read poetry, do my calligraphy, read, and listen to opera."

But he hadn't told me anything about Grandmother! And he hadn't said anything that would help me decide what to do tonight or help me understand what I was feeling.

"Baba . . ." I said shyly.

"Yes," he answered, without looking up.

"I've been thinking about the opera and Liniang's

lovesickness," I blurted in a rushed tumble. "Do you think that could happen in real life?"

"Absolutely. You've heard of Xiaoqing, haven't you?"

Of course I had. She was the greatest lovesick maiden ever.

"She died very young," I prompted. "Was it because she was beautiful?"

"In many ways she was a lot like you," Baba answered. "She was graceful and elegant by nature. But her parents, members of the gentry, lost their fortune. Her mother became a teacher, so Xiaoqing was well educated. Perhaps too well educated."

"But how can anyone be too well educated?" I asked, thinking of how happy I had just made my father by showing interest in his books.

"When Xiaoqing was a little girl, she visited a nun," Baba answered. "In one sitting, Xiaoqing learned to recite the *Heart Sutra* without missing a single character. But as she was doing this, the nun saw that Xiaoqing did not have good fortune. If the girl could keep from reading, then she'd live to thirty. If not . . ."

"But how could she die of lovesickness?"

"When she turned sixteen, a man in Hangzhou acquired her to be a concubine and secreted her away just out there"—he gestured to the window—"on Solitary Island to keep her safe from his jealous wife. Xiaoqing was all alone and very lonely. Her only comfort came from reading *The Peony Pavilion*. Like you, she read the opera constantly. She became obsessed, caught a case of lovesickness, and wasted away. As she weakened, she wrote poems likening herself to Liniang." His voice softened and color came to his cheeks. "She was only seventeen when she died."

My cousins and I sometimes talked about Xiaoqing. We

made up explanations for what we thought "being put on earth for the delights of men" might mean. But as Baba spoke, I saw that somehow Xiaoqing's frailty and dissipation excited and fascinated him. He wasn't the only man who'd been captivated by her life and death. Lots of men had written poems to her, and more than twenty had written plays about her. There was, I realized now, something about Xiaoqing and how she died that was deeply attractive and enthralling to men. Did my stranger feel the same way too?

"I often think of Xiaoqing as she reached the end of her days," Baba added, his voice dreamy. "She drank only one small cup of pear juice a day. Can you imagine?"

I was beginning to feel uncomfortable. He was my father, and I didn't like thinking he might have feelings and sensations similar to the ones I'd had since last night when I had always told myself that he and my mother were distant with each other and that he received no real joy from his concubines.

"Just like Liniang, Xiaoqing wanted to leave behind a portrait of herself," Baba went on, oblivious to my unease. "It took the artist three attempts to get it right. Xiaoqing grew more pathetic with each passing day, but she never forgot her duty to be beautiful. Each morning she dressed her hair and clothed herself in her finest silks. She died sitting up, looking so perfect that those who came to see her believed her still to be alive. Then her owner's terrible wife burned Xiaoqing's poems and all but one of the portraits."

Baba gazed out the window to Solitary Island, his eyes glassy and filled with . . . pity? desire? longing?

Into the heavy silence, I said, "Not everything was lost, Baba. Before Xiaoqing died, she wrapped some jewelry in discarded paper and gave it to her maid's daughter. When the girl opened the package, she found eleven poems on those abandoned sheets."

"Recite one of them for me, will you, Peony?"

My father hadn't helped me understand what I was feeling, but he did give me a glimmer of the romantic thoughts my stranger might be experiencing as he waited for me to come to him. I took a breath and began to recite.

"The sound of cold rain hitting the forlorn window is not bearable—"

"Please close your mouth!" Mama ordered. She never came here, and her appearance was startling and unsettling. How long had she been listening? To my father, she said, "You tell our daughter about Xiaoqing, but you know perfectly well she was not the only one to die upon reading *The Peony Pavilion.*"

"Stories tell us how we should live," my father responded easily, covering the surprise he must have felt at my mother's presence and her accusatory tone.

"The story of Xiaoqing has a lesson for our daughter?" Mama asked. "Peony was born into one of the finest families in Hangzhou. That other girl was a thin horse, bought and sold like property. One girl is pure. The other was a—"

"I'm aware of Xiaoqing's profession," my father cut in. "You don't need to remind me. But when I speak to our daughter about Xiaoqing, I'm thinking more of the lessons that can be learned from the opera that inspired her. Surely you see no harm in that."

"No harm? Are you suggesting our daughter's fate will be like that of Du Liniang?"

I glanced furtively at the servant standing by the door. How long before he reported this—gleefully, probably—to another servant and it spread throughout the compound?

"Peony could learn from her, yes," Baba answered evenly. "Liniang is fair, her heart kind and pure, her vision farsighted, and her will steadfast and true."

"Waaa!" Mama responded. "That girl was stubborn in love! How many girls need to die from this story before you see the perils?"

My cousins and I whispered about these unfortunates late at night when we thought no one was listening. We spoke of Yu Niang, who became enamored of the opera at the age of thirteen and died by seventeen, with the text at her side. The great Tang Xianzu, heartbroken at the news, wrote poems eulogizing her. But soon came many many more girls, who read the story, became lovesick like Liniang, wasted away, and died, hoping that true love would find them and bring them back to life.

"Our daughter is a phoenix," Baba said. "I will see her married to a dragon, not a crow."

This answer did not satisfy my mother. When she was happy, she could change ice crystals into flowers. When she was sad or angry—as she was now—she could turn dark clouds into swarms of biting insects.

"An overeducated daughter is a dead daughter," my mother announced. "Talent is not a gift we should wish on Peony. All this reading, where do you think it will end—in nuptial bliss or in disappointment, consumption, and death?"

"I've told you before, Peony will not die from words."

Mama and Baba seemed to have forgotten I was in the room, and I didn't move for fear they would notice me. Just yesterday I'd heard them argue about this subject. I rarely saw my parents together. When I did, it was for festivals or religious rites in the ancestral hall, where every word and action was set in advance. Now I wondered if they were like this all the time.

"How will she learn to be a good wife and mother if she keeps coming here?" Mama demanded.

"How will she not?" Baba asked, no concern in his voice. To my great surprise and my mother's disgust, he loosely quoted Prefect Du speaking about his daughter. "A young lady needs an understanding of letters, so that when she marries she will not be deficient in conversation with her husband. And Peony's role is to be a moral guardian, is it not? You should be happy that she cares little for pretty dresses, new hairpins, or painting her face. While she is lovely, we need to remember that her face is not what distinguishes her. Her beauty is a reflection of the virtue and talent she keeps inside. One day she will offer comfort and solace to her husband through reading to him, but ultimately we are training our daughter to be a good mother—no more, no less. Her role is to teach her daughters to write poetry and perfect their womanly skills. Most of all, she will help our grandson in his studies, until he is old enough to leave the women's chambers. When he completes his studies, she will have her day of glory and honor. Only then will she shine. Only then will she be recognized."

My mother could not argue this point; she acquiesced. "Just so long as her reading doesn't cause her to cross any boundaries. You wouldn't want her to become unruly. And if you must tell our daughter stories, can't you tell her of the gods and goddesses?"

When my father wouldn't agree, Mama's eyes came to rest on me. She said to my father, "How much longer will you keep her?"

"Just a little while."

As quietly as she'd come, my mother disappeared. My father had won the argument, I think. At least he didn't seem particularly perturbed as he made a notation in an account book and then set down his calligraphy brush, got up, and walked to the window to look out to Solitary Island.

A servant came in, bowed to my father, and handed him a sealed letter with an official red chop. My father fingered it thoughtfully, as though he might already know what was written inside. Since he didn't seem to want to open it with me sitting there, I rose, thanked him again for giving me the edition of *The Peony Pavilion,* and left the library.

Desire

ANOTHER LUSH AND WARM NIGHT. IN OUR WOMEN'S chambers we enjoyed a banquet that included beans dried in spring sunshine and then steamed with dried tangerine peel, and red seventh-month crabs, which were the size of hen's eggs and available from our local waters only at this time of year. Special ingredients were added to the married women's dishes to help them get pregnant, while others were left out for those who were or might be with child: rabbit meat, because everyone knows it can cause a hare lip, and lamb, because it can cause a baby to be born ill. But I wasn't hungry. My mind was already in the Riding-the-Wind Pavilion.

When the cymbals and drums called us to the garden, I lagged behind, doing my best to be gracious and make small talk with my aunts, the concubines, and the wives of my father's guests. I joined the last group to leave our chambers. Only cushions on the outer edge of the women's area remained. I took one and looked around to make sure

I'd made the right decision. Yes, my mother, as the hostess, sat in the middle of the group. Tonight all the unmarried girls but me had been clustered together. Tan Ze—whether of her own accord or because my mother had insisted on it—had been relegated to the section with girls her own age.

Once again my father had chosen highlights for this evening's performance, which began three years after Du Liniang's death with the scholar Liu Mengmei falling ill on his long journey to take the imperial exams. Liniang's old tutor gives Mengmei shelter at her shrine near the plum tree. As soon as the next piece of music started, I could tell that we'd gone with Liniang to the afterworld for Infernal Judgment. Since tonight I couldn't see the performers, I had to imagine the judge, fearful in his aspect, as he talked about reincarnation and how souls scatter like sparks from a firecracker. They're sent to any of 48,000 fates in the realms of desire, of form, and of the formless, or to one of the 242 levels of Hell. Liniang pleaded with the judge, telling him a terrible mistake had been made, for she was too young to be there, had neither married nor drunk wine, but had fallen into longing and then lost her life.

"When in the world did anyone die from a dream?" The judge's voice tore into me as he demanded an explanation from the Flower Spirit, who had brought about Liniang's lovesickness and death. Then, after checking the Register of Marriages, he determined that indeed Liniang had been destined to be with Mengmei, and—since her ancestor tablet hadn't been dotted—granted her permission to wander the world as a ghost in search of the husband she'd been fated to marry. After this, he charged the Flower Spirit with keeping Liniang's physical body from decaying. As a ghost, Liniang returned to the earthly realm to live near her tomb under the plum

tree. When Sister Stone, the old nun charged with caring for the tomb, made offerings on a table under the tree, Liniang was so grateful that she scattered plum blossoms into which she infused her loving thoughts.

As Mengmei recovered at the shrine, he grew restless and strolled through the gardens. Quite by accident—except that it had to be fate interfering—he found the box with Liniang's rolled-up self-portrait scroll. He believed he'd found a painting of the goddess Guanyin. He took the scroll back to his room and burned incense before it. He delighted in Guanyin's soft mist of hair, her tiny mouth shaped like a rosebud, and the way love's longing seemed to be locked between her brows, but the closer he looked, the more convinced he became that the woman on the silk couldn't be the goddess. Guanyin should be floating, but he saw tiny lily feet poking out from beneath the woman's skirts. Then he saw the poem that had been written on the silk and realized that this was a self-portrait painted by a mortal girl.

As he read the lines, he recognized himself as Liu, the willow; the girl in the painting also held a sprig of plum in her hand, as though she were embracing Mengmei—Dream of Plum. He wrote a poem in reply and then called upon her to step down from the painting and join him.

Quiet expectancy settled over the women on our side of the screen as Liniang's dark ghostly side emerged from her garden tomb to tempt, woo, and seduce her scholar.

I waited until she began tapping at Mengmei's window and he started asking her questions about who she was, and then I rose and swiftly left. My feelings mirrored Liniang's as she glided around her scholar, calling to him, teasing him with her words. *"I am a flower you brought to bloom in the dark of night,"* I heard Liniang sing. *"This body, a thousand pieces of gold, I offer to you without hesitation."* I was an unmarried girl, but I understood her wish. Mengmei accepted her offer. Again and again, he asked Liniang's name, but she refused to give it. It was easier for her to give her body than reveal her identity.

I slowed as I neared the zigzag bridge that led to the Riding-the-Wind Pavilion. I envisioned my lily feet—hidden under my flowing skirt—blooming with each step. I smoothed the silk, let my fingers play across my hair to make sure that all my pins were in place, and then for a few moments I held my palms over my heart, trying to still its desperate, anxious beating. I had to remember who and what I was. I was the only daughter in a family that had produced imperial scholars of the highest rank for nine generations. I was betrothed. I had bound feet. If anything untoward happened, I would not be able to run away as a big-footed girl might, nor would I be able to float away on a ghostly cloud as Liniang could have done. If I was caught, my betrothal would be broken. A girl couldn't do anything worse than bring embarrassment and disgrace on her family in this way, but I was foolish and stupid and my mind was dulled by desire.

I pressed my fingers hard against my eyes and brought my mother into that pain. If I had any reason left, I would have seen her disappointment in me. If I had any sense, I would have known how severe her anger would be. Instead, I tried to bring into my mind her dignity, her beauty, her stature. This was my home, my garden, my pavilion, my night, my moon, my life.

I stepped across the zigzag bridge and into the Riding-the-Wind Pavilion, where he waited for me. At first we didn't exchange words. Perhaps he was surprised that I had come; it didn't say much about my character, after all. Perhaps he was as afraid as I was that we'd be caught. Or perhaps he was breathing me in just as I was letting him come into my lungs, my eyes, my heart.

He spoke first. "The portrait doesn't just represent Liniang," he said, using formality as a way to keep us both from making a terrible mistake. "It holds the key to Mengmei's destiny with her—the plum blossom in her hand, the words of invitation to someone named Willow in her poem. He sees his future wife in that fragile piece of silk."

These were hardly the romantic words I longed for, but I was a girl and I followed his lead.

"I love the plum blossoms," I responded. "They appear again and again. Did you stay to see the scene where Liniang scatters the petals on the altar under the plum tree?" When he nodded, I went on. "Would the blossoms sprinkled by Liniang's ghost appear different from those brought there by the wind?"

He didn't answer my question. Instead he said, his voice thick, "Let us look at the moon together."

I let Liniang's courage come into my heart and then I took small steps across the pavilion until I reached his side. Tomorrow would be the quarter moon, so it was little more than a sliver hanging low in the sky. A sudden breeze came off the lake, cooling my burning face. Tendrils of hair came loose, caressing my skin and sending shivers along my spine.

"Are you cold?" he asked, moving behind me, putting his hands on my shoulders.

I wanted to turn and face him, look into his eyes, and . . . ? Liniang had seduced her scholar, but I didn't know what to do.

Behind me, he dropped his hands. I felt slightly adrift. The only thing keeping me from running or fainting was the warmth emanating from his body, that's how close we stood. And I didn't move.

From the distance came the opera. Mengmei and Liniang continued to meet. Always he asked her name; always she refused to give it. Always he asked: *"How can your footfall be so soundless?"* And always Liniang admitted that it was true she left no footprints in the dust. Finally, one night, the poor ghost girl arrived, fearful and trembling, because at last she was going to tell him who and what she was.

In the Riding-the-Wind Pavilion two people stood paralyzed, too afraid to move, too afraid to speak, too afraid to flee. I felt my young man's breath on my neck.

From the garden, Mengmei sang in question, *"Are you betrothed?"*

Even before I could hear Liniang's answer, a whispered voice came into my ear. "Are you betrothed?"

"I've been betrothed since infancy." I barely recognized my voice, because all I could hear was the blood pounding in my ears.

He sighed behind me. "A wife has been chosen for me too."

"Then we shouldn't be meeting."

"I could say good night," he said. "Is that what you want?"

From the stage, I heard Liniang confide to her scholar her worries that now that they had done clouds and rain together he would only want her as a concubine and not as a wife. Hearing this, indignation suddenly bubbled up inside me. I wasn't the only one doing something wrong here. I turned to face him.

"Is this what your wife can expect in her marriage, that you would meet strange women?"

He smiled guilelessly, but I thought about how he had prowled through our garden when he should have been watching the opera with my father, my uncles, Commissioner Tan, and the other male guests.

"Although men and women are different, in love and desire they are the same," he recited the popular saying. Then he added, "I'm hoping not only for a companion in the home but in the bedchamber as well."

"So you're looking for concubines even before you're married," I responded tartly.

Since marriages were arranged and neither the bride nor the groom had any say in the match, concubines were every wife's fear. Husbands fell in love with concubines. They came together by choice, had no responsibilities, and could delight in each other's company, while marriages were a matter of duty and a way to provide sons who, in time, would perform rites in the ancestral hall.

"If you were my wife," he said, "I would never have need of concubines."

I lowered my eyes, oddly happy.

Some might say all this is too ridiculous. Some might say it could never have happened this way. Some might say this was in my imagination—a fevered imagination that would eventually lead to my obsessed writings and no-good end. Some might even say, if everything happened the way I've recounted, that I deserved my no-good end and had earned *worse* than death, which in truth is what I got. But at the time I was joyous.

"I think we were destined to meet," he said. "I didn't know you would be here last night, but you were. We can't fight fate. Instead, we must accept that fate has given us a special opportunity."

I blushed deeply and looked away.

All the while, the opera played in our garden. I knew it so well that even though I was distracted by what was happening with my stranger, a part of me was letting the story seep into my consciousness. Now at last I heard Liniang admit who she was: a spectral image locked between life and the afterworld. Mengmei's terrified screams echoed through the Riding-the-Wind Pavilion. I shivered again.

My young man cleared his throat. "I think you know this opera very well."

"I'm just a girl and my thoughts are of no importance," I answered, trying to be modest, which was foolish given our circumstances.

He looked at me quizzically. "You are beautiful, which pleases me, but it is what is inside here"—without touching me, he reached out and brought the tip of his finger to a spot over my heart, the seat of all consciousness—"that I'd like to know."

The place on my chest where he'd almost touched me burned. We were both bold and reckless, but where Liniang's enticing words and her scholar's equally suggestive actions eventually ended in consummation, I was a living girl who could never give herself away so easily without paying a severe price.

In the garden, Mengmei overcame his fear of the ghost, proclaimed his love, and agreed to marry Liniang. He painted the dot on Liniang's ancestor tablet, something her father had been too hurried with his promotion to do. Mengmei opened the grave and removed the jade funeral stone that had been placed in Liniang's mouth. With that, her body once again breathed the air of the living.

"I must go," I said.

"Will you meet me again tomorrow?"

"I can't," I said. "They'll miss me."

I considered it a miracle that no one had come after me on either night. How could I take one more chance?

"Tomorrow, but not here," he went on as though I hadn't just refused him. "Is there another place? Perhaps somewhere farther from the garden?"

"Our Moon-Viewing Pavilion is by the shore." I knew where it was, but I'd never been there. I wasn't even allowed to go there with my father. "It is the farthest from the halls and the garden."

"Then I will wait for you there."

I longed for him to touch me, but I was afraid.

"You will come to me," he said.

It took great willpower for me to turn away and head back to the opera. I was fully aware of his eyes on me as I crossed back and forth across the zigzag bridge.

No girl—not even the spoiled Tan Ze—could meet her future husband like this, let alone a strange man, of her own volition, of her own choosing, with no watchful eyes, no condemnation. I had been carried away by the story of Liniang, but she was not a living girl who would suffer any consequences.

Spring Sickness in Summer

ALL GIRLS THINK ABOUT THEIR WEDDINGS. WE WORRY that our husbands will be cold, mean, indifferent, or neglectful, but mostly we imagine something wonderful and joyous. How can we not create a fantasy in our minds when the reality is so hard? So, during the darkness as the nightingales sang, I imagined my wedding, my husband waiting for me in his home, and everything leading up to the moment we would be united—only, in place of a faceless man, I envisioned my handsome stranger.

I dreamed of the final bride-price gifts arriving. I imagined the sparkle and weight of the hairpins, earrings, rings, bracelets, and loose jewels. I thought of the Suzhou silks that would rival even what my father made in his factories. I dreamed of the last pig that would be part of the livestock my father would receive in exchange for me. I imagined the way my father would have the pig butchered and how I would wrap the head and tail to send back to the Wu family as a sign of respect. I thought of the gifts my father would send with the pieces of pig: sprigs of artemisia to expel evil influences before my arrival, pomegranates to symbolize my fertility, jujubes because the word sounded like *having children quickly,* and the seven grains, because the character for kernel was identical in writing and sound to *offspring.*

I dreamed of what the palanquin would look like when it came to fetch me. I thought about meeting my mother-in-law for the first time and how she would hand me the confidential wedding book that would instruct me on what to do when the time came for clouds and rain. I imagined my first night alone in bed with my stranger. I conjured our future years together unhampered by worries about money or officialdom. We would enjoy the day, the night, a smile, a word, a kiss, a glance. All lovely thoughts. All pointless dreams.

When morning came—my birthday and the Double Seven Festival—I had no appetite. My mind was dense with memories of the young man's breath against my cheek and his whispered words. This was, I realized with great happiness, lovesickness.

Today I wanted everything I did—from the moment I got up until I met him in the Moon-Viewing Pavilion—to be of my own choosing. I had Willow unwrap my bindings, letting her hold my right ankle in her palm and watching as her fingers unwound the cloth over, under, and around my foot in a hypnotic motion. She set my feet to soak in a bath of pomelo leaves, to keep my flesh soft and easy to bind, and then washed away the old skin. She used powder made from the root bark of the wolfberry to smooth away rough spots, sprinkled alum between my toes to ward off infection, and finished with a fine dusting of fragrant powder to entice.

My bound feet were extremely beautiful—my best feature—and I took great pride in them. Ordinarily I paid strict attention to Willow's ministrations, making sure that my deep crease was fully cleaned, calluses cut away, any fragments of broken bone that poked through my skin sanded down, and my nails kept as short as possible. This time, I relished the sensitivity of my skin to the warmth of the water and the cool of the air. A woman's feet were her greatest mystery and gift. If some miracle happened and I married my stranger, I would care for them in secret, powdering them to accentuate their odor, and then rewrapping them tightly so they would appear as small and delicate as possible.

I had Willow bring me a tray laden with several pairs of slippers. I gazed at them pensively. Which pair would he prefer, the magenta silk embroidered with butterflies or the pale green with the tiny dragonflies?

I looked at the silks Willow brought out for me and wondered if he might like them. Willow put me into my clothes, combed my hair, washed my face, and applied powder and rouge to my cheeks.

I was hopelessly lost in thoughts of love, but I still had to make offerings to my ancestors on Double Seven. I was not the first in my family to go to the ancestral hall this morning. We all wish for wealth, good harvests, and offspring, and already offerings of food had been made to encourage reciprocal gifts of fecundity from our ancestors. I saw whole taro roots—a symbol of fertility—and knew that my aunts and the concubines had been here to ask my ancestors to bring sons to our line. My grandfather's concubines had left little piles of fresh loquats and lichee. They tended to be excessively extravagant, knowing that in the afterworld they would maintain their status as my grandfather's property and hoping Grandmother was whispering good words about them in his ear. My uncles had brought rice to ensure peace and plenty, while my father had offered a warm platter of meats to encourage more wealth and a good crop of silkworms. Chopsticks and bowls had been provided for my ancestors as well, so they might dine with elegant ease.

I had started toward the Spring Pavilion for breakfast when I heard Mama call me. I followed her voice to the room for little girls. When I entered, I was assailed by the unique scent of a special broth of frankincense, apricot kernel, and white mulberry that my old amah used for all the Chen daughters during the footbinding process. I saw Second Aunt holding Orchid, her youngest daughter, on her lap, my mother kneeling before the two of them, and all the other little girls who lived in this room—not one of them older than seven—clustered around them.

"Peony," Mama said when she saw me, "come here. I need your help."

I'd heard Mama complain that Orchid's footbinding wasn't going fast enough and that Second Aunt was too soft-hearted for the job. Mama held one of the little girl's feet lightly in her hand. All the required bones had broken, but no effort had been made to mold them into a better shape. What I saw looked like the body of an octopus filled with broken and jagged little sticks. In other words, a useless, ugly, purple-and-yellow mess.

"You know the men in our household are weak," Mama scolded Second Aunt. "They resigned their commissions and came home after the Cataclysm. They refuse to work for the new emperor, so they no longer wield any real power. They've been forced to shave their foreheads. They no longer ride horses, preferring the comfort of palanquins. In place of battle, the hunt, and argument, they collect delicate porcelains and paintings on silk. They have retreated and become more . . . feminine." She paused before going on briskly. "Since this is so, we have to be more womanly than ever before."

With this she shook Orchid's foot. The girl whimpered, and tears rolled down Second Aunt's cheeks. Mama paid no attention.

"We must follow the Four Virtues and the Three Obediences. Remember, when a daughter, obey your father; when a wife, obey your husband; when a widow, obey your son. Your husband is Heaven," she said, quoting the *Classic of Filial Duty for Girls*. "You know what I'm saying is true."

Second Aunt didn't speak, but these words scared me. Since I was the eldest girl in our household, I remembered all too clearly each time one of my cousins had had her feet bound. Too often my aunts were merciful and Mama would rewrap the feet herself, making both the girl and her mother weep in pain and misery.

"These are difficult times," Mama said sternly to the crying pair. "Our footbinding helps us to be softer, more languid, smaller." She paused again, and then added, in a kinder but no less adamant tone, "I will show you how this is done. I expect you to do this for your daughter four days from now. Every four days, tighter and tighter. Give your daughter the gift of your mother love. Do you understand?"

Second Aunt's tears dripped from her cheeks into her daughter's hair. All of us in the room knew that in four days Second Aunt would be no stronger than she was now and a variation of this scene would be repeated.

Mama turned her attention back to me. "Come sit beside me." Once we were eye to eye, she gave me a lovely mother smile. "These will be the last set of feet to be bound in our household before your marriage. I want you to go to your husband's home with the proper skills to bind your own daughter's feet one day."

The other little girls looked at me in admiration, hoping their mothers would do this for them too.

"Unfortunately," Mama said, "we first have to fix what has been neglected here." She then forgave Second Aunt by gently adding, "All mothers are cowardly when it comes to this job. There were times when I was as feeble as you. It's tempting not to wrap the bindings tight enough. But then what happens? The child walks and the bones begin to move within their bindings. Don't you see, Second Aunt, that while you think you're doing your daughter a favor, you're only prolonging her ordeal and worsening her pain? You must remember that a plain face is given by Heaven, but poorly bound feet are a sign of laziness, not only of the mother but of the daughter as well. What kind of message does this send to prospective in-laws? Girls should be as delicate as flowers. It is important that they walk elegantly, sway gracefully, and show their respectability. In this way girls become precious gems."

Mama's voice hardened again as she spoke to me.

"We have to be strong and correct mistakes when they occur. Now take your cousin's ankle with your left hand."

I did as I was told.

Mama folded her hand over my own and squeezed. "You're going to have to hold on very tight, because . . ." She glanced up at Orchid and decided not to finish her sentence. "Peony," she continued, "we don't do washing, but surely you've seen Willow or one of the other servants wash your clothes or linens."

I nodded.

"Good, so you know that when they're done rinsing they wring the clothes as tightly as possible to get out all the remaining water. We're going to do something like that. Please follow exactly what I do."

The written character for *mother love* is composed of two elements: *love* and *pain*. I had always thought this emotion was felt by daughters for their mothers, who inflict pain on us by binding our feet, but looking at Second Aunt's tears and my mother's courage I realized this emotion was for them. A mother suffers deeply to give birth, bind feet, and say goodbye to a daughter when she marries out. I wanted to be able to show my daughters how much I loved them, but I felt sick to my stomach—in sympathy for my little cousin and in fear that I would fail in some way.

"Mother"—Mama addressed her sister-in-law—"hold your daughter firmly." She looked at me, gave me a nod of encouragement, and said, "Put one hand around the foot so that it meets your other hand . . . as though you were about to wring clothes."

The pressure on Orchid's broken bones caused her to squirm. Second Aunt wrapped her arms even more tightly around her daughter.

"I wish we could do this quickly," Mama went on, "but haste and a soft heart are what caused this problem in the first place."

She kept her grip on the ankle with her left hand, while her right slowly pulled away toward the toes. My cousin began to scream.

I felt light-headed but exuberant too. Mama was showing me much mother love.

I followed her movement and my cousin's screams intensified.

"Good," Mama said. "Feel the bones straighten beneath

your fingers. Let them fall into place as they squeeze through your hand."

I came to the toes and let go. Orchid's feet were still horribly misshapen. But instead of strange bumps poking against the flesh, the feet looked like two long chilies. Above me, Orchid's body heaved with sobs as she tried to catch her breath.

"This next part will be painful," Mama observed. She looked to one of the cousins standing to her right, and said, "Go and find Shao. Where is she anyway? No matter. Just bring her. And quickly!"

The girl returned with my old wet nurse. She had once been part of a good family, but she came to work for us when she became a widow at an early age. The older I'd grown, the less I liked her, because she was so strict and unforgiving.

"Hold the child's legs in place," Mama ordered. "I don't want to see any movement from the knees down, except what comes from either my daughter's hands or my own. Understood?"

Shao had been through this many times and knew what needed to be done.

Mama glanced around at the cluster of girls. "Step back. Give us some room."

Although those girls were as curious as mice, Mama was the head woman in our household and they did as they were told.

"Peony, think of your own feet when you do this. You know how the toes are tucked under and how your mid-foot is folded in on itself? We accomplish this by rolling the bones under the foot as if you were rolling a sock. Can you do that?"

"I think so."

"Mother," Mama asked Second Aunt, "are you ready?"

Second Aunt, who was known for her pale skin, appeared almost translucent, as though her soul was barely in her body.

To me, Mama said, "Once again, just follow me."

And I did. I rolled the bones under, concentrating so hard that I barely noticed my cousin's shrieks. Shao's knobby hands held the legs with such strength that her knuckles went white. In her agony, Orchid vomited. The putrid mess shot from her mouth and spattered my mother's tunic, skirt, and face. Second Aunt apologized profusely, and I heard the bitter shame in her voice. Wave after wave of nausea washed over me, but Mama didn't flinch or waver for one moment in her task.

Finally, we were done. Mama looked at my work and patted my cheek. "You did an excellent job. This may be your special gift. You will make a fine wife and mother."

Never had my mother offered such approval for anything I'd done.

Mama wrapped the foot she'd worked on first. She did what Second Aunt couldn't do; she made the bindings very tight. Orchid was beyond tears by now, so the only sounds were my mother's voice and the soft swish of the cloth as she passed it up and over and under the foot, again and again, until all three meters had been used on the one tiny foot.

"More girls are having their feet bound than ever before in the history of our country," Mama explained. "The Manchu barbarians believe our women's practice to be backward! They see our husbands and we worry for them, but the Manchus can't see us in our women's chambers. We wrap our daughters' feet as an act of rebellion against those foreigners. Look around; even our maids, servants, and slaves have bound feet. Even the old, the poor, and the frail have bound feet. We have our women's ways. This is what makes us valuable. It's what makes us marriageable. And they cannot make us stop!"

Mama sewed the bindings shut, set the foot on a cushion, and began working on the foot I'd reshaped. When she finished, she set this foot on the cushion as well. She batted her sister-in-law's comforting fingers away from Orchid's still-wet cheeks and added a few final thoughts.

"Through our footbinding we have won in two ways. We weak women have beaten the Manchus. Their policy failed so badly that now the Manchu women try to emulate *us*. If you went outside, you would see them with their big ugly shoes with tiny platforms built in the shape of bound-foot slippers tacked under the soles to give them the *illusion* of bound feet. Ha! They cannot compete with us or stop us from cherishing our culture. More importantly, our bound feet continue to be an enticement to our husbands. Remember, a good husband is one who brings you pleasure too."

With the sensations I'd had in my body since meeting my stranger, I felt I knew what she was talking about. Strangely, though, I'd never seen my mother and father touch. Did this come from my father or my mother? My father had always been affectionate with me. He hugged me and kissed me whenever we saw each other in the corridors or I visited him in his library. The physical distance between my parents had to come from some lack in my mother. Had she gone to her marriage with the same apprehension I would now take to mine? Was this why my father had concubines?

Mama stood up and pulled her wet skirt away from her legs. "I'm going to change. Peony, please go ahead to the Spring Pavilion. Second Aunt, leave your daughter here and go with Peony. We have guests. I'm sure they're waiting for us. Ask them to start breakfast without me." To Shao, she added, "I'll send *congee* for the child. Make sure she eats it, and then give her some herbs to ease the pain. She may rest today. I'm counting on you to let me know what transpires four days from now. We can't allow this to happen again. It's unfair to the child and it frightens the younger girls."

After she left, I stood up. For a moment, the room went dark. My head finally cleared, but my stomach was far from calm.

"Take your time, Auntie," I managed to say. "I'll meet you in the corridor when you're ready."

I hurried back to my room, shut the door, lifted the lid off the half-full chamber pot, and threw up. Fortunately, Willow was not there to see me, because I don't know how I would have explained myself. Then I got up, rinsed my mouth, walked back down the corridor, and arrived just as Second Aunt emerged from the girls' hall.

I'd finally done something that made my mother truly proud, but it had also made me sick. For all my desire to be strong like Liniang, I was softhearted like my aunt. I wouldn't be able to show my mother love to my daughter. I'd be a disaster when it came to binding her feet. I hoped that Mama would never know. My mother-in-law might not let the news of my failure pass beyond the Wu family gates, just as Mama wouldn't let anyone know of Second Aunt's continued weakness. This fell under the admonition of never doing anything that would allow the family to lose face, and the Wus—if they were good and kind—would do their part by keeping the secret within the four walls of their home.

I expected hushed tones when Second Aunt and I entered the Spring Pavilion, for surely every woman in the villa had heard Orchid's screams, but Third Aunt had taken the opportunity to play at being head woman. Dishes had been set out and the women were busily eating and gossiping as though nothing out of the ordinary had happened on the morning of Double Seven in the Chen Family Villa.

I forgot to harden myself against my cousins' predictable biting comments that came over breakfast, but oddly their words fell away from me like the old skin that Willow had washed from my feet. I couldn't eat, however, not even the special dumplings that Mama had Cook prepare for my birthday. How could I put food in my mouth and swallow it when my stomach was still so unsettled—from the binding, from my secret happiness, and from my worries about being caught tonight?

After breakfast, I went back to my room. Later, when I heard the soft padding of lily feet as the others left their rooms and headed for the Lotus-Blooming Hall, I wrapped one of my paintings in a piece of silk for today's contest, took a deep breath, and stepped out into the corridor.

When I got to the Lotus-Blooming Hall, I sought my mother's side. Her warm feelings from earlier seemed to have evaporated, but I didn't worry. She would be exceptionally busy today between the guests, the contests, and the celebration, I thought, as she walked away from me.

We started with an art contest. If I was sloppy at embroidery and awkward at the zither, I was even worse when it came to painting. The contest's first category was peonies. Once it seemed all the paintings had been displayed, expectant eyes turned to me.

"Peony, where is *your* peony?" one of our guests asked.

"It's her name," Third Aunt confided to the others, "but she never practices her petal work."

This contest was followed by one for chrysanthemums, another for plum blossoms, and finally for orchids. I surreptitiously laid my painting on the table. My orchids were too heavy and another girl won the competition. Next came paintings with butterflies, and finally butterflies and flowers together. I didn't enter either of those categories.

Always the same flowers and butterflies, I thought to myself. But what else could we paint? Our paintings were about what we could see in the garden: butterflies and flowers. Standing there, looking at the beautifully powdered faces of my aunts, cousins, and our female guests, I saw wistful longing. But if I was looking at them, they were observing me too. My mooning did not escape the notice of the other women, who were all trained to spot weakness and vulnerability.

"Your Peony seems to have been overcome by spring sickness in summer," Fourth Aunt remarked.

"Yes, we have all noticed the heightened color on her cheeks," Third Aunt added. "What could be on her mind?"

"Tomorrow I will pick herbs and brew a tea to ease her spring sickness," Fourth Aunt offered helpfully.

"Spring sickness in summer?" my mother echoed. "Peony is too practical."

"We like to see your daughter this way," Second Aunt said. "Perhaps she will confide her secrets to the other girls. They all wish to have romantic thoughts too. Every girl should look this pretty on her sixteenth birthday. Five more months to her marriage. I think we can all agree she is ready to be plucked."

I tried as hard as possible to make my face as unfathomable as a pond on a humid summer night. I failed, and some of the older women tittered at my girlish embarrassment.

"Then it's a good thing she's marrying soon," my mother agreed, in a deceptively light tone. "But you're right, Second Aunt, maybe she should speak to your daughter. I'm sure that Broom's husband would be grateful for any improvement on their wedding night." She clapped her hands softly. "Now come, let us go to the garden for our final contests."

As the other women filed out, I felt my mother's eyes on me— weighing and considering what had been said. She didn't speak and I refused to meet her eyes. We were like two stone statues in that room. I was grateful she'd protected me, but to say that would be to admit . . . what? That I was lovesick? That I'd met someone in the Riding-the-Wind Pavilion the last two nights? That I planned to meet him tonight in the Moon-Viewing Pavilion, a place on our property I was not allowed to go? Suddenly I realized I'd changed in a fundamental way. Monthly bleeding doesn't turn a girl into a woman, nor does betrothal or new skills. Love had turned me into a woman.

I called upon my grandmother's poise and dignity, and without saying a word I lifted my head and walked out the door and into the garden.

I sat on a porcelain jardinière. The garden looked very pretty, and much of the inspiration for this last round of contests would come—as usual—from what we could see. My cousins and aunts offered bits of poetry from famous women poets that invoked the plum blossom, chrysanthemum, orchid, and peony. So many lovely words for such beautiful and evocative flowers, but I scrolled through my memory until I came to a dark poem that had been written on a wall in Yangzhou by an unknown woman during the Cataclysm. I waited until the others had recited their poems and then I began to speak in what I imagined to be the sorrowful voice of that desperate writer:

"The trees are bare.
In the distance, the honks of mourning geese.
If only my tears of blood could dye red the blossoms of the
plum tree.

But I will never make it to spring.
My heart is empty and my life has no value anymore.
Each moment a thousand tears."

This poem—considered one of the saddest of the Cataclysm—reached deep into everyone's hearts. Second Aunt, still upset over her daughter's footbinding, once again shed tears, but she wasn't the only one. Great feelings of *qing* filled the garden. We shared in the despair of that lost and presumably dead woman.

Then I felt my mother's eyes piercing me. All color had drained from her face, making her rouge stand out like bruises on her cheeks. Her voice was barely audible as she said, "On this beautiful day my daughter brings misery into our midst."

I didn't know why Mama was upset.

"My daughter isn't feeling well," Mama confided to the mothers around her, "and I'm afraid she's forgotten what's proper." She looked back at me. "You should spend the rest of the day and evening in bed."

Mama had control over me, but was she really going to keep me from the opera because I recited an unhappy poem? Tears gathered in my eyes. I blinked them back.

"I'm not sick," I said, rather pathetically.

"That is not what Willow tells me."

I flushed with anger and disappointment. When she'd emptied the chamber pot, Willow must have seen that I'd thrown up and told my mother. Now my mother knew I'd failed—once again—as a soon-to-be wife and mother. But this knowledge didn't chasten me. It made me very determined. I wouldn't let her keep me from my meeting in the Moon-Viewing Pavilion. I brought a forefinger to my cheekbone, inclined my head, and drew my features into the prettiest, blankest, most harmless picture of a Hangzhou maiden.

"Oh, Mama, I think it is as my aunties have said. On the day we honor the Weaving Maid I have let my mind drift to the celestial bridge that will be formed tonight for the two lovers to meet. I may have had a momentary case of spring feelings, but I don't have spring fever, aches of any sort, or any womanly complaints. My lapse is only an indicator of my maiden status, nothing more."

I appeared so innocent, and the other women looked at me with such benevolence, that my mother would have had a hard time sending me away.

After a long moment, she asked, "Who can recite a poem with *hibiscus* in it?"

Everything—as it was every day in our women's quarters —seemed a test of some sort. And every test reminded me of my inferiority. I didn't excel at anything—not footbinding, or embroidery, painting, zither playing, or reciting poetry either. How could I go to my marriage now when I loved someone else so deeply? How could I be the wife my husband deserved, needed, and wanted? My mother had followed all the rules, yet she'd failed to give my father sons. If Mama had been unsuccessful as a wife, how could I ever succeed? Maybe my husband would turn away from me, embarrass me in front of my mother-in-law, and find delights in the singing girls around the lake or by taking in concubines.

I recalled something Mama liked to repeat: "Concubines are a fact of life. What matters is that *you* choose them before your husband does, and then how *you* treat them. Don't hit them yourself. Let him do it."

That was not what I wanted for my life.

Today was my sixteenth birthday. Tonight, in the heavens, the Weaving Maid and the Cowherd would be reunited. In our garden, Liniang would be resurrected by

Mengmei's love. And in the Moon-Viewing Pavilion, I would meet my stranger. I may not have been the most perfect young woman in all of Hangzhou, but under his gaze I felt I was.

Soiled Shoes

CONFUCIUS WROTE: *ESPECT THE GHOSTS AND SPIRITS but keep them at a distance.* On Double Seven, people forgot about ghosts and ancestors. Everyone just wanted to enjoy the celebration—from our special games to the opera performance. I changed into a silk gauze tunic embroidered with a pair of birds flying above summer flowers to evoke the happiness I felt when my stranger and I were together. Under this I wore a skirt of silk brocade with a band of snow-crabapple blossoms embroidered around the hem, which attracted the eye to my fuchsia-colored silk bound-foot shoes. Gold earrings dangled from my ears, and my wrists were heavy with gold and jade bangles that had been given to me over the years by my family. I was not in the least over-dressed. Everywhere I looked I saw lovely women and girls who tinkled and jangled as they swayed across the room to greet one another in their rhythmic lily gaits.

On the altar table, set up for the occasion in the Lotus-Blooming Hall, sticks of incense burned in bronze tripods, filling the room with a deliciously pungent odor. Piles of fruit—oranges, melons, bananas, carambolas, and dragon eyes—sat in cloisonné dishes. On one end of the table stood a white porcelain bowl filled with water and pomelo leaves to symbolize the ritual bath given to brides. In the middle of the table lay a circular tray—nearly one meter across—with a round center surrounded by six sections. The middle depicted the Weaving Maid and the Cowherd, with his buffalo wading nearby in the stream to remind us of the place the goddess had hidden her nakedness. The surrounding sections showed the Weaving Maid's other sisters. One by one, Mama invited the unmarried girls to place an offering for each sister in the corresponding section.

After the ceremony, we sat down to an extravagant banquet. Each dish had a special meaning, so we ate "dragon hoof that sends child"—pig leg with ten kinds of patrimonial seasonings braised over a slow fire—which was reputed to bring sons. The servants brought in a beggar's chicken for each table. With a strong *thwack,* the baked clay crust for each chicken was broken and an aroma of ginger, wine, and mushrooms escaped into the room. Course after course arrived, each flavored to satisfy one of the tastes: good, bad, fragrant, stinky, sweet, sour, salty, and bitter. For dessert, our servants presented us with malt cakes made with sticky rice, red beans, walnuts, and river-bank grass, to help us digest, reduce fat, and prolong life. It was a sumptuous meal, but I was too nervous to eat.

The banquet was followed by one last contest. The lanterns were turned down and each of the unmarried girls had a chance to thread a needle by the light from the tip of a single stick of incense. A needle successfully threaded meant that the girl would give birth to a son upon marriage. There had been much drinking of Shaoxing wine, so considerable laughter accompanied each failed attempt.

I joined in the laughter as best I could, but I was already plotting how I was going to meet my stranger without getting caught. I would have to use the scheming ways of the inner realm and make up what I thought might serve me well from the outside realm. I could only guess and hope and think about each move, as I did when I played chess with my father.

Unlike the first night, I didn't want to sit in the front row where I'd be closest to the opera but would also be in the one place where all the women could see me. I also couldn't linger behind as I had last night. If I did that again, my mother would suspect something. She knew I loved the opera too much to be late again. I had to appear as though I were trying to please her, especially after what had happened this afternoon. As my mind searched for the possibilities, my eyes fell on Tan Ze. I began to play out my moves. Yes, I could use the child to cloak myself in innocence.

As Lotus successfully threaded the needle and everyone applauded, I moved across the room to Ze, who perched on the edge of a chair, hoping my mother would choose her to take a turn at the game. That was never going to happen. Ze wasn't waiting for her wedding ceremonies to take place; she was a little girl who had yet to be matched.

I tapped her on the shoulder.

"Come with me," I said. "I want to show you something."

She slipped off the chair and I took her hand, making sure my mother saw what I was doing.

"You know I've already been betrothed," I said, as we walked to my room.

The little girl nodded, her face serious.

"Would you like to see my bride-price gifts?"

Ze squealed. Inside, I did practically the same thing but for a very different reason.

I opened pigskin chests and showed her the bolts of airy gauzes, lustrous satins, and heavy brocades that had already been sent.

When the crash of cymbals and the bang of drums began calling us to the garden, Ze got to her feet. Outside my room, women gathered in the corridor.

"You have to see my wedding costume," I rushed on. "You'll love the headdress."

The girl sat back down, eagerly wiggling her bottom into my bedding.

I brought out my embroidered red silk wedding skirt, which had dozens of tiny pleats. The women my father had hired to make it had adjusted their stitches so that the pattern of flowers, clouds, and interlocking good-luck symbols were perfectly aligned. On my wedding day the design would break apart only if I took too large a step. The tunic was equally exquisite. Instead of just four frogs to hold it shut—at my neck, across my breast, and under my arm—the seamstresses had made dozens of tiny braided frogs to confound my husband and prolong the wedding night. The headdress was simple and elegant: a garden of thin gold leaves that would quiver as I moved and shimmer in the light, with a red veil to cover my face so I wouldn't see my husband until he removed it. I had always loved my wedding costume, but the emotions it now stirred in me were very dark. What was the purpose of being wrapped like a present if you had no feelings for the person you were being given to?

"It's beautiful, but *my* father has promised I will have pearls and jade in my headdress," Ze boasted.

I barely heard her, because I was listening so hard to what was happening outside my room. The drums and cymbals still called the audience, but the corridor was quiet. I put my wedding costume away. Then I took Ze's hand and we left my room.

We wandered together to the garden. I saw my cousins grouped together behind the screen. Unbelievably, they'd saved a place for me. Lotus waved to me to join them. I smiled back and then bent to whisper in Ze's ear.

"Look, the unmarried girls want you to sit with them."

"They do?"

She didn't even wait for me to give her more encouragement but threaded her way through the cushions to the other girls, sat down, and immediately began talking nonstop to my cousins. They had shown me a little kindness and this was how I repaid them.

I made a great show of looking around for an available cushion near the front or in the middle, but of course by now there were none. I feigned a look of disappointment and then delicately sank to a cushion on the edge at the back of the women's section.

Tonight's opening scene was one I would have liked to have seen but could only hear from my spot at the back of the audience. Liniang and Mengmei eloped—something completely unheard of in our culture. As soon as they were married, Liniang confessed that she was a virgin—this despite her ghostly nocturnal unions with Mengmei. As a ghost, the maiden status of her body in its grave had been preserved. The scene ended with Liniang and Mengmei departing for Hangzhou, where he would complete his studies for the imperial exams.

There was very little in the final third of the opera that I liked. It was mostly about the world beyond Liniang's garden—with great battle scenes, where everyone was on the move—but it completely captivated the audience on my side of the screen. Around me the women sank deeper into the story. I waited until I couldn't stand it any longer; then, with my heart pounding, I slowly rose, smoothed my skirts, and walked back as casually as possible toward the women's chambers.

But I didn't go to the Unmarried Girls' Hall. I turned off the main path and then hurried along the south wall of our property, past small ponds and viewing pavilions, until I reached the trail by the lakeshore. I had never been on this path before and was unsure how to proceed. Then I saw the Moon-Viewing Pavilion and sensed my stranger there already. Only the quarter moon illuminated the night, and I searched the darkness until I found him. He perched on the balustrade that lined the farthest edge of the pavilion, looking not out at the water but at me. My chest constricted with that knowledge. The path had been inlaid with pebbles in designs that created bats for happiness, tortoise backs for longevity, and *cash* for prosperity. Each step thus brought joy, a long life, and more wealth. My ancestors had also constructed these pathways for health reasons. As they aged, the pebbles massaged their feet as they walked. This must have been in long-ago days when women weren't allowed in the garden, because I found the surface hard to walk on with my bound feet. I focused on making each foot find purchase on a pebble, balancing just so before committing myself to moving forward, knowing that this accentuated the delicacy of my lily walk.

I hesitated before stepping into the Moon-Viewing Pavilion. My courage faded. This place had always been forbidden to me because three sides were surrounded by water. Technically, it was *outside* our garden walls. Then I remembered Liniang's determination. I took a breath, walked into the middle of the pavilion, and stopped. He wore a long gown of midnight-blue silk. Next to him on the balustrade were a peony and a sprig of willow. He didn't stand. He just stared at me. I tried to keep perfectly still.

"I see you have a three-ways viewing pavilion," he said. "I have the same in my home, only ours is on our pond and not the lake."

He must have seen my confusion, so he explained. "From here you can see the moon three ways: in the sky, reflected in the water, and refracted from the lake into the mirror." He lifted his hand and languorously pointed to a mirror that hung above the only piece of furniture in the pavilion: a carved wooden bed.

"Oh!" slipped from my mouth. Until this instant I had never considered a bed in a pavilion as anything other than a place for the lazy to rest, but now I trembled at the thought of the bed, the mirror, and the languid nights I wished I could have in his moon-viewing pavilion.

He smiled. Had he found humor in my embarrassment or were his thoughts the same as mine? After a long and to me discomforting moment, he rose and came to my side. "Come. Let's look out together."

When we reached the balustrade, I gripped a pillar to steady myself.

"It's a beautiful night," he said, looking out across the glassy water. Then he turned to me. "But you are far more beautiful."

I felt overwhelming happiness and then a horrible wave of shame and fear.

He stared questioningly into my face. "What's wrong?"

Tears welled in my eyes, but I forced myself to contain them. "Perhaps you see only what you want to see."

"I see a real girl whose tears I want to kiss away."

Twin drops overflowed and ran down my cheeks.

"How can I be a good wife now?" I gestured around me hopelessly. "After this?"

"You've done nothing wrong."

But of course I had! I was *here*, wasn't I? But I didn't want to talk about it. I stepped away, folded my hands in front of me, and said in a steady voice, "I always miss notes when I play the zither."

"I don't care for the zither."

"But you won't be my husband," I responded. A pained look came over his face. I'd hurt him. "My stitches are too large and ungainly," I blurted quickly.

"My mother does not sit in the women's hall all day for needlework. If you were my wife, the two of you would do other things together."

"My paintings are weak."

"What do you paint?"

"Flowers—the usual."

"You are not the usual. You shouldn't paint the usual. If you could paint anything you wanted, what would you choose?"

No one had asked me that before. In fact, no one had ever asked me anything quite like it. If I had been thinking, if I had been at all proper, I would have answered that I would keep practicing my flowers. But I wasn't thinking.

"I would paint this: the lake, the moon, the pavilion."

"A landscape then."

An actual landscape, not a landscape found hidden in cold slabs of marble like the ones in my father's library. The idea intrigued me.

"My home across the lake is high on the hill," he went on. "Every room has a view. If we were married, we'd be companions. We'd go on excursions—on the lake, on the river, to see the tidal bore."

Everything he said made me happy and sad at the same time as I longed for a life I would never have.

"But you shouldn't worry," he continued. "I'm sure your husband isn't perfect either. Look at me. Since the Song dynasty it has been the ambition of every young man to achieve distinction in official life, but I have not taken the imperial exams and I have no ambition to take them."

But this was how it was supposed to be! A man today—one who was loyal to the Ming—would always choose an interior life over one of civil service in the new regime. Why had he said that? Did he think I was old-fashioned or just plain stupid? Did he think I wished him to be in business? Making money as a merchant was vulgar and low.

"I'm a poet," he said.

I grinned. I had intuited it the first moment I saw him through the screen. "The greatest calling of all is to have a literary life."

"I want a marriage of companions—one of shared lives and shared poems," he murmured. "If we were husband and wife, we would collect books, read, and drink tea together. As I told you before, I'd want you for what's in here."

Again he pointed to my heart, but I felt it in a place far lower in my body.

"So tell me about the opera," he said after a long moment. "Are you sad not to see Liniang reunite with her mother? I understand that girls love that scene."

It was true. I did love that scene. As the battles wage on between the brigand and the empire's forces, Madame Du and Spring Fragrance seek shelter at an inn in Hangzhou. Madame Du is amazed—frightened—to see what she believes is her daughter's ghost. But of course, by now the three parts of Liniang's soul have been brought back together and she is a girl once again, of flesh and blood.

"Every girl hopes her mother would recognize her and love her, even if she were dead, even if she were a ghost, even if she eloped," I said.

"Yes, it is a good *qing* scene," my poet agreed. "It shows us mother love. The other scenes tonight . . ." He jutted his chin indifferently. "Politics don't interest me. Too much *li,* don't you agree? I much prefer the scenes in the garden."

Was he mocking me?

"Mengmei brought Liniang back to life through passion," he went on. "He *believed* her back into existence."

His understanding of the opera was so close to my own that I was emboldened to ask, "Would you do that for me?"

"Of course I would!"

Then he brought his face close to mine. His breath was redolent of orchids and musk. The desire we both felt warmed the air between us. I thought he might kiss me and I waited to feel his lips on mine. My body flooded with blood and emotion. I didn't move, because I didn't know what to do or what he expected me to do. That's not quite true. I was not expected to be doing *any* of this, but when he stepped away and regarded me with his deep black eyes, I trembled with longing.

He didn't seem much older than me, but he was a man and lived in the outside world. For all I knew, he had much experience with the teahouse women whose voices I sometimes heard floating across the lake. To him, I must have seemed like a child, and in some ways he dealt with me that way, by retreating just far enough to give me a chance to steady myself.

"I can never decide if the opera has a happy ending or not," he said.

His sentence startled me. Had that much time passed since I'd come here? He must have sensed my alarm, because he added, "Don't worry. There are several more scenes." He picked up the peony that he'd brought with him with one hand and laid its blossom in his other. "Mengmei wins the top honors in the imperial exams."

My mind and body were far, far away from the opera and I had to force myself to concentrate, which I suppose is what he wanted.

"But when he presents himself to Prefect Du as his new son-in-law, he's arrested," I said. When he smiled, I understood I was doing the exact right thing.

"The Prefect orders Mengmei's baggage searched, and—"

"The guards find Liniang's self-portrait," I finished for him. "Prefect Du has Mengmei beaten and tortured, believing the scholar has defiled his daughter's tomb."

"Mengmei insists he brought Liniang back from the spirit world and that the two of them have married," he said. "Outraged, Prefect Du orders Mengmei's decapitation."

The fragrance from the peony in his palm filled my head. I remembered all the things I wished I'd done last night. I picked up the willow sprig from the balustrade. Slowly I began to walk around him, speaking softly all the while, caressing him with my words.

"Will the story end sorrowfully?" I asked. "Everyone is brought to the imperial court to present their problems to the emperor." I came full circle, stopped to glance up to his eyes, and then glided around him again, this time letting the willow leaves brush against his torso.

"Liniang is presented to her father," he said gruffly, "but he can't accept that she's alive, not even when he's looking at her."

"In this way, the great Tang Xianzu illustrated how men can be limited by *li*." I kept my voice low, knowing my poet would have to work hard to hear me. "When something so miraculous happens, people can't be rational anymore." He sighed and I smiled. "The Prefect insists that Liniang pass many tests—"

"She casts a shadow and leaves footprints when she walks under blossoming trees."

"That's right," I whispered. "And she also answers questions about the Seven Emotions—joy, anger, grief, fear, love, hate, and desire."

"Have you experienced these emotions yourself?"

I stopped before him. "Not all of them," I admitted.

"Joy?" He brought the peony he'd been holding in his hand to my cheek.

"Just today when I woke up."

"Anger?"

"I told you I'm not perfect," I answered as he brought the petals along my jaw.

"Grief?"

"Every year on the anniversary of my grandmother's death."

"But you have not truly experienced it yourself," he said, taking the blossom away from my face and letting it trail down my arm. "Fear?"

I thought of the fear I felt coming here, but I said, "Never."

"Good." He kept the peony against the inside of my wrist. "Love?" I didn't answer, but the feel of the flower on my skin caused me to shiver, and he smiled. "Hate?"

I shook my head. We both knew I hadn't lived long enough or seen enough to hate anyone.

"Only one left," he said. He brought the peony back up along my arm and then pulled it away, to drop again to a spot just below my ear. Then he slowly let the blossom glide down across my neck to the top of my collar and forward to my throat. "Desire?"

I had stopped breathing.

"I see your answer in your face," he said.

He brought his lips to my ear.

"If we married," he whispered, "we would not have to waste time drinking tea and making conversation." He stepped back and looked out across the lake. "I wish . . ." His voice quavered, which I saw embarrassed him. He felt this moment as deeply as I did. He cleared his throat and swallowed hard. When he next spoke, it was as though nothing had happened between us. I was loose again, on my own.

"I wish you could see my home. It's just across the lake on Wushan Mountain."

"Isn't that it right there?" I asked, pointing to the hill on the other side of the lake.

"That is the hill, yes, but Solitary Island—as beautiful as it is—obstructs the view of the house. My home is just behind the tip of the island. I wish you could see it, so that you could look across the water and think of me."

"Perhaps I'll be able to see it from my father's library."

"You're right! Your father and I have talked politics there many times. I can see my home from the windows. But even if you can see the mountain, how will you know which house is mine?"

My mind, in such a turbulent state, could not think clearly enough to come up with a possible solution.

"I'm going to show you the house, so you can find it. I promise to look out from there every day to find you, if you will look for me."

I agreed. He led me to the right side of the pavilion near the shore. He took the willow sprig from my hand and put it together with the peony blossom on the balustrade. When he sat down next to them and swung his legs over the edge, I understood that he intended me to do the same. He jumped down, stood on a rock, and reached his arms up to me.

"Give me your hands."

"I can't." And I truly couldn't. I had done a lot of improper things this evening, but I wasn't going to follow him. I'd never been outside the Chen Family Villa. On this one thing my mother and father were adamant.

"It's not far."

"I've never been beyond my garden. My mother says—"

"Mothers are important, but—"

"I can't do this."

"What about the promise you just made?"

My will wavered. I was as weak as my cousin Broom when presented with a plate of dumplings.

"You will not be the only girl—woman—outside a garden wall tonight. I know many women who are boating on the lake this evening."

"Teahouse women." I sniffed.

"Absolutely not," he said. "I'm referring to women poets and writers who have joined poetry and writing clubs. Like you, they want to experience more of life than what is available inside their gardens. By leaving their inner chambers they've become artists of worth. It is this outside world that I would show you if you were my wife."

He left unsaid that tonight was as far as that dream would go.

This time when he extended his arms, I sat down on the balustrade and, as delicately as possible, drew my legs across the stonework and let myself be pulled from the safety of the villa. He led me to the right along the rocks that lined the shore. What I was doing was beyond bad. Amazingly, nothing terrible happened. We weren't caught, and no ghosts leaped from behind a bush or tree to scare or kill us for this infraction.

He held my elbow, since some of the rocks were slick with moss. I felt the heat of his hand through the silk of my sleeve. Warm air lifted my skirt as though it were a cicada's wing carried by the wind. I was *out*. I was seeing things I'd never seen before. Here and there, bits of vines and branches draped over our compound wall, hinting at what was hidden inside. Weeping willows hung over the lake, their tendrils teasing the water's surface. I brushed against wild roses blooming on the bank and their scent infused the air, my clothes, my hair, the skin on my hands. The feelings that rushed through my body were nearly overwhelming: fear that I would be caught, exhilaration that I was out, and love for the man who had brought me here.

We stopped. I wasn't sure how long we'd been walking.

"My house is there," he said, pointing across the lake, past the newly built pavilion on Solitary Island that I could see from my father's library. "There's a temple on the hill. It's lit by torches this evening. Do you see it? The monks open their doors for all festivals. Just a little up and to the left is the house."

"I see it."

The moon was just a sliver, but it was enough to cast a path across the lake from my toes to his doorstep. It felt as though the heavens had agreed that we were meant to have this time together.

In this most extraordinary circumstance, I was distracted by a peculiar sensation. My lily shoes were thoroughly soaked and I could feel water being drawn up into the hem of my skirt. I took a tiny step back from the water's edge, which sent ripples out across the peaceful surface. I thought about those ripples hitting the hulls of boats that carried other lovers on the lake and lapping at the edges of moon-viewing pavilions where young husbands and wives had sought refuge from the watchful eyes of the household.

"You'd like my home," he said. "We have a nice garden—not as large as yours—with a small rockery, a moon-viewing pavilion, a pond, and a plum tree whose blossoms in spring fill the entire compound with an enticing fragrance. Whenever I see it, I'll think of you."

I wished we would have a wedding night. I wished it would happen right now. I blushed and looked down. When I looked up, he stared into my eyes. I knew he longed for the same thing I did. And then the moment was over.

"We must return," he said.

He tried to hurry us, but my shoes were now slippery and I was slow. As we got closer to the villa, the sounds of the opera came more fully into my consciousness. Mengmei's pained cries as he was tortured and beaten by Prefect Du's guards told me we were close to the end.

He lifted me up and back into the Moon-Viewing Pavilion. This was it. Tomorrow, I would go back to preparing for my marriage, and he would go back to whatever young men do to get ready to greet their wives.

"I liked talking to you about the opera," he said.

They may not seem like the most romantic words a man could have spoken, but to me they were, for they showed that he cared for literature, the concerns of the inner chambers, and that he truly did want to know what I thought.

He picked up the willow sprig and handed it to me. "Keep this," he said, "to remind you of me."

"And the peony?"

"I'll keep it forever."

I smiled inwardly, knowing that the flower and I shared the same name.

He brought his lips close to mine, and when he spoke

his voice trembled with emotion. "We had three nights of happiness. That's more than most married couples have in a lifetime. I will remember them forever."

As my eyes filled with tears, he said, "You must go back. I won't leave here until there's a safe distance between us."

I bit my lip to keep from crying and turned away. I walked alone toward the main garden, stopping by the pond to tuck the willow sprig inside my tunic. Only when I heard Prefect Du accuse his daughter, who'd been brought before him, of being a disgusting creature of the dead did I remember how sullied my shoes, leggings, and the bottom of my skirt had become. I needed to get back to my room and change without being seen.

"Here you are," Broom said, stepping out of the shadows. "Your mother sent me to look for you."

"I was . . . I had to . . ." I thought of Willow that first night as she played the role of Spring Fragrance. "I had to use the chamber pot."

My cousin smiled knowingly.

"I've been to your room. You weren't there."

Having caught me in a lie, Broom regarded me suspiciously. I watched her smile broaden as her eyes traveled from my face down across my torso to my skirt, my dirty hem, and my soiled shoes. She pasted a bright mask on her face, looped her arm affectionately through mine, and said in a pretty tone, "The opera is nearly finished. I don't want you to miss the end."

I was light-headed enough with my own private happiness to believe she wanted to help me. Whatever hidden strength had surfaced when I allowed myself to go over the balustrade of our Moon-Viewing Pavilion had retreated to a hidden corner deep inside me, because I didn't break away from Broom and sit down on my cushion at the back of the audience but allowed myself to be led—helplessly, stupidly, but with the ridiculous invincibility that came with the bliss I felt—through the seated women, right past my mother, and on to the front row of cushions, where I was squeezed in between little Ze and my cousin. And because I was seated next to Ze, I found myself once more before the crack in the screen that allowed me to peek out to the stage.

I looked across the sea of black-haired men until I found my poet, sitting next to my father. After a few minutes, I forced myself to look away from him and to the stage, where the emperor tried to bring the two factions together. Proclamations were read; honors bestowed. There was great rejoicing for the two young lovers—a truly happy ending—and yet nothing had been or would ever be reconciled between Prefect Du and his daughter.

The men on the other side of the screen jumped to their feet with applause and whoops of appreciation. The women on our side nodded at the truth of this ending.

As he had on the first night, my father took the stage. He thanked everyone for coming to our meager home for our inadequate production. He thanked the visiting actors and those on our household staff who'd been pulled from their regular duties for the performance.

"This is a night of love and destiny," he said. "We have seen how Liniang and Mengmei's story has ended. And we know how the story of the Weaving Maid and the Cowherd will end later tonight. Now let us have a preview of another love story."

Waaa! He was going to announce something about my marriage. My poet put his head down. He didn't want to hear this either.

"Many of you know that I'm fortunate to have as my

future son-in-law a good friend," Baba said. "I have known Wu Ren for so long, he is like a son to me."

As my father lifted his arm to point out the man I was to marry, I closed my eyes. Three days ago, I would have followed his gesture to get a glimpse of my future husband, but right now I couldn't abandon the tender emotions swimming inside me. I wanted to hold on to them a little longer.

"I'm lucky Ren has such a love of words," my father went on. "I'm not so lucky when he beats me in chess."

The men laughed appreciatively as they were meant to. On our side of the screen, there was silence. I felt stares of disapproval and disdain from the women behind me driving into my back like daggers. I opened my eyes, peered to my right, and saw Ze staring through the crack in the screen, her mouth set in an alarmed *oh*. Then Ze quickly averted her gaze. My husband had to be really ugly, hideous.

"Many of you are guests tonight and have not met my daughter," my father continued, "but I also have my whole family here and they've known Peony for her entire life." He addressed my future husband, confiding in front of everyone, "I have no doubt she will be a good wife to you . . . except for one thing. Her name is not suitable. Your mother's name is also Peony."

My father looked out across the audience of men, but he spoke to us behind the screen. "From now on, we will call my daughter Tong—*Same*—for she is the same as your mother, my young friend."

I shook my head in disbelief. Baba had just changed my name forever and ever. I was now Tong—a common *Same*— because of my mother-in-law, someone I had yet to meet but who would have control over me until the day she died. My father had done this without asking me, without even warning me. My poet was right. Three beautiful nights would have to sustain me for a lifetime. But this night was not over, and I refused to sink into despair just yet.

"Let this be a night of celebration," my father announced. He signaled toward the screen where we women sat. Servants came to escort us back to the Lotus-Blooming Hall. I leaned on Willow's arm for support and was prepared to let her guide me back to the women's chambers, when my mother came to my side.

"It seems you are a chosen one tonight," she said, but the graciousness of her words could not hide the disappointment in her voice. "Willow, allow me to take my daughter back to her room." Willow let go of me and my mother took my arm in hers. How she managed to look so beautiful and delicate when her fingers were digging into my flesh through my silk tunic, I don't know. The others parted, and let the head woman of the Chen Family Villa lead her one and only child back to the Lotus-Blooming Hall. The others trailed behind us, quiet as scarves floating on the wind. They didn't know what I'd done, but clearly I'd been somewhere I shouldn't have been because they could all see that my feet—those most private of a woman's parts—were soiled.

I don't know what caused me to look back, but I did. Little Ze was walking with Broom. My cousin had a trace of smugness and triumph at the corners of her mouth, but Ze was still too young and unsophisticated to hide her emotions. Her face was red, her jaw clenched, her whole body rigid with anger. I didn't know why.

We reached the Lotus-Blooming Hall. My mother paused for a moment to tell the others to enjoy themselves; she would return in a few minutes. Then, without another word, she took me to my room in the Unmarried Girls' Hall, opened the door, and gently pushed me inside. After she closed the door, I heard something I'd never heard before. It sounded like metal scraping. Only when I tried to open the door again to see what it was did I realize that for the first time my mother had used one of her locks to confine me.

That Mama was angry with me didn't change the words my poet had spoken in my ear, nor did they alter the feeling that still lingered on my flesh from where he had touched me with the peony. I brought out the willow sprig he'd given me and used it to caress my cheek. Then I put it in a drawer. I undressed my wet feet and wrapped them again in clean bindings. From my window, I did not see the celestial bridge that was supposed to unite the Weaving Maid and the Cowherd, but I did still smell the fragrance of wild roses in my hair and on my skin.

Closing Doors,
Opening Heart

MAMA NEVER AGAIN MENTIONED THE WETNESS AND DIRT on my shoes, skirt, and leggings. A servant took those things away, they were never brought back, and I continued to be locked in my room. During the long weeks of my confinement, I would begin to question everything. But at first I was just a sad girl locked in her room with no one to talk to. Even Willow was barred, except to bring me meals and fresh water for washing.

I spent hours at my window, but my view was limited to a small patch of sky above and the courtyard below. I leafed through my copies of The Peony Pavilion. I sought out the scene of The Interrupted Dream, trying to decipher what Liniang and Mengmei were doing together in the grotto. At every moment, I thought about my stranger. The feelings that filled my chest dampened my appetite and emptied my head. I constantly brooded about how I would continue to hold on to my emotions once I got out of this room.

One morning, a week into my confinement, Willow

opened the door, padded quietly across the floor, and set down a tray with tea and a bowl of *congee* for breakfast. I missed her company and the way she cared for me—brushing my hair, washing and wrapping my feet, keeping the air between us lively with conversation. These past days, she'd been very quiet when she brought my meals, but now she smiled in a way I'd never seen before.

She poured my tea, knelt before me, and looked up into my face, waiting for me to question her.

"Tell me what's happened," I said, expecting to hear that my mother had decided to release me or that she was going to let Willow stay in my room again.

"When Master Chen asked me to play the part of Spring Fragrance, I said yes, hoping that one of the men in the audience might see me, approach your father, and ask if he would sell me to another household," she answered, her eyes bright with happiness. "The offer came last night and your father agreed. I'm to leave this afternoon."

I felt like Willow had just slapped my face. Never in ten thousand years would I have guessed or imagined this.

"But you belong to me!"

"Actually, until yesterday I was your father's property. Today, I belong to Master Quon."

That she smiled when she said this unlocked a pocket of anger in me.

"You can't leave. You can't *want* to leave."

When she didn't answer, I knew she truly wanted to go. But how could this be? She was my maid and companion. I had never thought about where she'd come from or how she'd come to be my servant, but I'd always believed her to be mine. She was a part of my everyday life like the chamber pot. She was at my feet when I fell asleep; she was the first person I saw in the morning. She started the brazier before

I opened my eyes and fetched hot water for bathing me. I had thought she would go with me to my husband's home. She was supposed to care for me when I got pregnant and had sons. Since she was my age, I had expected her to be with me until I died.

"Every night after you fall asleep, I lie here on the floor and hide my tears in my handkerchief," she confessed. "For years, I have hoped your father would sell me. If I'm lucky, my new owner will make me a concubine." She paused, considered, and then added in a practical tone, "A second, third, or fourth concubine."

That my servant had longings like this shocked me. She was far ahead of me in her thinking, in her desires. She had come from the world outside our garden—the world I was suddenly obsessed with—and I had never once asked her about it.

"How can you do this to me? Where is your gratitude?"

Her smile faded. Did she not answer because she didn't want to or because she didn't feel she owed it to me?

"I'm thankful your family took me in," she admitted. She had a pretty face, but in that moment I saw how much she disliked me, how much she had probably disliked me for years. "Now I can have a different life than the one I was born to as a thin horse."

I had heard the term before, but I didn't want to admit that I didn't fully understand what it meant.

"My family was from Yangzhou, where your grandmother died," she went on. "Like so many families, mine suffered greatly. The old and ugly women were massacred along with the men. Women like my mother were sold like salted fish—in sacks, by weight. My mother's new owner was an enterprising man. I was the fourth daughter to be sold. Since then I have been like a leaf in the wind."

I listened.

"The thin-horse trader bound my feet and taught me to read, sing, embroider, and play the flute," she continued. "In this way my life was not unlike yours, but in other ways it was very different. Those people grew girls on their land instead of crops." She lowered her head and glanced at me furtively. "Spring came, autumn went. They could have kept me until I was old enough to sell into pleasure, but inflation and a glut on the market lowered prices. They had to unload some of the crop. One day, they dressed me in red, painted my face white, and took me to market. Your father examined my teeth; he held my feet in his hands; he patted my body."

"He wouldn't do that!"

"He did, and I was ashamed. He bought me for a few bolts of cloth. These last years I hoped that your father might take me as his fourth concubine and that I might bring him the son your mother and the others can't give him."

The thought curdled my stomach.

"Today I go to my third owner," she said matter-of-factly. "Your father has sold me for pork and *cash*. It's a good deal, and he's happy."

Sold for pork? I was to be married in exchange for bride-price gifts, which included pigs. Perhaps Willow and I were not so different after all. Neither of us had any say in our futures.

"I'm still young," Willow said. "I may change hands again if I don't bear a son or I stop making my master smile. The thin-horse trader taught me that buying a concubine adds to a man's garden. Some trees bear fruit, some give shade, some give pleasure to the eye. I'm hopeful that I will not be weeded out and sold again."

"You're like Xiaoqing," I said in wonder.

"I don't have her beauty or talent, but I hope my future

(95)

is better than hers and that in my next life I will not be born in Yangzhou."

This was my first true understanding that my existence in our garden villa was not at all like that of girls in the outside world. Terrifying and horrible things happened out there. This had been kept a secret from me, and I was grateful but curious. My grandmother had been out there and now she was worshipped as a martyr. Willow had come from out there and her future was as set as my own: Make the man in her life happy, bear him sons, and excel in the Four Virtues.

"So I'm going," Willow said abruptly, as she got up off her knees.

"Wait." I stood, crossed to a cabinet, and opened a drawer. I fingered my jewelry and hair ornaments, looking for a piece that would be neither too ordinary nor too extravagant. I settled on a hairpin of blue kingfisher feathers shaped into a soaring phoenix, its tail flowing delicately behind it. I placed it in Willow's hand.

"To wear when you meet your new owner."

"Thank you," she said, and with that she left the room.

Not two minutes later, Shao, my old wet nurse and our head amah, entered. "I will be taking care of you from now on."

I could not have received worse news.

MY MOTHER HAD plans for me, and Shao, who now lived in my room, had to make sure they were fulfilled. "Tong—Same—you will prepare for your wedding, nothing else," Shao announced, and she meant it.

Hearing my new name, I had an inward shiver of despair. My place in the world was set by label and designation;

through my name I was already changing from a daughter into a wife and daughter-in-law.

For the next seven weeks, Shao brought my meals, but my stomach had become an abyss of anguish and I ignored the food or stubbornly pushed it away. As time passed, my body changed. My skirts started to hang on my hips instead of my waist, and my tunics swung loose and free.

My mother never visited.

"She's disappointed in you," Shao reminded me every day. "How could you have come from her body? I tell her a bad daughter is a typical daughter."

I was book-smart but no match for my mother. Her job was to control me and see me married out to a good family. Although she still did not want to see my face, she sent emissaries. Every morning, Third Aunt arrived just before dawn to teach me to embroider properly.

"No more sloppy or clumsy stitches allowed," she said, her voice tinkling like white carnelian. If I made a mistake, she made me pull out the stitches and start again. With no distractions and Third Aunt's exacting instruction, I learned. And with every stitch, I ached for my poet.

As soon as she swept out of the room, Shao let in Second Aunt, who drilled me on my zither. Despite her indulgent reputation, she was very strict with me. If I erred in my plucking, she struck my fingers with a stalk of green bamboo. My zither playing improved surprisingly quickly, becoming clear and limpid. I imagined each note floating out the window and traveling across the lake to my poet's home, where the music would make him think of me as I was thinking of him.

In the late afternoons, as the colors of evening began to appear in the west, Fourth Aunt, widowed and childless, came to teach me the purpose of clouds and rain.

"A woman's greatest strength is to give birth to sons," Fourth Aunt instructed. "It gives a woman power and it can take it away. If you give your husband a son, you might keep him from entering the pleasure quarters on the lake or bringing in concubines. Remember, a woman's purity grows through seclusion. This is why you're in here."

I listened hard to what she said, but she told me nothing about what to expect on my wedding night or how I could participate in clouds and rain with someone I didn't love, like, or know. I relentlessly conjured the hours leading up to it: my mother, aunts, and cousins washing and dressing me in my wedding clothes; the five grains, the piece of pork, and the pig heart they'd hide in the underskirt I'd wear next to my skin; the tears shed by everyone as I was led outside to the palanquin; stepping over the Wu family threshold and letting that underskirt with its hidden treasures drop to the floor to ensure the fast and easy births of sons; and finally being led into the wedding chamber. These thoughts, which had once filled me with happy expectation, now made me want to run away. That I had no way to escape my fate made me feel even worse.

After dinner, Fifth Aunt took time from the nightly gathering in the women's chambers to improve my calligraphy. "Writing is a creation of the outer world of men," she said. "It is by its nature a public act—something that we, as women, should avoid—but you need to learn it so that one day you can help your son with his studies."

We worked through sheet after sheet of paper, copying poems from the *Book of Songs,* doing drills from *Pictures of Battle Formations of the Brush,* and limning lessons from the *Women's Four-Character Classic* until my fingers were stained with ink.

Apart from perfecting my brushstrokes, Fifth Aunt's

lessons were pure and simple: "The best you can do is take the ancients as your teachers. Poetry is on earth to make you serene, not corrupt your mind, thoughts, or emotions. Make yourself presentable, speak gently but don't say anything, wash yourself diligently and frequently, and keep a harmonious mind. In this way you will wear your virtue on your face."

I dutifully obeyed, but each stroke of my brush was a caress I gave my poet. Each swish of my brush was my fingers on his skin. Each character completed was a gift to the man who had so invaded my thoughts.

Every moment of the day and night that one of my aunts wasn't in my room I still had Shao. Like Willow, she slept on the floor at the foot of my bed. She was there when I woke up, there when I used the chamber pot, there when I did my lessons, there when I went to sleep. I was there for her too, listening to her snoring and farting, smelling her breath and what left her body and went into the chamber pot, watching her scratch her rump or clean her feet. No matter what she did, she was unrelenting in what spewed from her mouth.

"A woman—and your mother has recognized this in you—becomes unruly through knowledge," she told me, contradicting my aunts' teachings. "In your mind you go too far beyond the inner chambers. It's dangerous out there; your mother needs you to understand that. Forget what you've learned. *Instructions from Mother Wen* tells us that a girl should know only a few written characters, like *firewood, rice, fish,* and *meat.* These words will help you run a household. Anything more is perilous."

Just as door after door was closing me in, my heart was opening wider and wider. A dream visit to the Peony Pavilion had given Liniang a case of lovesickness. Visits to pavilions in the Chen Family Villa had given me my lovesickness. I had no control over my activities—how I dressed or my future life with this Wu Ren—but my emotions remained untrammeled and free. I've come to believe that part of lovesickness comes from this conflict between control and desire. In love we have no control. Our hearts and minds are tormented, teased, enticed, and delighted by the over-whelming strength of emotions that make us try to forget the real world. But that world does exist, so as women we have to think about how to make our husbands happy by being good wives, bearing sons, running our households well, and being pretty so they don't become distracted from their daily activities or loiter with concubines. We are not born with these abilities. They must be instilled in us by other women. Through lessons, aphorisms, and acquired skills we are molded . . . and controlled.

My mother controlled me through her instructions even as she refused to see me. My aunts controlled me through their lessons. My future mother-in-law would control me after marriage. Together, these women—from the time I was born until the day I died—would control every single minute of my life.

Yet for every effort at control, I was spinning away. At every moment, my poet invaded my thoughts—during every stitch, every strum, every didactic lesson. He was in my hair, my eyes, my fingers, my heart. I daydreamed about what he was doing, thinking, seeing, smelling, feeling. I could not eat for thoughts of him. Each time petal-scented air came through my window, my emotions were thrown into turmoil. Did he long for a traditional wife or a new wife, like the one he talked about the night we met in the Moon-Viewing Pavilion? Would his future wife give him what he wanted? And what about me? What would happen to me now?

At night, as moonlight sent scattered shadows of bamboo

leaves across my silk bedding, I dwelled in these dark thoughts. Sometimes I would get up, step over Shao, and go to the drawer where I kept the sprig of willow my poet had given me on our last night together. As the weeks went by, leaf after leaf fell away and crumbled to nothing, until all that was left was the twig. My little speck of a heart was soaked through with sadness.

Over time I improved on the zither, memorized rules, and worked on my embroidery. Two months into my seclusion, Third Aunt announced, "You are ready to make shoes for your mother-in-law."

Every bride does this as a sign of respect, but for years I'd dreaded this task, knowing my needlework would instantly reveal my flaws. Now I dreaded it even more. While I would no longer embarrass myself or bring shame on my family through my stitches, I had no feelings for this woman and felt no need to impress her. I tried to imagine she was my poet's mother. What else could I do to protect myself from the hopelessness I felt? My mother-in-law's name was the same as mine—Peony—so I incorporated that flower, the hardest of all to paint or stitch, into my design. I spent hours on each petal and leaf until after a month the shoes were completed. I held the pair in my hand and showed them to Third Aunt.

"They are perfect," she said, and she meant it. I may not have woven in strands of my hair or made them as airy as she would have, but by any other standard they were splendid. "You may wrap them."

ON THE NINTH day of the ninth month, when we commemorate Lady Purple, who was treated so badly by her mother-in-law that she hanged herself in the privy she was required to clean each day, the door to my room opened and my mother entered. I bowed deeply to show my respect, and then I stood still, my hands clasped before me, my eyes cast down.

"*Waaa!* You look . . . !" The surprise in Mama's voice caused me to glance up. She must have still been angry with me, because her face was disturbed. But she had perfected the art of hiding her feelings, and her features quickly settled. "Your final bride-price gifts have arrived. You might like to see them before they're put away. But I expect you to—"

"Don't worry, Mama. I've changed."

"I see that," she said, but again I did not detect pleasure in her tone. Rather, I heard concern. "Come. Take a look. Then I want you to join us for breakfast."

As I left my room, a single thread held together my emotions—loneliness, despair, and my unwavering love for my poet. I had learned to vent my sorrows through sighs.

I followed my mother at a respectful distance to the Sitting-Down Hall. My bride-price gifts had been brought to our home in lacquer-framed boxes that looked like glass coffins. My family had received the usual items: silks and satins, gold and jewelry, porcelains and ceramics, cakes and dumplings, jars of wine and roast pork. Some of these things were for me; most were for my father's coffers. Ample gifts of *cash* were for my uncles. This was physical proof that my marriage was going to happen—and soon. I pinched the bridge of my nose to keep from crying. Once my emotions were under control, I planted a placid smile on my face. I was out of my room at last and my mother would be watching for any lapse in the proprieties. I had to be wary.

My eyes fell on a package wrapped in red silk. I glanced at my mother, and she nodded to let me know I could open it. I peeled back the soft folds. Inside was a two-volume set of *The Peony Pavilion*. It was the only edition I didn't already own, the one from Tang Xianzu's private press. I opened the note that came with the set. *Dear Same, I look forward to staying up late with you, drinking tea, and talking about the opera.* It was signed by my future husband's sister-in-law, who already lived in the Wu household. The bride-price payments were fine, but this gift told me that there was at least one person in the Wu family's women's chambers with whom I might find companionship.

"May I keep this?" I asked my mother.

Her brow furrowed and I thought she would say no.

"Take it to your room and then come straight away to the Spring Pavilion. You need to eat."

I clutched the volumes to my chest, walked slowly back to my room, and set them on my bed. Then, following my mother's orders, I went to the Spring Pavilion.

I'd been locked away for two months, and I looked at the room and everyone in it with new eyes. The usual tensions bubbled among my aunts, my cousins, my mother, and those women and girls who were unseen in the morning—the concubines and their daughters. But because I'd been away I saw and felt an undercurrent that I'd never fully noticed before. Every woman is expected to be pregnant at least ten times during her lifetime. The women in the Chen Family Villa had trouble getting pregnant, and when they did they seemed incapable of dropping a son. This lack of sons weighed on everyone. The concubines were supposed to rescue our dying family line, but even though we fed, clothed, and housed them, none of them had birthed a boy either. They may not have been allowed physically to join us for breakfast, but they were with us nonetheless.

My cousins seemed to have a new attitude toward me. Broom, who'd orchestrated my confinement, used her chopsticks to put a few dumplings on my plate. Lotus poured my tea and handed me her bowl of *congee*, which she'd flavored with salted fish and scallions. My aunts came by the table, welcomed me back with smiling faces, and urged me to eat. But I didn't take a single bite. I even ignored the sweet-bean paste dumplings that Shao delivered from my mother's table.

When the meal ended, we moved to the Lotus-Blooming Hall. Little clusters formed: one group to embroider, another to paint and do calligraphy, yet another to read poetry. The concubines arrived and came to peck at me, present me with treats, and pinch my cheeks to bring in color. Only two of my grandfather's concubines were still alive, and they were very old. Their face powder accentuated their wrinkles. Their hair ornaments did not make them look younger but only highlighted the white. Their waists were big, but their feet were still as tiny and beautiful as they were on those nights when my grandfather had eased his mind by holding the delicate morsels in his hand.

"You look more like your grandmother every day," Grandfather's favorite said.

"You are as kind and good-natured as she was," the other added.

"Please join us for embroidery," the favorite went on. "Or choose another activity. It would please us to keep you company in whatever activity you desire. We are a sisterhood in this room, after all. When we were hiding from the Manchus in Yangzhou, your grandmother was very clear on this point."

"From the afterworld she looks to your future," the lesser concubine said, in an obsequious tone. "We've been making offerings to her on your behalf."

After so many weeks of solitude, the chatter and competitiveness—all hidden behind the activities of embroidery, calligraphy, and reading poetry—clearly revealed to me the shadow darkness of the women who lived in the Chen Family

Villa. I felt tears gather from the exertion of trying to be a good daughter, of listening and protecting myself from their false concern, and of realizing that this was my life.

But I could not fight my mother.

I wanted to submerge myself in my feelings. I wanted to bury myself in thoughts of love. I had no way to get out of my marriage, but maybe I could escape from it in the same way I had here in my natal home, by reading, writing, and imagining. I wasn't a man and could never compete with the writings of men. I had no desire to write an eight-legged essay, even if I could have taken the imperial exams. But I did have a certain kind of knowledge—all those things I had learned sitting on my father's lap when I was a small girl and later when he gave me editions of the classics and volumes of poetry to study—that most girls didn't, and I would use it to save myself. I wouldn't write poetry about butterflies and flowers. I had to find something that would not only be meaningful to me but would sustain me for the rest of my life.

A thousand years ago, the poet Han Yun wrote, "All things not at peace will cry out." He compared the human need to express feelings in writing to the natural force that impelled plants to rustle in the wind or metal to ring when struck. With that I realized what I would do. It was something I'd already worked on for years. With the outside world stripped away, I had spent my life looking inward and my emotions were finely tuned. My poet wanted to know my thoughts about the Seven Emotions; now I would find all those places in *The Peony Pavilion* that illustrated them. I would look inside myself and write not what the critics had observed or what my aunts discussed about these emotions but how *I* felt them myself. I would finish my project in time for my marriage, so I could go to Wu Ren's home with something that would remind me forever of the three nights of love I'd spent with my poet. My project would be my salvation in the coming dark years. I might be locked in my husband's home, but my mind would travel to the Moon-Viewing Pavilion, where I could meet my poet again and again without interruption or fear of being caught. My poet would never read it, but I could always imagine presenting it to him—me unclothed on his bed and naked in my heart and mind.

I stood up abruptly, scraping my chair against the floor. The sound caused the women and girls to stare at me. I saw the way their hate and jealousy hid behind pretty faces filled with false worry and concern.

"Tong," my mother said, addressing me by my new name.

My head felt like ants were crawling inside it. I composed my face as best I could.

"Mama, may I go to Baba's library?"

"He's not there. He's gone to the capital."

The news shocked me. He had not been back to the capital since the Manchus took over.

"Even if he were here," she went on, "I would say no. He's a bad influence. He thinks a girl should know about Xiaoqing. Well, look what that kind of lesson has brought you." She said this in front of every woman who lived in our compound. This is how great her scorn and contempt for me was. "The Cataclysm is over. We have to remember who we are: women who belong in our inner chambers, *not* wandering in the garden."

"I only want to look up something," I said. "Please, Mama, let me go. I'll return shortly."

"I'll accompany you. Let me hold your arm."

"Mama, I'm fine. Really. I'll be right back."

Nearly everything I said to my mother was a lie, but she let me go anyway.

I left the Lotus-Blooming Hall feeling light-headed and wandered through the corridors until I could step out and into the garden. It was the ninth month. The blossoms had faded, their pitiful petals fallen. The birds had left for warmer climates. With spring feelings so strong in me, it hurt to see this reminder of the frailty of youth, life, and beauty.

When I came to the edge of our pond, I sank to my knees so I might see my reflection on the glassy surface. Lovesickness had caused my face to grow thin and pale. My body looked less substantial, as if it could no longer bear the weight of my tunic. My gold bracelets hung loosely on my wrists. Even my jade hairpins seemed too heavy for the lightness of my frame. Would my poet recognize me if he saw me now?

I stood again, lingering for a moment to see my reflection one last time, and then I retraced my steps until I was back in the corridor. I walked to the front gate. Over the last sixteen years I'd come here many times but had never stepped through it or been carried over the threshold. That would happen only on my wedding day. I ran my fingers along its surface. My father had once explained to me that we had a wind-fire gate. The side that faced the outside world was composed of solid wood. It protected us from all kinds of weather, but it also shielded us from ghosts and bandits by tricking them into believing that nothing of importance or interest resided on our side. The inside of the gate was sheathed in shaved stone to protect us from fire and give us extra fortification against whatever evils might try to penetrate our garden home. Touching those stone sheets was like touching the cold *yin* of the earth. From there I went to the ancestral hall, made obeisance to my grandmother, lit incense, and begged her to make me strong.

Finally, I went to my father's library. When I stepped inside I could see that my father had been away for some time. I smelled no tobacco or incense floating on the air. The trays that held his summer ice had been removed, but no braziers had been brought in to heat the room against the autumn chill. More than anything, the energy of his mind was gone not only from this room but—I felt it now—from the compound. He was the most important person in the Chen Family Villa. How had I not noticed his absence, even alone in my room?

I went to the shelves and selected the best collections of poetry, history, myth, and religion I could find. I made three trips to my room to drop them off. I came back to the library and sat for a few minutes on the edge of Baba's daybed to think if there was anything else I might want. I chose another three books from a stack in the corner, and then I left the library and made my way back to my room. I entered, and this time I closed the door of my own accord.

Jade Shattering

I SPENT THE NEXT MONTH PORING OVER EACH OF THE
twelve editions of *The Peony Pavilion* I'd collected
and transcribing all the notes I'd ever written in
those copies into the margins of Tang Xianzu's original two-
volume edition my future sister-in-law had sent me. Once
I finished that, I gathered my father's books around me and
looked through them until, after another month, I'd identified
all but three of the original authors of the pastiches in Volume
One and most of those in Volume Two. I didn't explain
terms or allusions, comment on the music or performance,
or try to compare *The Peony Pavilion* to other operas. I wrote
in tiny characters, packing them tightly between the lines of
the text.

I didn't leave my room. I allowed Shao to wash and dress
me, but I turned away from the food she brought. I wasn't
hungry; being light-headed seemed to make me think and
write more clearly. When my aunts or cousins came to invite
me to take a walk in the garden or join them for tea and

dumplings in the Spring Pavilion, I graciously thanked them but said no. Not surprisingly, my attitude did not agree with my mother. I didn't tell her what I was doing and she didn't ask. "You cannot learn to be a good wife by hiding in your room with your father's books," she said. "Come to the Spring Pavilion. Have breakfast and listen to your aunts. Come for lunch and learn how to treat your husband's concubines. Join us at dinner and perfect your conversation."

Suddenly everyone wanted me to have a meal, but for years my mother had told me to beware of becoming chubby like Broom and to eat little so I would be slim at my wedding. But how can you eat anyway when you're in love? Every girl has this experience. Every girl knows this is so. My heart was dreaming of my poet, my head was filled with this project that I was sure would protect me in my married loneliness, and my stomach? It was empty and I didn't care.

I began to stay in bed. All day I read from the two volumes. All night I read by the flickering light of the oil lamp. The more I read, the more I began to think about the small links that Tang Xianzu had used to create a deeper whole. I pondered the key moments in the opera, the foreshadowing, the special motifs, and how every word and action illuminated the one thing I was obsessed with: love.

The plum tree, for example, was an arbor of life and love. It was the place where Liniang and Mengmei first met, where she would be buried, and where he would bring her back to life. In the very first scene, Mengmei changed his name because of a dream, becoming Dream of Plum. But the tree also evoked Liniang, for plum blossoms are delicate, ethereal, almost virginal in their beauty. When a girl falls into marriage, she exhales her beauty and loses forever her romantic image. She still has many obligations to fulfill— giving birth to sons, honoring her husband's ancestors, becoming a chaste widow—but she has already begun her glide into death.

I pulled out my ink, ground it into the inkstone, added water, and then in my finest hand wrote my thoughts in the upper margin of Volume One:

> Most of those who grieve over spring are especially moved by fallen blossoms, as I was when I last walked in our garden. Liniang sees the petals and understands that her youth and her beauty are fleeting. She doesn't know that her life is frail too.

What had always captured my imagination about the opera was its portrayal of romantic love, which was so different from the arranged loveless marriages that I'd grown up with in the Chen Family Villa or the one I was going to. To me, *qing* was noble, the highest ambition a man or woman could have. Although my experience of it was limited to three nights under the light of the quarter moon, I believed it gave meaning to life.

> Everything begins with love. For Liniang, it begins with her tour of the garden, then her dream, and it never ends.

Liniang's ghost and Mengmei enjoyed clouds and rain. They were both so honest in their love for each other—as my poet and I were—that this was not some ugly thing between a concubine and a man.

> Theirs is a purely divine love. Liniang always behaves like a lady.

As I wrote this, I thought of myself on the last night in the Moon-Viewing Pavilion.

I wrote about dreams—Liniang's, Mengmei's, and my own. I also thought about Liniang's self-portrait and compared it to what I was doing with my project. In the upper margin, I wrote in my finest hand:

A painting is form without shadow or reflection, just as a dream is shadow or reflection without form. A painting is like a shadow without a frame. It is even more of an illusion than a dream.

Shadows, dreams, reflections in mirrors and ponds, even memories were insubstantial and fleeting, but were they any less real? They weren't to me. I dipped my brush in the ink, smoothed off the excess, and wrote:

Du Liniang sought pleasure in a dream; Liu Mengmei sought a mate in a painting. If you don't consider such things illusion, then illusion will become real.

I worked so hard and ate so little that I began to doubt I had ever met a stranger in the Riding-the-Wind Pavilion for two nights. Had the poet and I actually left the Moon-Viewing Pavilion to walk along the lakeshore? Was all that a dream or real? It had to be real, and very shortly I would be sent into a marriage with someone I did not love.

When Liniang goes to the library, she passes by a window and wants to fly out to meet her lover. Naturally, she is too afraid to do so.

Tears came to my eyes, rolled down my cheeks, and fell onto the paper as I wrote this.

Visions of love consumed me. What little appetite that

had survived my first confinement left me completely. Xiao-qing used to drink half a cup of pear juice each day; I took only a few sips. Not eating stopped being about maintaining control over my life. It even stopped being about my poet and the tumultuous feelings of love and longing I felt were consuming me. One of the sages once wrote: *Only when you are suffering in extremity will the poetry you write be any good.* Gu Ruopu, the great woman poet, responded to this when she commented: *Officials and scholars will engrave their very flesh and carve into bone, turning white-haired and using up their lives contriving to produce dark and melancholy lines.*

I traveled to a place deep within myself where everything worldly was stripped away and I felt only emotion: love, regret, longing, hope. I sat propped up in bed, wearing my favorite gown with the pair of mandarin ducks flying above flowers and butterflies, and allowed my mind to travel to the Peony Pavilion. Had Liniang's dreams compromised her chastity? Had my dreams—my wandering in our family garden—compromised my own? Was I no longer pure because I'd met a stranger and let him touch me with the petals of a peony?

WHILE I FEVERISHLY wrote, wedding preparations swirled around me. One day a seamstress put me into my wedding costume and then took it away to make it smaller. Another day Mama arrived with my aunts. I was in bed, my books spread about me on the silk coverlet. They had smiles on their faces, but they weren't happy.

"Your father has sent word from the capital," Mama said, in her melodious voice. "He's going back into service for the emperor as soon as you are married."

"Have the Manchus left?" I asked. Had I missed a dynastic change during my confinement?

"No, your father will be serving the Qing emperor."

"But Baba is a loyalist. How can he—"

"You should eat." Mama cut me off. "Wash your hair, put on powder, and be prepared to greet him when he returns, as a proper daughter should. He has brought great honor to our family. You need to show him respect. Now get up!"

But I didn't.

My mother left the room, but my aunts stayed. They tried to get me out of bed and make me stand, but I was as slippery and formless as an eel in their hands. My thoughts were just as elusive. How could my father serve the emperor when he was a loyalist? Would my mother leave the compound and follow him to the capital, as she once had to Yangzhou?

The next day, Mama brought the family diviner to discuss how to bring more color to my cheeks before my wedding.

"Do you have spring tea from Longjing?" he asked. "Brew it with ginger to improve her stomach and build her strength."

I tried the tea, but it didn't help. A light wind would have kept me from walking. Even my bed dress seemed heavy on me.

He gave me ten sour apricots—the common prescription for young women whose thoughts are considered a little overripe—but my mind did not go in the prescribed direction. Instead, I thought about being married to my poet and the salted plums I would eat when I got pregnant with our first son, knowing they would help me with morning sickness.

The diviner returned to sprinkle pig's blood on my bed in an attempt to exorcise the spirits he was convinced hovered there. When he was done, he said, "If you start eating again, on your wedding day your skin and hair will exceed all earthly models of beauty."

But I wasn't interested in marrying Wu Ren and I certainly

didn't care to eat as a way to make him happier on our wedding day. It barely mattered anyway. My future was set and I had already done everything I needed to do to prepare for my wedding. I had perfected my embroidery. I could now play the zither. Every day Shao dressed me in tunics embroidered with flowers and butterflies or two birds in flight as an outward expression of the love and happiness I was supposedly feeling for my coming life in my husband's home. I just didn't eat, not even fruit; rarely anything beyond a few sips of juice. I fed myself by ingesting mystic breath, by thinking of love, by remembering my adventure with my poet outside the garden walls.

The diviner left instructions to keep the door to the hall closed at all times, to prevent any malevolent spirits from entering, and to readjust the stove in the kitchen and shift the direction of my bed to take advantage of more favorable aspects of *feng shui*. Mama and the servants made sure these things were done, but I didn't feel any different. The moment they left the room, I went back to my writing. You cannot cure a longing heart by changing the direction of the bed.

A few days later, Mama arrived with Doctor Zhao, who listened to the various pulses in my wrist and announced, "The heart is the seat of consciousness, and your daughter's is congested with too much yearning."

I was happy to be officially diagnosed as lovesick. A fanciful thought entered my mind. What if I died from my lovesickness as Liniang did? Would my poet find me and bring me back to life? The idea pleased me, but my mother had a very different reaction to the doctor's news. She buried her face in her hands and wept.

The doctor led her away from my bed and lowered his voice. "This kind of melancholy syndrome is also associated with spleen dysfunction. It can cause someone to stop eating.

What I'm telling you, Lady Chen, is that your daughter could die from her congested *qi*."

Aiya! Doctors always try to scare mothers. This is how they make money.

"You must force her to eat," he said.

And that's exactly what they did. Shao and Mama held down my arms, while the doctor pushed clumps of cooked rice into my mouth and held my jaw shut. A servant brought in stewed plums and apricots. The doctor shoved the soggy pieces into my mouth until I vomited out everything.

He looked at me in disgust, but to my mother he said, "Do not worry. This stasis is related to the passions. If she were a wife already, I would say that a night of clouds and rain would cure her. Since she is not yet married, she must silence her desires. Good Mother, on her wedding night she will be cured. But you may not have enough time to wait for that. I'm going to recommend that you try something different." He took her elbow again, pulled her close, and whispered in her ear. When he let her go, a mask of grim determination covered her fear. "Anger is often enough to release the stasis," he added reassuringly.

Mama escorted the doctor out of the room. I laid my head back on the pillow, my books spread out about me on the bedclothes. I picked up Volume One of *The Peony Pavilion,* closed my eyes, and let my mind drift across the lake to my poet's home. Was he thinking of me as I was thinking of him?

The door opened. Mama entered with Shao and a couple of other servants.

"Start with those over there," Mama said, pointing to the stack of books I had on a table. "And you, get those on the floor."

Mama and Shao approached my bed and gathered up the books nestled near my feet.

"We're removing the books," Mama announced. "The doctor has instructed me to burn them."

"No!" Instinctively I tightened my arms around the book I was holding. "Why?"

"Doctor Zhao says it will cure you. On this he has been very clear."

"You can't do this!" I cried. "They belong to Baba!"

"Then you won't mind," Mama replied calmly.

I dropped the book I was holding and frantically scrambled free of my silk quilt. I tried to stop Mama and the others, but I was too weak. The servants left with their first piles of books. I screamed, my arms stretched out to them as though I were a beggar instead of the privileged daughter in a family of nine generations of imperial scholars. These were our books! Precious with learning! Divine with love and art!

On the bed I had my editions of *The Peony Pavilion*. Mama and Shao started to take those too. The horror of what they were about to do sent me into a frenzied panic.

"You can't! They're mine!" I screamed, gathering together as many of the volumes as I could reach, but Mama and Shao were suprisingly strong. They ignored me, slapping away my efforts to save my books as easily as they might a pesky gnat.

"My project, please, Mama," I cried. "I've worked so hard."

"I don't know what you're talking about. You have only one project: to get married," she said, as she swooped up the edition of *The Peony Pavilion* that Baba had given me for my birthday.

Outside, in the courtyard below my room, I heard voices.

Mama said, "You need to see what your selfishness has created."

She nodded to Shao and the two of them pulled me from the bed and dragged me to the window. Below, the servants had lit a fire in a brazier. One by one they dropped Baba's books into the flames. The lines of the Tang dynasty poets he loved disappeared into the air as smoke. I saw a volume of women's writings burn and curl into nothing. My chest heaved with sobs. Shao released me and went back to the bed to gather up the rest of the books.

When she left the room, Mama asked, "Are you angry?"

I was not that. I felt nothing but despair. Books and poems can't keep away hunger, but without them I didn't have a life.

"Please tell me you are angry," Mama pleaded. "The doctor said you'd get angry."

When I didn't answer, she spun away from me and sank to her knees.

Below, I watched as Shao dropped the editions of *The Peony Pavilion* I'd collected into the flames. As each one was eaten by the fire, I shriveled inside. Those were my most treasured possessions. Now they'd been reduced to tiny feathers of ash that drifted up on the wind and out and away from our compound. My project and all my hopes for it disappeared. I was numb with despair. How could I go to my husband's home now? How would I survive my loneliness?

Next to me, Mama cried. Her body bent forward until her forehead was on the ground, and then she shuffled to me, as submissive as a servant. She gathered the hem of my skirt into her fingers and buried her face in the silk.

"Please be angry with me." Her voice was so soft I could barely hear her. "Please, daughter, please."

I let my hand rest lightly on the back of her neck, but I didn't say a word. I just stared at the fire.

A few minutes later, Shao came and took Mama away.

I stayed by the window, my arms resting on the sill. The

garden was bleak in winter. Storms and frost had stripped the trees bare. The shadows lengthened and the light dimmed. I didn't have the strength to move. Everything I'd been working on had been destroyed. At last, I pulled myself up. My head spun. My legs trembled. I thought my lily feet wouldn't be able to bear my weight. Slowly I made my way across the room to the bed. The silk quilt was twisted and rumpled from my futile attempts to save my books. I pulled back the quilt and climbed back in the bed. As my legs slipped down under the cool silk I felt them bump into something. I reached under the fabric and pulled out Volume One of the copy of *The Peony Pavilion* that my future sister-in-law had sent me. In the madness of the purge, this one book with all the writing in the margins had been saved. I sobbed in gratitude and grief.

SOMETIMES LATE AT night after that horrible day I'd leave my bed, step over Shao's sleeping form, and go to the window, where I'd pull aside the heavy curtains that kept out the winter cold. The snows had come and the thought of once-fragrant blossoms being crushed by the bitter whiteness troubled me. I stared at the moon and watched its slow trek across the sky. Night after night, dew dampened my gown, weighted my hair, chilled my fingers.

I could no longer bear the endlessness of the frigid days. I thought of Xiaoqing and how she had dressed every day, smoothing her skirts about her. She had sat up in bed so as not to muss her hair, she had tried to remain beautiful, but the bleak gloom I felt about my future life paralyzed me and I did none of these things. I even stopped caring for my feet. Shao washed and wrapped them with great tenderness. I was grateful but wary too. I kept my saved volume of *The Peony*

Pavilion hidden in the silks around me, afraid that she would find it and tell Mama, and it would be taken away to be burned.

Doctor Zhao came again. He examined me, frowned, but then said, "You took the correct action, Lady Chen. You exorcised the curse of literacy from your daughter. Burning those inauspicious books has helped ward off the evil spirits that surround her."

He listened to my pulses, watched me breathe in and out, asked me a few meaningless questions, and then announced, "Maidens, particularly at the moment of marriage, are susceptible to the evil attention of malevolent spirits. Young girls often lose their minds to these apparitions. The more beautiful the girl, the more she will suffer from chills and fever. She'll stop eating, much as your daughter has stopped eating, until she dies." He squeezed his chin thoughtfully before going on. "This, as you might expect, is not something a future husband wants to hear. And I can say from experience that many girls in our city have used this claim to keep from having conjugal relations upon marrying into their husbands' homes. But, Lady Chen, you should be grateful. Your daughter is clear of such debauchery. She claims no improper relations with any gods or spirits. She is still pure and ready for marriage."

These words did not cheer my mother, and I felt even worse. I saw no way out of my wedding night or the unhappy years that would come afterward.

"Tea brewed from fresh snow will cause her cheeks to bloom in time for the ceremony," Doctor Zhao said as he left.

Every day Mama came to stand by my bed, her face wan with dread. She begged me to get up, visit my aunts and cousins, or eat a little. I tried to laugh lightly at her concern.

"I'm fine here, Mama. Don't worry. Don't worry."

But my words gave her no comfort. She brought back the diviner. This time he slashed the air around my bed with a sword, trying to scare away the evil spirits he claimed lurked there. He hung an amulet of stone around my neck to prevent my soul from being stolen by a hungry ghost. He asked my mother for one of my skirts into which he tied bundles of peanuts, telling her that each peanut would serve as a prison for predatory spirits. He shouted out incantations. I pulled the bedclothes up over my face so he wouldn't see my tears.

FOR DAUGHTERS, MARRYING out is a little like dying. We say goodbye to our parents, our aunts and uncles, our cousins, and the servants who cared for us, and go into an entirely new life, where we live with our true families, where our names will be listed in our in-laws' ancestral hall. In this way, marriage is like experiencing death and rebirth without having to travel to the afterworld. These are morbid thoughts for any bride, I know, but mine were compounded by my unhappy situation. That morbidity sent my mind into darker and darker places. Sometimes I even believed—hoped—I might be dying like Xiaoqing or the other lovesick maidens. I let my mind dwell in theirs. I used my tears to mix the ink, and then I took up my brush. Lines of poetry flowed from the tip:

> I have learned to use the pattern of butterflies and flowers
> in my embroidery.
> I have been doing this for years, because I'm expecting my
> wedding day.
> Do people know that once I go to the afterworld
> The flowers will not be fragrant, nor the butterflies fly for
> me?

For days my mind burned with words and emotions. I wrote and wrote. When I felt too tired and weary to lift my brush I had Shao write down my poems for me. She did as she was told. Over the next few days, I dictated another eight. My words floated out one by one, like peach flowers floating on a grotto stream.

We reached the twelfth month. Charcoal burned all day and night in the brazier, but I was never warm. I was to be married in ten days.

My silk slippers are only seven centimeters long.
My waistband is loose even though I fold it in half.
Since my fragile being does not allow me to walk to the
    afterworld,
I have to lean on the wind to go there.

I worried that someone would find them and laugh at my melodrama or say my words had as much importance and permanence as the songs of insects. I folded the pieces of paper and looked around the room for a place to hide them, but all my furniture would eventually be taken to my husband's home.

I was adamant that my poems not be found, but I didn't have the strength of will to set fire to them. Too many women burn their words in a fit of thinking them not worthy, only to regret it later. I wanted to keep these, imagining that one day, after I was a married lady with children of my own, I might forget my poet. I would come to visit my family, find my poems, read them again, and remember my lovesick girlhood. Wouldn't that be for the best?

But I would never forget what had happened. This made me even more determined to find a safe place for my poems. No matter what the future held, I would always be able to come here and relive my sentiments. I forced myself out of bed and went into the corridor. It was early evening and everyone was at dinner. I made my way—and it seemed to take forever to get there as I steadied myself by holding on to the walls, grasping pillars, or clinging to the balustrades—to my father's library. I pulled out a book no one would ever look at, on the history of dam building in the southern provinces, and tucked my poems between its pages. I put the book back and stared at it to remember the title and its place on the shelf.

When I returned to my room, I picked up my brush for the last time before my marriage. On the outside of my volume of *The Peony Pavilion,* I painted my interpretation of The Interrupted Dream, the scene where Mengmei and Liniang first meet. My painting showed the two of them before the rockery, just moments before they would disappear into the grotto for clouds and rain. I waited until my ink dried, and then I opened the book and wrote:

> When people are alive, they love. When they die, they keep loving. If love ends when a person dies, that is not real love.

I closed the book and called for Shao.

"You saw me when I came into the world," I said. "Now you see me as I leave for my new home. I can trust no one else."

Tears ran down Shao's stern face. "What do you want me to do?"

"You must promise to obey, no matter what Mama or Baba say. They have taken away so much from me, but I have things that must go with me to my new home. Promise you will bring them three days after my marriage."

I saw hesitation in her eyes. She shivered once, and said, "I promise."

"Please bring me the shoes I made for Madame Wu."

Shao left the room. I lay very still, staring at the ceiling, listening to the honking of orphaned geese as they crossed the sky. They made me think of Xiaoqing's poems and the way she'd invoked that sorrowful sound. Then I remembered the nameless woman who'd written her despair on a wall in Yangzhou. She too had heard the calling of geese. I sighed as I remembered her line, *If only my tears of blood could dye red the blossoms of the plum tree. But I will never make it to spring. . . .*

A few minutes later, Shao returned with the shoes, still in the silk I'd wrapped them in.

"Put them in a safe place. Don't let Mama know you have them."

"Of course, Peony."

I had not been called by my milk name since my father changed it on the final night of the opera.

"There is one more thing," I said. I reached under my bedclothes and pulled out my saved copy of *The Peony Pavilion*.

Shao drew back in alarm.

"This is the most important item in my dowry. Mama and Baba don't know about it and you must never tell them. Promise!"

"I promise," she mumbled.

"Keep it safe. Only you can bring it to me. Three days after my marriage. Don't forget."

BABA RETURNED FROM his trip to the capital. For the first time in my life he came to visit me in my room. He hesitated by the door, too nervous to approach.

"Daughter," he said, "your marriage is only five days away. Your mother tells me you refuse to rise and perform your toilette, but you must get up. You don't want to miss your wedding."

When I hung my head in resignation, he crossed the room, sat on the bed, and took my hand.

"I pointed your husband out to you on the last night of the opera," he said. "Were you unhappy with what you saw?"

"I didn't look," I answered.

"Oh, Peony, I wish now I'd told you more about him, but you know how your mother is."

"That's all right, Baba. I promise to do what's expected of me. I won't embarrass you or Mama. I'll make Wu Ren happy."

"Wu Ren is a good man," Baba went on, ignoring what I'd said. "I've known him since he was a boy and I have never seen him do anything improper." He smiled lightly. "Except for one time. That night after the opera he approached me. He gave me something to give you." Baba shook his head. "I may be master of the Chen family, but your mother has her rules and already she was angry with me about the performance. I didn't give it to you then. Even I knew it was improper. So I saved what he gave me in a book of poetry. Knowing both of you, I thought that was the right place."

A gift five months ago or now wouldn't change how I viewed my future husband or my marriage. I saw duty and responsibility, nothing more.

"And now here we are, just a few days before . . ." Baba shook his head as though he was driving out an unpleasant thought. "I don't think your mother will mind if I give it to you now."

He let go of my hand, reached into his tunic, and pulled out something small folded in rice paper. I didn't have the strength to lift my head off the pillow, but I watched as he unfolded the paper. Inside was a dried peony, which he set in my palm. I stared at it in disbelief.

"Ren is just two years older than you," Baba said, "but he's done so much already. He's a poet."

"A poet?" I echoed. My mind was having a hard time accepting what I held in my hand, while my ears seemed to be hearing Baba's words from the bottom of a cave.

"A successful one," Baba added. "His work has already been published, even though he's so young. He lives on Wushan Mountain just across the lake. If I hadn't left for the capital, I would have shown you his home from my library window. But I was gone, and now you are—"

He was talking about *my* stranger, *my* poet. The dried flower I held in my hand was the one he'd caressed me with in the Moon-Viewing Pavilion. Everything I had been dreading was wrong. I was going to marry the man I loved. Fate had brought us together. We truly were like two mandarin ducks mated for life.

My body began to shake uncontrollably, and tears streamed from my eyes. Baba lifted me up as though I weighed no more than a leaf and held me in his arms.

"I'm so sorry," he said, trying to comfort me. "Every girl is afraid to marry out, but I didn't know how bad it was with you."

"I'm not crying because I'm sad or scared. Oh, Baba, I am the happiest girl ever."

He didn't seem to have heard me, because he said, "You would have been happy with Ren."

He laid me gently back down on my pillow. I tried to bring the flower up to my nose to see if its scent still lingered, but I was too weak. Baba took the flower and placed it on my chest. It felt as heavy as a stone on my heart.

Tears gathered in Baba's eyes. How perfect that father and daughter should be united in their happiness.

"I need to tell you something," he said urgently. "It's a secret about our family."

He had already given me the greatest wedding gift possible.

"You know I once had two other younger brothers," he said.

I was so elated—because Wu Ren was my poet, we were to be married shortly, and we were living a miracle—that it was hard for me to focus on who Baba was talking about. I had seen these uncles' names in the ancestral hall, but no one ever went to clean their graves at Spring Festival. I'd always supposed they'd died at birth, which was why so little attention was paid to them.

"They were just boys when my father got his posting to Yangzhou," Baba went on. "My parents trusted me to take care of this villa and the family in their absence, but they took the youngest boys with them. Your mother and I went to Yangzhou for a visit, but we couldn't have chosen a worse time. The Manchus came."

He paused to gauge my reaction. I didn't know why he was telling me something so grim at this wonderful moment. When I didn't say anything, he continued.

"My father, my brothers, and I were herded along with the other men to a gated area. We didn't know what happened to the women, and your mother to this day has not spoken of it, so I can only tell you what I saw. My little brothers and I had one duty as sons, and that was to make sure our father survived. We stood around him, shielding him not only from the soldiers but also from the other desperate prisoners, who would easily have turned him over to the Manchus if they thought it might save them."

This was more than I had ever known. But as happy as I was, my mind was troubled. Where were my mother and grandmother?

Snatching this thought from my head, my father said, "I did not have the privilege of witnessing my mother's bravery, but I saw my brothers die. Oh, Peony, men can be very cruel."

He suddenly seemed unable to speak. And again I wondered, Why tell me all this now?

After a long while, he went on. "When you meet them, please tell them I'm sorry. Tell them we try to honor them as best we can. Our offerings have been great, but they still have not granted our family sons. Peony, you've been a good daughter. Please see how you can help."

I was confused and I think my father was too. My responsibility was to bring sons to my husband's family, not to my natal family.

"Baba," I reminded him, "I'm marrying into the Wu family."

He closed his eyes and turned his face away. "Of course," he said gruffly. "Of course. Please forgive my mistake."

I heard people coming down the hall. Servants entered and removed my furniture, clothes, draperies, and dowry—everything but my bed—from my room to take to my husband's home.

Then Mama, my aunts, uncles, cousins, and the concubines entered and gathered around my bed. Baba must have made a mistake in counting how many days were left until my wedding. I tried to stand so that I could properly kowtow to them, but my body was weak and tired even as my heart was full of happiness. Servants hung a sieve and a mirror in the doorway of my room to render favorable every inauspicious element.

I wouldn't be allowed to eat during the course of my

wedding ceremonies, but I needed to taste a bit of the special foods my family had prepared for my wedding-day breakfast. I wasn't hungry, but I would do my best to obey, because every bite would be an omen of a long life in harmony with my husband. But no one offered me pork spareribs, which I was supposed to eat to give me the strength to have sons, while refraining from gnawing the bones to protect the vitalization of my husband's fertility. They would want me to eat the seeds of the water lily, pumpkin, and sunflower to bring many sons. But they didn't offer these things either. Instead, my family stood around my bed and wept. They were all sad to see me marry out, but I was ebullient. My body felt so light and unburdened that I thought I might just float away. I took a deep breath to steady myself. I would be with my poet before the sun set. Between now and then, I would enjoy all the traditions and customs for marrying out a beloved daughter. Tonight—much, much later tonight—and at intimate times in years to come, I would entertain my husband with my memories of these beautiful moments.

The men left, and my aunts and cousins washed my limbs, only they forgot to add pomelo leaves to the water. They brushed my hair and pinned it up with jade and gold hairpins, forgetting to put on my wedding headdress. They put white powder on my face, ignoring the pots of color that would brighten my lips and cheeks. They placed the dried peony in my hand. They dressed me in a thin white silk underskirt with sutras printed on it. With so many tears around me, I didn't have the wherewithal to point out that they'd forgotten to tie the pig's heart into my underskirt.

Next they would help me into my outer wedding costume. I smiled at them. I would miss them. I cried as I was supposed to. I'd been selfish and stubborn to hide away with my project when my time with my family was so limited. But before they brought out my wedding skirt and tunic, Second Aunt called for the men to return. I watched as servants took the door off the frame and brought it to my bedside. I was gently lifted onto the door. Whole taro roots were placed around me as symbols of fertility. I looked like an offering to the gods. It seemed I would not even have to walk to my palanquin. Tears of gratitude ran from the corners of my eyes, down my temples, and into my hair. I didn't know I could be so happy.

They carried me downstairs. A beautiful procession formed behind me as we moved along the covered corridors. We needed to go to the ancestral hall so I could thank all the Chen family ancestors who'd looked out for me, but we didn't stop there. We went straight to the courtyard just before the Sitting-Down Hall that lay before our main gate. The bearers set me down and stepped aside. I looked at our wind-fire gate and thought, It will just be moments now. The gate will open. I'll step into my palanquin. One last goodbye to Mama and Baba, and then I'll go to my new home.

One by one, all the fingers in our household—from my parents down to the lowest servant—passed by me and performed obeisance. And then strangely, peculiarly, they left me alone. My heart calmed. Around me were my belongings: my chests filled with silks and embroideries, my mirrors and ribbons, my quilts and clothes. The courtyard at this time of year was desolate and cold. I heard no firecrackers. I heard no cymbals or voices raised in celebration. I heard no bearers bringing the palanquin that would carry me to my husband's home. Melancholy thoughts started to unreel, ensnaring me like tangled vines. With terrible sadness and desperate panic, I realized I was not going to Ren. My family—following the custom for all unmarried daughters—had brought me outside to die.

"Mama, Baba," I called, but my voice was too faint to be heard. I tried to move, but my limbs were at once too heavy and too light to stir. I closed my hand into a fist and felt the peony crumble into dust.

It was the twelfth month and bitterly cold, but I survived the day and the night. As pink light began to infuse the sky, I felt like a pearl sinking beneath the waves. My heart felt like jade shattering. My mind was like powder fading, perfume melting, clouds drifting away. My life force became as thin as the lightest silk. As I took my last breath, I thought of lines from the last poem I'd written:

It is not so easy to wake from a dream.
My spirit, if sincere, will stay forever under the moon or
    by the flowers. . . .

And then in an instant I was flying on and on for thousands of *li* across the sky.

PART II

Roaming with the Wind

The Separated Soul

I DIED IN THE SEVENTH HOUR ON THE SEVENTH DAY OF the twelfth month in the third year of Emperor Kangxi's reign. I was just five days from my wedding. In those first moments of death, much of what had happened in the last few weeks and days became clear to me. Obviously I had no idea I was dying, but my mother had understood it when she first entered my room after not seeing me for so long. When I'd gone to the Spring Pavilion, my cousins, my aunts, and the concubines had tried to get me to eat, recognizing I was already starving myself. In my final days, I'd been obsessed with writing just as Liniang had been obsessed with painting her self-portrait. I'd thought my poems had emerged from love, but deep inside I think I knew I was dying. What the body knows and what the mind chooses to believe are two different things, after all. Baba had come to give me the peony because I was dying and the proprieties didn't matter anymore; I'd been happy to find out I was marrying my poet, but I was too close to death to recover.

The drapes in my room had been taken down not for me to take to my new home but because they resembled fishing nets and my family didn't want me to be reborn as a fish. My father told me about my uncles because he wanted me to carry a message to them in the afterworld. "One day you may meet them," he'd said. He couldn't have been more direct than that, and yet I hadn't understood. My family had placed taro around me. Taro is carried by a bride to her new home, but it is also offered to the dead to ensure future sons and grandsons. Tradition demands that an unmarried girl be taken outside when there is "only one breath left." But how can anyone gauge these things? At least I wasn't a baby when I died. I would have been left to be eaten by dogs or buried in a shallow grave and quickly forgotten.

As children, we learn about what happens to us after we die from our parents, didactic tales, and all the traditions we perform for ancestor worship. Certainly much of what I knew about death came from *The Peony Pavilion*. Still, the living can't know everything, so I was often bewildered, lost, and unsure as I began my journey. I had heard that death is darkness, but that's not how I experienced it. It would take forty-nine days to push me out of the earthly realm and pull me into the afterworld. Every soul has three parts, and each must find its proper home after death. One part stayed with my body to be buried, another part traveled toward the afterworld, while the last part remained in the earthly realm, waiting to be put in my ancestor tablet. I was rent through with terror, sadness, and confusion as my three parts began their separate journeys, each fully aware of the other two at all times.

How could any of this be?

Even as I flew across the sky, I was conscious of the wailing that began in the courtyard when my body was discovered. Great sadness filled me when I saw my relatives and the servants who'd cared for me stamp their feet in grief. They loosened their hair, took off their jewelry and ornaments, and dressed themselves in white sackcloth. A servant adjusted the sieve and mirror that hung in the doorway to my room. I thought they'd been placed there to protect me as I went to Ren's home in marriage, but these items had actually been used in preparation for my death. Now the sieve would allow goodness to pass through, while the mirror would change my family's misery back to happiness.

My first concern was for that part of my soul that would stay with my body. Mama and my aunts stripped my corpse and I saw how horrifyingly emaciated I was. They washed me an uneven number of times and dressed me in layers of longevity clothes. They put me in padded undergarments so I might be warm in winter, and then they slipped my limbs into the silk gowns and satin tunics that had been made for my dowry. They took great care to make sure no fur trimmed my clothes, for fear I might be reborn an animal. For my outer layer, I wore a padded silk jacket with sleeves embroidered in an elaborate and very colorful kingfisher feather pattern. I was dazed—as any spirit is who has just left its body—but I wished they had used my wedding costume for one of my longevity layers. I was a bride, and I wanted my wedding clothes in the afterworld.

Mama placed a thin sliver of jade in my mouth to safeguard my body. Second Aunt tucked coins and rice in my pockets so I might soothe the rabid dogs I'd meet on my way to the afterworld. Third Aunt covered my face with a thin piece of white silk. Fourth Aunt tied colored string around my waist to prevent me from carrying away any of our family's children and around my feet to restrain my body from leaping about should I be tormented by evil spirits on my journey.

Servants hung sixteen white paper streamers on the right

side of the Chen Family Villa's main gate, so our neighbors would know that a girl of sixteen years had died. My uncles crisscrossed the city to shrines for local gods and deities, where they lit candles and burned spirit money, which the part of my soul that was traveling to the afterworld used to bribe my way through the Demon Barrier. My father hired monks—not many, just a few, because I was a daughter—to chant every seventh day. In life, no one is allowed to wander at will, and so it is in death. My family's job now was to tie me down so I would not be tempted to roam.

On the third day after my death, my body was placed in my coffin, along with ashes, copper coins, and lime. Then the unsealed coffin was set in a corner of an outer courtyard to wait until the diviner found the right date and place for me to be buried. My aunts put cakes in my hands, and my uncles laid sticks on either side of my body. They gathered together clothes, binding cloth for my feet, money, and food—all made from paper—and burned them so they would accompany me to the afterworld. But I was a girl, and soon enough I learned they hadn't sent enough.

At the beginning of the second week, the part of my soul that was journeying toward the afterworld reached the Weighing Bridge, where demon bureaucrats went about their duties without pity. I stood in line directly behind a man named Li, watching as those ahead of us were weighed before being forwarded to the next level. For seven days, Li quivered and shook, even more terrified than I was by what we were seeing and hearing. When his turn came, I watched in horror as he sat on the scale and all the misdeeds he had done in life caused it to drop several meters. His punishment was instantaneous. He was ripped into pieces and ground into powder. Then he was brought back together and sent on his way with an admonition.

"This is just a sample of the suffering that is waiting for you, Master Li," one of the demons declared mercilessly. "Don't cry or beg for leniency. It is too late for that. Next!"

I was petrified. Hideous demons surrounded me, herding me to the scale with their terrible faces and screeching cries. I was not lighter than air—the sign of the truly good—but my misdeeds in life had been minor and I continued on my journey.

The whole time I stood in line at the Weighing Bridge, friends and neighbors paid their condolences to my parents. Commissioner Tan gave my father spirit money for me to spend in the afterworld. Madame Tan brought candles, incense, and more paper objects to be burned for my comfort. Tan Ze inspected the offerings, measuring their modesty, and offered my cousins empty words of sorrow. But she was only nine years old. What could she possibly know about death?

In my third week, I passed through the Bad Dogs Village, where the virtuous are met with wagging tails and licking tongues and the evil are torn apart by powerful jaws and ragged teeth until their blood flows in rivers. Again, I had not been so bad in life, but I was very happy for the cakes my aunts had placed in my coffin to appease the beasts of two, four, and more legs and for the sticks my uncles had given me to beat away the truly unruly. In the fourth week, I arrived at the Mirror of Retribution and was told to look into it to see what my next incarnation would be. If I had been wicked, I would have seen a snake slithering in the grass, a pig wallowing in muck, or a rat nibbling on a corpse. If I had been good, I would have glimpsed a new life better than my last. But when I looked in the mirror, the image was murky and unformed.

• • •

THE FINAL THIRD of my soul was roaming, lingering on earth until my ancestor tablet was dotted and I would come to a final rest. My thoughts about Ren never left me. I blamed myself for my stubbornness in not eating and I grieved for the wedding we would not have, but I never once despaired that we wouldn't be joined. In fact, I believed more than ever in the strength of our love. I expected Ren to come by the house, weep over my coffin, and then ask my parents for a pair of bound-foot slippers I'd recently worn. These he would carry home with three lighted sticks of incense. At each corner, he'd call out my name and invite me to follow. Once he reached home, he would put my shoes on a chair, along with the incense. If he burned incense for two years and remembered me every day, he would be able to honor me as his wife. But he didn't do these things.

Since it is against nature for even the dead to be without a spouse, I began to dream about a ghost wedding. It wasn't as easy or romantic as an Asking-for-the-Shoes ceremony, but I didn't care, as long as it brought me quickly into marriage with Ren. After our ghost wedding was held—with my ancestor tablet sitting in for me—I would pass forever out of the Chen family and into my husband's clan, where I belonged.

When I didn't hear talk about this happening either, the third of my soul that was not with my body or traveling to the afterworld decided to visit Ren. My whole life had been about going in. As I died, I felt myself going in, in, in, until there was nothing left. Now I was free from my family and the Chen Family Villa. I could go anywhere, but I didn't know the city or how to find my way, and I found it difficult to walk on my lily feet. I could go no more than ten steps without swaying in the breeze. But for all my pain and confusion, I had to find Ren.

The outside world was both far more beautiful and uglier than I'd imagined. Colorful fruit stands were sandwiched between stalls that sold pig carcasses and plough parts. Beggars with dripping sores and amputated limbs entreated passersby for food and money. I saw women—from noble families!—walking on the street as though it were nothing, laughing on their way to restaurants and teahouses.

I was lost, curious, and excited. The world was in constant movement, with carts and horses rolling through the streets, salt wagons drawn by lumbering water buffaloes, flags and pennants flapping from buildings, and too many people pushing and shoving in great eddies of humanity. Hawkers sold fish, needles, and baskets in piercing voices. Construction sites battered my ears with their hammering and shouting. Men argued about politics, gold prices, and gambling debts. I covered my ears, but the wisps of vapor that were my hands could not keep out the raucous, torturous sounds. I tried to get off the street, but as a spirit I couldn't navigate around corners.

I went back to my family home and tried a different street. This brought me to a shopping area, where they sold fans, silks, paper umbrellas, scissors, carved soapstone, prayer beads, and tea. Signboards and trappings of one kind and another blocked the sunlight. I continued on, passing temples, factories for making cotton, and mints where the sound from the stamping machines pounded at my ears until tears poured from my eyes. The streets of Hangzhou were paved with cobblestones, and my lily feet bruised and tore until spirit blood oozed through my silk slippers. They say that ghosts feel no physical pain, but this is not true. Why else would dogs in the afterworld tear the evil limb from limb or demons spend eternity eating the heart of a miscreant again and again and again?

After another long straight line that led nowhere, I returned to my family home. I set off in a new direction, walking along the edge of the exterior wall until I came to the crystal waters of West Lake. I saw the causeway, lagoons with shimmering ripples, and verdant hillsides. I listened to doves croon for rain and magpies bicker. I glimpsed Solitary Island and remembered how Ren had pointed out his house on Wushan Mountain, but I couldn't figure out how to get from here to there. I sat on a rock. The skirts from my longevity clothes draped about me on the shore, but I was now of the spirit world and they didn't get wet or muddy. I no longer had to worry about soiled shoes or anything like that. I left no shadow or footprints. Did this make me feel free or uncontrollably lonely? Both.

The sun set over the hills, turning the sky crimson and the lake deep lavender. My spirit trembled as a reed in the breeze. Night draped itself over Hangzhou. I was alone on the bank, separated from everyone and everything I knew, sinking deeper and deeper into despair. If Ren wouldn't come to my family's home for any of my funeral activities and I couldn't go to his since I was hampered by corners and noises, how would I find him?

In the houses and business establishments around the lake, lanterns were turned down and candles blown out. The living slept, but the shore shimmered with activity. Spirits of trees and bamboo breathed and quivered. Poisoned dogs came to the lake desperate for a final drink of water before death shudders took them. Hungry ghosts—those who'd drowned in the lake or had resisted the Manchus, refused to shave their foreheads, and lost their heads as punishment—dragged themselves through the underbrush. I also saw others like myself: those just dead and still roaming before the three parts of their souls found their proper resting places. There would be no peaceful nights filled with beautiful dreams for us ever again.

Dreams! I leaped to my feet. Ren knew *The Peony Pavilion* nearly as well as I did. Liniang and Mengmei first met in a dream. Surely since I'd died Ren had tried to reach me in his dreams, only I hadn't known where or how to meet him. Now I knew exactly where to go, but I'd have to turn right to get there. I tried several times to go around the corner of the compound, each time widening my turn until finally I arced out wide enough to make it. I crept along the water's edge, stepping on rocks, not worrying about puddles, pushing aside the rock roses and other bits of shrubbery that impeded my way until I reached my family's Moon-Viewing Pavilion. Just as the tiniest sliver of sun peeked over the mountain, I spotted Ren, waiting for me.

"I've been coming here, hoping to see you," he said.

"Ren."

When he reached for me, I didn't shy away. He held me for a long time without speaking, and then he asked, "How could you die and leave me?" His anguish was palpable. "We were so happy. Did you decide you didn't care for me?"

"I didn't know who you were. How could I know?"

"At first, I didn't know it was you either," he answered. "I knew my future wife was Master Chen's daughter and that her name was Peony. I didn't want an arranged marriage, but like you I had accepted my fate. When we met, I thought you might be one of the cousins in the household or one of the guests. My heart changed, and I thought, Let me have these three nights, believing they were as close as I'd ever get to what I wanted from marriage."

"I felt the same way too." I was filled with regret as I added, "If only I had said my name."

"I didn't say my name either," he said ruefully. "But what

about the peony? Did you get it? I gave it to your father. You had to know it was me then."

"He gave it to me when it was too late to save me."

He sighed. "Peony."

"But I still don't understand how you knew it was me."

"I didn't until your father made the announcement about our marriage. To me, the girl I was going to marry had no face and no voice. But when your father spoke your name that night I heard it in a whole new way. Then when he said your name had to change because it was the same as my mother's, somehow I felt—understood—he was talking about *you*. You don't look like my mother, but the two of you share the same sensibility. I hoped when he made the announcement and pointed to me that you would see me."

"I had my eyes shut. After meeting you, I was afraid to see the man who would be my husband."

Then I remembered opening my eyes and seeing Tan Ze with her mouth pulled into a taut *oh*. She had seen exactly who it was. She had told me on the first night of the opera that she had set her heart on the poet. No wonder she was furious when we were walking back to the women's quarters.

Ren stroked my cheek. He was ready for something more, but I had to try to make sense out of what had happened.

"So you decided it was me based on intuition?" I persisted.

He smiled, and I thought, If we had married, this is how he would have responded to me at those times when I couldn't release my obstinacy.

"It was very simple," he said. "After the announcement, your father dismissed the women. When the men stood up, I quickly separated myself from them and hurried through the garden until I saw the procession. You were at the front. The women were treating you as a bride already." He bent down and whispered in my ear. "I thought how lucky we were that we wouldn't be strangers on our wedding night. I was happy—with your face, your golden lilies, your manner." He straightened up again and said, "After that night, I dreamed about our future life. We were to spend our days in words and in love. I sent you *The Peony Pavilion*. Did you get it?"

How could I tell him that my obsession with it had caused my death?

So many mistakes. So many errors. So much tragedy as a result. In that moment I understood that the cruelest words in the universe are *if only*. If only I hadn't left the opera on the first night, I would have gone to my marriage and met Ren on my wedding night without incident. If only I had kept my eyes open when my father pointed out Ren. If only my father had given me the peony the next morning or a month or even a week before I died. How could fate be so merciless?

"We can't change what's happened, but maybe our future isn't hopeless," Ren said. "Mengmei and Liniang found a way, didn't they?"

I didn't yet fully understand how things worked here, or what I would be allowed to do, but I said, "I won't leave you. I'll stay with you forever."

Ren tightened his arms around me and I buried my face in his shoulder. This was where I needed to be, but then he pulled away and gestured to the rising sun.

"I've got to go," he said.

"But I have so many things to tell you. Don't leave me," I pleaded.

He smiled. "I hear my servant in the hall. He's bringing my tea."

Then, just as he had on the first night of the opera, he asked me to meet him again. With that, he was gone.

I stayed right there all day and into the night, waiting for him to come to me in his dreams. Those hours gave me a lot of time to think. I wanted to be an amorous ghost. In *The Peony Pavilion,* Liniang had done clouds and rain with Mengmei first in her dream and then later as a ghost. When she became human again, she still had her virginity and was unwilling to compromise her chastity before marriage. But could that happen in real life? Apart from *The Peony Pavilion,* almost every other ghost story involved a female spirit who ruined, maimed, or killed her lover. I remembered a story my mother told me in which the ghost-heroine kept herself from touching her scholar with the words "These moldering bones from the grave are no match for the living. A liaison with a ghost only hastens a man's death. I could not bear to harm you." I couldn't risk hurting Ren in this way either. Like Liniang, I was destined to be a wife. Even in death—especially in death—I couldn't show my husband that I was anything less than a lady. As Liniang observed, *A ghost may be deluded by passion; a woman must pay full attention to the rites.*

That night, when Ren came again to the Moon-Viewing Pavilion, we talked about poetry and flowers, about beauty and *qing,* about lasting love and the temporary love of teahouse girls. When he left at daybreak, I was disconsolate. The whole time I was with him, I wanted to reach inside his tunic and touch his skin. I wanted to whisper the messages of my heart into his ear. I wanted to see and touch what he kept hidden inside his trousers, just as I wanted him to peel away my layers of longevity clothes until he found that place that was yearning, even in death, to be touched.

The following night, he brought with him paper, ink, inkstone, and brushes. He took my hand and together we ground the ink against the stone, and then we walked to the lake, where he cupped my hands so that I might bring back water to mix the ink.

"Tell me," he said. "Tell me the words to write."

I thought of my experiences of the last weeks and then began to compose.

"Soaring across the sky in never-ending sleeplessness.
The mountains are fresh with dew,
The lake glimmers.
You draw me to you from across the clouds."

When the last words fell from my lips, he set down the brush and removed my padded jacket with the sleeves embroidered in the kingfisher pattern.

He wrote the next poem, his calligraphy as sumptuous as a caress. He called it "Visitation from a Goddess," and it was about me.

"Unable to express the sadness of your parting,
Darkness without end.
You come to me in a dream.
I am flooded by thoughts of what should have been.
But I find it here, with you, goddess of my heart.
A sudden sob wakes me from my dream.
Alone again."

Together we wrote eighteen poems. I'd say one line and he'd come up with the next, often borrowing from the opera that we loved. *"Tonight I come to you whole in body, full of love, yours in every desire,"* I quoted Liniang after her secret marriage. Each line was a revealed intimacy. Each line brought us closer together. And each poem got shorter and shorter as layer after layer of my longevity clothes fell to the ground. I forgot my concerns. Everything was reduced to words like *pleasure, ripples, temptations, surging, clouds*.

Dawn broke, and he was ripped away from me. Simply gone. The sun was fully up in the sky and I was down to my last layers of clothes. The dead don't feel heat and cold in the usual way. Rather, we feel something deeper, something connected to the *emotions* of these sensations. I shivered uncontrollably, but I didn't dress again. I waited all day and into the night for Ren to come back to me, but he didn't. The next thing I knew, strong forces pulled me away from the Moon-Viewing Pavilion. I wore only my inner garment and a gown embroidered with birds flying in a pair above flowers.

I HAD BEEN dead five weeks, and the three aspects of my soul began to wrench apart irrevocably. One part settled forever in my corpse, the roaming part began to drift to the ancestor tablet, while my afterworld soul arrived at the Viewing Terrace of Lost Souls. At this point, the dead are so sad and filled with longing that they are given one last chance to look at their homes and listen to their families. From my great distance, I searched along the shore of West Lake until I came to my family home. At first all I could see were trivial things: the servants emptying my mother's chamber pot, the concubines arguing over a dish of lion's head, Shao's daughter hiding her embroidery patterns between the folds of my copy of *The Peony Pavilion*. But I also saw my parents' sorrow and was stabbed through with remorse. I had died from too much *qing*. I had left the world because an abundance of emotion had overwhelmed me, sapped my strength, and clouded my thoughts. Below me, Mama cried and I realized she'd been right. I should have stayed away from *The Peony Pavilion*. It had brought out too much passion, despair, and hope in me, and now here I was, separated from my family and my husband.

Baba, as the eldest son, was in charge of all the rites. His main duty and responsibility now were to see me properly interred and my ancestor tablet dotted. My family and our servants prepared more paper offerings—all those things they thought I might need for my new life. They made clothes, food, rooms, and books for my entertainment. They did not provide a palanquin, because even in death Mama did not want me to go abroad. On the eve of my funeral, these offerings were burned in the street. From the Viewing Terrace, I saw Shao use a stick to beat at the fire and the leaves of paper as they twisted in the flames to keep away the spirits who wanted to take my belongings. My father should have had one of my uncles do this to show he meant business and my mother should have thrown rice around the edges of the fire to attract the attention of the hungry ghosts who craved the food, because Shao did not scare away the spirits and nearly everything was stolen before I had a chance to receive it.

When my coffin reached the wind-fire gate, I saw Ren. Even as my Second Uncle broke a cup with holes in it just over where my head rested—from now on I would only be allowed to drink the water I'd wasted in life—I rejoiced. Fire-crackers exorcised from around the compound inauspicious influences associated with me. I was placed in a palanquin, not a red one for marriage but a green one to represent death. The procession started. My uncles tossed spirit money to secure my right of way to the afterworld. Ren, his head bent, walked between my father and Commissioner Tan. They were followed by palanquins holding my mother, aunts, and girl cousins.

At the cemetery, my coffin was lowered into the ground. The wind soughed through the poplars in ghostly song. Mama, Baba, and my aunts, uncles, and cousins each picked up a handful of dirt and threw it on my coffin. As the soil covered the lacquer surface, I felt that third of my soul disappear from me forever.

From the Viewing Terrace, I watched and listened. No ghost marriage ceremony was performed. No banquet was presented at the graveside, which would introduce me to my new companions in the afterworld and pave the way for good understanding between me and my new associates. Mama was so weak from grief that my aunts had to help her back into the palanquin. Baba led the procession, and once again Ren and Commissioner Tan were beside him. For a long while, no one spoke. What comfort could anyone give a father who has lost his only child? What could anyone say to a groom who has lost his bride?

Finally, Commissioner Tan addressed my father: "Your daughter is not the only one to be affected by this terrible opera."

What kind of solace was this?

"But she loved the opera," Ren mumbled. The other men stared at him, and he added, "I heard this about your daughter, Master Chen. If I'd been fortunate enough to marry her, I never would have kept it from her."

It's hard to describe my feelings at seeing him there when so recently we had been in each other's arms, composing poetry, letting *qing* flow between us. His mourning was real, and once again I was filled with regret for the stubbornness and foolishness that had brought me to this place.

"But she died from lovesickness, just as that sorry girl died in the opera!" Commissioner Tan spat out. It seemed he was unaccustomed to anyone disagreeing with him.

"It's true that life's tendency to imitate art is not always a comfort," my father admitted, "but the boy is right. My daughter could not live without words and emotion. And you, Commissioner, don't you sometimes wish you could visit the women's chambers and experience the true depths of *qing*?"

Before Commissioner Tan could respond, Ren said, "Your daughter is not without words or emotion, Master Chen. For three nights, she visited me in my dreams."

No! I shouted from my spot on the Viewing Terrace. Didn't he know what revealing this would mean?

My father and Commissioner Tan looked at him in concern.

"Truly we have met," Ren said. "A few nights ago, we were together on your Moon-Viewing Pavilion. When she first came to me, her hair was pinned for marriage. The sleeves of her outer jacket were embroidered the color of kingfisher feathers."

"You describe her perfectly," my father agreed suspiciously. "But how did you know her if you had not met her before?"

Would Ren give away our secret? Would he ruin me in my father's eyes?

"My heart recognized her," Ren answered. "We composed poems together: *Soaring across the sky in never-ending sleeplessness. . . .* When I woke, I wrote down eighteen poems."

"Ren, you have proved once again that you are a man of sentiment," my father said. "I could not have asked for a better son-in-law."

Ren reached into his sleeve and pulled out several folded pieces of paper. "I thought you would like to read these."

Ren was wonderful, but he'd made a terrible, nearly irreversible, mistake. When we're alive, we're told that if a dead one appears to someone in a dream and that person tells others about it—or, worse, if he shows through writing the words of the dead—then the spirit will be driven away. This is why fox spirits, ghosts, and even immortals beg their human lovers not to reveal their existence to the world. But humans cannot keep a secret. Of course, the spirit—whatever form it takes—doesn't "disappear." Where would it go? But the ability to visit in dreams becomes nearly impossible. I was devastated.

IN THE SIXTH week after my death, I should have crossed the Inevitable River. In the seventh week, I should have entered the realm of the Prince of the Wheel, where I would be brought before judges who would decide my fate. But none of these things happened; I remained on the Viewing Terrace. I began to suspect that something was terribly wrong.

I never saw Baba approach Ren about a ghost marriage. My father was too busy, preparing to move to the palace in Beijing to take up his new post. I should have been distressed about this—how could he allow himself to make obeisance to the Manchu emperor?—and I was. I should have worried for my father's soul when he decided to give up his morals in exchange for making a fortune—and I did. But I was far more anxious that Baba would try to trap a husband other than Ren to accept me as a ghost bride. It would have been easy for Baba to throw some money on the road outside our gate, wait for some passerby to pick it up, and tell the man that in picking up the "bride price" he had accepted me as a wife. But this didn't happen either.

Mama said she wouldn't follow Baba to Beijing, refusing to waver in her steadfastness never to leave the Chen Family Villa. I took comfort in this. For Mama, the joys and laughter of our once happy days in the Spring Pavilion before I retired to my room had disappeared, only to be replaced by tears of blood and woe. She spent hours in the storeroom where my belongings were kept, finding my scent clinging to my clothes, touching the brushes I'd handled, letting her eyes rest on the items I'd embroidered for my dowry. I had resisted my mother for so long; now I longed for her all the time.

Forty-nine days after my death, my family crowded into our ancestral hall for the dotting of my ancestor tablet and a final goodbye. Storytellers and a handful of singers gathered in the courtyard. Someone of great distinction—a scholar or member of the literati—is always given the honor of placing the final precious dot on the ancestor tablet. Once this was done, a third of my soul would be transferred to the tablet, where it would watch over my family. The dotting would allow me to be worshipped as an ancestor and give me a place to inhabit on earth for all eternity. My dotted ancestor tablet would also be the object through which my family would send their offerings to sustain me in the afterworld, make requests for my help, and provide comfort to me as a way of averting potential hostility. In the future, when my family embarked on a new business venture, named a child, or considered a marriage proposal, they would consult me through my tablet. I was sure Commissioner Tan, who was the highest-ranked person my father knew in Hangzhou, would perform the dotting. But my father chose the one person who would mean more to me than anyone else: Wu Ren.

He was more distraught than he'd been on the day of my funeral. His hair was tousled as though he'd given up sleep altogether. Pain and regret filled his eyes. Now that I'd been banned from his dreams, he understood his loss all too clearly. That part of me that was to reside in my ancestor tablet came to rest next to him. I wanted him to know I was there at his side, but neither he nor anyone else seemed aware of my presence. I was less substantial than a whiff of incense smoke.

My ancestor tablet stood on an altar table. It had been inscribed with my name, the hour of my birth, and the hour of my death. Next to the tablet stood a small dish of cock's blood and a brush. Ren dipped the brush in the blood. He lifted the brush to animate my tablet, hesitated, and then dropped the brush, groaned, and ran from the hall. Baba and the servants followed him outside. They had him sit under a ginkgo tree. They brought him tea. They comforted him. Then Baba noticed my mother was missing.

We all followed him back into the hall. Mama lay on the floor, sobbing and clutching my tablet. Baba stared at her, helpless. Shao crouched down next to Mama and tried to pry the tablet from her hands, but she wouldn't let it go.

"Husband, let me keep this," Mama sobbed.

"It needs to be dotted," he said.

"She's my daughter, let me do it," she begged. "Please."

But Mama was not someone of distinction! She was not a writer or a member of the literati. Then to my absolute bafflement, a look of deep understanding passed between my parents.

"Of course," Baba said. "That would be perfect."

Then Shao wrapped her arms around my mother and led her away. My father dismissed the storytellers and singers. The rest of my family and the servants dispersed. Ren went home.

All through the night, my mother cried. She refused to let go of the tablet, despite Shao's constant coaxing. How could I have not seen how much she loved me? Was this why Baba had given her permission to dot my tablet? But that didn't make sense. This was Baba's duty.

In the morning, he stopped by Mama's room. When Shao opened the door, he saw Mama hidden under quilts, moaning her sadness. Sorrow pierced his eyes.

"Tell her I had to leave for the capital," he whispered to Shao.

Reluctantly, he turned away. I went with him to the front gate, where he got in a palanquin to carry him to his new post. After the palanquin disappeared from view, I returned to my mother's room. Shao knelt on the floor next to Mama's bedside, waiting.

"My daughter's gone," Mama whimpered.

Shao hummed her sympathy and smoothed away strings of damp hair from my mother's wet cheeks.

"Give me the tablet, Lady Chen. Let me take it to the master. He must perform the rite."

What was she thinking? My father was gone.

Mama didn't know that, but she tightened her arms around the tablet, refusing to let go of it, of me.

"You know the ritual." Shao spoke sternly. How like her to rely on tradition to try to relieve my mother's sorrow. "This is a father's duty. Now give it to me." When she saw my mother waver, she added, "You know I'm right."

Against her will, Mama gave the tablet to Shao. As Shao left the room, Mama buried her face in the quilts again to cry. I followed my old wet nurse as she walked to a storage room at the back of the compound and watched helplessly as she tucked the tablet on a high shelf behind a jar of pickled turnips.

"Too much trouble for the mistress," she said, and cleared her throat as if getting rid of a bad taste. "No one wants to see this ugly thing."

Without the dot I was unable to enter the tablet, and the part of my soul that was supposed to settle there united with me on the Viewing Terrace.

The Viewing Terrace
of Lost Souls

I WAS UNABLE TO JOURNEY BEYOND THE VIEWING terrace so I had no opportunity to plead my case before the panel of infernal judges. As the days went by, I discovered that I still had all the needs and wants I had when I was alive. Death, rather than quelling my emotions, had intensified them. The Seven Emotions we talk about on earth—joy, anger, grief, fear, love, hate, and desire—had traveled with me to the afterworld. These ancestral emotions, I saw, were more commanding and enduring than any other force in the universe: stronger than life, more persistent than death, more powerful than what the gods can control, floating about us without beginning and without end. And while I was awash in them, none was stronger than the sorrow I felt for the life I'd lost.

I missed the Chen Family Villa. I missed the smells of ginger, green tea, jasmine, and summer rain. After so many months without an appetite, suddenly I hungered for lotus roots braised in sweet soy, preserved duck, lake crabs, and crystal shrimps. I missed the sound of nightingales, the chatter of the women in our inner quarters, and the lapping of the lake along the shore. I missed the feel of silk on my skin and the warm wind coming through my bedroom window. I missed the smell of paper and ink. I missed my books. I missed being able to step into their pages and into another world. But what I missed most was my family.

Every day I looked over the balustrade to watch them. I saw Mama, my aunts, my cousins, and the concubines go back to their usual routines. I was happy when Baba came home to visit, have meetings in the Hall of Abundant Elegance with young men in handsome robes in the afternoons, and sip tea with my mother in the evenings. I never heard them talk about me, however. Mama didn't mention that she hadn't dotted my ancestor tablet, because she thought Baba had done it. And he didn't bring it up, because he thought *she'd* done it. Which meant, of course, that Baba didn't invite Ren back to dot my tablet either. With my tablet hidden away, I might be stuck here forever. When I got too scared about that, I comforted myself with the knowledge that Prefect Du had left for his appointment right after Liniang's death and had forgotten to dot her tablet too. With so many parallels between Liniang and me, surely I would also be brought back to life through true love.

I began to look for Ren's home. Finally, after countless attempts, my vision found the way by skimming across the surface of West Lake, passing over Solitary Island, and crossing onto the north shore. I located the temple where torches had burned so brightly on the night of the opera and from there located Ren's family compound.

I was supposed to be a jade maiden marrying a golden boy—meaning that our family status and wealth matched—but the Wu family's villa had just a few courtyards, a handful of pavilions, and only 120 fingers. Ren's older brother had moved to a posting in a distant province, where he lived with his wife and daughter, so the Wu compound was home now only to Ren, his mother, and ten servants. Did I question this? No. I was lovesick and saw only what I wanted to see, which was a small but tasteful villa. The main doors were painted the color of cinnabar. The green tile roof blended beautifully with the willow trees that surrounded the compound. The plum tree Ren had told me about stood in the central courtyard, but it had lost its leaves. And then there was Ren, composing in his library during the day, taking his meals with his widowed mother, and wandering in the garden and along the dark corridors at night. I watched him all the time and forgot about my own family, which is why I was unprepared when Shao came to call at the Wu home.

My old wet nurse was escorted to a hall and told to wait. Then a servant brought Ren and his mother into the room. Madame Wu had been a widow for many years and dressed appropriately in somber hues. Her hair was shot through with strands of gray and her face showed the suffering of the loss of her husband. Shao bowed several times, but she was a servant, so they did not exchange pleasantries and Madame Wu did not offer tea.

"When Little Miss was dying," Shao said, "she gave me some things to give to your family. The first—" She peeled back the corners of a silk kerchief that lined a basket and brought out a tiny package also wrapped in silk. Shao lowered her head and held out the bundle cupped in the palms of her hands. "Little Miss intended these for you as a token of filial piety."

Madame Wu took the package and slowly opened it. She picked up one of the shoes I'd made for her and examined it with a mother-in-law's shrewd eyes. The peonies I'd embroidered were striking against their deep blue background. Madame Wu turned to her son, and said, "Your wife was very talented with a needle."

Would she have said that to me if I'd been alive? Or would she have criticized me as a proper mother-in-law should?

Shao reached back into the basket and pulled out my copy of *The Peony Pavilion*.

Here's a truth about death: Sometimes you forget things that you once thought were important. I'd asked Shao to bring Volume One to my new home three days after my marriage. She hadn't done that for obvious reasons, and I'd forgotten about her promise and my project. Even when I'd seen her daughter hiding her embroidery patterns in the folds, I didn't remember.

After Shao explained that I'd stayed up late at night reading and writing, that my mother had burned my books, and that I'd hidden the volume in my bedclothes, Ren took it in his hands and opened it.

"My son saw the opera, and then he searched the city to find this particular copy," Madame Wu explained. "I thought it best if my daughter-in-law gave it to your Peony. But this is only part one. Where is the second volume?"

"As I said, the girl's mother burned it," Shao repeated.

Madame Wu sighed and pursed her lips in disapproval. Ren leafed through the pages, stopping here and there.

"Do you see?" he asked, pointing to characters blurred by my tears. "Her essence glistens on the paper." He began to read. A few moments later he looked up and said, "I see her face in every word. The ink looks vivid and new. Mother, you can sense her hand's moisture on the pages."

Madame Wu regarded her son sympathetically.

I felt sure Ren would read my thoughts about the opera and know what he had to do. Shao would help him by telling him to dot my tablet.

But Shao mentioned nothing about my missing dot, and Ren didn't look hopeful or inspired in any way. Rather, sadness deepened his features. My pain was so deep I felt as though my heart was shredding.

"We're grateful to you," Madame Wu said to Shao. "In your mistress's brushstrokes, my son finds his wife. In this way, she continues to live."

Ren closed the book and abruptly stood. He gave Shao an ounce of silver, which she pocketed. Then, without another word, he stalked out of the room with my book under his arm.

That night I watched him in his library as he sank deeper and deeper into melancholy. He called for servants and ordered wine. He read my words, delicately touching the pages. He held his head, drank, and let tears fall down his cheeks. Distraught at this reaction—this was not at all what I wanted—I looked for Madame Wu and found her in her bedchamber. We shared the same name and we both loved Ren. I had to believe that she would do whatever she could to ease her son's mind. In this we had to be "sames."

Madame Wu waited until the household grew quiet, and then she padded along the corridor on her lily feet. She quietly opened the door to the library. Ren had put his head down on the desk and fallen asleep. Madame Wu picked up *The Peony Pavilion* and the empty bottle of wine, and then she blew out the flickering candle and left the room. Back in her bedchamber, she slipped my project between two folded gaily colored silk gowns that, as a widow, she would never wear again, and closed the drawer.

●   ●   ●

MONTHS WENT BY. Since I couldn't leave the Viewing Terrace, I saw everyone who stopped here on their journey through the seven levels of the afterworld. I saw chaste widows dressed in layer upon layer of longevity clothes meet their long-dead husbands in joyful reunions and knew that they would be treasured and honored for decades to come. However, I saw no mothers who'd died in childbirth. They'd gone straight to the Blood-Gathering Lake, a place where women suffered in a perpetual hell for the pollution of their failed childbearing. But for all the others who passed this way, the Viewing Terrace gave the newly dead a chance to say goodbye to those below and at the same time be reminded of what their duties were now as ancestors. From now on, they would return to this spot to look down on the world, weigh how their descendants were doing, and then grant wishes or send punishments. I saw angry ancestors, who taunted, teased, or humiliated those left behind; I saw other ancestors—plump with offerings—reward their families with plentiful harvests and numerous sons.

But for the most part I watched the newly dead. None of them knew yet where they would end up once they passed through all seven levels. Would they be sent to one of the ten *yamens* with all its different hells? Would they wait hundreds of years before being allowed to return to earth and inhabit another body? Would they be reincarnated quickly, as educated men if they were lucky, or transmigrated into a woman, a fish, or a worm if they weren't? Or would Guanyin whisk them to the Western Paradise, ten thousand million *li* from here, where they would escape all further rebirths and spend the rest of eternity in a blissful haven of everlasting happiness, feasting, and dancing?

Some of the other lovesick maidens I'd heard about when I was alive came to meet me: Shang Xiaoling, the actress who died onstage; Yu Niang, whose death inspired Tang Xianzu to write poems eulogizing her; Jin Fengdian, whose story was almost identical to mine, except that her father had been a salt merchant; and a few others.

We commiserated. In life, we had all known the danger that emanated from the opera's pages—reading it, reading *anything,* could be fatal—but we'd each been bewitched by the allure of dying young, beautiful, and talented. We were seduced by the pain and pleasure of contemplating the other lovesick maidens. We read *The Peony Pavilion,* we wrote poems about it, and we died. We thought our writing would live beyond the ravages of time and the decay of our bodies, thereby proving the power of the opera.

The lovesick maidens wanted to know about Ren, and I told them I believed two things: first, Ren and I were a match made in Heaven; second, *qing* would bring us back together.

The girls looked at me pityingly and murmured among themselves.

"We all had dream lovers," the actress finally confided, "but that's all they were—dreams."

"I believed my scholar was real too," Yu Niang admitted. "Oh, Peony, we were just like you. We had no say in our lives. We were all to be married to husbands unknown into families unknown. We had no hope for love, but we longed for it. What girl doesn't meet a man in her dreams?"

"Let me tell you about my love. In my dreams, we used to meet at a temple. I loved him very much," said another of the girls.

"I too thought I was like Liniang," the salt merchant's daughter added. "I expected that after I died my young man would find me, fall in love with me, and bring me back to life. We would have real love, not obligation or duty love." She sighed. "But he was just a dream, and now here I am."

I looked from pretty face to pretty face. Their sad expressions told me that they each had nearly identical stories.

"But I actually met Ren," I said. "He touched me with a peony blossom."

They looked at me in disbelief.

"All girls have dreams," Yu Niang repeated.

"But Ren was real." I pointed over the balustrade to the earthly realm below. "Look there. That's him."

A dozen girls—not one over the age of sixteen—looked over the edge and followed my finger to Ren's home, where they saw him writing in his library.

"That's a young man, but how do we know he's the one you met?"

"How do we know you met him at all?"

In the afterworld, we are sometimes able to be transported back through the years to relive our experiences or see them through another's eyes. This is one reason that the hells are so terrible. People are given the opportunity to relive their misdeeds forever. But now I relived very different kinds of memories so the lovesick maidens could see them. I carried the girls back to the Riding-the-Wind Pavilion, the Moon-Viewing Pavilion, and to my final visit as a spirit to Ren. They cried at the beauty and truth of my story, and below us a storm fell on Hangzhou.

"Only in death did Liniang prove her undying passion," I said, as the girls wiped their eyes. "You'll see. One day Ren and I will be married."

"How is that going to happen?" the actress asked.

"How can the moon be scooped from the water's surface, or flowers be plucked from the void?" I asked in return, quoting Mengmei. "The scholar didn't know how he was going to bring Liniang back from the dead, but he did it. Ren will figure it out too."

The girls were lovely and sweet, but they didn't believe me.

"You may have met and talked to this man, but your lovesickness was just like ours," Yu Niang said. "We all starved ourselves to death."

"All you can hope is that your parents will publish your poems," the salt merchant's daughter offered helpfully. "In this way you may live again a little. That's what happened to me."

"And me too."

The others chimed in that their families had also published their poetry.

"Most of our families don't make offerings to us," the merchant's daughter confided, "but we receive some sustenance because our poems are in print. We don't know why this happens, but it does."

This was hardly good news. I'd hidden my poems in my father's library and Ren's mother now had Volume One hidden in one of her drawers. The girls shook their heads disconsolately when I told them this.

"Perhaps you should talk to Xiaoqing about these matters," Yu Niang suggested. "She has more experience than we do. Maybe she can help you."

"I would love to meet her," I said eagerly. "I would appreciate her advice even more. Please bring her the next time you come."

But they didn't bring her. And the great Tang Xianzu didn't come to visit either, although the lovesick maidens said the author was nearby.

So mostly I was alone.

IN LIFE, I'D been told many things about the afterworld; some were right, some were wrong. Most people call it the underworld, but I prefer to call it the afterworld, because it isn't really *under,* although some parts are. Beyond the actual geography of the place, where I was seemed to be *after*— simply a continuation. Death doesn't terminate our associations to our families, and the positions we held in life don't change either. If you were a peasant in the earthly realm, you continued your work in the fields here; if you were once a landowner, a scholar, or a member of the literati, you spent your days reading, writing poetry, drinking tea, and burning incense. Women still had bound feet, were obedient, and focused their attention on their families; men still oversaw the outer realm by navigating through the infernal judges' bureaus upon bureaus of darkness.

I continued to learn what I could and couldn't do. I could float, drift, melt. Without Shao or Willow to help me, I learned to care for my feet with the spirit bindings my family had burned for my use in the afterworld. I could hear from a great distance, but I hated noise. I couldn't turn sharp corners. And when I looked over the balustrade, I could see a lot, but I was unable to look beyond Hangzhou's environs.

After I'd been on the Viewing Terrace for many months, an old woman came to visit. She introduced herself as my grandmother, but she didn't look at all like the stern-faced woman in the ancestor portrait that hung in our ancestral hall.

"*Waaa!* Why do they make ancestors look like that?" she cackled. "I never looked so disapproving in life."

Grandmother was still handsome. Her hair was pinned with ornaments made of gold, pearls, and jade. Her gown was of the lightest silk. Her lily feet were smaller even than my own. Her face was etched with fine lines but her skin was luminous. Her hands were covered in long water sleeves in the old style. She seemed delicate and ladylike, but when she sat down next to me and pressed against my thigh I felt surprising strength.

Over the next few weeks, she came to visit often but she never brought Grandfather and always evaded questions about him.

"He's busy in another place," she might say. Or, "He's helping your father with a negotiation in the capital. People at court are devious and your father is out of practice." Or, "He's probably visiting one of his concubines . . . in her dreams. He likes to do that sometimes, because in their dreams the concubines are still young and beautiful, not the old hens they've become."

I liked listening to her wicked comments about the concubines, because in life I'd always heard that she'd been kind and generous toward them. She'd been an exemplar of what a head wife should be, but here she liked to tease and banter.

"Stop looking at that man down there!" she snapped at me one day, several months after her first visit.

"How do you know who I'm looking at?"

She jabbed me with her elbow. "I'm an ancestor! I saw it *all*! Think about that, child."

"But he's my husband," I offered lamely.

"You were never married," she retorted. "You can be happy for that!"

"Happy? Ren and I were fated to be together."

My grandmother snorted. "The idea is ridiculous. You weren't fated to be together. You simply had a marriage arranged by your father, like every other girl. There's nothing special in that. And in case you've forgotten, you're here."

"I'm not worried," I said. "Baba's going to arrange a ghost marriage for me."

"You should consider more carefully what you see below."

"You're testing me. I understand—"

"No, your father has other plans."

"I can't see Baba when he's in the capital, but what does it matter anyway? Even if he doesn't arrange a ghost marriage, I'll wait for Ren. That's why I'm stuck here, don't you think?"

She ignored my question.

"Do you think this man will wait for *you*?" Her face crinkled as though she had opened a jar of stinky tofu. She was my grandmother—a cherished ancestor!—so I couldn't contradict her. "Don't worry so much about him," she said, patting my face through the water sleeve that covered her hand. "You were a good granddaughter. I appreciated the fruit you brought me all those years."

"Then why didn't you help me?"

"I had nothing against you."

It was a strange comment, but often she said things I didn't understand.

"Now pay attention," Grandmother ordered. "You need to think about why you're stuck here."

ALL THROUGH THIS time, important dates came and went. My parents forgot to include me in their New Year's offerings, which were just days after my death. On the thirteenth day of the first month after the New Year, they were supposed to place a lighted lamp at my tomb. At Spring Festival, they should have cleaned my grave, exploded firecrackers, and burned spirit money for me to use in the afterworld. On the first day of the tenth month, the official start of winter, they should have burned padded jackets, woolen caps, and fur-lined boots all made of paper to keep me warm. Throughout the year, my family should have been making offerings to me of cooked rice, wine, plates of meat, and spirit money on the first and fifteenth of every moon. All these offerings had to be presented to my dotted ancestor tablet for me to receive them in the afterworld. But when Shao didn't bring it out of its hiding place and no one asked for it, I concluded that everyone was still too upset by my absence to look at my ancestor tablet.

Then, during the Festival of the Bitter Moon, which occurs during the darkest, cruelest days of winter, I discovered something that shattered me. Just before the first anniversary of my death, my father returned home for a visit and my mother prepared special Bitter-Moon porridge with various grains, nuts, and fruits, flavored with four different kinds of sugar. My family gathered in the ancestral hall and offered the porridge to Grandmother and others in the family. Once again, my ancestor tablet wasn't brought out of its hiding place in the storage room and I didn't receive an offering. I knew I hadn't been "forgotten"; Mama cried bitter tears for me every night. This neglect meant something far worse.

Grandmother, who must have been somewhere eating her porridge with Grandfather, saw what happened and came to me. She was a plain speaker, but I didn't want to hear or accept what she had to say.

"Your parents will never worship you," she explained. "It goes against nature for a parent to worship a child. If you'd been a son, your father would have beaten your coffin to punish you for being so unfilial as to die before him, but eventually he would have relented and seen that you were provided for. But you're a girl—unmarried at that. Your family will never make offerings to you."

"Because my tablet isn't dotted?"

Grandmother snorted. "No, because you died unmarried. Your parents raised you for your husband's family. You belong to them. You are not considered a Chen. And even if your tablet were dotted, it would be kept out of sight behind a door, in a drawer, or in a special temple, which is what happened to those girls who visit you."

I'd never heard any of this before, and for a moment I believed Grandmother. But then I shook her bad thoughts out of my head.

"You're wrong."

"Because no one told you before you died that this would happen? *Ha!* If your mother and father put your tablet on the family altar, they would risk punishment from the other ancestors." She held up a hand. "Not from me, but there are others here who hold to the traditional ways. No one wants to see such an ugly thing on the family altar."

"My parents love me," I insisted. "A mother who didn't love her daughter wouldn't have burned her books to try to keep her alive."

"This is true," Grandmother agreed. "She didn't want to do it, but the doctor hoped it would spark anger in you so strong that you'd be shaken from your path."

"And Baba wouldn't have mounted the opera for my birthday if he hadn't loved me like a precious pearl."

Even as the words left my mouth I felt they were wrong.

"The opera wasn't for you," Grandmother said. "It was for Commissioner Tan. Your father was lobbying for his appointment."

"But Commissioner Tan disapproves of the opera."

"So he's a hypocrite. Men in power often are."

Was she suggesting my father was a hypocrite too?

"Political loyalty is a natural extension of personal loyalty," Grandmother went on. "I'm afraid your father—my son—has neither."

She said nothing more, but the expression on her face

caused me to look back—to finally *see*—and understand what I'd ignored in life.

My father was not a Ming loyalist or the man of integrity I'd always believed him to be, but from my perspective this was minor. In life, I'd known my father regretted I was a girl. Despite that, in my heart I'd believed, truly believed, that he cherished, adored, and loved me, but the fact of my tablet and all it implied—that I was an unmarried girl being raised for another family—had proved otherwise. With no one to care for me through my tablet in the earthly realm, my soul was in terrible trouble. I was like a torn-off remnant of silk. That I'd been abandoned— orphaned—in this way provided one explanation for why I was stuck on the Viewing Terrace.

"What's going to happen to me?" I cried. Only a year had passed, and already my gown had faded and I'd grown thinner.

"Your parents could send your tablet to a maiden's temple, but this is a distasteful idea, since those places house not only the tablets of unmarried daughters but those of concubines and prostitutes as well." Grandmother drifted across the terrace and sat down next to me. "A ghost marriage would remove the ugly thing from the Chen Family Villa—"

"I could still marry Ren. My tablet would be used in the ceremony. Everyone would see my missing dot," I said hopefully. "It would be dotted, and from then on my tablet would be worshipped on the Wu family altar."

"But your father hasn't arranged that. Think, Peony, think. I've been telling you to look, really look. What have you seen? What do you see right now?"

Time is strange here: sometimes fast, sometimes slow. Now it was days later, and another succession of young men visited my father.

"Baba has appointments. He's an important man."

"Don't you listen, child?"

Business belonged to the outer realm. I'd deliberately not listened to my father's conversations, but I did now. He was interviewing those young men. Instantly I was terrified that he was trying to arrange a ghost marriage for me to someone other than Ren.

"Will you be loyal and filial?" he inquired of one young man after another. "Will you sweep our graves at New Year and make offerings in our ancestral hall every day? And I need grandsons. Can you give me grandsons to care for us after you're gone?"

Hearing these questions, Baba's intention became clear. He was going to adopt one of those young men. My father couldn't have sons—an embarrassment for any man and a disaster when it came to ancestor worship. Adopting one for purposes of filial piety was common enough and Baba could afford it, but I was being replaced in his heart completely!

"Your father did a lot for you," Grandmother said. "I saw how solicitous he was of you—teaching you to read, write, and question. But you weren't a son, and he needed one."

My father had shown me devotion, love, and many kindnesses over the years, but I now saw that my being a girl had diminished me in his affections. I cried and Grandmother held me.

Barely able to accept any of this, I looked down to Ren's home, hoping *his* family might have offered me porridge. Naturally, they hadn't. Ren stood beneath an awning in the pouring rain, relacquering in cinnabar red the front gate to his family compound as a symbol of the rebirth of the coming New Year, while in my father's library a young man with small eyes signed a contract of adoption. My father patted the young man on the back and said, "Bao, my son, I should have done this many years ago."

The Cataclysm

IT IS SAID THAT DEATH IS EVER FOLLOWED BY LIFE AND the end is always a new beginning. Clearly that is not how it was for me. Before I knew it, a river of seven years rolled past. Holidays and feast days—especially the New Year—were particularly hard for me. I had been thin when I died, and without offerings I became frailer and more translucent with each passing year until now I was little more than a wraith. The single gown I'd worn here was faded and frayed. I'd become a pathetic creature, always hovering by the balustrade, unable to leave the Viewing Terrace.

The lovesick maidens came to visit for New Year, knowing how sad I would be. I enjoyed their company, because—unlike in the Chen Family Villa—we had no petty jealousies between us. After all this time, they finally brought Xiaoqing. She was exquisite. Her forehead was high, her eyebrows were painted, her hair was festooned with ornaments, and her lips were soft and pliant. She wore a gown of the old style—

elegant, flowing, decorated with flowers—and her feet were so tiny that she appeared weightless as she swayed delicately onto the terrace. She was too beautiful ever to have been a wife, and I could see why so many men had been entranced by her.

"I titled the poems I left behind *Manuscripts Saved from Burning,*" Xiaoqing said, in a voice that sounded as melodious as wind chimes, "but what's extraordinary in that? The men who write about us call us lovesick. They say we are the sickly sex, always suffering from blood loss and body depletion. The result, they conclude, is that our fates must match those of our writings. They don't understand that fires aren't always an accident. Too often women—and I count myself among them—doubt their words and skill, so they decide to burn their work. This is why so many collections have the exact same title."

Xiaoqing regarded me, waiting for me to say something. The other lovesick maidens also looked at me expectantly, urging me with their kind eyes to be clever.

"Our writings don't always pass away like a spring dream," I said. "Some remain in the earthly realm where people weep over them."

"May they do so for ten thousand years," the salt merchant's daughter added.

Xiaoqing looked at us benignly. "Ten thousand years," she repeated. She shivered and the air around her trembled in response. "Don't be so sure. They're beginning to forget about us already. When that happens . . ." She stood. Her gown billowed around her. She nodded to each of us, then drifted away.

The lovesick maidens left when Grandmother arrived, but what comfort could that old woman offer me? "There is no such thing as love," she liked to say, "only obligation and responsibility." Her words about her husband were always bound by duty, not love or even affection.

Forlorn and disconsolate, I listened to Grandmother—she talked about nothing in particular—and watched the New Year's preparations in Ren's home. He paid his family's debts; his mother swept and cleaned; servants prepared special foods; and the picture of Kitchen God, which hung above the stove, was burned and sent here to report on the good and bad deeds of the family. No thought was given to me.

Reluctantly, I turned my eyes to my natal family home. My father had returned from his posting in the capital to perform his filial duties. Bao, my brother of seven years, had married in. Disappointingly, his wife had only succeeded in birthing three stillborn sons. Whether it was from this failure or from a general weakness of character, Bao had taken to spending most of his time with pleasure women along the shores of West Lake. My father didn't seem perturbed by this, as he and my mother went to the family graveyard on New Year's Eve to invite the ancestors home for the holiday.

Baba wore his mandarin robes with great dignity. The elaborately embroidered emblem on his chest told anyone who saw him of his rank and importance. He carried himself with far greater assurance than he had when I'd been a daughter in the household.

My mother seemed far less secure. Mourning had caused her to age. Her hair was now streaked with white and her shoulders seemed thin and brittle.

"Your mother still cares for you," Grandmother said. "This year she will break with tradition. She's a very brave woman."

I couldn't imagine my mother doing anything that strayed from the Four Virtues and Three Obediences.

"You left her childless," Grandmother went on. "Her heart

fills with grief whenever she sees a book of poetry or catches the scent of peonies. These things remind her of you and are a heavy burden on her heart."

I didn't want to hear this. What good would it do me? But my grandmother didn't often attend to my feelings.

"I wish you'd known your mother when she first married into our family," Grandmother continued. "She was just seventeen. She'd been highly educated and her womanly skills were flawless. It's a mother-in-law's duty, obligation, and reward to complain about her daughter-in-law, but your mother did not allow me this gift. I didn't mind. I had a house full of sons. I was happy to have her company. I came to look at her not as a daughter-in-law but as a friend. You can't imagine the places we went and the things we did."

"Mama doesn't go out," I reminded her.

"She did in those days," she countered. "In the years leading up to the fall of the Ming emperor, your mother and I questioned the true nature of a woman's calling. Was it the traditional womanly arts that she so excelled at or was it her adventurousness, her curiosity, and her beautiful mind? Your mother, not your father, was the first to take an interest in the women poets. Did you know that?"

I shook my head.

"She felt it was the responsibility of women to collect, edit, anthologize, and critique the work of others like ourselves," Grandmother continued. "We traveled many places in search of books and experience."

This seemed far-fetched. "How did the two of you go? Did you walk?" I asked, trying to make her stop her exaggerations.

"We practiced walking in our rooms and in the corridors in the villa," she answered, smiling at the memory. "We toughened our golden lilies so they wouldn't hurt, and what pain we still experienced was soothed by the pleasures of what we saw and did. We found men who were so proud of the women in their families that they published their writings to memorialize the domestic bliss in their households, establish the family's sophistication, and honor their wives and mothers. Like you, your mother stored in her heart all the plunder of her readings, but she was modest in her own writing. She refused to use ink and paper, preferring instead to mix powder with water and then write on leaves. She wanted to leave behind no trace of herself."

Below us, New Year's Day arrived. In our ancestral hall, my parents laid out trays of meats, fruits, and vegetables, and I watched as my grandmother's flesh began to fill out. After the ceremony, Mama took three small rice balls, went to my old room, and left them on the windowsill. For the first time in seven years I was fed. Just three rice balls and I was strengthened.

Grandmother looked at me and nodded knowingly. "I told you she still loves you."

"But why now?"

Grandmother ignored my question and continued her earlier topic with renewed fervor. "Your mother and I went to poetry parties held under the full moon; we traveled to see jasmine and plum blossoms in bloom; we went to the mountains and made rubbings of stone stelae at Buddhist retreats. We rented pleasure boats and journeyed on West Lake and along the Grand Canal. We met women artists who supported their families with their paintings. We dined with professional women archers and celebrated with other gentry women. We played instruments, drank late into the night, and wrote poetry. We had fun, your mother and I."

When I shook my head in disbelief, Grandmother observed, "You're not the first girl not to know her mother's true nature." She seemed pleased that she'd surprised me, but her pleasure was brief. "Like so many women in those days, we enjoyed the outer realm, but we knew nothing about it. We employed our calligraphy brushes and had our parties. We laughed and sang. We didn't pay attention to the Manchus' southward trek."

"But Baba and Grandfather knew what was coming," I cut in.

Grandmother tightened her arms over her chest. "Look at your father now. What do you think?"

I hesitated. I'd come to regard my father as someone without loyalty, either to our Ming emperor or to his only child. His lack of deep feelings for me still hurt, but my emotions hadn't kept me from observing him. No, not at all. Some perverse place inside me wanted to see him. Watching Baba was like picking at a sore. I turned to look for him now.

In these past few years, my abilities had expanded and I could now see beyond Hangzhou. As part of my father's New Year's duties, he ventured into the countryside to visit his lands. Not only had I read the Speed the Plough scene in *The Peony Pavilion,* I had seen it performed in our family garden. What I saw now was a visual echo. The farmers, fishermen, and silk laborers brought him dishes prepared by the best cooks in each village. Acrobats tumbled. Musicians played. Big-footed peasant girls danced and sang. My father praised his workers and ordered them to provide good harvests of crops, fish, and silk in the coming year.

Even though I'd become disillusioned by my father, I still hoped to discover I was wrong and that he was a benevolent man. After all, I'd heard about our lands and these workers for years. But what I saw was extreme poverty. The men were thin and wiry from their labors. The women had been used up from a lifetime of hauling water, having babies, keeping house, spinning silk, and making clothes, shoes, and meals. The children were small for their ages and dressed in clothes handed down by older brothers and sisters. Many of them also worked; the boys were in the fields while their sisters used their unprotected fingers to unravel silk cocoons in boiling water. For these people, the only purpose in life was to provide for my father and those who lived in the Chen Family Villa.

My father stopped at the house of the headman of Gudang Village. The husband was a Qian, as were all the people who lived in the village. His wife was unlike the other women. She had bound feet and carried herself as though she were once from the gentry class. Her words showed refinement and she did not cower before my father. She held a baby in her arms.

My father tweaked one of the infant's pigtails, and said, "This one is very pretty."

Madame Qian stepped back, out of my father's reach.

"Baby Yi is a girl—another worthless branch on the family tree," her husband said.

"Four daughters," my father said sympathetically. "And now this fifth one. You are unlucky."

I hated to hear those words spoken so bluntly, but were they worse than what I'd experienced? My father had spoken to me with a smiling face but to him, it seemed, I too had been just a worthless branch on the family tree.

Feeling bereaved, I looked at Grandmother.

"No," I said, "I don't think he would pay attention to anything beyond his own enterprises."

She nodded sadly. "This is how it was with your grandfather too."

Although Grandmother had been visiting me for years, I'd been careful not to ask certain questions. Partly I'd been afraid of her unpredictable moods, partly I hadn't wanted to appear unfilial, and partly I didn't want to know the answers. But I'd held on to my blindness for too long. I took a deep breath and let my questions flow, fearing I might not survive her truths, whatever they were.

"Why don't you ever bring Grandfather to visit me? Is it because I'm a girl?" I asked, remembering that as a small child he hadn't cared very much for me.

"He's in one of the hells," she answered, in her usual brusque way.

I took this to be her customary wifely rancor. "And my uncles? Why do they not come?"

"They died away from home," she said, and this time her voice held no edge, only sorrow. "They have no one to clean their graves. They roam the earth as hungry ghosts."

I shrank into myself. "Hungry ghosts are horrible, disgusting creatures," I said. "How could we have them in our family?"

"Are you finally asking this question?"

Her impatience was obvious, and I drew farther away. Would she have been this way in the earthly realm, treating me as the insignificant girl I was? Or would she have indulged me with sesame sweets and little treasures from her dowry?

"Peony," she went on, "I love you. I hope you know that. I listened to you in life. I tried to help you. But these last seven years have left me wondering. Are you only a lovesick maiden, or is there something more inside you?"

I bit my lip and turned away. I'd been right to keep a respectful distance. My mother and grandmother may have been friends, but it seemed my grandmother also saw me as nothing more than a worthless branch on our family tree.

"I'm glad you're here on the Viewing Terrace," she contin-ued. "For years I've come here to look over the balustrade for my sons. For these last seven years, I've had you at my side. They're down there somewhere"—she gestured with her long water sleeves to the land below us—"wandering as hungry ghosts. In twenty-seven years, I haven't found them."

"What happened to them?"

"They died in the Cataclysm."

"Baba told me."

"He didn't tell you the truth." Her eyes narrowed and she crossed her water sleeves over her chest. I waited. Grandmother said, "You won't like the story."

I didn't say anything, and for a long time neither of us spoke.

"On the day you and I first met here," she began, "you said that I wasn't like my portrait. The truth is, I wasn't at all like what you've been told. I wasn't tolerant of my husband's concubines. I hated them. And I didn't commit suicide."

She gave me a sideways look, but I kept my face impassive and untroubled.

"You have to understand, Peony, that the end of the Ming dynasty was terrible and wonderful at the same time. Society was collapsing, the government was corrupt, money was everywhere, and no one was paying attention to women, so your mother and I went out and did things. As I told you, we met other wives and mothers: women who managed their families' estates and businesses, teachers, editors, and even some courtesans. We were brought together by a failing world and found companionship. We forgot about our embroidery and our chores. We filled our minds with beautiful words and images. In this way we shared our sorrows and joys, our tragedies and triumphs, with other women across great distances and time. Our reading and writing allowed us to form a world of our own that was very much against what our fathers, husbands, and sons wanted. Some men—like your father and grandfather—were attracted to this change. So when your grandfather got his official posting in Yangzhou, I went with him. We lived in a lovely compound, not as grand as our family home in Hangzhou but spacious and with plenty of courtyards. Your mother often came to visit. Oh, did we have adventures!

"For one of those visits, your mother and father came together. They arrived on the twentieth day of the fourth month. We had four lovely days together, feasting, drinking, laughing. None of us—not even your father or grandfather—gave any thought to the outer world. Then, on the twenty-fifth day, Manchu troops entered the city. In five days, they killed over eighty thousand people."

As Grandmother told her story, I began to experience it as though I'd been at her side. I heard the clang of swords and spears, the clatter of shield against shield and helmet against helmet, the pounding of horses' hooves on cobble-stones, and the screams of terrified residents as they sought safety when there was none. I smelled smoke as houses and other buildings were set on fire. And I began to smell blood.

"Everyone panicked," Grandmother remembered. "Families climbed onto roofs, but the tiles crumbled and people fell to their deaths. Some hid in wells, only to drown. Others tried to surrender, but that was a serious miscalculation; men lost their heads and women were raped to death. Your grandfather was an official. He should have tried to help the people. Instead, he ordered our servants to give us their coarsest clothes. We changed into them and then the concubines, our sons, your parents, and your grandfather and I went to a small outbuilding to hide. My husband gave us women silver and gems to sew into our garments, while the men tucked pieces of gold into their topknots, shoes, and waistbands as so many families did in those days. On the first night, we hid in the dark, listening as people were killed. The cries of those who were not blessed with a quick death, but suffered for hours as their blood ran out of them, were pitiful.

"On the second night, when the Manchus slaughtered our servants in the main courtyard, my husband reminded me and his concubines that we were to safeguard our chastity with our lives and that all women should be prepared to make sacrifices for their husbands and sons. The concubines were still concerned with the fate of their gowns, powders, jewels, and ornaments, but your mother and I did not need to hear this admonition. We knew our duty. We were prepared to do the correct thing."

Grandmother paused for a moment and then continued. "The Manchu soldiers looted the compound. Knowing they would eventually come to the outbuilding, my husband ordered us onto the roof, a tactic that had already proved fatal to many families. But we all obeyed. We spent the night in the pouring rain. When dawn broke, the soldiers saw us huddled together on the roof. When we refused to come down, the soldiers set fire to the building. We scrambled quickly back to the ground.

"Once our feet touched the earth," Grandmother went on, "they should have killed us, but they didn't. For this we can thank the concubines. Their hair had fallen loose. They weren't accustomed to such rough clothes, so they'd loosened them. Like all of us, they were soaked, and the weight of the water pulled their garments away from their breasts. This, in addition to the pretty tears on their eyelashes, made them so alluring that the soldiers decided to keep us alive. The men were herded to an adjacent courtyard. The soldiers used rope to bind us women together around our necks, as if we were a string of fish, and then they led us into the street. Babies lay on the ground everywhere. Our golden lilies, which your mother and I had tried so hard to strengthen, slipped in the blood and smashed organs of those who'd been trampled to death. We walked next to a canal filled with the floating dead. We passed mountains of silks and satins that had been looted. We reached another compound. When we walked in, we saw perhaps a hundred naked women, wet, muddy, crying. We watched men pull women out of that quivering mass and do things to them—in the open air, in front of everyone, with no regard to propriety."

I listened in horror. I felt terrible shame as my mother, my grandmother, and the concubines were told to strip and the rain pelted their naked bodies. I stayed by my mother's side as she took the lead and wormed her way safely into the center of the crowd, all the while attached by the rope around her neck to her mother-in-law and the concubines. I saw that women in these circumstances no longer lived in the human world. Mud and excrement were everywhere, and my mother used them to smear the faces and bodies of the women in our family. All day they held on to one another, always shifting to the center as women from the edges were grabbed, raped, and killed.

"The soldiers were very drunk and very busy," Grandmother went on. "If I could have killed myself, I would have, because I'd been taught to value my chastity above all else. In other parts of the city, women hanged themselves and cut their own throats. Others locked themselves in their chambers and set fire to the rooms. In this way whole households of women—babies, little girls, mothers, grandmothers—burned to death. Later they would be venerated as martyrs. Some families would argue over who would claim this or that dead woman for her virtuous suicide, knowing of the honors that would be bestowed on them by the Manchus. We are taught that only in death can we preserve our virtue and integrity, but your mother was different. She was not going to die, and she wouldn't allow herself or any of us to be raped. She made us crawl through the other naked women until we reached the back edge, and then through sheer will she convinced us to attempt an escape through the rear of the compound. We made it and were once again outside. The streets were lit by torches, and we scurried together like rats from one dark alley to another. We stopped when we thought it was safe, freed ourselves of the rope, and stripped the dead and clothed ourselves. Several times we dropped to the ground, grabbing loose entrails to drape over our bodies and pretending to be corpses. Your mother insisted that we return to find your father and grandfather. 'It is our duty,' she kept saying, even as my courage wavered and the concubines cried and whimpered."

Grandmother paused again. I was grateful. I reeled from what I was seeing, feeling, and hearing. I fought back the tears I felt for my mother. She'd been so brave and suffered so much, and she'd kept it all a secret from me.

"On the morning of the fourth day," Grandmother continued, "we reached our compound and miraculously found our way to the girls' lookout pavilion, which your mother was sure would be unattended. We used it as girls and women have before and since, to see but not be seen. Your mother held her hands over my mouth to muffle my screams when we saw my sixth and seventh sons hacked to pieces with sabers and then hauled out to the street in front of the compound, where they—like so many others—were trampled until there was nothing left but mush and fragments of bone. My eyes were parched by the horror."

This is how my uncles came to be hungry ghosts. With no bodies, they couldn't be buried properly. The three parts of their souls were still roaming, unable to complete their journeys, unable to find rest. Tears dripped down Grand-mother's cheeks, and I let mine flow as well. Below us in the earthly realm a terrible storm lashed Hangzhou.

"Your mother could not sit and wait," Grandmother remembered. "She had to do something—with her hands, if nothing else. At least that's what I thought. She told us to rip out the stitches from our stolen clothes to see if they held silver or gems. We did as we were told and then she held out her hands to take the glittering pieces. 'Stay here,' she said. 'I will send help.' Then, before any of us could stop her—we were paralyzed with fear and grief—she got to her feet and stepped out of the girls' lookout pavilion."

I felt sick and filled with dread.

"An hour later, your father and grandfather came to us," she said. "They'd been beaten and they looked frightened. The concubines threw themselves on your grandfather's feet, sobbing and thrashing on the ground. Making noise is what they were doing, attracting attention. I had never loved your grandfather. It was an arranged marriage. He did his duty, I did mine. He had his business and left me alone to follow my own interests. But in that moment I felt nothing but contempt for him, because I could see there was a part of him—in this most terrible of circumstances—that enjoyed having those pretty girls slithering like greased snakes all over his shoes."

"And Baba?"

"He did not say a word, but he had a look on his face that no mother should see—guilt for having left your mama behind, combined with a desire for survival. 'Hurry!' he said. 'Get up! We must move quickly.' And we did as we were told, because we were women and we now had men to tell us what to do."

"But where was Mama? What happened to her?"

But Grandmother was reliving what happened next. As she continued speaking, I searched for my mother, but she remained hidden. It seemed I could only follow this story through my grandmother's eyes.

"We crept back downstairs. Your mother may have procured your father and your grandfather's freedom, but that didn't mean we were safe. We edged along a passageway lined with severed heads until we reached the back of the compound, where we kept our camels and horses in corrals. We crawled under the animals' bellies through more filth, blood, and death. We didn't dare risk going back out on the streets, so we waited. Several hours later, we heard men coming. The concubines panicked. They slipped back under the bellies of the horses and camels. The rest of us decided to hide in a pile of straw."

Grandmother's voice swelled with remembered bitterness. " 'I know your foremost concern is for me and our eldest son,' your grandfather said to me. 'My mouth wants to go on eating for a few more years. It is good of you to choose death, protect your chastity, and save your husband and son.' "

She cleared her throat and spit. "*Go on eating for a few more years!* I knew my duty and I would have done the right thing, but I hated being volunteered by that selfish man. He hid in the back of the pile of straw. Your father went in next to him. As the wife and mother, I had the honor of lying on top of them. I covered myself as best as I could. The soldiers came in. They were not dumb. They'd been killing for four days already. They used their lances to stab into the pile. They stabbed and stabbed until I died, but I saved my husband and my son, I preserved my chastity, and I learned I was expendable."

My grandmother loosened her gown and for the first time

pulled her water sleeves up and over her hands. She was horribly scarred.

"Then I was flying across the sky," she said, a slight smile on her face. "The soldiers got bored and wandered away. Your grandfather and father stayed hidden for another full day and night with my cold body as their protection, while the concubines retreated to a corner and stared for hours at the silent, bloody pile of straw. Then, like that, the Manchus' lesson ended. Your father and grandfather crawled out of the straw. The concubines washed and wrapped my body. Your father and grandfather performed all the proper rites for me to become an ancestor, and in time they took me back to Hangzhou for burial. I was honored as a martyr." She sniffed. "This was a piece of Manchu propaganda that your grandfather was happy to receive." She gazed around the Viewing Terrace appraisingly. "I think I have found a better home."

"But they capitalized on your sacrifice!" I said indignantly. "They let you be canonized by the Manchus so they wouldn't have to acknowledge the truth."

Grandmother looked at me as though I still didn't understand. And I didn't.

"They did what was proper," she admitted. "Your grandfather did the right and sensible thing for the entire family, since women have no value. You still don't want to accept this."

I was disappointed in my father yet again. He hadn't told me anything resembling the truth about what happened during the Cataclysm. Even when I was dying and he'd come to me to beg forgiveness from his brothers, he hadn't mentioned that his mother had saved his life. He didn't ask for her absolution or send his thanks.

"But don't think I've been happy with the result," she added. "The imperial support of my female virtues brought many rewards to my descendants. The family is wealthier than ever and your father's new post is very powerful, but our family still lacks something it wants desperately. That doesn't mean I have to give it to them."

"Sons?" I asked. I was angry on my grandmother's behalf, but had she really denied our family this most important treasure?

"I don't see it as revenge or retribution," she confided. "It's just that all those who had real value and honor in our family were women. For too long our daughters have been pushed aside. I thought that might change with you."

I was appalled. How could my grandmother be so cruel and vindictive as to keep sons from our family? I forgot my manners and demanded, "Where is Grandfather? Why hasn't he given the family sons?"

"I told you. He's in one of the hells. But even if he were by my side right now, he would have no power in this regard. The affairs of the inner chambers belong to women. The other ancestor women in our family—even my mother-in-law—have acquiesced to my desires, because even here I'm honored for my sacrifice."

Grandmother's eyes were clear and at peace. But I was broken, torn apart by conflicting feelings. All this was truly beyond me. I had uncles who languished in the earthly realm as hungry ghosts, a grandfather who suffered in a dark and painful hell, and a grandmother who was so far from benevolent that she was actually hurting our family by not giving us sons. But above all, I couldn't stop thinking about my mother.

"You must have seen Mama after you died," I prompted. "When your soul was roaming."

"The last time I saw her was when she left us that terrible night with her hands full of jewels and silver. I didn't see

{ 189 }

her again until I arrived here at the Viewing Terrace, five weeks after I died. By then the whole family was back in the Chen Family Villa and she'd changed. She'd become the woman you know as your mother, adhering to the old ways, so afraid she could no longer venture out, divorced from the world of words and books, and unable anymore to feel or express love. Since that time your mother has never spoken of the Cataclysm, so I've been unable to travel there with her in her mind."

My thoughts went back to why Grandmother had come here today. Tears rolled down my cheeks as I thought of my two boy uncles' deaths. Grandmother took my hand and looked at me with great kindness.

"Peony, my sweet girl, if you ask your question, I will help you find the answer."

"What am I?"

"I think you know."

My uncles had not found peace because they hadn't been buried properly; I hadn't been able to move beyond the Viewing Terrace because my ancestor tablet hadn't been dotted. The three of us had been denied proper burial rites. For us, even access to the hells was denied. Now, as the words came out of my mouth, my last bit of blindness fell away.

"I am a hungry ghost."

Red Palanquin

I HAD NOWHERE TO GO. I WAS BEREFT AND LONELY. I had no embroidery to work on and for years I hadn't had brush, paper, and ink to write. I was hungry, but I had nothing to eat. I no longer wanted to fill the long empty hours by staring over the balustrade at the earthly realm below. It hurt too much to see my mother, because now all I could sense was her secret suffering; it hurt to see my father, knowing I'd never been as precious to him as I'd believed. And when Ren entered my mind, my heart constricted in pain. I was alone as no human or spirit should be, unloved and unconnected. For weeks, I cried, sighed, screamed, and moaned. The monsoon was particularly bad that season in my hometown.

Slowly, tentatively, I began to feel better. I folded my arms on the balustrade, leaned over the edge, and looked out. I shielded my eyes from my parents' home and instead watched the laborers in my father's mulberry fields. I looked at the girls spinning silk thread. I peeked in on the headman's family in Gudang. I liked Madame Qian; she was erudite and refined. In other times, she wouldn't have been married to a farmer, but in the aftermath of the Cataclysm she was lucky to have a husband and a home. The five daughters were disappointment upon disappointment. She couldn't even teach them to read since their futures were tied to work in silk production. She had little time to call her own, but late at night she might light a candle and read from the *Book of Songs,* the one thing she'd saved from her former life. She had many desires and no way to attain them.

But truthfully she and her family were just a distraction. They were what I looked at until I couldn't stand it anymore. Then I would give in to my desires and let my eyes travel to Ren's home. I teased myself, letting one image after another caress me—the plum tree that still refused to bloom, the peonies heavy-headed with passion, the moonlight glistening on the lily pond—until finally I would seek out Ren, who was twenty-five and still unmarried.

One morning I was going through my ritual when I came upon Ren's mother walking to the front gate. She looked around to make sure nobody was watching and then tacked something to the wall just above the door. When she was done, Madame Wu glanced around again. Convinced nobody could see her, she cupped her hands together and bowed three times in the four directions of the compass. Finished with her rite, she wended her way back through the courtyards toward her inner chamber. Her shoulders were hunched and she shifted her gaze furtively from side to side. Clearly she'd done something she didn't want anyone to see, but her pitiable human actions couldn't be hidden from me.

I was far away, but by now my eyes were very strong. I focused them until my vision was as solid and as straight as an embroidery needle. I pierced through the great distance, focusing on the spot above the door, and found the tip of a fern frond. I sat back, surprised and startled, because everyone knows that ferns are supposed to blind spirits. I pressed my fingers over my eyes, worried that they'd been damaged. But they hadn't been harmed at all. In fact, I felt nothing. I gathered my courage and peeked at the fern again. I felt no pain this time either. That frail piece of greenery was useless against me.

Now I was the one to glance around surreptitiously. Madame Wu was trying to protect her house from a ghost or ghosts, but I didn't see anyone spying on the compound other than myself. Did she know I was watching? Was she trying to protect her son from me? But I would do nothing to hurt him! And even if I could, why would I want to? I loved him. No, the only reason she would try to keep me away was if there was something she didn't want me to see. After so many weeks of feeling despondent and without purpose, I burned with curiosity.

I observed the Wu household for the rest of the day. People came and went. Tables and chairs were set up in the courtyard. Red lanterns were hung in the trees. In the kitchen, servants chopped ginger and garlic, strung peas, cleaned ducks and chickens, carved pork. Young men came to visit. They played cards and drank with Ren late into the night. They made jokes about his sexual prowess, and even so far away I blushed in embarrassment but also in desire.

The next morning, couplets on red and gold paper were festooned on the front gate. Some type of celebration was about to take place. For so long I hadn't taken care with my appearance, but now I brushed my hair and pinned it up. I smoothed my skirt and tunic. I pinched my cheeks to bring in color. All this, as though I were going to the party myself.

I'd just settled down to watch the events unfold when I felt something graze my arm. Grandmother had come.

"Look below!" I exclaimed. "So much merriment and joy."

"That's why I'm here." She looked down at the compound and frowned. After a long moment, she said, "Tell me what you've seen."

I told her about the decorations, the late-night drinking, and the cooking. I smiled the whole while, still feeling as though I were going to be a guest and not just an observer.

"I'm happy. Can you understand that, Grandmother? When my poet is happy, I feel so—"

"Oh, Peony." She shook her head, and her headdress tinkled as softly as whispering birds. She took my chin in her palm and turned my face away from the world of the living so she could look into my eyes. "You're too young to have such heartbreak."

I tried to pull away, irritated that she wanted to turn my happiness into something dark and unpleasant, but her fingers held me with surprising strength.

"Don't look, child," she cautioned.

With that warning, I yanked away from her. My eyes fell to the Wu family compound just as a palanquin draped in red silk and carried by four bearers stopped before the front gate. A servant opened the palanquin's door. A perfectly bound foot in a red slipper emerged from the dark interior. Slowly a figure stepped out. It was a girl, dressed from head to toe in wedding red. Her head drooped from the weight of her headdress, which was encrusted with pearls, carnelian, jade, and other gems. A veil hid her face. A servant used a mirror to flash rays of light on the girl to ward off any malevolent influences that might have accompanied her.

I frantically tried to come up with an explanation other

than what my eyes now told me and other than what my grandmother already seemed to understand.

"Ren's brother must be marrying today," I said.

"That boy is already married," Grandmother responded softly. "His wife sent you your special edition of *The Peony Pavilion.*"

"Then perhaps he's taking a concubine—"

"He no longer lives in this house. He and his family have gone to Shanxi province, where he's a magistrate. Only Madame Wu and her younger son live here now. And look, above the door someone has placed a fern."

"Madame Wu put it there."

"She's trying to protect someone she loves very much."

My body shook, not wanting to accept what Grandmother was trying to tell me.

"She's protecting her son and his bride from you," she said.

Tears poured from my eyes, fell down my cheeks, and dripped over the balustrade. Down below, on the north shore of West Lake, mists formed, partially obscuring the bridal party. I wiped my eyes, blinking back my emotions. Once again the sun broke through the mists and I clearly saw the palanquin and the girl who was taking my place. She stepped over the threshold. My mother-in-law led her through the first courtyard, and then the second. From here, Madame Wu escorted the girl into the bridal chamber. Soon the girl would be left in seclusion to calm her thoughts. To prepare her for what was coming, Madame Wu would do what many mothers-in-law do by giving the girl a book, a kind of confidential text that would outline the intimate demands of married life with a man she knew not at all. But all this should have been happening to me!

I'll admit it. I wanted to kill that girl. I wanted to tear off her veil and see who would dare to replace me. I wanted her to see my ghostly face and then rip her eyes from their sockets. I thought of the story my mother used to tell me about the man who brought in a concubine, who'd laughed at the first wife behind her back and taunted her for how her appearance had changed over the years. The wife turned into a tiger and ate the concubine's heart and innards, leaving behind her head and limbs for the husband to find. That's what I wanted to do, but I couldn't leave the Viewing Terrace.

"When we're alive we believe many things that we only learn are wrong when we get here," Grandmother said.

I didn't absorb her words. I was completely transfixed by what I was seeing. It couldn't be happening, yet it was.

"Peony!" Grandmother's voice was sharp. "I can help you!"

"There is no help or hope for me," I cried.

Grandmother laughed. The sound was so foreign that it jarred me from my tragic circumstances. I turned to her and her face practically danced with mirth and mischievousness. I had never seen that before, but I was too heartbroken to be hurt by that old woman's amusement at my desperate circumstances.

"Listen to me," she continued, seemingly oblivious to the torture I felt. "You know I don't believe in love."

"I don't want your bitterness," I said.

"I'm not offering it. Instead, I'm saying that perhaps I was wrong. You love this man; I understand that now. And surely he must love you still or his mother wouldn't be trying to protect that girl from you." She glanced over the balustrade and smiled knowingly. "See that?"

I looked and saw Madame Wu present her future daughter-in-law with a hand mirror, which was a traditional gift given to a bride to protect her from troublesome spirits.

"Today when I saw what was happening," Grandmother went on earnestly, "everything became clear. You must go back to your rightful place."

"I don't think I can," I said, but inside my mind began to spin with the possibilities of how I would seek revenge on the girl dressed in red, sitting in seclusion, waiting to go to her husband.

"Think, child, think. You're a hungry ghost. Now that you know what you are, you're free to roam wherever you want."

"But I'm stuck—"

"You can't go forward and you can't go back, but that doesn't mean you can't go down. You could have returned at any time, but I interceded with the judges. I selfishly wanted you to stay here with me." She tossed her head defiantly. "With men there's always a bureaucracy, and it's no different here. I bribed them with some of the offerings I received at New Year."

"Will I ever meet them? Will I ever have a chance to plead my case?"

"Only when your ancestor tablet is dotted. Otherwise"— she gestured below—"that's where you belong."

She was right . . . again. As a hungry ghost, I should have been roaming in the earthly realm these last seven years.

My mind at that moment was so twisted between my desire to harm the girl and the realization that I should have been roaming all this time that for a second I didn't comprehend what she was saying. I took my eyes away from the girl in red and looked at Grandmother.

"Are you saying I could also get my tablet dotted?"

Grandmother leaned forward and took my hands in hers. "You should hope for that to happen, because then you'll come back here and become an ancestor. But you won't be able to *make* it happen. You'll have a lot of tricks that you can use with people in the earthly realm to get them to do what you want them to do, but you will be powerless when it comes to your tablet. Remember all the ghost stories you heard as a little girl? There are a lot of different ways people become ghosts, but if all those creatures who didn't have their tablets dotted could force humans to complete this task, there wouldn't be very many ghost stories, would there?"

I nodded, taking it all in, thinking first I would ruin the wedding, then I would make Ren remember me, then I would make him to go my father's house and dot my tablet, then we would have a ghost marriage, and then . . . I shook my head. Vengeance and confusion were so clouding my mind that I wasn't thinking clearly. In reality, I'd heard a lot of ghost stories, as Grandmother said, and the happy endings only came when those creatures were wounded, maimed, and destroyed.

"Won't it be dangerous?" I asked. "Mama used to tell me that she would cut any evil spirits that visited me with scissors and that if I wore charms I'd be safe when I walked in the garden. What about ferns and mirrors?"

Grandmother laughed once more, and it was no less extraordinary than the first time.

"A fern will not protect the living from someone such as you. And mirrors?" She snorted at their relative insignificance. "They can hurt you if you get too close, but they won't destroy you." She stood and kissed me. "You won't be able to come back until you've settled things in the earthly realm. Do you understand?"

I nodded.

"Rely on the lessons you learned when you were alive." She began to drift away from me. "Use common sense and be wary. I'll watch out for you from here and protect you as best I can."

And then she was gone.

I looked down at the Wu household. Madame Wu was walking to her inner chamber, where I was sure she would retrieve the confidential book to give to her future daughter-in-law.

I took one last look around the terrace, and then I lifted myself up and over the balustrade and dropped down into the main courtyard of the Wu compound. I went straight to Ren's room. I spotted him by the window, staring at a stand of bamboo as it swayed in the breeze. I was sure he would turn to me, but he didn't. I swirled around him so that I floated just before the bamboo. The light played on his high cheekbones. The ends of his black hair hung over his collar. His hands rested on the windowsill. His fingers were long and tapered, perfect for holding a calligraphy brush. His eyes—as black and limpid as the waters of our West Lake—stared out the window with an expression I couldn't read. I was right before him, but he didn't see me; he didn't even sense me.

A band began to play. This meant Ren would soon meet his bride. If I was going to stop this, I had to try someone else. I went quickly to the bridal chamber. The girl sat on her wedding chair, the mirror held securely in her lap. Even alone, she hadn't pushed aside her veil. She was dutiful and obedient, this one. She was also strong. I don't know how to explain it, but in her absolute stillness I felt her fighting against me—me personally—as though she knew I'd be here.

I hurried to Madame Wu's bedchamber. She was on her knees before an altar. She lit incense, prayed wordlessly to herself, and then put her forehead to the ground. Her actions didn't frighten me or drive me away. Instead, I was filled with resolve and a kind of peace I hadn't felt in years. Madame Wu rose and crossed to a cabinet. She slid open a drawer. Inside, two books nestled in silk: to the right, her confidential book on marriage; to the left, Volume One of *The Peony Pavilion*. Her hands reached down and touched the confidential book.

"No!" I screamed. If I couldn't stop the wedding, at least Ren and his wife's first night together would be miserable.

Madame Wu's hands drew back as though the book were in flames. She tentatively reached down again.

I whispered this time: "No, no, no."

It was all so sudden—that I was here, that the marriage would happen in minutes—that I acted without thinking about the consequences.

"Take the other one," I whispered impulsively. "Take it. Take it!"

Madame Wu stepped away from the open drawer and looked around the room.

"Take it! Take it!"

Seeing nothing, she adjusted a pin in her hair and then, in the most indifferent way possible, picked up my book as though it were the one she'd come for and carried it out through the courtyards to the bridal chamber.

"Daughter," she said to the seated girl, "this helped me on my wedding night. I'm sure it will help you too."

"Thank you, Mother," the bride said.

Something about the girl's voice chilled me, but I shrugged it off, believing I was finding my powers and that my revenge would come soon.

Madame Wu backed out of the room. The girl stared at the cover of the book where I'd painted my favorite scene from *The Peony Pavilion*. It was The Interrupted Dream, where Du Liniang meets the scholar and they become lovers. This scene had to be a common one used to decorate women's confidential books, for the girl didn't seem distressed or surprised by the subject.

Now that *The Peony Pavilion* was in her hands, I realized I'd acted rashly when I told Madame Wu to take it. I didn't want this girl to read my private thoughts, but then a plan slowly began to form in my mind. Maybe I could use my written words to scare this bride away from her marriage. As I'd done with Madame Wu, I began whispering.

"Open it and see who's here with you. Open it and run away. Open it and admit you can never do what you need to do to be a wife."

But she wouldn't open the book. I raised my voice and repeated my orders, but she sat as still as a vase on a nightstand. Even if I'd done nothing, she hadn't planned on opening the confidential wedding book. Putting my destructive desires aside, what kind of wife did she think she'd be if she didn't read the instructions for her wedding night?

I perched on a carved chair across the room from the girl. She didn't move, sigh, cry, or pray. She didn't push aside her veil to look around the room. With her sitting so quietly, I could see that she'd obviously followed all the rituals for a girl of good breeding and great wealth. Her tunic was of bright red silk, and the embroidery on it was so exquisite that I was sure she'd done none of it herself.

"Open the book," I tried again. "Open it and run away."

When nothing happened, I got up, crossed the room, and knelt before her. Our faces were just inches apart, separated only by her opaque red veil. "If you stay, you will not be happy."

A tiny tremor rippled through her body.

"Go now," I whispered.

She took a deep breath and let it out slowly, but other than this she did not move. I went back to my chair. I was as ineffectual with this girl as I'd been with Ren.

I heard the band outside the door. Someone came into the room. The bride took the book from her lap, set it on the table, and left to meet her future husband.

DURING THE WEDDING ceremony and the celebrations that followed, I tried to intervene in many ways. Always I was unsuccessful. I'd been so sure that Ren and I were meant to be together. How could fate be so cruel and so wrong?

After the banquet, Ren and his wife were escorted back to the bridal chamber. Red candles nearly a meter long burned, filling the room with a golden glow. If they burned all night, that would be seen as an auspicious sign. The trickling down of the wax was like the shedding of a bride's tears on her first night alone with her husband. If one of the candles went out—even by accident—it would be an omen of a premature death for one or both parties. The band and the party were raucous and loud. Each crash of the cymbals terrified me. Each beat of the drum pounded fear into me. Bands played noisily at weddings and funerals to scare away bad spirits, but I wasn't a bad spirit. I was a heartbroken girl, deprived of my destiny. I stayed at Ren's side until the firecrackers were lit. The rattling pops tossed me from side to side. It was more than I could bear and I floated up and away from him.

From a safe distance, I saw my poet raise his hands to his wife's headdress and veil, take out the pins that held them in place, and lift the covering from her head.

Tan Ze!

I was doubly incensed. On the first night of the opera all

those years ago, she'd said she wanted her father to make inquiries about Ren. Now she'd gotten what she wanted. How I would make her suffer! My spirit would haunt her. I'd fill her worldly days with misery. I'd felt much pain and wretchedness these past years, but seeing Ze—her perfect white breasts now bared—filled me with excruciating agony and raging despair. How could Ren's mother have chosen Tan Ze? I didn't know why she'd done it, but the result was that out of all the women in Hangzhou, my home country of China, and the world, she'd arranged for her son to marry the one person who would hurt me the most. Was this why Ze had been so still when she was waiting in the bridal chamber? Had she put up hard defenses around herself, knowing I'd be there? The *Book of Female Filial Piety* calls jealousy the sickest of all the ancestral emotions, and I was sinking in it.

Ren untied the knots at Ze's waist. Her silk skirt slipped through the fingers I'd so admired, that I'd so longed to touch me when we were alone in the garden. Tormented, I pulled at my hair. I tore at my clothes. I cried, terrified that I would miss this, ashamed that I had to see it. No mists formed over the lake and no rains fell. The musicians in the courtyard didn't have to cover their instruments and run for cover. The guests didn't stop laughing or telling jokes. My tears had nowhere to fall but on my tunic.

Earlier I'd wished for quiet so I could return to Ren's side. But this silence was worse, because it heightened and accelerated what was happening in the bridal chamber. If I'd been in Ze's place, I would have unbuttoned the frogs that held Ren's tunic closed. I would have used my hands to push away the fabric from his chest, I would have let my lips linger on his smooth skin—but Ze did none of these things. She stood there as passively as she had when she should have been reading the confidential book. I looked into her eyes and saw no emotions there. A realization came to me in a way that perhaps only those who reside in the afterworld can understand. She'd wanted Ren, but she didn't love him. She had thought she was cleverer and prettier than I, and that she deserved him more. She had won: She was sixteen and alive, and she'd taken what was supposed to be mine. But now that she had Ren, she didn't know what to do with him. I don't think she even wanted him anymore.

I made myself watch as they got in bed. He took one of her hands and brought it under the quilt so she might touch him, but she pulled away. He tried to kiss her, but she turned her face so that his lips fell on her jaw. He rolled onto her. Ze was either too afraid or too unknowledgeable to feel anything herself or give him pleasure. This should have made me want to do even more evil to her, but another feeling began to creep into my heart. I felt sorry for Ren. He deserved more than this.

Ren's face tightened at the moment of release. For a moment, he stayed on his elbows, trying to read Ze's features, but they were as bland and pale as slivers of bean curd. Without a word, he got off her. When she turned on her side away from him, his face settled into that same expression I'd seen just before the marriage ceremony, when he gazed out the window at the stand of bamboo. I couldn't believe I hadn't recognized that look before, because it was one that I'd worn for years. He felt the same loneliness and sense of detachment from family and life that I felt.

I shifted my attention back to Ze. I still hated her, but what if I could use her like a puppet to reach Ren and make him happy? As a ghost, I could use my abilities to inhabit Ze and turn her into a perfect wife. If I worked hard enough, he would feel me in her body, recognize me in her caresses, and come to realize that I loved him still.

Ze's eyes were tightly shut. I could see she longed for sleep, believing it would provide an escape from . . . what? Her husband, physical pleasure, her mother-in-law, her wifely duties, me? If she was truly frightened of me, sleep was a terrible mistake. I might not have been able to reach her yet in the earthly realm—perhaps she wore an amulet or had received a blessing I was unaware of, or maybe the stubborn selfishness she'd shown when I was alive was really only a hardness of personality that kept her emotions, softness, and vulnerability at bay—but in the world of dreams she'd have no defenses against me.

AS SOON AS Ze drifted off to sleep, her soul left her body and began to roam abroad. I trailed at a safe distance behind her, seeing where she would go, trying to decipher her intentions. I'd be lying if I didn't say a part of me still longed for revenge, and I thought of all the ways I could attack her in her dreams when she was most vulnerable. Maybe I could become a barber ghost. In life, we all fear visits from these demons, who come in the night and shave portions of a person's head when he or she is defenseless. The hair never grows back on those spots, which remain bald and shining, reminders of the touch of death. We also fear traveling very far in our dreams, knowing that the farther we are from home the easier it is to become disoriented and lost. It wouldn't take much for me to scare Ze into the woods, where I could make sure she never escaped from the dank darkness.

But I did none of these things. Instead, I waited on the periphery of her vision, hiding behind a pillar in the temple she visited, concealing myself in the depths of the pond into which she gazed, and lurking in the shadows when she returned to her new bedchamber, which she freely explored now that she was in the mistaken safety of her dream. She looked out the window and saw a nightingale perched on a camphor tree and a lotus in bloom. She picked up the mirror her mother-in-law had given her and smiled at her reflection, which was much prettier than what she saw by day. She sat on the edge of the bed, her back to her sleeping husband. Even in her dream she would not look at him or touch him. Then I saw what she was staring at. Her eyes were on *The Peony Pavilion,* which was on the table.

I fought my desire to step out from the shadows that hid me in Ze's dream, guessing that a little prudence now would serve me well in the long run. My mind raced. What could I do to catch her attention but not frighten her too much? The lightest, most innocent thing I could think of was air. In my hiding place, I stayed as still as possible, and then softly let out a small breath that I sent in Ze's direction. As quiet and gentle as it was, it had the power to cross the room and brush against her cheek. Her fingers rose to the place where my breath had kissed her skin. In the darkness, I smiled. I had made contact, but in doing so I had learned just how cautiously I needed to proceed.

I mouthed words. "Go home. Wake up. Pick up the book. You will know the right page to read." No sound came out, only breath, which once again traveled across the room to Ze. Her body trembled as the words wafted about her.

Back in the earthly realm, Ze tossed from side to side, woke up, and then sat up abruptly. Her face shone with a thin sheen of sweat and her naked body shivered uncontrollably. She seemed unsure of where she was, and her eyes searched the darkness until they came to rest on her husband. Instinctively, it seemed to me, she drew back in surprise and alarm. For a moment she remained absolutely still, afraid perhaps that he might waken. Then, as quietly and slowly as possible, she slipped out of the bed. Her bound feet seemed too tiny to hold her upright, and the pale flesh that rose from her red wedding slippers shook with the effort of standing. She went to where her wedding clothes lay in a rumpled heap on the floor, picked up her tunic, put it on, and then wrapped her arms around herself as if to hide her nakedness even more.

On unsteady legs, she crossed to the table, sat down, and pulled one of the wedding candles closer. She stared at the cover of *The Peony Pavilion,* possibly thinking of her own interrupted dream. She opened the book and flipped through the pages. She came to the page I intended, smoothed the paper with her delicate fingers, glanced one more time back at Ren, and then whispered the words I'd written under her breath.

"Liniang and the scholar's love is divine, not carnal. But this does not—and should not—stop them from experiencing carnal pleasure. In the bedchamber, Liniang knows how to behave like a lady by bringing desire, amusement, enjoyment, and satisfaction to her lover. This is perfectly fitting for a respectable woman." How I had known that, as an unmarried girl, I couldn't say, but these were my words and thoughts and I believed them now more than ever.

Ze shivered, closed the book, and blew out the candle. She covered her face with her hands and began to weep. The poor girl was frightened, unintelligent, and uninformed about what she could do to bring gratification to her husband and herself. Given time—and that was all I had—I would be even bolder than I'd been with her today.

Clouds and Rain

THE *BOOK OF RITES* TELLS US THAT THE MOST IMPORtant duty in marriage is to have a son who will feed and care for his parents once they go to the afterworld, since only he can do this. Beyond that, marriage is for the joining of two surnames, thereby bringing prosperity to both families through the exchange of bride-price gifts, dowries, and mutually beneficial connections. But *The Peony Pavilion* was about something completely different: sexual attraction and physical passion. Liniang began as a shy girl, but she flowered through love, becoming more openly sensuous as a ghost. Having died a virgin, she took her unfulfilled desires with her to the grave. During the worst of *my* lovesickness, Doctor Zhao had said I needed clouds and rain. He'd been right about that. If I'd lived long enough, my wedding night would have cured me. Now my yearnings—long kept hidden on the Viewing Terrace—were as ravenous and greedy as my stomach. I wasn't a frightening, malignant, or predatory creature; I was merely in need of my husband's sympathy, protection, and touch. My longing for Ren was as great as on the first night we'd met. It was as strong as the moon, reaching through the clouds, over the waters, clear to the man who should have been my husband. But of course I had nothing of the moon's powers. Since I couldn't connect to Ren directly anymore, I used Ze to reach him. She resisted at first, but how can a living girl win against someone from the afterworld?

Ghosts, like women, are creatures of *yin*—cold, dark, earthy, and feminine. For months I made things easy on myself by staying in Ren's bedchamber, where I didn't have to worry about the suddenness of sunrises or strategize as to how to navigate an impossibly tight corner. I was a nocturnal creature. I spent my days nesting in the rafters or curled in a corner of the room. When the sun set, I became more brazen, lounging like a concubine on my husband's bed, waiting for him and his second wife to come to me.

Refusing to leave the room also permitted me less time with Ze. Her dowry had greatly increased the Wu family's riches—which is why Ren's widowed mother had agreed to the arrangement—but it barely made up for Ze's disagreeable personality. As I'd suspected all those years ago, she'd grown up to be mean-spirited and petty. During the day, I would hear her in the courtyard, complaining about this or that. "My tea has no flavor," she scolded a servant. "Did you use the tea of this household? Do not do that again. My father sent tea of the highest grade for me to drink. No, you may not use it for my mother-in-law. Wait! I haven't dismissed you! I want my tea hot this time. I don't want to say this again!"

After lunch, she and Madame Wu retired to the women's quarters, where they were supposed to read, paint, and write poetry together. Ze wouldn't participate in these activities, nor would she play the zither, although she was reputed to be quite adept. She was too impatient for embroidery and more than once threw her project against the wall. Madame Wu tried scolding, but that only made matters worse.

"I don't belong to you!" Ze screamed at her mother-in-law one day. "You can't tell me what to do! My father is the Commissioner of Imperial Rites!"

Under ordinary circumstances, Ren would have had the authority to return Ze to her natal home, sell her to another family, or even beat her to death for being unfilial to his mother, but she was correct. Her father was important and the dowry had been plentiful. Madame Wu did not reprimand Ze, nor did she report the girl to her husband. The silences that visited the women's chambers were rare, but they were heavy with bitterness and reproach.

I heard Ze in the late afternoons, her voice so shrill and loud that it carried all the way from Ren's library to the bedchamber. "I've been waiting for you all day," she carped. "What are you doing in here? Why do you always keep to yourself? I don't want your words and poems. I need money. A silk merchant is bringing samples from Suzhou today. I do not ask for gowns for myself, but surely you agree that the hangings in the main hall are shabby. If you worked harder, we wouldn't have to rely so much on my dowry."

When the servants brought dinner to the table, criticism poured from her mouth. "I don't eat fish from West Lake. The waters there are too shallow and the fish tastes like earth." She picked at the pan-fried goose with lemons and ignored the double-boiled chicken with lotus seeds. Ren ate the seeds, which were a well-known aphrodisiac, and put a lot of them in Ze's bowl, which she pointedly ignored. I was the only one who knew that she was secretly burning lotus leaves and eating the ashes to prevent pregnancy. Same plant, different purposes. I was happy for her choice. A son would solidify her position in the household.

Every marriage encompasses six emotions: love, affection, hatred, bitterness, disappointment, and jealousy. But where were Ze's love and affection? Everything she said and did was insulting to her mother-in-law and her husband, but Ze seemed impervious. Neither of them dared protest, because daughters of powerful men were allowed to nag their husbands and make their families feel inconsequential. But this was not marriage.

Ze's parents came to visit. The bride threw herself at their feet and begged to be taken home.

"This was a mistake," she cried. "This house and the people in it are too low. I was a phoenix. Why did you marry me to a crow?"

Was this how she saw my poet? Was this why she pecked at him all the time?

"You turned down all offers," the commissioner answered coldly. "I was deep into negotiations with the son of Suzhou's magistrate. They had a beautiful garden compound, but you wouldn't consider it. It is a father's duty to find the right husband for his daughter, but you decided whom you wanted to marry when you were nine years old. What girl chooses her husband by peeking through a screen? Well, you wanted—no, demanded—a mediocre man who lived in a mediocre house. Why? I have no idea, but I gave you what you wanted."

"But you're my baba! And I don't love Ren. Buy me back. Arrange a different marriage."

Commissioner Tan was unyielding. "You have always been selfish, spoiled, and strong-minded. I blame your mother for that."

This hardly seemed fair. A mother can spoil her daughter

with too much affection, but only a father has the money and power to give a girl the things she wants.

"You've been nothing but a blight on our family from the moment you were born," he went on, and pushed her away with his shoe. "The day you married out was a happy one for your mother and me."

Madame Tan didn't deny this or try to intervene on her daughter's behalf. "Stand up and stop acting so foolish," she said in disgust. "You wanted this marriage, and now you have it. You've made your fate. Start acting like a wife. Obedience is the only way for a wife. *Yang* is on top; *yin* is on the bottom."

When pleading and tears didn't work, Ze turned vicious. Her face grew red and horrible words spewed from her mouth. She was like a first-born son—absolutely sure of her position and her right to demand—but Commissioner Tan remained unmoved.

"I won't lose face for you. We did our best to raise you for your husband's family. You belong to them now."

The commissioner and his wife instructed their daughter to behave, gave Madame Wu gifts as compensation for having to accept the company of their unruly daughter, and left. Ze's disposition did not improve; if anything it got worse. During the day, when she treated the fingers in the household with utter disdain, I didn't interfere. The nights, however, belonged to me.

At first I didn't know what to do and Ze often fought against me. But I was so much stronger she had no choice but to obey me. Pleasing Ren was another matter altogether. I learned by trying and failing, by trying and succeeding. I began to follow his cues and react to his sighs, his internal trembling, and the subtle shifting of his body to give me better access. I directed Ze's fingers along his muscles. I urged her to use her breasts to caress his skin, his lips, his tongue. I made her use the wetness of her mouth to tantalize his nipples, his belly, and that part lower down. I finally understood what Tang Xianzu meant when he wrote about Liniang "playing the flute." As for that dark moist part of Ze that Ren desired most of all, I made sure it was open and available to him at any moment he chose.

All the while I whispered in her ear the things I'd learned about marriage from *The Peony Pavilion* and how a wife had to be *"agreeable, accommodating, and compliant."* When I was a girl, listening to my mother's and aunts' endless drills and recitations about marriage, I'd thought I'd never be like them. I'd planned to reject the past, those lessons, and the rigidity of custom and tradition. I'd wanted to be modern in my thinking, but like all girls who've just moved sight unseen to their husbands' homes, I imitated my mother and aunts, calling on all those things I'd so resisted. If I'd been alive, I was sure that eventually I would have come to carry locks in my pockets and insist that my daughters follow the Three Obediences and the Four Virtues. I would have become my mother. Instead, my mother's voice came out of my mouth and entered Ze's ears.

"Don't track your husband's activities all the time," I instructed. "No man likes to feel his wife watching over him. Don't eat too much. No man wants to see a wife putting too much food in her mouth. Show respect for the money he earns. Generosity in spending is very different from wasting money. Only a concubine likes to regard a man as a money printer."

Ze gradually succumbed to my lessons, while I grew out of the girlish romanticism that had made me lovesick. I came to believe that true love meant physical love. I enjoyed making my husband suffer the pain of desire. I spent hours thinking of new ways to prolong that agony. I used Ze's body freely and without regret, remorse, or guilt. I made her do what she was supposed to do as a wife, and then I watched—smiling, laughing, loving with my entire spirit—as my husband found release in her hands, mouth, and hidden crevice. By now I knew my husband's greatest desire was to hold Ze's bound feet dressed in embroidered red silk slippers in his hands, where he could fully appreciate their delicacy, their fragrance, and the pain she had gone through to give him this pleasure. When I saw Ren could do even more with them, I prevented her from pushing him away. With Ze as my emissary, I experienced sexual love.

That she didn't feel anything didn't bother me. That I didn't know what she was thinking didn't disturb me either. Even when she was tired, even when she was afraid, even when she was embarrassed, I pushed and used her. Ze's flesh was there for Ren to taste, fondle, tease, pinch, nuzzle, and penetrate. But over time I saw that her look of indifference and her lack of response disturbed my husband. Whenever he asked what would please her, she shut her eyes and turned her face away from him. For all my efforts, she was less present in the bed with him than she'd been on her marriage night.

Ren began to stay in his library to read until Ze fell asleep. When he came to the room and got in bed, he did not wrap his arms around her to seek warmth, comfort, and companionship for his sleeping hours. He stayed on his side of the bed; she stayed on hers. At first, this satisfied me greatly, because it allowed me to drape my ghostly form around his body like a shroud. I'd stay that way all night, moving as he moved, letting his warmth seep into my coldness. But when he called for the windows to be shut and extra quilts to be brought, I retreated back up to the rafter above him.

He started visiting the teahouses on the shore of West Lake. I accompanied him, staying with him when he gambled, when he drank too much, and when—eventually—he started amusing himself with the women whose specialty was men's delight and satisfaction. I watched, fascinated, entranced. I learned a lot. Mostly I learned that Ze was as selfish and self-centered as ever. How could she not do what she was supposed to do, as a woman and as a wife? Did she have no feelings, emotional or physical? And putting aside Ren's pleasure, had she forgotten that he might fall in love with one of those women and bring her home as a concubine?

After she'd done clouds and rain with my husband, I journeyed with Ze in her dreams. Since her wedding night, she no longer visited pretty spots. Rather, her dreams took place in fog and shadows. She concealed the moon. She refused to light candles or lanterns. This suited me well. From my hiding place behind trees or pillars or from the darkness of caves or corners, I haunted her, bullied her, lectured her. The next evening, she would stay awake in bed, pale and shivering, until our husband came to her. She did everything I told her to do, but the look on her face still did not please him.

Finally, one night as she ventured in a dream garden, I stepped out of the black shadows and met her face-to-face. Naturally, she screamed and ran away, but how far could she go? Even in her dream, she tired. I never tired. I couldn't tire.

She sank to her knees and rubbed her scalp, trying to produce sparks, hoping those bursts of illumination would scare me. But this was a dream and I had no fear of friction static here.

"Leave me alone!" Ze cried, and then bit the tip of her middle finger, doing her hardest to bring blood. "Go away!"

She pointed her finger at me, trying to place blame but also knowing that gore in any form was terrifying to ghosts. But again, this was a dream and her teeth hadn't the strength to tear her skin. Her powers of conjuration, as harmful to me as they could be in the earthly realm, had no power over me in a dream.

"I'm sorry," I said amiably, "but I'll never leave you."

She covered her mouth with her hands to smother her petrified screams. No, *petrified* is the wrong word. It was as though all the fears she'd refused to acknowledge were true.

I was a ghost, so I was aware of what was happening to her in the earthly realm. There she whimpered and struggled against the covers.

In the dream, I took several steps back. "I'm not here to hurt you," I said. I extended my hand and sent in her direction a shower of petals. I smiled and flowers bloomed around us. I gently twirled toward her, sending away the shadows and darkness until we were two pretty girls in a garden on a pleasant spring day.

In her bed, Ze's breathing calmed and her features settled. Here, in her dreams, her hair shone in the sunlight. Her lips were full with promise. Her hands were slim and pale. Her lily feet were delicate, an enticement even to me. I saw no reason why she couldn't bring this hidden self back to the earthly realm.

I lowered myself before her.

"People say you are selfish," I said. She closed her eyes against the truth of this and her face began to pinch again. "I want you to be selfish. I want you to be selfish here." I used the tip of my index finger to touch the seat of consciousness that lay embedded in her chest. Under my finger, I felt something open. I drew my finger away and thought about the women I'd spied in the pleasure houses. Emboldened, I reached out with both hands and grazed her nipples hidden under her gown. I felt sudden hardness beneath my fingertips; in the earthly realm, Ze stirred. I remembered the deepest source of sensation I had when Ren had caressed me with the peony blossom. This was a dream and Ze couldn't get away from me, so I trailed a finger down, down, down until I touched the spot that I knew was the source of pleasure. Through the silk I felt warmth begin to radiate until Ze shuddered and sighed. In her bed, she trembled too. "Be selfish about this," I whispered in her ear. Remembering what my mother used to say about clouds and rain, I added, "Women should have pleasure too."

Before I let her waken, she had to promise me something. "Don't mention our talk or that you saw me," I said. She had to remain silent about our visits for my connection to her to continue. "No one, especially your husband, wants to hear about your dreams. Ren will think you superstitious and ignorant if you talk nonsense about his first wife."

"But he's my husband! I can't keep secrets from him."

"All women keep secrets from their husbands," I said. "Men keep secrets from their wives too."

Was this true? Fortunately, Ze had as little experience as I had and didn't question me. Still, she resisted.

"My husband wants a new kind of wife," Ze said. "He's looking for a companion."

At those words—which were so close to what Ren had told me—rage, deep and inhuman, roared out of me. For a moment, I became fearful in my aspect: hideous, repulsive, and frightening. After that, I had no more trouble from Ze. Night after night I visited her in her dreams until she no longer fought against me.

This is how Tan Ze became my sister-wife. Every night I waited for her, coiled in the rafters, when she came to the bedchamber. Every night I slipped down from my perch to the marital bed to guide her hips, arch her back, and help her open to our husband. I relished each moan that escaped her lips. I enjoyed tormenting her as much as I did him. When she resisted, all I had to do was reach out and touch this or that exposed piece of flesh to make desperate warmth seep into her body until she was nothing more than raw sensation, until her hair became disarrayed and her combs and ornaments littered the bed, until she reached her moment of sweet melting and the rains came.

Ze's sudden fervor brought our husband back home from the pleasure houses. He grew to love his earthly wife. For every moment of enchantment she brought him—and there were many, as I thought of new and varied ways to please him—he challenged her right back with his ingenuity. There were many places on Ze's body to explore and he found them all. She did not resist, because I wouldn't let her. Now when she left the room, I did not hear complaints, criticisms, or angry words fly about the compound. She began to take tea to Ren's library. His interests became her interests. She started treating the servants kindly and fairly.

How happy all this made Ren. He brought her little gifts. He asked the servants to prepare special foods that would entice and stimulate her. After clouds and rain, he stayed on top of her, looked into her beautiful dream face, and let words of adoration cascade from his mouth and drench her in love. He loved her in the way I'd hoped he would have loved me. He loved her so much that he forgot about me. But a part of her remained cold and distant, because for every shiver I sent through her body, for every sigh I let escape her wet and open mouth, for all the delights I gave her unselfishly— after all, I was wife number one—there was one thing I could not make her do. She would not meet his eyes.

But I never wavered in my determination to make her the wife I wanted her to be. Ren had said he wanted a marriage of companions, so I filled Ze's belly with books. I made her read volumes of poetry and history. She became such a good and deep reader that she kept books on her dressing table, along with her mirror, cosmetics, and jewelry.

"Your desire for knowledge is as strong as your need to maintain your looks," Ren observed one day.

His words inspired me to be even more persistent. I got Ze interested in *The Peony Pavilion*. Again and again, she read my saved copy of Volume One. Soon she was never seen without it. She could recite whole portions of my commentary from memory.

"You never miss a word," Ren said to her in admiration, and I was happy.

Eventually, Ze began writing notes about the opera on little pieces of paper. Were these her original thoughts or mine fed to her? They were both. Remembering what had happened when Ren told my father about his dreams and how we wrote together, I took care to remind Ze never to mention her writing—or me—to anyone. In this regard, she was an obedient second wife, acquiescing to the needs of wife number one.

Nevertheless, although everything was going well, I had a big problem. I was a hungry ghost and I was becoming less and less.

Festival of Hungry Ghosts

AS LIVING GIRLS, CERTAIN THINGS HAPPEN ON SCHEDULE whether we like them or not. We get our monthly bleeding. The moon waxes and wanes. New Year comes, followed by the Spring Festival, Double Seven, the Festival of Hungry Ghosts, and the Autumn Moon Festival. We have no control over these things, yet our bodies are set in motion by them. At New Year, we clean our homes, prepare special foods, and make offerings not out of duty or custom but because the change in season and the hint of spring prods us, lures us, and compels us to those actions. The same is true in many ways for ghosts. We have the freedom to wander, but we're also driven and called by tradition, instinct, and a desire to survive. I wanted to stay with Ren every second, but in the seventh month my hunger came on as strong and uncontrollable as bad cramps, a harvest moon, or firecrackers sending the Kitchen God to Heaven to report on a family. Even as I curled around my rafter or hovered over my sister-wife's bed, I felt myself being beckoned, enticed, *pulled* outside.

Driven by hunger so powerful I couldn't stand it, I left the security of the bedchamber. I needed a straight line, and I had it, drifting right through the courtyards and out the gate of the Wu family compound behind two servants holding paper and pots. The minute I passed through the gate I heard it close behind me and watched horrified as the servants pasted protective talismans on the doors and locked them to protect those inside from such as me. It was the fifteenth day of the month set aside for the Festival of Hungry Ghosts. I was as much a victim of my desires as my sister-wife; my actions, like hers, were uncontrolled and uncontrollable.

I banged on the gate. "Let me in!"

Around me I heard cries and wails echo my wish: "Let me in! Let me in! Let *me* in!"

I swirled around to see creatures whose clothes were in shreds, whose faces were gaunt, gray, and wrinkled, and whose bodies sagged with loneliness, bereavement, and remorse. Some had missing limbs. Others reeked of fear, terror, or revenge. Those who'd died by drowning dripped rank fluids and smelled of rotten fish. But the children! Dozens of small children—mostly girls who'd been abandoned, sold, abused, and ultimately forgotten by their families—scampered together in packs like so many rats, their eyes filled with an eternity of sadness. All these creatures had two things in common: hunger and anger. Some were angry because they were hungry and homeless; some were hungry and homeless because they were angry. Horrified, I swung back to the gate and banged on it as hard as I could.

"Let me in!" I screamed again.

But my fists had no strength against the talismans and protective couplets the servants had used to seal the door against me and my kind. *My kind.* I put my forehead against the gate, closed my eyes, and let that knowledge seep into my consciousness. I was one of those disgusting creatures, and I was deeply, overwhelmingly, and ravenously hungry.

I took a deep breath, pushed myself away from the wall, and forced myself to turn around. The others had lost interest in me and gone back to their main business: stuffing their faces with the Wu family offerings. I tried to edge my way through their violently writhing bodies, but they easily pushed me away.

I walked along the road, stopping before every house where an altar table had been set up, but either I was too late or the others were too fierce for me. I was reduced to an open mouth and an empty stomach.

Gods and ancestors are worshipped and cared for as social superiors. They give protection and grant wishes; the celestial aspect of their souls is associated with growth, procreation, and life. Their offerings are carefully cooked and presented on beautiful platters with plenty of serving and eating implements. But ghosts are despised. We're social inferiors, worse than beggars or lepers. We're believed to offer nothing but misfortune, unhappiness, and disaster. We're blamed for accidents, barrenness, illnesses, crop failures, bad luck in gambling, business losses, and, of course, death. So does it come as a surprise that offerings for us during the Festival of Hungry Ghosts are vile and disgusting? Instead of trays of ripe peaches, fragrant steamed rice, and whole soy-sauce chickens, we receive uncooked rice, vegetables that should have been fed to the pigs, chunks of turned meat with hair still on it, and no bowls or chopsticks. We're expected to shove our faces into this food like dogs, rip it apart with our teeth, and carry it away to dark nether corners.

People don't understand that many of us are from refined homes, lonely for our families, and as concerned for others as those ancestors they so cherish. As ghosts, we can't escape our essential natures, but that doesn't mean we deliberately try to do harm; we're dangerous in the same way that a hot stove is dangerous. So far I hadn't purposely used the darkness of my condition to hurt, maim, or be cruel, had I? But as I wended my way around the lake, I fought off others more timid than myself for the peel of a mildewed orange or a piece of bone that hadn't already been sucked of its marrow. I walked, drifted, crawled, and dragged myself from house to house, eating what I could, slurping the remains from tables already ravaged by those like myself until I arrived at the wall of the Chen Family Villa. Unknowingly, I'd come all the way around the lake. That's how deep and unfulfilled my hunger was.

I'd never been right outside my family compound's wind-fire gate on this festival, but I remembered how the servants had worked for days, chattering among themselves about the wealth of food that they'd placed, tied, or strapped to the altar before our gate: chickens and ducks, dead and alive; slices of pork and pigs' heads; fish, rice cakes, and whole ripe pineapples, melons, and bananas. When the festival was over and the ghosts had eaten their share of the spiritual meal, beggars and the destitute would come to partake of the carnal leavings in the form of an ample banquet courtesy of the Chen family.

Just as at every house, the competition for the offerings was brutal, but this was *my* home. I was entitled to these things. I pushed my way forward. A ghost in a tattered mandarin robe with an embroidered insignia on his chest that showed him to be a scholar of the fifth rank tried to elbow me away, but I was small and slipped under his arm.

"This is ours!" he roared. "You have no rights here. Go away!"

I held on to the table—as though that would help someone

who has no substance—and addressed him with the respect due his rank.

"This is my family home," I said.

"Your status in life has no importance here," a creature to my right growled.

"If you had any status at all, you would have been buried properly. Another worthless branch," sniffed a woman, her flesh so corrupted that bits of her skull had broken through her skin.

The man in the mandarin robe dropped his odorous, yawning mouth down to my face. "Your family has forgotten about you and they have forgotten about us. We've been coming here for years, but look what they give us now! Almost nothing. Your new brother seems not to understand his mistake. *Jaaaaa!*" He spewed his putrid breath on me, and I smelled the rotten offerings in his gullet. "With your baba in the capital, Bao thinks this festival is not necessary. He took the best offerings, such as they were, to his room to share with his concubines."

With that, the creature in the mandarin robe picked me up by the back of my neck and tossed me away. I hit the wall of the compound across the street, slid to the ground, and watched as the others gnawed and tore at the paltry offerings. I crept around them and knocked futilely on our wind-fire gate. In life, all I had wanted was to leave the compound and go on an excursion; now all I wanted was to get in.

For so long I hadn't thought about my natal family. Lotus and Broom had to be living in their own homes now, but my aunts were inside. The concubines were still there. My little cousin Orchid would be preparing for her betrothal. I thought of all the hundreds of fingers—the amahs, the servants, the cooks, and most of all my mother—who lived behind the gate. There had to be a way for me to see my mother.

I walked around the compound, making wide turns to avoid the sharpness of the corners. But it was hopeless. The Chen Family Villa had only one gate and it was closed against hungry ghosts. Was Mama in the Lotus-Blooming Hall thinking about me? I looked up into the sky, trying to glimpse the Viewing Terrace. Was Grandmother looking down at me? Was she shaking her head and laughing at my stupidity?

Ghosts, like living people, do not like to accept the truth. We delude ourselves to save face, maintain a measure of optimism, and keep going forward in truly untenable situations. I didn't like to think of myself as a hungry ghost, who was so famished she would shove her face into a platter of moldy fruit to feed her ravenous emptiness. I sighed. I was still hungry. I had to eat enough on this one day to sustain me for a year.

When I was still on the Viewing Terrace, I'd periodically looked in on the Qian family in Gudang that my father had visited during New Year's Festival soon after I died. I set off in the right direction, fighting off others like myself when I had to, making wide turns when necessary, and getting lost in the twisting pathways between rice fields just as the farmers intended.

Night fell, the time when even more creatures should have come out to fill their bellies, but in the countryside I met few other ghosts. Out here, most people met undesirable demises from earthquake, flood, famine, and plagues of various sorts. They died near or in their homes, so their bodies weren't lost. Rarely did accidents occur where a body disappeared entirely; perhaps an occasional house fire consumed a whole family or the collapse of a bridge during flood season carried away a man going to market with his pig. So most of the dead in the countryside were carefully buried and the three parts of their souls sent to their proper resting places.

I did, however, encounter a few perturbed spirits: a mother who'd been interred improperly so that her body had been pierced by tree roots, causing her unbearable pain; a man who'd been driven from his coffin because it had flooded; a young wife whose body had shifted when her coffin was placed in the ground so that her skull was so twisted that the rest of her soul was unable to proceed to her next incarnation. These spirits were agitated and troubled; in trying to find help, they caused problems for their families. No one likes to hear ghostly wails of unspeakable anguish when trying to fall asleep, feed the baby, or make clouds and rain with your husband. But except for these few souls, my journey was uneventful and lonely.

I reached the Qian family home. Although they were poor, they had good hearts; their offerings were modest, but the quality was better than anything I'd eaten so far. Once I was sated, I drifted closer to the house, wanting to rest before my journey back to the city, enjoying the sensation of being full, and wishing to connect for just a few moments to people who were closely tied to my natal family.

But during the Festival of Hungry Ghosts, wooden screens covered the Qians' windows and the doors were locked from the inside. I smelled rice cooking. Lantern light leaked from under the doorjamb. I heard the low murmur of voices. I listened very hard, and then the sound of Madame Qian's voice coalesced. *"Since I stopped gathering kingfisher feathers along the emerald river, I have kept to my poor and humble abode, just chanting my poems."* I knew this poem well, and it made me sad and homesick. But what was I to do? I was alone, deprived of my family, companionship, and the gift of words and art.

I buried my face in my hands and sobbed. From inside the house I heard the scraping of chairs and sounds of consternation. These people had comforted me, and now I'd terrified them with my netherworld cries.

WHEN THE FESTIVAL was over and I returned to Ren and Ze's bedchamber, I was fortified, strong, and unexpectedly focused. Being full for the first time since long before I died brought back a different hunger, the one I had once reserved for my project about The Peony Pavilion. What if I could add to what I'd written in the margins and turn it into a self-portrait that Ren would recognize as symbolizing everything I held inside of me? Didn't Liniang's self-portrait and my writings harbor our souls?

Suddenly, I was as selfish as my sister-wife. I'd educated Ze about The Peony Pavilion. I'd touched her thoughts enough so that she'd written on those slips of paper and hidden them in our bedchamber. Now she had to do something for me.

I began to keep Ze in the bedchamber by day, preferring that she stay with me rather than join her husband and mother-in-law in the eating hall for breakfast or lunch. I did not love light, so I forced her to keep the doors closed and the windows covered. During the summer, the room stayed cool, the way I liked it. In fall, quilts were brought in. In winter, Ze took to wearing padded jackets or jackets lined with fur. The New Year came, followed by spring. In the fourth month, the flowers opened their faces to the sun, but inside we found companionship in our shared darkness that refused to warm even by day.

I made Ze reread what I'd written in Volume One. Then I sent her to Ren's library to find the sources for the three pastiches I hadn't found before I died. I helped her pick up her brush and write these answers and my thoughts about them on the pages right next to my other writing. If I could make Ze play the flute with my husband, how hard was making her pick up a brush and write? Nothing. Easy.

But I was not remotely satisfied. I desperately needed Volume Two, which begins with Mengmei and Liniang's ghost swearing eternal love. Then he dots her ancestor tablet, exhumes her body, and resurrects her. If I could make Ze write down my thoughts and make her give them to Ren to read, wouldn't he be inspired to follow Mengmei's example?

At night, in Ze's dreams, we met by her favorite pond and I said to her, "You need Volume Two. You must get it." For weeks I was like a cockatoo, repeating these lines again and again. But Ze was a wife. She could no more go out to find this volume than I could have if I'd been alive. She had to rely on her wiles, her charm, and her husband's love to bring it into our home. Ze had my help, but she also had her own abilities. She could be stubborn, petty, and spoiled. Our husband responded beautifully.

"I long to read Volume Two of The Peony Pavilion," she might say, as she poured him a cup of tea. "I saw the opera long ago and now I would love to read the great writer's words and discuss them with you." As Ren sipped the hot liquid, she would look into his eyes, run her fingers along his sleeve, and add, "Sometimes I don't understand what the writer meant with his metaphors and allusions. You are such a fine poet. Maybe you could tell me."

Or at night, in bed, with Ren lying between us and the quilts piled high to keep them warm, she might whisper in his ear, "I think of my sister-wife each day. The missing second half of the opera is a vivid reminder to me that Same is gone. Surely you miss her too. If only we could bring her back to us." And then her tongue would dart from her lips and tease his earlobe until other things began to happen.

I grew bolder. By summer I began to leave the bedchamber by placing my hands on Ze's shoulders and letting her pull me from room to room. Drifting this way, I didn't have to worry about corners. I was merely a breath of air that trailed behind my sister-wife. When we arrived in the eating hall for dinner, Madame Wu would put away her fan, call to the servants to close the doors against the sudden chill, and order coal to be lit in the brazier even though these were the hottest months.

"Your lips are growing thin again," Madame Wu said to Ze one evening.

Such a common mother-in-law complaint, since everyone knows that thin lips show a thinness of personality and this thinness can translate to a thinness of the womb. The unspoken message: *Where is my grandson?* So typical, so old-fashioned.

Under the table Ren took Ze's hand. A look of concern came over his face.

"And your hand is cold. Wife, it's summer. Come outside with me tomorrow. We'll sit by the pond, look at the flowers and butterflies, and let the sun warm your skin."

"These days, it is my fate to despise blossoms," Ze murmured, "while butterflies remind me of dead souls. When I see water, I think only of drowning."

"I think," my mother-in-law observed caustically, "that the sun will not help her either. She brings coldness with her wherever she goes. We should not wish the sun to run from her as well."

Tears welled in Ze's eyes. "I should return to my room. I have reading to do."

Madame Wu pulled her shawl more tightly around her

shoulders. "Perhaps that is best. I will send a doctor tomorrow to make a diagnosis."

Ze squeezed her thighs together. "That won't be necessary."

"How will you bring a son if . . . ?"

A son? Ze was worth more to me than her ability to give a son! She was helping me. We did not need a son.

But this was not Doctor Zhao's concern when he came to visit us. I'd not seen him since I died, and I can't say I was happy to see him again.

He took the usual pulses, looked at Ze's tongue, took Ren outside, and pronounced, "I have seen this many times before. Your wife has stopped eating and she spends hours alone brooding in darkness. Master Wu, I can draw only one conclusion: Your wife is lovesick."

"What can I do?" Ren asked in alarm.

The doctor and Ren sat on a bench in the garden.

"Usually a night alone with her husband will cure a wife's lovesickness," the doctor said. "Has she been unwilling to perform clouds and rain? Is this why she has not yet conceived? You've been married for well over a year now."

I was incensed that the doctor would even suggest this. I wished I had the abilities of a vengeful ghost, for I would have made the doctor pay for those accusations.

"I could not ask for a better wife in this regard," Ren said.

"Have you"—and here the doctor hesitated before going on—"been giving her your vital essence? A woman must take this internally to maintain good health. You cannot just spend it between the scented softness of her bound feet."

After much prompting, Ren confided the activities that took place each day and night in the bedchamber. Once everything was revealed, the doctor could not fault one party or the other for a lack of enthusiasm, knowledge, frequency, or ingestion.

"Perhaps something else is causing your wife's lovesickness. Is there something else she wants?" the doctor asked.

Ren left town the next day. I didn't try to follow him, because I was busy with Ze. Madame Wu, on instructions from the doctor, entered the bedchamber, opened the doors, and took away the heavy curtains that covered our windows. The heat and humidity so common in Hangzhou during the summer months filled our room. It was horrible, but we tried our best to be dutiful daughters-in-law by adapting, putting our personal feelings and comfort aside, and complying. I stayed as close as possible to Ze to offer her solace from the intrusion. I was gratified to see her put on another coat over her jacket. Mothers-in-law can tell you what to do, and we can appear to submit, but they can't watch us every minute.

Three mornings later, Ren returned.

"I went to every village between the Tiao and Zha rivers," he said. "My persistence paid off in Shaoxi. I'm sorry I didn't do this sooner." From behind his back he brought out a copy of *The Peony Pavilion,* with parts one and two together in one volume. "This is the best gift I could ever give you." He hesitated then, and I knew he had to be thinking of me. "I give you the entire story."

Ze and I collapsed in his arms with happiness. What he said next convinced me that I was still very much in his heart.

"I don't want you to be lovesick," he said. "You'll be better now."

I thought, Yes, yes, I will be better. Thank you, Husband, thank you.

"Yes, yes," Ze echoed and sighed.

We had to celebrate.

"Let us celebrate," she said.

Though it was still morning, servants brought a bottle of wine and jade drinking cups. My sister-wife was not accustomed to drinking and I'd never had wine, but we were happy. She drank the first cup even before Ren picked up his. Each time she set down her cup, I touched the rim and she'd fill it again. It was broad daylight and the windows were open to the heat, but there was another kind of light and heat that husband and wife began to feel. A cup, another cup, and another cup. Ze drank nine cups. Her cheeks were dizzied by the tide of wine. Ren was far more chaste, but he'd made his wife glad and she repaid him with our combined gratitude.

The two of them fell asleep in the early afternoon. The next day, Ren woke up at his usual time and went to his library to compose. I let my sister-wife, so unused to wine, continue to sleep, because I needed her to be fresh and ready.

Dreams of the Heart

WHEN THE SUN STRUCK THE HOOKS OF THE BED curtains, I roused Ze. I had her gather up all the small pieces of paper she'd been writing on during the last few months and sent her to Ren's library. She bowed her head and showed him the papers in her hands.

"Might I be allowed to copy my commentary, along with that of Sister-Wife Tong's, into our new copy of *The Peony Pavilion*?" she asked.

"I'll allow it," he said, not even looking up from his papers.

I thought how lucky I was that marriage had not closed the door to his broad-mindedness, and my love for him deepened.

But let me be clear: It was my idea for Ze to copy my commentary into the new volume. It was my idea for her to add her comments to my comments. And it was my idea for her to continue the work I hadn't finished when my mother burned Volume Two. It made sense for everything to be in the one new book.

It took two weeks for Ze to finish copying my commentary neatly into the first half of our new volume. It took another two weeks for her to organize her little pieces of paper and transcribe them onto the clean pages of the second half. Then we began to add new comments in both halves.

The Dao tells us that we should write what we know from experience and that we have to move outside the mind and come in contact with real things, people, and experiences. I also believed what Ye Shaoyuan wrote in his introduction to his daughter's posthumous literary collection: *It may be that the numinous spirit of the written word does not perish and so, too, bestows life after death.* So when I had Ze write, her expressions about the opera's structure and plot were more extensive than what I'd written as a lovesick girl in my bed. I hoped Ren would see Ze's handwriting, hear me, and know he could have me still.

Three months passed. The sun stayed behind clouds and sank early in the day. Windows were closed and draperies hung. Doors shut out the constant chill and braziers were lit. This change in the environment was good for me and stimulated my mind. For weeks I stayed transfixed by my project, barely allowing Ze out of the room, but one night I watched and listened to Ren as he talked to my sister-wife before retiring. He sat on the edge of the bed with his arm around her shoulders. She seemed very small and delicate next to him.

"You've grown pale," he said. "And I see you're thinner."

"Your mother complains about me still, I see," she commented dryly.

"Forget your mother-in-law. This is your husband speaking." He touched the circles that hung like dark moons beneath her eyes. "You didn't have these when we married. It hurts me to see them now. Are you unhappy with me? Do you need to visit your parents?"

I helped Ze with the proper response.

"A girl is only a guest in her parents' home," she recited weakly. "I belong here now."

"Would you like an excursion?" he asked.

"I'm content here with you." She sighed. "Tomorrow I will pay more attention to my toilet. I'll try harder to please you—"

He cut her off sharply. "This isn't about pleasing me." When she trembled in response, he went on in a gentler tone. "I want to make you happy, but when I see you at breakfast you do not eat or speak. I rarely see you during the day anymore. You used to bring me tea. Do you remember that? We used to chat in my library."

"I'll serve you tea tomorrow," she promised.

He shook his head. "This is not about you serving me. You're my wife and I'm troubled. The servants bring dinner and you do not eat. I'm afraid we'll have to ask the doctor to come again."

I couldn't bear his distress. I slipped down from my place in the rafters, hovered just behind Ze, then reached out with my fingertip and touched the back of her head. We were so close now, so intimate, that she followed my directions without resistance. She turned her head and without a word covered his mouth with her own. I didn't want him to worry and I didn't want to hear his concerns.

My methods for silencing him had always worked in the past, but not tonight. He pulled away, and said, "I'm serious about this. I thought bringing you the copy of the opera would cure your illness, but it seems only to have made it worse. Believe me, this is not what I intended." There I was again, sneaking into his mind. "Tomorrow I'm going out and will return with the doctor. Please be ready to receive him."

When they got in bed, Ren wrapped his arms around Ze, pulled her back against his chest, and held her protectively.

"Beginning tomorrow things will be different," he whispered. "I'll read to you by the fire. I'll have the servants bring our meals and we'll eat alone. I love you, Ze. I will make you better."

Men are so sure of themselves, and they have such courage and conviction. They believe—truly believe—that they can make things happen just by speaking words, and in many cases they can. I loved Ren for this and I loved seeing his effect on my sister-wife. When I saw the way the warmth of his body bled into hers, I thought of Mengmei caressing Liniang's cold ghostly flesh back into existence. As Ren's breathing slowed and deepened, Ze's breathing responded in kind. I could barely wait for him to fall asleep. As soon as he did, I dragged Ze from the marital bed and made her light a candle, mix ink, and open our project. I was excited, invigorated. This was my way back to Ren and our life together.

I wouldn't make Ze write much, just a little:

What is amazing about the opera is not Liniang but the scholar. There are many love-crazed women in the world like Liniang, who dream of love and die, but they do not return to life. They do not have Mengmei, who laid out Liniang's portrait, called out to her, and worshipped her; who made love to her ghost and believed that it was flesh and blood; who conspired with Sister Stone to open her coffin and carried her corpse without fear; who traveled far to beg his father-in-law and suffered at his hands. The dream was so real to him that opening her grave did not frighten him. He cried for her without shame. All this he did with no regrets.

I smiled, pleased with my accomplishment. Then I let Ze return to the comfort and warmth of her husband's arms. I slithered back up the wall and resumed my perch in the rafters. I had to keep Ren satisfied with his wife or I wouldn't be able to keep using her to write; if I couldn't use her, Ren wouldn't hear me. All through the night as I watched the two of them sleep, I searched my memory for the things that Mama and my aunts had said about being wives. "Every morning get up a half hour earlier than your husband," Mama used to say. So the next morning I made Ze get up before Ren wakened.

"Losing a half hour of sleep doesn't harm your health or beauty," I whispered to Ze when she sat down at her dressing table. "Do you think your husband likes to see you sleeping soundly? No. Take fifteen minutes to wash your face, brush your hair, and dress." I drew on the pampered ways of the women's chamber to help her mix her powder, put on rouge, coil her hair, and set it with feather adornments. I made sure she dressed in pink. "Take the other fifteen minutes to prepare your husband's clothes and lay them beside his pillow. Be ready when he wakes with fresh water, a towel, and a comb."

After Ren left the room, I reminded Ze, "Never stop improving your taste and style as a woman. Don't bring into our home your toughness, your stubbornness, or your jealousy. He can see that on the street. Instead, keep learning. Reading will enrich your conversation, the art of pouring tea will warm him, and playing music and flower arranging will deepen your powers of emotion and enliven him at the same time." Then, remembering my mother on the day I helped her bind Orchid's feet, I added, "Your husband is Heaven. How could you not serve him?"

Today, for the first time, I pushed her out the door and guided her to the kitchen. Needless to say, Ze had never been there before. When she squinted at a servant in disapproval, I pulled on her lashes to keep her eyes open and carefree. She may have been a spoiled girl and an absentminded wife, but surely her mother had taught her to make something. I kept Ze there until the simplest of all recipes came to her mind. The servants watched nervously as Ze set a pot of water to boil, poured in a handful of rice, and stirred constantly until it turned into creamy *congee*. She looked through baskets and cupboards until she found fresh greens and raw peanuts, which she chopped and put into condiment bowls. She poured the *congee* into a serving dish, put it and the side dishes, bowls, and soup spoons on a tray, and carried it to the breakfast hall. Madame Wu and her son sat speechless as Ze served them, her head bowed, her face prettily pink from the steam and the reflected color from her tunic. Later, Ze followed her mother-in-law to the women's chamber, where the two of them sat together to embroider and make conversation. I did not allow sniping words to come out of either of their mouths. And Ren did not feel the need to call for the doctor.

I insisted Ze follow these rituals to appease her husband's anxiety and earn her mother-in-law's respect. When Ze cooked, she made sure that all the flavors were compatible and that the food was fragrant. She brought to the dinner table fish from West Lake and watched quietly to make sure the others enjoyed the taste. She poured tea when her mother-in-law's or husband's cup was low. Once these obligations were fulfilled, I drew her back to the bedchamber and we'd get back to work.

By now I'd learned a lot about married life and sexual love. It was not the sordid thing that Sister Stone joked about or that the Flower Spirit liked to make bawdy innuendo about in *The Peony Pavilion*. I now understood it to be about spiritual connection through physical touch. I made Ze write:

Liniang says, "Ghosts can be careless about passion, but humans must affect propriety." Liniang cannot and should not be considered ruined for having made clouds and rain with Mengmei in her dream. She could not become pregnant in a dream nor could she become pregnant as a ghost. Clouds and rain in a dream is without consequence, demands no responsibility, and should bring no shame. All girls have dreams of this sort. This does not soil them, far from it. A girl who dreams of clouds and rain is preparing herself for the fulfillment of *qing*. As Liniang says, "Betrothal makes a wife, elopement only a concubine." Between a husband and wife, what some consider lascivious becomes elegant.

But *qing* couldn't just be limited to husbands and wives. What about mother love? I still missed my mother and longed for her. Across the lake, she had to be missing me too. Wasn't that *qing* also? I had Ze turn to the scene of Mother and Daughter Reunited, when Liniang—once again alive—meets her mother by accident in the Hangzhou guesthouse. Years ago, I'd considered this scene merely a respite from all the battles and political intrigue that riddled the last third of the opera. Now, when I read it, I was drawn into the world of *qing*—feminine, lyrical, and very emotional.

Madame Du and Spring Fragrance are horrified when Liniang emerges from the shadows, believing they're seeing a ghost. Liniang weeps, while the other two women shrink back in fear and disgust. Sister Stone steps into the room with a lamp. Quickly assessing the situation, she takes Madame Du's arm. *Let the lamplight aid the moon to show your daughter's features.* From the darkness of misunderstanding, Madame Du sees that the girl before her truly is her daughter and not just a ghost. She recalls the desperate sadness she felt at Liniang's death; now she must overcome her fear of an otherworldly creature. That's how deep her mother love is, but it was even more than that.

I held Ze's hand as she wrote:

> In believing that the creature before her is human, Madame Du not only acknowledges Liniang as human but also gives her back her place in the human world.

To me, this was the purest definition of mother love. For all the pain, for all the suffering, for all the disagreements between the generations, a mother gives the child her place in the world, as a daughter and as a future wife, mother, grandmother, aunt, and friend.

Ze and I wrote and wrote and wrote. By spring, after six obsessed months, I was finally worn out. I thought I'd written everything I could about love. I looked at my sister-wife. Her eyes were swollen with fatigue. Her hair hung limp and stringy. Her skin had gone very pale from our work, the sleepless nights, and keeping her husband and mother-in-law happy. I had to acknowledge her role in my project. I gently blew at her. She shivered and automatically picked up the brush.

On two blank pages at the front of the opera, I helped Ze compose an essay explaining how the commentary had come to be written, leaving out anything that would seem strange or improbable in the earthly realm.

There had once been a lovesick girl who loved *The Peony Pavilion*. This girl, Chen Tong, was betrothed to the poet Wu Ren, and at night she wrote her thoughts about love in the margins of the opera. After she died, Wu Ren married another girl. This second wife came upon the copy of the opera with her predecessor's gentle words. She was compelled to finish what her sister-wife had started, but she didn't have the second part of the opera. When her husband came home with a text of the entire opera, she got drunk with happiness. After that, whenever Wu Ren and Tan Ze passed time appreciating flowers, he teased her about the time she drank too much, fell asleep, and slept all one day and into the next. Tan Ze was diligent and thoughtful. She completed the commentary and decided to offer it to those who embrace the ideals of *qing*.

It was a simple explanation, pure and mostly true. Now all I needed was for Ren to read it.

I WAS SO accustomed to having Ze obey me that I didn't pay attention when, after Ren left the house to meet friends at a lakeshore teahouse, she pulled out my original copy of Volume One. I didn't give a moment's thought when she took it outside. I believed she was going to reread my words and think about everything I'd taught her about love. I wasn't even concerned when she crossed the zigzag bridge that led across the water to the summer pavilion in the middle of the Wu family's pond. Under no circumstances could I navigate the sharp corners of the bridge. Still, I heard no alarms. I sat on a jardinière near the edge of the pond, under the plum tree that refused to leaf, bloom, or bear fruit, and prepared myself to enjoy the serenity of the scene. It was the fifth month in the eleventh year of Emperor Kangxi's reign, and I thought how tranquil the late-spring day was, with Ze—a pretty if thin-lipped young wife—enjoying the lotus blooms on the pond's placid surface.

But when she pulled out a candle from her sleeve and lit it outside in daylight, I jumped to my feet. I paced back and forth anxiously, and the air around me swirled in response. I watched in absolute horror as she tore a page out of Volume

One and slowly and deliberately placed it in the flame. Ze smiled as the paper crinkled into blackness. When she could hold it no longer, she dropped the tiny shred that remained over the railing. The last of the paper trailed down, burning into nothing before hitting the water.

She tore out another three pages from the book. Again she set them on fire and dropped them over the edge of the pavilion. I tried to run to the bridge, but my bound feet were useless. I fell, scraping my chin and hands. I scrambled back to my feet and hurried to the zigzag bridge. I stepped onto it, made my way to the first turn, and stopped cold. I couldn't walk wide around this corner. Zigzag bridges were designed this way as a barrier to spirits like me.

"Stop!" I screamed. For a moment the whole world shivered. The carp stilled in the pond, the birds went quiet, and flowers lost their petals. But Ze didn't even look up. She methodically tore out another few pages and burned them.

I ran, tripping, scrambling, flailing, back to the shore. I shouted across the pond, sending waves against the zigzag bridge and the pavilion, spinning the air in hopes of blowing out the candle. But Ze was wily. She took the candle from the ledge and sank to her knees on the pavilion floor where she'd be sheltered from the breezes and gusts I sent her way. Once she was settled, a new even crueler idea seized her mind. She tore out all the pages from the book, crumpled them, and put them into a pile. She tipped the candle, and then hesitated for a moment, letting the wax drip down onto the wadded sheets. She glanced around, her eyes furtively scanning the shore and the surrounding halls to make sure no one was looking, and then she touched the flame to the paper.

So often we hear about this or that Manuscript Saved from Burning. This wasn't an accident or even a momentary loss of faith in the quality of the writing. This was a deliberate act committed against me by the woman I'd come to see as my sister-wife. I wailed in agony, as though I'd been set on fire myself, but she didn't care. I whirled my body and thrashed my arms until spring leaves fluttered down around us like snow. But this was the worst thing I could have done; the frenzied air fed the flames. If I'd been on the pavilion, I would have swallowed the smoke, sucking in all my words. But I wasn't there. I was on the shore, on my knees, sobbing with the knowledge that the writing that had come from my own hand and been stained by my tears had disappeared into ash, smoke, nothing.

Ze waited on the pavilion until the ashes grew cold and then she brushed them into the pond. She came back across the bridge not with worry or remorse in her heart but with a quickness to her step that made me apprehensive. I followed her back to the bedchamber. She opened the copy of *The Peony Pavilion* into which she'd transcribed my comments and added her own. With every page she turned, I trembled with fear. Would she destroy this too? She thumbed back to the first two pages that explained the "true" authorship of the commentary. In a movement as sharp, brutal, and quick as the stabbing of a knife, she ripped out those pages. This was worse than when my mother had burned my books. Soon there'd be nothing left of me on earth beyond an undotted ancestor tablet lost in a storage room. Ren would never hear me, and I would be completely forgotten.

Then Ze took the two ripped pages and hid them in the folds of another book.

"For safekeeping," she said to herself.

With that, I was saved. That is what I felt: saved.

But I was physically and spiritually wounded. In the time it took Ze to perform her wickedness, I became almost nothing. I crawled out of the room. Hand over hand I pulled myself along the covered corridor. When I felt I could go no farther, I dropped over the edge, made myself very small, and slipped under the foundation.

I skittered out two months later to find nourishment during the Festival of Hungry Ghosts. There was no roaming for me, no visit to my old home, no trek out to the countryside to see my father's lands and sample the Qian family's offerings. I had only the energy to uncoil myself from my hiding place, slither down to the pond, and eat the pellets the gardener dropped in the water for the carp. Then I scuttled back up the bank and once again hid myself in the dank darkness.

How was it that I—who'd been born into privilege, who'd been educated, who was pretty and clever—had had so many bad things happen? Was I paying for misdeeds committed in a former life? Did I go through these things to amuse the gods and goddesses? Or was it merely my fate as a woman to suffer? During the following months, I found no answers, but I began to regain my strength, find my resolve, and once again remember that I, like all women and girls, wanted—needed—to be heard.

The Good Wife

ANOTHER FIVE MONTHS PASSED. ONE DAY I HEARD people scurrying back and forth on the corridor above me: rushing to meet guests, calling out propitious greetings, and bearing fragrant offerings on trays and platters to celebrate the New Year. The clang of cymbals and the burst of firecrackers brought me back out into the daylight. My eyes burned from the harshness of the bright rays. My limbs were stiff from being folded for so many months. My clothes? They were too pathetic even to consider.

Ren's brother and wife returned from Shanxi province for the festivities. Ren's sister-in-law had sent me Tang Xianzu's edition of *The Peony Pavilion* all those years ago. I hadn't lived long enough to meet her. Now here she was, small and graceful. Her daughter, Shen—just sixteen and already married to a landowner in Hangzhou—came to visit too. Their gowns were exquisitely embroidered and personalized with scenes from antiquity to show mother and daughter's individuality and sensitivity. Their soft voices carried refinement, education, and a love of poetry. They sat with Madame Wu and talked about their excursions during the holiday. They'd visited monasteries in the hills, they'd walked in the Bamboo Forest, and they'd visited Longjing to see tea leaves harvested and cured. They made me long for the life I'd missed.

Ze entered. During the last seven months as I lay under the corridor, I hadn't heard much from her. I expected to see thin lips, a set jaw, and scornful eyes. I *wanted* her to look that way and she did, but when she opened her mouth, only charming words came out.

"Shen," Ze said, addressing Ren's niece, "you must make your husband proud with your entertaining. It's good for a wife to display her elegant taste and style of manners. I understand you're a wonderful hostess and that you make the literati feel comfortable."

"Poets often come to our home," Shen conceded. "I'd love for you and Uncle to visit one day."

"When I was a girl, my mother took me on excursions," Ze replied. "These days I prefer to stay home and make meals for my husband and mother-in-law."

"I agree, Auntie Ze, but—"

"A wife needs to be extra careful," Ze went on. "Would I try to walk across the lake after the first winter freeze? Under the full sun, there are those who will report on you. I don't want to humiliate myself or bring shame on my husband. The only safe place is within our inner chambers."

"The men who visit my husband are important," young Shen replied calmly, ignoring everything Ze had said. "It would be good for Uncle Ren to meet them."

"I have nothing against excursions," Madame Wu cut in, "if my son will benefit from new connections."

Even after two years of marriage she refused to openly

criticize her daughter-in-law, but in every gesture and look she made it plain that this wife was not a "same" in any way.

Ze sighed. "If Mother agrees, we shall come. I'll do anything to make my husband and mother-in-law happy."

What was this? When I'd been in hiding, had the lessons I'd drilled into Ze somehow taken hold?

During the weeklong visit, the four women spent their mornings together in the women's quarters. Madame Wu, inspired by her daughter-in-law and granddaughter, invited other relatives and friends to visit. Li Shu, Ren's cousin, arrived with Lin Yining, whose family had been tied to the Wus for generations. Both women were poets and writers; Lin Yining was a member of the famous Banana Garden Five Poetry Club, which had been founded by the woman writer Gu Ruopu. The members of the club, seeing no conflict between the writing brush and the embroidery needle, had taken the idea of the Four Virtues in a new direction. They believed the best exemplar of "womanly speech" was women's writing, so Li Shu and Lin Yining's visit was a time of strong incense, open windows, and active calligraphy brushes. Ze played the zither for everyone's entertainment. Ren and his brother performed all the rites to appease, feed, and clothe the Wu ancestors. Ren was affectionate with his wife in front of the others. I was not the merest glimmer of a thought for any of them. I could only watch and bear it.

And then my fortunes changed. I call it fortune, but maybe it was fate. Shen picked up *The Peony Pavilion* and began to read my words, the ones Ze had transcribed onto the pages. Shen opened her heart to the sentiments and touched on all seven ancestral emotions. She reflected on her own life and the moments of love and longing she'd experienced. She imagined herself growing old and harboring feelings of loss, pain, and regret.

"Auntie Ze, may I borrow this?" Shen asked innocently. How could my sister-wife deny her?

And so *The Peony Pavilion* left the Wu family compound and traveled to another part of Hangzhou. I didn't follow Shen, believing my project was safer in her hands than in Ze's.

AN INVITATION ARRIVED for Ren, Ze, Li Shu, and Lin Yining to visit Shen and her husband. When the palanquins came to pick them up, I held on to Ze's shoulders as she walked through the compound. When we reached her palanquin, she stepped inside and I climbed up to the roof. We were carried down Wushan Mountain, past the temple, and around the lake to Shen's home. This wasn't the haphazard roaming of a dead girl on her way to the afterworld or the frantic search for food and scraps during the Festival of Hungry Ghosts. At last I was doing the very thing that Ren had promised would happen once we were married: I was on an excursion.

We arrived at Shen's house, and for the first time I stepped over a threshold that did not belong to my father or my husband. Shen met us in a pavilion covered by a wisteria vine that she said was two hundred years old. Huge clusters of the violet flowers hung down and swelled the air with the freshness of their scent. As promised, Shen had also invited established members of the literati. Her tutor, who had a long thin beard to show his age and wisdom, was given the chair of honor. The poet Hong Sheng and his pregnant wife arrived with gifts of wine and nuts. Several married women, some of them poets, congratulated Li Shu on the recent publication of her new drama. I was most impressed by the appearance of Xu Shijun, who'd written *Reflection on the Spring*

Wave about Xiaoqing. He was known for supporting the publication of women's writings. Today he'd been invited to discuss the Buddhist sutras. My mother-in-law was right; Ren would make some interesting connections here today. He and Ze sat side by side, looking like the handsome young married couple they were.

The *Book of Rites* says that men and women should never use the same hangers, towels, or combs, let alone sit together. But here men and women—strangers—commingled with no regard to the old ways of thinking. Tea was poured. Sweetmeats were passed. I sat on the balustrade and got drunk on the vivid fragrance of the wisteria and the lines of poetry that flew back and forth across the pavilion like birds soaring in the clouds. But when Shen's tutor cleared his throat, everyone in the pavilion fell silent.

"We can recite and compose all afternoon," he said, "but I'm curious about what Shen has let us read these past few weeks." A few of the guests nodded in agreement. "Tell us"—the tutor addressed Ren—"about your commentary on *The Peony Pavilion.*"

Surprised, I slipped from my perch. A gust of wind blew through the pavilion, causing the wives to pull the silk of their gowns closer to their bodies and the men to hunch their shoulders. I had little control over the effect my actions had on the natural world, but I tried to be quiescent. When the air stilled, Shen looked at Ren, smiled, and asked, "How did you come to write the commentary?"

"Modesty doesn't allow me to admit the depth of my feelings for the opera," Ren answered, "but I haven't written about it."

"You *are* being modest," the tutor said. "We know you're an accomplished critic. You've written a lot about theater—"

"But never about *The Peony Pavilion*," Ren finished.

"How can this be?" the tutor asked. "My student returned from your home with a copy of *The Peony Pavilion*. Surely it is you who wrote your thoughts in the margins."

"I haven't written a thing," Ren swore. He glanced questioningly at his wife, but she said nothing.

"After Shen read it, she passed it to me," Hong Sheng's wife commented lightly. "I don't think a man could have had such sentiments. Those words were written by a woman. I imagined a young one like me," she added, blushing.

The tutor waved away the idea as though it were a bad smell. "What I read couldn't have been written by a girl—or a woman, for that matter," he said. "Shen allowed me to show the commentary to others here in Hangzhou. To a man, to a woman"—and here he gestured to the others sitting in the pavilion—"we've been touched by the words. We've asked ourselves, Who could have had such amazing insights about tenderness, devotion, and love? Shen invited you here to answer that question for us."

Ren touched Ze's hand. "Is this your copy of *The Peony Pavilion*? The one you worked on for so long? The one started by . . . ?"

Ze stared into the middle distance as though he were speaking to someone else.

"Who wrote these beautiful words?" Hong Sheng asked.

Even he had read my commentary? I forced myself not to move or cry out from happiness. Ren's niece had done something extraordinary. She'd taken my thoughts not just to her home and to her tutor but to one of the country's most popular writers.

Ze, meanwhile, had put a look of utter confusion on her face, as though she'd somehow forgotten who'd written in the margins.

"Was it your husband?" the tutor prompted.

"My husband?" Ze inclined her head in the way of all humble wives. "My husband?" she repeated sweetly. Then after a long pause, she said, "Yes, my husband."

Was there no end to this woman's torture of me? She had once been docile and easy to control, but she'd learned my lessons too well. She'd become too much of a good wife.

"But, Ze, I've written nothing about the opera," Ren insisted. He looked at the others and added, "I know of the commentary, and I did not write it. Please," he said to Shen. "May I see it?"

Shen nodded to a servant to get the book. Everyone waited, feeling awkward that husband and wife were in disagreement. Me? I balanced on my lily feet, trying to remain as still as possible, while inside my emotions were in a storm of fear, astonishment, and hopefulness.

The servant returned with the book and placed it in Ren's hands. The guests watched as he turned the pages. I wanted to run to him, kneel before him, and stare into his eyes as he read my words. *Do you hear me?* But I kept myself in a grip of serenity. To interfere in any way— willfully or negligently—would have destroyed the moment. He flipped the pages, stopping here and there, and then he looked up with a curious expression of longing and loss.

"I didn't write this. This commentary was begun by a woman who was to be my wife." He turned to Lin Yining and Li Shu, the two women to whom he was related. "You remember that I was to marry Chen Tong. She started this. My wife picked up the project and added her comments in the second half. Surely you who are of my blood know I speak the truth."

"If what you say is true," the tutor cut in before the

women could respond, "why is Ze's style so similar to Chen Tong's that we cannot tell them apart?"

"Perhaps only a husband—a man who has known both women well—would hear the two voices."

"Love grows only when a couple is intimate," Hong Sheng agreed. "When the moon shines on West Lake, you do not see a husband alone in his room. When a jade hairpin falls onto the pillow, you do not see a wife alone. But please explain to us how an unmarried girl could know so much about love. And how is it you would know her voice if you were never married?"

"I think Master Wu speaks the truth," one of the wives interrupted shyly, saving Ren from answering the awkward questions. "I found Chen Tong's words to be romantic. Her sister-wife has also done a good job adding her thoughts about *qing*."

A few of the other wives nodded in agreement; Ze remained oblivious.

"I'd be happy to read these thoughts even without the opera," Shen proclaimed.

Yes! This was exactly what I wanted to hear.

Then Xu Shijun snorted his skepticism. "What wife would want her name to be known outside the bedchamber? Women have no reason to get caught up in the degrading quest for fame."

This, coming from a man who was known as an educator of women, who'd shown such sympathy for Xiaoqing's plight, who'd been known to support the publication of women's writings?

"No woman—let alone two wives—would want to exhibit her private thoughts in such a public way," one of the husbands added, picking up on Xu's surprising stance. "Women have the inner chambers for that. Liberalism, women venturing out, men encouraging women to write and paint for profit, all these things led to the Cataclysm. We can be grateful that some women are returning to old traditions."

I felt sick. What had happened to the loyalists? Why didn't Li Shu and Lin Yining, both professional women writers, correct him?

"Wives need to be literate," Shen's tutor said, and for a moment I felt better. "They need to understand the highest principles so they can teach them to their sons. But, sadly, it doesn't always turn out that way." He shook his head despairingly. "We let women read and then what happens? Do they aspire to noble thoughts? No. They read plays, operas, novels, and poetry. They read for entertainment, which can only impair contemplation."

I was paralyzed by the brutality of these words. How could things have changed so dramatically in the nine years since I died? My father may not have let me venture outside the villa and my mother may not have liked me reading *The Peony Pavilion,* but these ideas were far more strident than what I'd grown up with.

"Then we can agree the mystery is solved," Shen's tutor concluded. "Wu Ren has accomplished something truly unique. He has opened a window for us on the meaning of and reasons for love. He is a great artist."

"So sensitive," one of the men said.

"*Too* sensitive," Lin Yining added, with an audible touch of bitterness.

Through it all Ze said nothing. She acted polite and sincere. She kept her eyes cast down and her hands hidden in her sleeves. No one could have accused her of being anything less than a perfect wife.

Xu Shijun took the commentary away with him and published it. He included a preface he wrote about Ren, praising him for his insights about love, marriage, and longing. And then he promoted the commentary, traveling around the country and endorsing Ren as the author of this great work. In this way, my words, thoughts, and emotions became extremely popular among members of the literati, not only in Hangzhou but across China.

Ren refused to accept any accolades.

"I did nothing," he said. "I owe everything to my wife and the girl who would have been my wife."

Always he got the same response: "You are too modest, Master Wu."

Despite his denials—perhaps because of his denials—he gained a solid reputation for what Ze and I had written. Editors sought him out to publish his poems. He was invited to gatherings of the literati. He traveled for weeks at a time as his name grew. He earned money, which made his mother and wife very happy. Eventually he learned to accept the compliments. When men said, "No woman could ever write anything this insightful," he bowed his head and said nothing. And not one of the women who'd been at Shen's home that day came to my defense. Clearly it was easier in these changing times not to speak out or celebrate another woman's accomplishment.

I should have been proud of my poet's success. In life, I might have done exactly the same as Ze, for a wife's duty is to bring honor to her husband in every way possible. But I was not of the living world, and I felt the anger, disappointment, and disillusionment of a woman whose voice has been taken away from her. For all my efforts, I felt Ren hadn't heard me at all. I was crushed.

Jealousy-Curing Soup

AFTER THE VISIT TO SHEN'S, ZE WENT HOME AND retired to her bed. She refused to light the lamps. She didn't speak. She turned down food even when it was brought to her. She stopped dressing and pinning her hair. After the things she'd done to me, I didn't do anything to help her. When Ren finally returned from his travels, she still didn't get up. They performed clouds and rain, but it was as though they'd gone back to the first days of their marriage, so disinterested was she. Ren tried to coax Ze from the room with promises of pleasant strolls in the garden or a meal with friends. Instead of accepting, she wrapped her arms around herself, shook her head no, and asked, "Am I your wife or your concubine?"

He stared at her propped up in the bed, her face blotchy, her skin sallow, her elbows and collarbones protruding from her seemingly fleshless body. "You're my wife," he answered. "Of course I love you."

When she burst into tears, Ren did the only sensible thing

a man could do. He sent for Doctor Zhao, who pronounced, "Your wife has had a relapse of her lovesickness."

But Ze couldn't be lovesick. She'd stopped eating, true, but she wasn't a maiden. She wasn't a virgin. She was an eighteen-year-old married woman.

"I'm not lovesick. I have no love in me!" Ze cried from the bed.

The two men regarded each other soberly and then looked back down at the bedridden woman.

"Husband, stay away from me. I've become an incubus, a vampire, an evil temptress. If you sleep with me, I'll pierce your feet with an awl. I'll suck the blood from your bones to feed the emptiness inside me."

This was one way of getting out of doing clouds and rain, but I no longer had a desire to interfere.

"Perhaps your wife is afraid for her position," Doctor Zhao reasoned. "Have you been unhappy with her?"

"Be careful," Ze warned the doctor, "or the next time you fall asleep I'll use a piece of silk to snap your neck."

Doctor Zhao ignored the outburst. "Does Madame Wu criticize too freely? Even an offhand remark by a mother-in-law can make a young wife anxious and unsure."

When Ren assured the doctor this wasn't possible, he prescribed a diet of pig's trotters to help restore Ze's *qi*.

She was not about to eat something so lowly.

Next the doctor ordered the cook to make a soup of pig's liver to help strengthen Ze's corresponding organ. Soon he was trying every organ of the pig to fortify his patient. None of them worked.

"You were supposed to marry someone else," the doctor said diffidently to Ren. "Perhaps she's come back to claim her rightful place."

Ren dismissed the idea. "I don't believe in ghosts."

The doctor jutted his jaw and went back to listening to Ze's pulses. He asked about her dreams, which she said were filled with vile demons and horrific sights.

"I see a woman with little flesh on her bones," Ze recounted. "Her longing reaches out to me, wraps itself around my neck, and takes away my breath."

"I have not been subtle enough in my diagnosis," Doctor Zhao now admitted to Ren. "Your wife has a different kind of lovesickness from what I originally thought. She has a bad case of that most common of all feminine disorders: too much vinegar."

This word sounded exactly the same as *jealousy* in our dialect.

"But she has no reason to be jealous," Ren objected.

To which Ze pointed a thin finger at him. "You don't love me."

"What about your first wife?" Doctor Zhao circled back.

"Ze is my first wife."

That stung. Could Ren have forgotten me so completely?

"Perhaps you forget that I took care of Chen Tong as she died," the doctor reminded him. "Tradition would tell you that she was your first wife.. Were your Eight Characters not matched? Were bride-price gifts not sent to her family home?"

"Your thinking is very old-fashioned," Ren said disapprovingly. "This is not a ghost infestation. Ghosts only exist to scare children into obeying their parents, give young men an excuse to explain away bad behavior with low women, or make girls languish over something they can never have."

How could he say these things? Had he forgotten how we'd talked about *The Peony Pavilion*? Had he forgotten Liniang was a ghost? If he didn't believe in ghosts, how was he ever going to hear me? His words were so terrible and cruel that I decided he could only be saying them to comfort and reassure my sister-wife.

"Many wives go on hunger strikes because they're jealous and ill-tempered," the doctor suggested, trying a different approach. "They try to push their anger onto others by making them suffer with guilt and remorse."

The doctor prescribed a bowl of jealousy-curing soup made from oriole broth. In one of the plays about Xiaoqing, this remedy had been used on the jealous wife. It had reduced the wife's emotional disease by half but left her pockmarked.

"You would ruin me?" Ze pushed away the soup. "What about my skin?"

The doctor put a hand on Ren's arm and spoke loudly enough for Ze to hear. "Just remember that jealousy is one of the seven reasons for divorce."

If I'd known more, I would have tried to do something. But if I'd known more, maybe I wouldn't have died myself. So I stayed up in the rafters when the doctor tried to expel the excess fire from Ze's belly with a less scarring remedy by flushing her bowels with a tonic of wild celery. Chamber pot after chamber pot was filled and taken away, but Ze didn't regain her strength.

The diviner arrived next. I stayed out of his way as he brandished a sword wet with blood over Ze's bed. I covered my ears when he shouted incantations. But no evil spirits haunted Ze, so his efforts produced no results.

Six weeks went by. Ze worsened. When she woke in the morning, she threw up. When she moved her head during the day, she threw up. When her mother-in-law came with clear soups, Ze turned her face away and threw up.

Madame Wu called for the doctor and the diviner to come together.

"We've had a lot of bother in our household over my daughter-in-law," she said cryptically. "But perhaps what is happening is only natural. Maybe you should check her again and this time consider that she is a wife and my son is a husband."

The doctor looked at Ze's tongue. He peered into her eyes. He listened yet again to the various pulses in her wrist. The diviner moved a limp orchid from one table to another. He consulted Ze's and Ren's horoscopes. He wrote a question on a piece of paper, burned it in a censer so the words would travel to Heaven, and consulted the ashes to receive his answer. Then the two men bent their heads together to confer and refine their diagnosis.

"Mother is very wise," Doctor Zhao declared at last. "Women are always the first to recognize the symptoms. Your daughter-in-law has the best type of lovesickness: She's pregnant."

After so many weeks of this and that diagnosis I didn't believe it, but I was intrigued. Could it be true? Despite the presence of the others in the room, I dropped onto Ze's bed. I sat astride her and peered into her belly. I saw the tiny speck of life, a soul waiting to be reborn. I should have spotted it earlier, but I was young and unknowing about these things. It was a son.

"It's not mine!" Ze shrieked. "Get it out!"

Doctor Zhao and the diviner laughed good-naturedly.

"We hear this often from young wives," Doctor Zhao said. "Madame Wu, please show her the confidential women's book again and explain what has happened. Mistress Ze, rest, avoid gossip, and eat the proper foods. Stay away from water chestnuts, musk deer, lamb, and rabbit meat."

"And make sure you wear a daylily pinned to your waist," the diviner added. "It will help relieve the pains of childbirth and ensure the birth of a healthy son."

With much jubilation, Ren, his mother, and the servants discussed the possibilities. "A son is best," Ren said, "but I would welcome a daughter." This was the kind of man he was. This is why I loved him still.

But Ze was not happy about the baby, and her condition did not improve. She had no opportunity to encounter a musk deer, and the cook completely banned rabbit meat and lamb from the household, but Ze sneaked into the kitchen late at night to nibble on water chestnuts. She crumpled the flower at her waist and threw it on the floor. She refused to feed the child growing inside her. She stayed up late writing that the baby was not hers on pieces of paper. Every time she saw her husband, she wailed, "You don't love me!" And when she wasn't crying, accusing, or turning away food, she was throwing up. Soon enough we could all see pink pieces of stomach lining in the bowls the servants took away from the room. Everyone understood the seriousness of the situation. No one wants a loved one to die, but for a woman to die pregnant or in childbirth consigned her to a terrible fate: deportation to the Blood-Gathering Lake.

The Autumn Moon Festival came and went. Ze stopped taking in even water. Mirrors and a sieve were hung in the room. Fortunately, neither of these things was pointed up to where I kept my vigil.

"Nothing is wrong with her," Commissioner Tan announced, when he came to visit. "She doesn't want a baby in her womb because she has nothing in her heart."

"She's your daughter," Ren reminded the man, "and she's my wife."

The commissioner was unimpressed and left with advice and a warning: "When the baby comes, keep it away from her. That will be safest. Ze does not like to see eyes on anyone but herself."

Ze had no peace. She seemed terrified by day—shivering,

crying, hiding her eyes. The nights gave her no respite. She tossed from side to side, cried out, and woke up in pools of sweat. The diviner made a special altar of peach wood and set incense and candles on it. He wrote a charm, burned it, and then mixed the ashes with water from a spring. With his sword in his right hand and the cup of watery ashes in his left, he prayed: "Purge this dwelling of all evil lurking here." He dipped a sprig of willow in the cup and sprinkled it to the four compass points. To reinforce the spell, he filled his mouth with the ashy water and spurted it onto the wall above Ze's bed. "Cleanse this woman's mind of the spirits of darkness."

But her nightmares did not cease and the effects grew worse. Dreams were something I knew about and I thought I could help, but when I went abroad with Ze in this way I found nothing frightening or unusual. She wasn't being hunted or harmed in her dreams at all, which mystified me greatly.

The first snows came and the doctor visited yet again. "This is not a good child your wife carries," he told Ren. "He is hanging on to your wife's intestines and won't let go. If you give me permission, I'll use acupuncture to get rid of it."

On the surface, this seemed like a logical explanation and a practical solution, but I could see the baby. He was not an evil spirit; he was just trying to survive.

"What if it's a son?" Ren asked.

The doctor wavered. When he saw Ze's writing scraps scattered about the room, he said sadly, "Every day I see it and I don't know what to do. Literacy is a grave threat to the female sex. Too often I've seen the health and happiness of young women fade because they will not give up their brush and ink. I'm afraid"—and here he put a comforting hand on Ren's arm—"that we will look back and blame the lovesickness caused by writing for your wife's death."

I thought, not for the first time, that Doctor Zhao knew very little about women or love.

AT THIS MOST grim moment, as the Wu household settled in for the deathwatch, my adopted brother arrived. Bao's appearance shocked us all, for we were all so focused on someone who was literally wasting away while he was abundantly fat. In his pudgy fingers he held the poems I'd written when I was dying and hidden in the book on dam building in my father's library. How had Bao found them? Looking at his soft white hands, he did not seem the type to be commissioning or designing a dam. His little eyes seemed too narrow and close together to find joy in reading out of intellectual curiosity, let alone pleasure. Something else had caused him to open that particular volume.

When he demanded money for my simple poems and I saw that this was no gift from one brother-in-law to another, I understood that things could not be well in the Chen Family Villa. I suppose I expected this. They couldn't ignore my death and not expect some consequences. Bao had to be dismantling the library and had come across the poems. But where was my father? He'd sell his concubines before selling his library. Was he ailing? Had he died? Wouldn't I have heard something if he had? Should I rush back to my natal home?

But *this* was my home now. Ren was my husband and Ze was my sister-wife. She was sick, right here, right now. Oh, yes, I'd been angry with her at times. I'd even hated her on occasion. But I would be at her side when she died. I would welcome her to the afterworld and thank her for being my sister-wife.

Ren paid my adopted brother. Things were so bad with Ze that he didn't even look at the poems. He selected a book from his library, tucked the papers inside, placed the volume back on the shelf, and returned to the bedchamber.

We went back to waiting. Madame Wu brought tea and snacks for her son, which he left mostly untouched. Commissioner Tan and his wife came again to see their daughter. Their harshness faded as they realized Ze was actually dying.

"Tell us what the matter is," Madame Tan begged her daughter.

Ze's body relaxed and color flushed her cheeks when she heard her mother's voice.

Encouraged, Madame Tan tried again. "We can take you away from here. Come home and sleep in your own bed. You'll feel better with us."

At these words, Ze stiffened. She pursed her lips and looked away. Seeing this, tears streamed down Madame Tan's face.

The commissioner stared at his intractable daughter.

"You've been stubborn forever," he observed, "but I always go back to the night we saw *The Peony Pavilion* as the moment your emotions congealed to stone. Since that time, you've never listened to a single warning or piece of advice I've given you. Now you pay the price. We will remember you in our offerings."

As Madame Wu showed the Tans back to their palanquins, the sick girl moaned the ailments she would not tell her parents. "I feel a floating numbness. My hands and feet will not move. My eyes are too dry for tears. My spirit is frozen by the cold."

Every few minutes she opened her eyes, stared up at the ceiling, shivered, and closed them again. All the while, Ren held her hand and spoke softly to her.

Later that night when all was darkness and I had no fear of reflection from the mirrors, I let myself down into the room. I blew open the curtains so that moonlight illuminated the bedchamber. Ren slept in a chair. I touched his hair and felt him shiver. I sat with my sister-wife and felt the cold piercing her bones. Everyone else in the household was wandering in their dreams, so I stayed at Ze's side to protect and comfort her. I placed my hand over her heart. I felt it slow, skip beats, race, and slow again. Just as darkness began to give way to pink, the air in the room shifted. Tan Ze's bones crumbled, her soul dissolved, and just like that she was flying across the sky.

The Blood-Gathering Lake

ZE'S SOUL BROKE INTO THREE. ONE PART BEGAN ITS journey to the afterworld, one part waited to enter its coffin, and the last part roamed until it was time to be placed in its ancestor tablet. Her corpse submitted humbly to the rites that had to be performed. The doctor cut the baby from Ze's stomach and threw it away, so it wouldn't go with her to the Blood-Gathering Lake and would have a chance at rebirth. Then her emaciated body was washed and dressed. Ren remained at her side, refusing to take his eyes off her pale face and still-red lips, seemingly waiting for her to waken. I waited in the bedchamber for the roaming part of her soul to appear. I was convinced she would be relieved to see someone familiar. I couldn't have been more wrong. The moment she saw me, her lips drew back and she bared her teeth.

"You! I knew I would see you!"

"Everything will be fine. I'm here to help you—"

"Help me? You killed me!"

"You're confused," I said soothingly. I too had been disoriented upon my death. She was lucky I was here to ease her mind.

"I knew even before my marriage that you would try to harm me," she went on, in a no-less-furious tone. "You were there on my marriage day, weren't you?" When I nodded, she said, "I should have smeared your tombstone with the blood of a black dog."

This was the worst thing a person could do to a dead soul, since this type of blood was believed to be as odious as a woman's monthly excretions. If she'd done that, I would have been set on a path to kill my natal family. I was surprised by her bitterness, but she wasn't done.

"You haunted me from the very beginning," she continued. "I heard you crying in the winds of stormy nights."

"I thought I made you happy—"

"No! You made me read that opera. Then you made me write about it. You made me imitate you in everything I did, until finally there was nothing left of me. You died from the opera, and then you made me copy you copying Liniang."

"I only wanted Ren to love you more. Couldn't you tell?"

This calmed her somewhat. Then she looked at her fingernails. They'd already turned black. The harsh reality of her situation crushed her remaining anger.

"I tried to protect myself, but what chance did I have against you?" she asked pitifully.

So many times I'd said the reverse of this to myself: My sister-wife didn't have a chance against me.

"I thought I could make him love me if he read the commentary and believed the work to be all mine," she continued, reproach creeping back into her voice. "I didn't want him reading about your lovesickness. I didn't want him believing I'd continued your project as a way of honoring the 'first' wife. *I* was the first wife. Didn't you hear my husband? You two were never married. He cares nothing for you."

She was ruthless in death.

"We are a match made in Heaven," I said, and I still believed it to be true. "But he loved you too."

"You were sick with cleverness. You made me cold, kept me in darkness, and hunted me in my dreams. You made me careless with my meals and careless with my rest—"

That this line came from *The Peony Pavilion* didn't reassure me, because I *had* made her careless.

"The only way I could escape you was in the safety of the pavilion on the pond," she went on.

"The zigzag bridge."

"Yes!" Her lips drew back again, showing her dead-white teeth. "I burned your copy of *The Peony Pavilion* to exorcise you from my life. I thought I'd succeeded, but you never left."

"I couldn't leave, not after what you did next. You let people believe our husband wrote the commentary."

"What better way to show my devotion? What better way to prove I was an ideal wife?"

She was right, of course.

"But what about me?" I asked. "You tried to make me disappear. How could you do that when we're sister-wives?"

Ze laughed at the stupidity of my question. "Men are the flowering of pure *yang*, but ghosts like you are all that is deathly and sick in *yin*. I tried to fight you, but your constant interference killed me. Go away. I have no need or want of your friendship. We are not friends. And we are not sister-wives. *I* will be remembered. *You* will be forgotten. I made sure of that."

"By hiding the missing pages that describe the true authorship—"

"Everything you made me write was a lie."

"But I gave you credit. Almost everything was about you—"

"I didn't pick up the commentary out of a desire to continue your work. I did not write from the heart. You made your obsession my obsession. You were a ghost and you wouldn't admit what you'd done, so I tore those pages out of the book. Ren will never find them."

I tried again to make her see the truth. "I wanted you to be happy—"

"So you used my body."

"I was happy when you got pregnant—"

"That child was not mine!"

"Of course he was yours."

"No! You brought Ren to my bed night after night against my will. You made me do things. . . ." She shivered with anger and disgust. "And then you put that baby inside me."

"You're wrong. I didn't put him there. I only watched that he'd be safe—"

"*Ha!* You killed me and the baby too."

"I didn't . . ."

But what was the use of denying her accusations when so many of them were true? I'd kept her up all night, first with her husband and then with writing. I'd made her room cold, closed her in the dark to protect my sensitive eyes, and sent breezes with her everywhere she went. When I forced her to work on my project, I'd kept her from joining her husband and mother-in-law for meals. Then, when she retired to her room after burning my original work and giving all credit to Ren, I hadn't encouraged her to eat because I was so dispirited. I'd been fully aware of all this even as I'd denied what I was seeing and doing to myself. I started to feel sick with the truth. What had I done?

She pulled back her lips, once again revealing her ugly essence. I turned my eyes away.

"You killed me," she proclaimed. "You hid in the rafters where you thought no one could see you, but I saw you."

"How could you?" All my earlier confidence was gone. Now I was the one who sounded pitiful.

"I was dying! I saw you. I tried to close my eyes to you, but every time I opened them you were there, staring at me with your dead eyes. And then you came down and put your hand on my heart."

Waaa! Had I truly played a part in her death? Had my obsession for my project made me so blind that first I had died and now I had killed my sister-wife?

Seeing the horror of understanding on my face, she smiled triumphantly. "You killed me, but I've won. You seem to have forgotten the deepest message of *The Peony Pavilion.* It's a story about fulfilling love through death, which is exactly what I've done. Ren will remember me and he will forget about the foolish unmarried girl in her inner rooms. You will waste away to nothing. Your project will be forgotten and no one—*no one*—will remember you."

Without another word, she turned away from me, left the room, and went back to roaming.

FORTY-NINE DAYS later, Ze's father came to dot her ancestor tablet, which was then set in the Wu family's ancestral hall. Since she'd died pregnant and married, one part of her soul was sealed inside her coffin, which would remain exposed to the elements until her husband's death, when the family would be reconstituted through simultaneous burial, as was proper. The last part of her soul was dragged to the Blood-Gathering Lake, which was reputed to be so wide that it would take 840,000 days to cross it, where she would experience 120 kinds of torture, where she would be required each day to drink blood or be thrashed with iron rods. This was her eternity, unless her family bought her freedom through proper worship, offerings of food to monks and gods, and prayers and bribes to the bureaucrats who governed the hells. Only then might a boat carry her from the lake of anguish to the bank where she might become an ancestor or be reborn into a blissful land.

As for me, I realized that if I'd helped Tan Ze and her baby die—knowingly or not—then I no longer had moral thoughts: no empathy, no shame, no sense of right and wrong. I thought I'd been very clever and even helpful, but Ze was right. I was a ghost of the worst sort.

PART III

Under the Plum Tree

Exile

MAMA USED TO SAY THAT GHOSTS AND SPIRITS WEREN'T bad by nature. If a ghost had a place to belong, it would not become evil. But many ghosts are roused to action by the desire to retaliate. Even a small creature like a cicada can bring about savage vengeance against those who have harmed it. I hadn't thought I wanted to hurt Ze, and yet if what she said was true I'd done just that. Filled with a desire for self-punishment and terrified that I might do something deadly to my husband by accident, I banished myself from Ren's home. In the earthly realm, I was twenty-five and I'd given up. I wasted away to almost nothing, just as Ze predicted.

Exile . . .

Not knowing where to go, I made my way around the lake to the Chen Family Villa. The house, to my surprise, was more beautiful than ever. Bao had added furniture, porcelains, and jade carvings to every room. Shimmering new silk tapestries hung on the walls. But as magnificent as it all was, a disturbing quiet infused everything. Far fewer fingers lived here now. My father was still in the capital. Two of his brothers had died. My grandfather's concubines had also died. Broom, Lotus, and some of my other cousins had married out. With fewer Chen family members in the compound, servants had been sent away. The villa and the grounds screamed beauty, abundance, and great wealth, but they were poor in the sounds of children, joy, and miracles.

Into the eerie silence came the haunting sound of a zither. I found Orchid, now fourteen, playing for my mother and the aunts in the Lotus-Blooming Hall. She was a pretty girl, and I had a momentary flash of pride that her bound feet had turned out so well. Sitting next to her was my mother. Only nine years had passed, but in that time her hair had gone gray. Deep sadness filled her eyes. When I kissed her, she shivered and rattled the locks hidden in the folds of her gown.

Bao's wife's face was pinched with the sadness of infertility. She hadn't been sold, but her husband had taken in two concubines. They too were infertile. The three women sat together, not fighting but mourning what they could not have. I didn't see Bao, but I had to consider that maybe I'd been wrong about him. He'd been perfectly within his rights to sell off these women, but he hadn't. These past years, I'd expected—wanted?—this adopted stranger to ruin my family through bad management, gambling, and opium. I'd envisioned the estate dwindling and Bao selling off my father's book, tea, rock, antiques, and incense collections. Instead, these things had been built up and enhanced. Bao had even replaced the volumes my mother had burned. I hated to admit it, but Bao had probably found my poems when he'd read that book on dam building. But why had he sold them? No one needed the money.

I went to the ancestral hall. Grandmother and Grandfather's ancestral portraits still hung above the altar. I was a ghost, but I paid obeisance to them. Then I bowed to the ancestor tablets for my other relatives. After that, I went to the storage room where my tablet had been hidden. I couldn't go in, because the corner was too sharp, but I saw a dusty edge of it on a shelf covered with mouse and rat droppings. Even though my mother mourned for me, I'd been forgotten by the rest of the family. I wished none of them ill, but there was nothing for me here.

Exile . . .

I had to go somewhere. The only other place I'd been was to Gudang Village during the Festival of Hungry Ghosts. The Qian family had fed me for two years. Maybe I could find a place with them.

I set out as night covered the land. Fireflies flitted about me, lighting my way. It was a long walk when I wasn't driven by hunger and had only my regrets for company. My feet hurt, my legs ached, and my eyes burned when dawn broke. I reached the Qian home as the sun hit the apex of the sky. The two eldest daughters worked outside under an awning, tending trays of silkworms that ate their way through freshly cut mulberry leaves. The next two daughters were in an open shed with another dozen or so girls, their hands in steaming water, washing the cocoons, and pulling and spinning the silk floss into thread. Madame Qian was inside the house, preparing lunch. Yi, the child I'd first seen as a baby in her mother's arms, was now three years old. She was a sickly little thing, thin and pale. She rested on a low wooden platform in the main room, where her mother could watch her. I sat down next to her. When she wiggled, I put a hand on her ankle. She giggled softly. It didn't seem possible that she would reach seven.

Master Qian, although it was hard for me to think of this farmer as a master of anything, came in from the mulberry grove and everyone sat down to lunch. No one gave anything to Yi; she was just another mouth to feed until she died.

As soon as the meal was done, Master Qian motioned to his oldest daughters. "Hungry worms do not produce silk," he snapped at them. With that, they got up and went back outside on their big flapping feet to resume their work. Madame Qian poured tea for her husband, cleared the table, and carried Yi back to the platform. She pulled out a basket and handed the child a piece of cloth with a needle and thread tucked into it.

"She doesn't need to learn to embroider," the girl's father said scornfully. "She needs to get strong so she can help me."

"She's not going to be the daughter you need and want," Madame Qian said. "I'm afraid she takes after her mother."

"You were cheap, but you've cost me a lot. Only girls—"

"And I'm no help with the worms," she finished for him.

I shivered in revulsion. It had to be hard for a woman of such refinement to have fallen so low.

"With Yi this way, I won't be able to marry her out," he complained. "What family would want a useless wife? We should have left her to die when she was born."

He took a last noisy sip of tea and left. Once he was gone, Madame Qian gave her full attention to Yi, showing her the stitches to make a bat, the symbol of happiness.

"My parents were once members of the gentry," Madame Qian said dreamily to her daughter. "We lost everything in the Cataclysm. For years we wandered as beggars. I was thirteen when we came to this village. Your baba's parents bought me out of pity. They didn't have much, but don't you see? If I'd lived so long on the road, I had to be strong. I was strong."

My despair grew deeper. Did every girl suffer?

"My bound feet kept me from working at your father's side, but I've brought him prosperity in other ways," Madame Qian continued. "I can make bedding, shoes, and clothes so fine they can be sold in Hangzhou. Your sisters will do physical labor their entire lives. I can only guess at the pain in their hearts, but I can do nothing for them."

She bowed her head. Tears of shame dripped from her eyes and stained her plain cotton skirt. I couldn't swallow any more sorrow. I slunk out of the house and away from the farm, embarrassed for my weakness and afraid of the harm I might do this family even unwittingly, when they were so miserable already.

Exile . . .

I sat down by the side of the road. Where could I go? For the first time in years I thought of my old servant, Willow, but there was no way for me to find her. Even if I could, what could she do for me? I had thought her a friend, but in our last conversation together I'd seen that she'd never felt the same about me. I hadn't had a single friend in life, and in death I'd hoped to be included in the circle of lovesick maidens. I'd tried to be a good sister-wife to Ze, and I'd failed there. My coming here was a mistake too. I was not part of the Qians nor were they a part of me. Maybe I'd been in exile my whole life . . . and death.

I had to find somewhere to live where I'd be assured I wouldn't hurt anyone. I returned to Hangzhou. For several days, I scouted along the lakeshore, but too many other spirits already inhabited the caves or had found comfort behind rocks or nestled in the roots of trees. I wandered aimlessly. When I came to the Xiling Bridge, I crossed over it and onto Solitary Island, where Xiaoqing had been banished long ago to keep her safe from a jealous wife. It was quiet and remote, a perfect place for me to languish in my sorrow and regret. I searched until I found Xiaoqing's tomb, hidden between the lake and the small pond where she'd contemplated her frail reflection. I curled in the tomb's doorway, listened to the orioles sing to one another in the canopy of trees above me, and brooded about what I'd done to an innocent wife.

OVER THE NEXT two years, however, I was rarely alone. Almost daily, women and girls left their chambers and came to Xiaoqing's tomb to consecrate the spot with wine, read poems, and talk about love, sadness, and regret. It seemed I was just one of hundreds of women and young girls who suffered for love, who thought about love, who desired love. They weren't as deeply affected as the lovesick maidens—like Xiaoqing or me—who'd died from too much *qing,* but they longed to be. They each wanted the love of a man or fretted about the love of a man.

Then one day the members of the Banana Garden Five came to the tomb to pay their respects. By every measure, they were famous. These five women liked to gather together, go on excursions, and write poetry. They didn't burn their manuscripts out of self-doubt or humility. They were published—not by their families as mementos but by commercial publishers who sold their works throughout the country.

For the first time in two years, curiosity drove me from the security of Xiaoqing's tomb. I followed the women as they strolled Solitary Island's tree-lined pathways, visited the temples, and sat together in a pavilion to sip tea and eat sunflower seeds. When they boarded their pleasure boat, I joined them, sitting on the deck as it sliced through the water. They laughed and drank wine. They engaged in games, challenging one another to compose poems under the open sky in broad daylight. When their outing was over and they went back to their homes, I stayed with the boat. The next time they gathered to meet on the lake, I was there, cheating my punishment, ready to go anywhere they wanted.

As a living girl, I'd longed to travel and go on excursions. When I first died, I'd roamed blindly. Now I spent lazy days sitting on the edge of the pleasure boat, listening and learning as we drifted past villas, inns, restaurants, and singsong houses. It seemed the whole world came to my home city. I heard different dialects and saw all manner of people: merchants who paraded their wealth; artists who were immediately recognizable by their brushes, inks, and rolls of silk and paper; and farmers, butchers, and fishermen who came to sell their wares. Everyone wanted either to sell or to buy something: Courtesans with tiny feet and lilting voices sold their private parts to visiting shipbuilders, professional women artists sold their paintings and poems to discriminating collectors, women archers sold their skills as entertainment to salt purveyors, and artisans sold scissors and umbrellas to the wives and daughters of fine families who'd come to my beautiful town for leisure, amusement, and, most of all, fun. West Lake was where legend, myths, and everyday life met, where the natural beauty and quiet of bamboo groves and towering camphor trees smacked up against noisy civilization, where men from the outer realm and women released from the inner realm conversed without a gate, a wall, a screen, or a veil to separate them.

On warm days, many pleasure boats—brightly painted with embroidered tents on their decks—plied the waters. I saw women lavishly dressed in silk gauze gowns with long trains, gold and jade earrings, and kingfisher-feather head-dresses. They stared at us. The women on my boat were not of low repute, new money, or too much money. They were from the gentry, like my mother and aunts. They were great ladies, who shared paper, brushes, and ink. They were modest in what they wore and how they dressed their hair. They inhaled and exhaled words, which floated on the air like willow floss.

The philosophers tell us to detach from the worldly. I couldn't fix all the wrongs I had done, but the Banana Garden Five helped me to understand that all the longing I felt and all the suffering I'd experienced had ultimately released me from everything material and mundane. But while I was relieved of my burdens, a kind of desperation tinged the Banana Garden Five's activities. The Manchus had disbanded most men's poetry clubs, but they hadn't found the women's groups yet.

"We've got to keep meeting," Gu Yurei, niece of the brilliant Gu Ruopu, said urgently one day as she poured tea for the others.

"We remain loyalists, but to the Manchus we're insignificant," Lin Yining responded, unconcerned. "We're only women. We can't bring down the government."

"But, Sister, we are a worry," Gu Yurei insisted. "My aunt used to say that the freedom of women writers had more to do with the freedom of their thoughts than the physical location of their bodies."

"And she inspired all of us," Lin Yining agreed, gesturing to the others around her, who were unlike the women in my family—who followed the lead dog with smiling faces because they had to—and unlike the lovesick maidens, who'd been brought together by obsession followed by early death. The members of the Banana Garden Five had come together by choice. They didn't write about butterflies and flowers—those things they could see in their gardens. They wrote about literature, art, politics, and what they saw and did on the outside. Through their written words, they encouraged their husbands and sons to persevere under the new regime. They bravely explored deep emotions, even when they were grim: the loneliness of a fisherman on a lake, the melancholy of a mother separated from her daughter, the despair of a girl living on the street. They had formed a sisterhood of friendship and writing, and then they built an intellectual and emotional community of women throughout the country through reading. In looking for solace, dignity, and recognition, they brought their quest to other women who still lived behind locked gates or were being pushed back inside by the Manchus.

"Why should having children and tending to our homes keep us from thinking about public affairs and the future of our country?" Lin Yining continued. "Marrying and having sons are not a woman's only way to have dignity."

"You say this because you wish you were a man," Gu Yurei teased.

"I was educated by my mother, so how could I wish this?" Yining countered, her fingers trailing in the water, sending quiet ripples across the lake. "And I'm a wife and mother myself. But if I'd been a man, I would have greater success."

"If we were men," one of the others cut in, "the Manchus might not let us write or publish at all."

"All I'm saying is that I also give birth to sons through my writing," Yining went on.

I thought about my failed project. Had it not been like a child I was trying to bring into the world to tie me to Ren? I shuddered at this. My love for him had never gone away but only changed, growing deeper like wine fermenting or pickles curing. It bore into me with the pervasiveness of water working its way to the center of a mountain.

Instead of letting my emotions continue to torture me, I began to use them for good. When someone got stuck composing a poem, I helped her. When Lin Yining began a line like, "I feel a kinship with . . ." I finished with "mists and fog." New moons could be grand up there beyond the clouds, but they could also move us to melancholy and remind us of our impermanence. Whenever we sank into sorrow, these poets remembered the voices of the lost and desperate women who'd written on walls during the Cataclysm.

"My heart is empty and my life has no value anymore. Each moment a thousand tears," Gu Yurie recited one day, recalling the poem that seemed to speak the sadness of my existence.

The members of the Banana Garden Five could joke about their relative unimportance to the Manchus, but they were clearly disrupting the moral order. How long would it be before the Manchus, and those who followed them, sent all women—from those who floated on the lake on a warm spring day to those who merely read to expand their hearts—permanently back to their inner chambers?

Mother Love

FOR THREE YEARS I WAS AFRAID TO SEE REN. BUT AS this year's Double Seven Festival approached, I found myself thinking about the Weaving Maid and the Cowherd and how all the magpies on earth formed a bridge so they could meet on this one special night. Couldn't Ren and I also have one night to reunite? I'd learned enough by now; I wouldn't hurt him. So two days before the Double Seven Festival—and the twelfth anniversary of Ren's and my first meeting—I left Solitary Island and glided up Wushan Mountain until I came to his home.

I waited outside the gate until he left the compound. To me, he was the same: man-beautiful. I relished his scent, his voice, his very presence. I attached myself to his shoulders so I could be pulled along as he went to a bookshop and later gave a talk to a gathering of men. Afterward, he was restless and unsettled. He spent the rest of the night drinking and gambling. I followed him when he went home. His bedchamber had been left untouched since Ze's death. Her zither rested in its stand in the corner. Her perfumes, brushes, and hair ornaments collected dust and spider silks on her dressing table. He stayed up late, pulling her books from the shelves and opening them. Was he thinking of her or me or both of us?

Ren slept until after lunch, woke up, and repeated the exact same pattern as the day before. Then, on Double Seven, on what would have been my twenty-eighth birthday, Ren spent the afternoon with his mother. She read poetry to him. She poured his tea. She patted his sad face. By now I was sure he was remembering me.

After his mother went to bed, Ren once again looked through Ze's books. I went back to my old place in the rafters, where my feelings of regret and remorse about Ren, Ze, and my own life and death rippled through me in wave upon wave. I'd failed in so many ways, and now seeing my poet like this—opening one book after another, his mind far into the past—hurt beyond measure. I closed my eyes against the pain of what I was seeing. I put my hands over my ears, which had never adapted to the sounds of the earthly realm, but I could still hear pages turning, each one a reminder of what Ren and I had lost.

When he moaned below me, the sound tore through my body. I opened my eyes and looked down. Ren sat on the edge of the bed, holding two sheets of paper, the book that they'd come from open next to him. I slipped straight down and came to rest at his side. He held the two pages Ze had so cruelly ripped out of our shared copy of *The Peony Pavilion* that described how our commentary had been written. Here was the proof Ren needed to know that Ze and I had worked together. I was delighted, but Ren didn't look happy or relieved in any way.

He folded the papers, tucked them into his tunic, and set out into the night with me hanging on to his shoulders. He pushed his way through the streets until he came to a house

I didn't know. He was let in and led to a room filled with men, who were waiting for their wives to finish their Double Seven customs and games so they could sit down to their banquet. The air was thick with smoke and incense, and at first Ren didn't recognize anyone. Then Hong Sheng, who had been at Ren's niece's house the day I had gone on my first ever excursion, stood and came forward. Seeing that Ren was not there for the festivities, Hong Sheng picked up an oil lamp with one hand and two cups and a bottle of wine with the other, and the two men walked outside to a pavilion on the property and sat down.

"Have you eaten?" Hong Sheng asked.

Ren politely declined and then began, "I have come—"

"Baba!"

A little girl, still so young her feet hadn't been bound, came running into the pavilion and climbed into Hong Sheng's lap. I remembered seeing the poet's wife pregnant with this child.

"Shouldn't you be with your mother and the others?" Hong Sheng asked.

The child squirmed her indifference to the games of the inner chamber. She reached up, put her arms around her father's neck, and buried her face in his shoulder.

"All right then," Hong Sheng said, "you can stay, but you must be quiet, and when your mother comes you'll have to go back with her. No arguments. No tears."

How many times had I sought refuge with my father? Was this girl as wrong about her father as I'd been about mine?

"Do you remember a few years ago when we visited my cousin's home?" Ren asked. "Cousin Shen and the others had read the commentary on *The Peony Pavilion*."

"I'd read it too. I was very impressed by your work. I still am."

"That day I told everyone I hadn't written it."

"You remain modest. It's a good quality."

Ren pulled out the two sheets of paper and gave them to his friend. The poet tilted them to the lamplight and read. When he was done, he looked up, and asked, "Is this true?"

"It was always true, but no one would listen." Ren hung his head. "Now I want to tell everyone."

"What good will it do if you change the story now?" Hong Sheng asked. "You will appear a fool at best and a man who is trying to promote women's fame at worst."

Hong Sheng was right. What I thought was a wonderful discovery locked Ren further into sadness and despair. He picked up the bottle of wine, poured himself a cup, and drained it. When he grabbed the bottle again, Hong Sheng took it from his hand.

"My friend," he said, "you need to get back to your own work. You need to forget about your suffering and the tragedies of that girl and your wife."

If Ren forgot, what would happen to me? But keeping us in his heart was torturing him. I'd seen this in his loneliness, his drinking, and in the way he handled Ze's books so lovingly. Ren had to get over his grief and forget about us. I left the pavilion, wondering if I would ever see him again.

A sliver of moon hung in the night sky. The air was damp and warm. I walked and walked, believing each step would take me farther into exile. I watched the sky the whole night, and I never saw the Weaving Maid and her Cowherd meet. And I didn't know what Ren did with those two pages.

JUST ONE WEEK later, the Festival of Hungry Ghosts arrived. After so many years, I knew what I was and what I needed to do. I pushed. I shoved. I stuffed my mouth with whatever

I could grab. I went from house to house. And as usual, as if I could have changed where I went even if I wanted to, I found myself again in front of the Chen Family Villa. I had my face in a bowl of melon rinds so old they'd gone soft and slimy when I heard someone call my name. I growled, spun around, and came face-to-face with my mother.

Her cheeks were painted white and she was dressed in layer upon layer of the finest silk. She recoiled when she saw it truly was me. Terror filled her eyes. She threw spirit money at me and took several steps back, tripping over her train.

"Mama!" I hurried to her side and helped her to her feet. How could she possibly see me? Had a miracle happened?

"Stay away!" She threw more money at me, which the other nether creatures scrambled to grab for themselves.

"Mama, Mama—"

She started to edge away again, but I stayed with her. Her back came up against the wall of the compound across the street. She looked from side to side, hoping to find a way to escape, but she was surrounded by those who wanted more money.

"Give them what they want," I said.

"I have nothing more."

"Then show them."

Mama held out her empty hands, and then reached into her clothes to show them she had nothing hidden beyond a couple of fish-shaped locks. The other ghosts and creatures— driven by their hunger—turned away and scurried back to the altar table.

I reached out to touch her cheek. It was soft and cold. She closed her eyes. Her whole body shook with fright.

"Mama, why are you out here?"

She opened her eyes and looked at me in bewilderment.

"Come with me," I said.

I led her by the elbow to the corner of our compound. I looked down. Neither of us cast shadows, but I refused to take in the knowledge. I arced out wide to navigate the corner by the shore. When I saw our feet left no prints in the soft mud, nor did our skirts get dirty, I·shut my heart to what I was seeing. Only when I realized Mama couldn't take more than ten steps without swaying did I accept the truth. My mother was dead and roaming, only she didn't know it.

We came to my family's Moon-Viewing Pavilion, I helped her up, and then I joined her.

"I remember this place. I used to come here with your father," Mama said. "But you shouldn't be here, and I should get back. I need to put out New Year offerings." Again confusion settled over her features. "But those are for ancestors and you're—"

"A ghost. I know, Mama. And this is not New Year." She had to have died very recently, because her confusion was still so powerful and complete.

"How can that be? You have an ancestor tablet. Your father had one made, even though it goes against tradition."

My tablet . . .

Grandmother had said I couldn't do anything to get it dotted, but maybe I could get my mother to help me.

"When did you last see it?" I asked, trying to keep my voice neutral.

"Your father took it with him to the capital. He couldn't bear to be parted from you."

I formed the sentences to tell her what had actually happened, but as hard as I tried, the words wouldn't come out of my mouth. A terrible feeling of helplessness washed over me. I could do many things but not this.

"You look exactly the same," Mama said, after a long

while, "but I see so much in your eyes. You've grown. You're different."

I saw a lot in her eyes too: desolation, resignation, and guilt.

WE STAYED IN the Moon-Viewing Pavilion for three days. Mama didn't say much and neither did I. Her heart needed to settle so she would understand she was dead. Gradually she remembered getting the feast for hungry ghosts ready and collapsing on the kitchen floor. Slowly she became aware of the other two parts of her soul, one waiting for burial, the other journeying to the afterworld. The third with me was free to roam, but Mama hesitated to leave the Moon-Viewing Pavilion.

"I don't go abroad," she said on the third night, as flower shadows trembled around us, "and you shouldn't either. You belong at home where you'll be safe."

"Mama, I've been roaming for a long time now. Nothing"—I considered my words carefully—"physically bad has happened to me."

She stared at me. She was still beautiful: thin, elegant, refined, but touched by sorrow so deep it gave her grace and dignity. How had I not seen this in life?

"I've walked to Gudang to see our mulberry groves," I said. "I've gone on excursions. I've even joined a poetry club. Have you heard of the Banana Garden Five? We go boating on the lake. I've helped them with their writing."

I could have told her about my project, how much I'd done on it and how my husband had received fame as a result. But she hadn't known about it when I was alive and in death I'd pursued it so hard that I'd caused Ze's death. Mama wouldn't be proud of me; she'd be disgusted and ashamed.

But it was as if she hadn't heard me at all when she said, "I never wanted you to go out. I tried hard to protect you. There was so much I didn't want you to know. Your father and I didn't want anyone to know."

She reached into her clothes and fingered her hidden locks. My aunts must have placed them there when preparing her for burial.

"Even before you were born, I dreamed of you and who you would be," she went on. "When you were seven, you wrote your first poem and it was beautiful. I wanted your talent to soar like a bird, but when it did I was frightened. I worried about what would happen to you. I saw your emotions were close enough to touch, and I knew you would have little happiness in life. This is when I realized the real lesson of the Weaving Maid and the Cowherd. Her gift of cleverness and her ability at weaving did not put an end to her sorrow, it caused it. If she hadn't been so good at weaving cloth for the gods, she could have lived forever with the Cowherd on earth."

"I always thought you told that tale because it was romantic. I didn't understand."

A long silence followed. Her interpretation of the story was dark and negative. There were so many things I didn't know about her.

"Mama, please. What happened to you?"

She looked away from me.

"We're safe now," I said, and gestured around us. We were in our family's Moon-Viewing Pavilion, the crickets were singing, and the lake spread out cool and still before us. "Nothing bad can happen to either of us here."

Mama smiled at that, and then she tentatively began. She reminisced about marrying into the Chen family and going on excursions with her mother-in-law, about her writing and what it meant to her, and about collecting the works of forgotten women poets who had been writing for nearly as long as our country's existence. I saw and felt everything as Mama spoke.

"Never let them tell you that women didn't write. They did," she said. "You can go back more than two thousand years to the *Book of Songs* and see that many of the poems were written by women and girls. Should we assume that they produced those poems by merely opening their mouths and mindlessly spouting words? Of course not. Men seek fame with their words—writing speeches, recording history, telling us how to live—but we are the ones who embrace emotions, who collect the leftover crumbs of seemingly meaningless days, who touch on the cycles of life and remember what happened in our families. I ask you, Peony, isn't that more important than writing an eight-legged essay for the emperor?"

She didn't wait for an answer. I don't think she even wanted one.

She talked about the days leading up to the Cataclysm and what happened when it arrived, and it all matched what my grandmother had told me. Mama stopped when they reached the girls' lookout pavilion and she had gathered all the jewels and silver from the other women.

"We'd been so happy to be out," Mama said, "but we didn't understand that there is a big difference between choosing to leave our inner chambers and being forced out. We are told many things about how we should behave and what we should do: that we should have sons, that we should sacrifice ourselves for our husbands and sons, that it is better to die than bring shame on our families. I believed all that. I still do."

She seemed relieved that she was finally able to talk

about this, but she still hadn't revealed what I wanted to know.

"What happened after you left the pavilion?" I asked gently. I took her hand and squeezed it. "No matter what you say or what you did, I'll love you still. You're my mama. I'll always love you."

She stared out across the lake to where it faded into mist and darkness.

"You were never married," she said at last, "so you don't know about clouds and rain. It was beautiful with your father—the building of the clouds, the rain that fell, the way we were together like one spirit, not two."

I knew more about clouds and rain than I would ever tell my mother, but I didn't quite understand what she was talking about.

"What the soldiers did to me was not clouds and rain," she said. "It was brutal, pointless, and unfulfilling even for them. Did you know I was pregnant then? You couldn't know. I never told anyone except your father. I was in my fifth month. The baby didn't show beneath my tunic and skirts. Your father and I thought we'd take this one last trip before my confinement. On our last night in Yangzhou we were to tell your grandparents. That never happened."

"Because the Manchus came."

"They wanted to destroy everything that was precious to me. When they took your father and grandfather, I knew what my duty was."

"Duty? What did you owe them?" I asked, remembering my grandmother's bitterness.

She looked at me in surprise. "I loved them."

My mind scrambled to shift with hers. She raised her chin in an offhand manner.

"The soldiers took the jewels and then they took me. I

was raped many times by many men, but that wasn't enough for them. They beat me with the sides of their swords until my skin split open. They kicked me in the stomach, taking care not to mar my face."

As she spoke, the mists gathering on the lake turned to drizzle and finally to rain. Grandmother had to be listening on the Viewing Terrace.

"It felt like a thousand demons driving me toward death, but I swallowed my sorrow and hid my tears. When I began to bleed from inside, they stepped back and watched me crab-crawl away from them into the grass. After that, they left me alone. The agony was so great it overpowered my hatred and fear. When my son spilled out of me, three of the men who'd put their organs inside me came forward. One cut the cord and took away my baby. Another lifted my body during the contractions to expel the placenta. And the last held my hand and murmured in his gruff barbarian dialect. Why didn't they just kill me? They'd killed so many already, what was one more woman?"

All this had happened on the last night of the Cataclysm, when men suddenly began to remember who they were. The soldiers burned some cotton and human bone together and used the ashes to treat my mother's wounds. Then they dressed her in a clean gown of raw silk and found cloth in the piles of looted goods to pack between her legs. But they were not so pure of heart.

"I thought they'd remembered their own mothers, sisters, wives, and daughters. But no, they were thinking of me as a prize." The locks in Mama's clothes rattled as she handled them anxiously. "They argued about which of them would take possession of me. One wanted to sell me into prostitution. One wanted to keep me in his household as a slave. The last one wanted me for a concubine. 'She's not repulsive,' the man who wanted to sell me said. 'I'll pay you twenty ounces of silver if you let me keep her.' 'I won't let her go for less than thirty,' barked the one who wanted me as a slave. 'She looks like she was born for singing and dancing, not weaving and spinning,' the first man reasoned. And it went on that way. I was only nineteen, and after everything that happened and everything that was still to happen this was my darkest moment. How was selling me as the bride of ten thousand men so very different from the general trade in women as wives, concubines, or servants? Was selling me or bartering me any different from dealing in salt? Yes, because as a woman I had even less value than salt."

The next morning, a high-ranking Manchu general dressed in red with a rapier at his waist arrived with a Manchu woman with big feet, her hair drawn back in a bun and a flower clipped to one temple. The two of them were scouts for a Manchu prince. They took Mama away from the soldiers, back to the compound where she'd been held the night before with her mother-in-law, the concubines, and all the other women who'd been separated from their families.

"After four days of rain and killing," Mama remembered, "the sun came out and cooked the city. The stench of corpses was staggering, but above us the sky blurred blue into forever. I waited my turn to be examined. All around me, women cried. Why hadn't we killed ourselves? Because we had no rope, no knives, no cliffs. Then I was brought before that same Manchu woman. She checked my hair, arms, palms, and fingers. She felt my breasts through my clothes and prodded my swollen belly. She lifted my skirts and looked at my lily feet, which said everything about who I was as a woman. 'I see where your talent lies,' she said disdainfully. 'You will do.' How could a woman do this to another woman? I was led away yet again and placed alone inside a room."

Mama thought this might be her chance to kill herself, but she found nothing she could use to cut her throat. She was on the first floor, so she couldn't throw herself from the window. She didn't expect to find rope, but she did have her gown. She sat down and tore at her hem. She made several long strips of cloth which she tied together.

"Finally I was ready, but I had one thing I still needed to do. I found a piece of charcoal by the brazier, picked it up and tested it on the wall, and then I started to write."

When my mother began to recite what she'd written, I was struck through the heart.

"The trees are bare.
In the distance, the honks of mourning geese.
If only my tears of blood could dye red the blossoms of the
    plum tree.
But I will never make it to spring. . . ."

I joined in for the last two lines.

"My heart is empty and my life has no value anymore.
Each moment a thousand tears."

Grandmother had told me my mother was a fine poet. I hadn't known she was the most famous poet of all—the one who'd left this tragic poem on the wall. I looked at my mother in wonder. Her poem had opened the gateway to the kind of immortality that Xiaoqing, Tang Xianzu, and other great poets had achieved. No wonder Baba had allowed Mama to take my ancestor tablet. She was a woman of great distinction and I would have been lucky—honored—to have her perform the dotting. So many mistakes, so many misunderstandings.

"I didn't know when I wrote those words that I would

live or that other travelers, mostly men, would chance upon them, copy them down, publish them, distribute them," Mama said. "I never wanted to be recognized for them; I never wanted to be branded a fame-seeker. Oh, Peony, when I heard you recite the poem that day in the Lotus-Blooming Hall, I could hardly breathe. You were my sole small vein of life's blood—my only child—and I thought you knew, because you and I, as mother and daughter, were so closely tied. I thought you were ashamed of me."

"I never would have recited that poem if I'd known. I never would have hurt you that way."

"But I was so afraid, I locked you in your room. I've lived with my regrets ever since."

I couldn't help it, but I blamed my father and grandfather for what happened in Yangzhou. They were men. They should have done something.

"How could you go back to Baba after he let you save him and after Grandfather used Grandmother to save them both?"

Mama's brow furrowed. "I didn't go back to Baba; he came for me. He's why I lived and how I came to be your mother. I finished my poem, looped my handmade rope over the beam, and tied it around my neck, but then that Manchu woman came to get me. She was very mad and slapped me hard, but it didn't shake me from my plan. If not now, I knew I would have a chance later. If they were going to keep me for some Manchu prince, I would have to be clothed, housed, fed. I would always be able to improvise a weapon."

The woman procurer led Mama back to the main hall. The general sat at the desk. My father was on his knees, his forehead on the floor, waiting.

"At first I thought they'd caught your father and were going to cut off his head," Mama went on. "Everything I'd done and everything I'd gone through was for nothing. But he'd come to buy me back. With the days of horror and murder over, the Manchus were trying to prove how civilized they were. Already they were hoping to create order out of disorder. I listened to them bargain. I was so numb with pain and grief that it took me a long time to find my voice. 'Husband,' I said, 'you can't take me back. I'm ruined.' He understood what I meant, but he was undeterred. 'And I have lost our son,' I confessed. Tears rolled down your father's cheeks. 'I don't care about that,' he said. 'I don't want you to die and I don't want to lose you.' You see, Peony, he kept me after what happened. I was so broken he could have sold me or traded me—just as those men who'd raped me wanted to do—or he could have discarded me completely."

Was Grandmother hearing this? She'd kept our family from having sons to punish my father and grandfather. Did she now see she was wrong?

"How can we blame the men when we made our own choices, your grandmother and I?" Mama asked, as if following my thoughts. "Your father saved me from a terrible fate that would have ended in suicide."

"But Baba went to work for the Manchus. How could he do that? Did he forget what happened to you and Grandmother?"

"How could he forget?" Mama asked, and smiled at me patiently. "He could never forget. He shaved his forehead, braided his hair, and put on Manchu clothes. This was nothing but a disguise, a costume. He'd proved to me who he was: a man who was loyal to his family above all else."

"But he went to the capital after I died. He left you all alone. He—" I must have been veering too close to the subject of my ancestor tablet, because I was unable to continue.

"That plan had long been in place." Mama scrolled back

in time to before my death. "You were supposed to marry out. He loved you so much. He couldn't bear to lose you, so he'd decided to take the appointment in the capital. After your death, his desire to be away from memories of you was even greater."

For too long I'd believed he was not a man of integrity. I'd been wrong, but then I'd been wrong about so many things.

Mama sighed, and again she abruptly changed the subject. "I just don't know what will happen to our family if Bao doesn't have a son soon."

"Grandmother won't allow it."

Mama nodded. "I loved your grandmother, but she could be vindictive. However, in this instance, she's wrong. She died in Yangzhou and didn't see what happened to me, and she wasn't here on earth when you were alive. Your baba loved you. You were a jewel in his hand, but he needed a son to care for the ancestors. What does your grandmother think will happen to her and all the other Chen family ancestors if we don't have sons, grandsons, and great-grandsons to perform the rites? Only sons can do this. She knows that."

"Baba *adopted* that man, that Bao," I said, doing little to cover the disappointment I still felt that my father had so easily replaced me in his affections.

"It took him a while to learn our ways, but Bao's been good to us. Look at how he cares for me now. I'm dressed for whatever eternity holds. I've been fed. And I was given plenty of spirit money for my journey—"

"He found my poems," I interrupted. "He went to Ren to sell them."

"You sound like a jealous sister," Mama said. "Don't feel that way." She touched my cheek. It had been a long time since I'd received a physical show of affection. "I found your poems by accident when I was reorganizing your father's bookshelves. When I read them, I asked Bao to take them to your husband. I told Bao to make sure Ren paid for them. I wanted to remind him of your worth."

She put an arm around me.

"The Manchus came to our region because as the richest area in the country we had much that was vulnerable to destruction," she said. "They knew we would make the best example, but that we also had the best resources for recovery. In many ways they were right, but how could we recover what had been lost in our families? I went home and shut the door. Now, when I look at you, I know that as much as a mother tries there's no way to protect a daughter. I kept you locked inside from birth, but that didn't keep you from dying too soon. And now look: You've been on pleasure boats, you've traveled—"

"And I've caused harm," I confessed. After everything she'd told me, didn't I owe her the truth about what I'd done to Tan Ze? "My sister-wife died because of me."

"I heard it differently," Mama said. "Ze's mother blamed her daughter for not performing her wifely duties. She was the kind who made her husband fetch water, isn't that true?"

When I nodded, she went on.

"You can't blame yourself for Ze's hunger strike. This strategy is as old as womankind. Nothing is more powerful or cruel than for a woman to make her husband watch her die." She took my face in her hands and looked into my eyes. "You're my beloved daughter, no matter what you think you've done."

But Mama didn't know everything.

"Besides, what choice did you have? Your mama and baba failed you. I feel especially responsible. I wanted you to excel at embroidery, painting, and playing the zither. I wanted you to keep your mouth shut, put on a smiling face, and learn to obey. But look what happened. You flew right out of the villa. You found freedom here"—she pointed to my heart—"in your seat of consciousness."

I saw the truth of her words. My mother made sure I was highly educated so I'd become a good wife, but in the process she'd inspired me to depart from the usual model of a young woman on the cusp of marriage.

"You have a big and good heart," Mama continued. "You don't have to be ashamed for anything. Think instead of your desires, your knowledge, and what's in here—your heart. Mencius was clear on this point: Lacking pity, one is not human; lacking shame, one is not human; lacking a sense of deference, one is not human; lacking a sense of right and wrong, one is not human."

"But I'm not human. I'm a hungry ghost."

There. I'd told her, but she didn't ask how it happened. Maybe it was too much for her to know right now, because she asked, "But you've experienced all that, haven't you? You've felt pity, shame, remorse, and sadness for everything that happened to Tan Ze, right?"

Of course I had. I'd driven myself into exile as punishment for what I'd done.

"How can one test for humanity?" Mama asked. "By whether or not you cast a shadow or leave prints in the sand? Tang Xianzu gave you the answers in the opera you love so well, when he wrote that no one can exist without joy, anger, grief, fear, love, hate, and desire. So, you have it from the *Book of Rites,* from *The Peony Pavilion,* and from me, that the Seven Emotions are what make us human. You still have these within yourself."

"But how can I change the wrongs I've done?"

"I don't believe you've done wrong. But if you do, you

have to take all your ghostly attributes and put them to good use. You need to find another girl whose life you can repair."

That girl came to my mind in a flash, but I needed Mama's help.

"Would you walk with me?" I asked. "It's very far. . . ."

Her smile radiated, sending beams across the dark surface of the lake. "That would be a good thing. I'm meant to be roaming."

She stood and looked around the Moon-Viewing Pavilion one last time. I helped her over the balustrade and down to the shore. She reached into the folds of her clothes and pulled out the fish-shaped locks. One after the other she threw them into the lake, each one hitting the water with a soundless splash that sent barely discernible ripples into infinity.

We began to walk. I guided Mama, her spirit skirts trailing on the ground behind her, through the city. By morning we reached the countryside, where fields stretched out around us like an intricately woven piece of brocade. The mulberry trees were dense with foliage. Big-footed women in straw hats and faded blue clothes climbed up in the branches to cut the leaves. Below them, other women—brown from the sun and strong from their labors—tilled the soil around the roots or carried away baskets of the leaves.

Mama was no longer afraid. Her face glowed with peace and happiness. In days long past, she'd come this way many times with my father and she relished the familiar landmarks. We traded confidences, compassion, and love—all those things that only a mother and daughter can share.

For so long I'd wished to be part of a sisterhood. I hadn't found it in the women's chambers with my cousins when I was alive, because they hadn't liked me. I hadn't found it on the Viewing Terrace with the other lovesick maidens, because their lovesickness was different from mine. I hadn't found it with the members of the Banana Garden Five, because they didn't know I existed. But I had it with my mother and grandmother. Despite our weaknesses and failings, a single thread bound us together: my grandmother, as confused as she was; my mother, as broken as she was; and me, a pathetic hungry ghost. As Mama and I walked on through the night, I understood at last that I was not alone.

A Daughter's Fate

WE REACHED GUDANG EARLY THE NEXT MORNING AND made our way to the house of the headman. I'd done so much roaming by now that these long distances no longer hurt me, but Mama had to sit down and massage her feet. A child squealed and ran barefoot out of the house. It was Qian Yi. Her hair had been tied up in little tufts, giving her an appearance of sparkle and liveliness that went against her thin frame and pale face.

"Is she the one?" Mama asked skeptically.

"Let's go inside. I want you to see her mother."

Madame Qian sat in a corner embroidering. Mama examined the stitches, looked at me in wonder, and said, "She's from our class. Look at her hands. Even in this place they're soft and white. And her stitches are delicate. How did she end up here?"

"The Cataclysm."

Mama's puzzlement turned to worry as she conjured up images of what might have happened. She reached into the folds of her skirts to find the locks she'd always relied on. Finding nothing, she clasped her hands together.

"Consider the girl, Mama," I said. "Should she suffer too?"

"Maybe she's paying for a bad deed in a past life," Mama suggested. "Maybe this is her fate."

I frowned. "What if it is her fate for us to interfere on her behalf?"

Mama looked doubtful. "But what can we do?"

I answered her question with one of my own. "Do you remember when you told me that footbinding was an act of resistance against the Manchus?"

"It was. It still is."

"But not here. This family needs its big-footed daughters to work. But this girl won't be able to do that."

Mama agreed with my assessment. "I'm surprised she's lived this long. But how can you help her?"

"I'd like to bind her feet."

Madame Qian called for her daughter. Yi obeyed and came to stand next to her mother.

"Footbinding alone won't change her fate," Mama said.

"If I'm to atone," I hurried on, "then I can't choose something easy."

"Yes, but—"

"Her mother moved down in the Cataclysm. Why can't Yi move up?"

"Up to what?"

"I don't know. But even if her destiny is only to be a thin horse, wouldn't that be better than this? If that's to be her course, perfectly bound feet will put her into a higher home."

Mama looked around the sparsely decorated room, then back at Madame Qian and her daughter. When she said, "This isn't the season for footbinding. It's too hot," I knew I'd won.

Putting the idea into Madame Qian's head was easy, but getting her husband to agree was another matter altogether. He listed his reasons against it: Yi wouldn't be able to help him raise silkworms (which was true), and no man in the countryside wanted to marry a useless woman with bound feet (which was a pointed insult directed at his wife).

Madame Qian listened patiently, waiting for an opportunity to speak. When it came, she said, "You seem to forget, Husband, that selling a daughter could bring a small fortune."

The next day, even as my mother reminded me again that we were in the wrong season, Madame Qian gathered together alum, astringent, binding cloths, scissors, nail clippers, needle, and thread. Mama knelt next to me as I placed my cold hands over Madame Qian's and helped her wash her daughter's feet and then put them in a softening bath of herbs. Then we cut Yi's toenails, daubed the flesh with the astringent, folded the toes under, wrapped the binding cloth up, over, and under the foot, and finally sewed the cloth shut so Yi wouldn't be able to free herself. Mama spoke softly into my ear, encouraging me, praising me. She gave me her mother love and I passed it through my hands into Yi's feet.

The child didn't begin to cry until later that night as her feet began to burn from the lost circulation and constant pressure of the bindings. Over the next few weeks, as we tightened the bindings every four days and made Yi walk back and forth to put added pressure on the bones that needed to break, I went forward with grim determination. Nights were the worst, when Yi sobbed, sucking in hiccuped breaths through her agony.

This would be a two-year process, and Yi inspired me with her bravery, inner strength, and persistence. The moment the bindings went on her feet, Yi automatically moved up a class from her father and her siblings. She could no longer run away from her mother or follow her sisters barefoot through the dusty village. She was an inside girl now. Her mother understood this too. The house had little ventilation, but my ghostliness brought coolness wherever I was, and on the hottest day of summer, when even I couldn't overcome the oppressive heat and humidity and Yi's suffering was great but not as great as it would be in a few more weeks, Madame Qian brought out the *Book of Songs*. The bright white pain in Yi's mind lessened as her mother recited love poems written by women tens of centuries ago. But after a while, the burning and throbbing in Yi's feet overpowered her again.

Madame Qian got up from the bed, swayed to the window on her golden lilies, and stared out over the fields for several minutes. She bit her upper lip and gripped the windowsill. Did she have the same thoughts as I, that this was a terrible mistake? That she was causing her daughter too much pain?

Mama came to my side. "Doubt comes to all mothers," she said. "But remember, this is the one thing a mother can do to give her daughter a better life."

Madame Qian's fingers loosened on the windowsill. She blinked back her tears, took a deep breath, and returned to the bed. She opened the book again.

"With your feet bound, you're no longer like your sisters," she said, "but there's an even more important gift I can give you. Today, little one, you will begin to learn to read."

As Madame Qian pointed out certain characters, explaining their origins and their meanings, Yi forgot her feet. Her body relaxed and the blinding whiteness of pain dulled. At six, Yi was old to start a proper education, but I was there to redeem myself, and reading and writing were things I knew very well. With my help, she would catch up.

A few days later, after seeing Yi's curiosity and aptitude, Mama announced, "I think the child's going to need a dowry. I'll be able to help with that once I'm settled."

With our energies so focused on Qian Yi, I'd stopped paying attention to the passage of time. Mama's forty-nine days of roaming had come to an end.

"I wish we had more time," I said. "I wish it had always been like this. I wish—"

"No more regrets, Peony. Promise me that." Mama hugged me and then held me away from her so she could look me straight in the face. "Soon you'll go home too."

"To the Chen Family Villa?" I asked, confused. "To the Viewing Terrace?"

"To your husband's home. That's where you belong."

"I can't go back there."

"Prove yourself here. Then go home." As she began to fade away and into her ancestor tablet, she called out, "You'll know when you're ready."

FOR THE NEXT eleven years I stayed in Gudang and dedicated myself to Qian Yi and her family. I perfected controlling my basest hungry-ghost qualities by building shields around myself, which I could raise and lower at will. In summer, I moved indoors with the family and cooled the house for them. When fall came, I mastered blowing on the coals in the brazier to make them hotter without singeing my skin or scorching my clothes.

It is said that a clean snow means prosperity in the coming year. Indeed, during my first winter in Gudang, a clean snow blanketed the Qian house and all that lay around it. At the New Year, when Bao came to survey my father's lands and exhort the workers to increase production, he had news: his wife was pregnant, and he was not increasing the rents and tributes due to the Chen family as usual.

The next winter more clean snow fell. This time when Bao came and announced that his wife had given birth to a son, I knew my mother had been hard at work in the afterworld. Bao did not deliver red eggs to everyone as a celebration for this miracle. He did something even better: He awarded each of the headmen of the villages that housed my father's workers a *mou* of land. The following year, another pregnancy, followed the year after that by another son. Now that the Chen family's future was secure, Bao could afford to be generous. With the birth of each new son, he gave another *mou* of land to the headmen. In this way, the Qian family's prosperity grew. The older sisters were given small dowries and married out. At the same time, bride-prices came in, increasing Master Qian's holdings.

Yi grew up. Her lily feet turned out beautifully: small, fragrant, and perfectly shaped. She remained sickly, even though I kept away other spirits who preyed on weakness. With her sisters gone from the house, I made sure she got more to eat, and her *qi* strengthened. Madame Qian and I turned the girl from a piece of unsculpted jade unfit for use into someone precious and refined. We taught her to dance on her lily feet so she looked like she was floating on clouds. She learned to play the zither in a clear style. Her strategy at chess became as ruthless as a pirate's. She also learned to sing, embroider, and paint. We lacked books, however. Master Qian didn't appreciate their purpose.

"Yi's education is part of a long-term investment," Madame Qian reminded her husband. "Think of her as a tray of silkworms that must be tended properly so they will spin their cocoons. You would not disregard that asset. If you tend a daughter, she will also become valuable." But

Master Qian was resolute, so we did the best we could with the *Book of Songs*. Yi could memorize and recite, but she didn't quite understand the poems' meanings.

All too soon Yi was a plum ready to be plucked. At seventeen, she was small, thin, and beautiful. Her features were delicate: jet-black hair, a wide-open forehead like white silk, lips the color of apricots, and cheeks as pale as alabaster. Dimples appeared with every smile. Her eyes shone bright with impudence. Her straight nose and questioning glances revealed her curiosity, independence, and intelligence. That she had survived illness, neglect, footbinding, and a generally weak constitution showed hidden tenacity and fortitude. She needed to be matched.

But her marriage possibilities were slim in the countryside. She could not do the hard labor required of her. She was still sickly, and she had a disconcerting habit of saying whatever came to her mind. She was educated but not to perfection, so even if a city family could be found that would consider a country girl, she would not be judged suitable or ready. And even in wealthy, some might say enlightened, families, no one wanted a second, third, fourth, let alone a *fifth* daughter, for it implied that only girls could come from the bloodline. For all these reasons, the local matchmaker pronounced Yi unmarriageable. I thought otherwise.

FOR THE FIRST time in eleven years, I left Gudang for Hangzhou and went straight to Ren's home. He had just reached forty-one years. In many ways he seemed the same. His hair was still black. He was still long, thin, and graceful. His hands still entranced me. While I'd been away, he'd stopped drinking and visiting the pleasure houses. He'd written his own commentary on *The Eternal Palace,* a play written by his friend Hong Sheng, which was published to great acclaim. Ren's poetry had been collected in editions featuring the finest poets of our region. He'd earned a reputation as a distinguished and respected drama critic. He'd been, for a time, secretary to a *juren* scholar. In other words, he'd found peace without me, without Tan Ze, and without the company of women. But he was lonely. If I'd lived, I would have been thirty-nine, we would have been married for twenty-three years, and it would have been time for me to start looking for a concubine for him. Instead, I wanted to bring him a wife.

I went to Madame Wu. We were "sames," and we both shared love for Ren. She had always been receptive to me, so I whispered in her ear. "A son's only duty in life is to give the family a son. Your first son has failed in this task. Without a grandson, you won't be cared for in the afterworld and neither will any of the Wu ancestors. Only your second son can help you now."

Over the next few days, Madame Wu watched Ren carefully, gauging his moods, seeing his solitary ways, and mentioning that it had been a long time since the sound of children had filled their compound.

I fanned my mother-in-law when she rested in the heat of the day. "Do not worry about class. Ren was not a golden boy when he was betrothed to the Chen daughter or when you married in the Tan girl. Both of those arrangements ended in disaster." I respected my mother-in-law by never sitting in her presence, but I had to rush her along. "This could be your last chance," I told her. "You have to do something now, while society is fluid and before the emperor has his way."

That evening, Madame Wu broached the subject of a new wife with her son. He did not object. After that, she called in the best matchmaker in the city.

Several girls were mentioned. I made sure they were all rejected.

"The girls in Hangzhou are too precocious and spoiled," I whispered in Madame Wu's ear. "You had someone like that once before in your household and it didn't suit you."

"You must go farther away," Madame Wu instructed the matchmaker. "Look for someone who has simple tastes and can keep me company in my old age. I don't have many years left."

The matchmaker got in her palanquin and traveled to the countryside. A few rocks pushed here and there on the road caused her bearers to follow my directions to Gudang. The matchmaker made inquiries and was shown to the Qian house, where two literate, bound-footed women lived. Madame Qian was remarkably composed and answered all questions about her daughter truthfully. She pulled out a card that recorded Yi's matrilineal ancestors for three generations, including her grandfather's and great-grandfather's titles.

"What has the girl learned?" the matchmaker asked.

Madame Qian listed her daughter's accomplishments, and then added, "I've taught her that a husband is the sun; a wife is the moon. The sun does not change in its fullness, but a woman waxes and wanes. Men act on their wills; women act on their feelings. Men initiate and women endure. This is why men visit the outside realm, while women remain inside."

The matchmaker nodded thoughtfully and then asked to see Yi. During the time it took for a single candle to burn down, Yi was brought in and inspected, a dowry was negotiated, and a possible bride-price discussed. Master Qian was willing to give five percent of his silk crop for five years, plus one *mou* of land. In addition, the girl would go to her new home with several trunks of bed linens, shoes, clothes, and other embroideries—all silk, all made by the bride.

How could the matchmaker not be impressed?

"It is often better for a wife to come from less standing and wealth so that she will more easily adjust to her new position as daughter-in-law in her husband's home," she observed.

When the matchmaker returned to Hangzhou, she went directly to the Wu compound. "I have found a wife for your son," she announced to Madame Wu. "Only a man who has already lost two wives would be willing to take her." The two women studied the times of birth for Ren and Yi and compared their horoscopes, making sure the Eight Characters were well matched. They discussed what a bride-price might be, considering that the father was only a farmer. Then the matchmaker went back to Gudang. She delivered silver, jewelry, four jars of wine, two bolts of cloth, some tea, and a leg of mutton to seal the agreement.

Ren and Qian Yi married in the twenty-sixth year of Emperor Kangxi's reign. Yi's father was relieved to be rid of his unwanted and useless daughter; her mother smiled at the reversal of fortune for her natal family line. I had many words of advice I wanted to give Yi, but at the moment of parting I let her mother do the talking.

"Be respectful and cautious," she advised. "Be diligent. Go to bed late and wake up early as you've always done. Make tea for your mother-in-law and treat her kindly. If they have domestic animals, feed them. Take good care of your feet, arrange your clothes, and comb your hair. Never be angry. If you do these things, you will have a good name."

She held her daughter in her arms.

"One more thing," she said gently. "This has happened very fast and we can't be sure the matchmaker has been completely forthright. If your husband turns out to be poor, don't blame him. If he has a clubfoot or is simpleminded, don't complain, become disloyal, or change your heart. You now have no one to rely on but him. The water is spilled and you can't take it back. Contentment is just a matter of chance." Tears streamed down her face. "You've been a good daughter. Try not to forget us entirely."

Then she pulled the opaque red veil down over Yi's face and helped her into the palanquin. A small band played, and the local *feng shui* man tossed grains, beans, small fruit, and copper *cash* to propitiate baleful spirits. But I could see there were none of those, only me, happy, and village children who scrambled for the corporeal treats to take home. Yi, who had no choice in any of this, left her home village. She had little expectation of love or affection, but she carried her mother's bravery in her heart.

Ren's mother greeted the palanquin at the front gate. She couldn't see the girl's face, but she inspected her feet and found them more than adequate. The two of them swayed together through the compound to the bedchamber. Here, Madame Wu placed the confidential book in her daughter-in-law's hands. "Read this. It will tell you what you need to do tonight. I look forward to a grandson in nine months."

Hours later, Ren arrived. I watched him lift Yi's veil and smile at the beautiful girl. He was pleased. I wished for them the Three Abundances—good fortune, long life, and sons—and then I left.

I wasn't going to make the same mistakes I'd made with Ze. I wouldn't live in Ren and Yi's bedchamber, where I might be tempted to interfere in ways I had in the past. I remembered how Liniang had been drawn to the plum tree she'd seen in the garden: *I should count it a great good fortune to be buried beside it when I die.* There she thought she might marshal her fragrant spirit through the dark rains of summer and keep company with the tree's roots. When she died, her parents honored her wishes. Later, Sister Stone put a sprig of flowering plum in a vase and placed it on Liniang's altar. Liniang's ghost had responded by sending a shower of plum petals. I went to the Wus' plum tree, which hadn't bloomed or borne fruit since I died. Its neglect suited me. I made a home for myself beneath the moss-covered rocks that surrounded the tree's trunk. From here, I'd be able to watch over Yi and Ren without intruding too much.

YI ADAPTED QUICKLY to being a wife. She had more wealth now than she ever could have imagined, but she showed no signs of extravagance. From childhood she'd sought inner calm, not outer beauty. Now, as a wife, she strove to be much more than just a pretty dress. Her charm was completely her own: Her skin was smoother than jade, each step she took with her lily feet was so dainty it seemed to cause other flowers to bloom, and her swaying gait was so soft that her skirts swirled about her like mist. She never complained, not even when loneliness for her mother overpowered her. At those times—instead of crying, yelling at the servants, or throwing a cup—she spent the day sitting at a northern window, practicing being quiet, with nothing but a single incense burner—and me—to keep her company.

She learned to love Ren and respect Madame Wu. There were no conflicts in the women's rooms, because Yi did all possible things to make her mother-in-law happy. Nor did Yi complain about the women who had preceded her. She didn't taunt us for dying so young. She didn't try to hurt the dignity of our memories. She preferred instead to entertain her husband and mother-in-law with her singing, dancing, and zither playing, and they enjoyed her innocence and lively manner. Her heart was like a great road with room for everyone. She treated the servants well, always had kind words for the cook, and dealt with tradesmen as though they were her kinsmen. For all this, she was appreciated by her mother-in-law and doted on by her husband. She had good food to eat, embroidered clothes to wear, and a much better house in which to live. However, she was not yet educated enough for this household. Now that I had access to Ren's library, I could teach her properly. But I was not alone in my efforts.

I remembered back to how my father taught me to read and understand, so one day I pushed Yi into Ren's lap. Beguiled by Yi's innocence and sincerity, Ren helped her by asking about her reading, forcing her to think and criticize. Yi became a conduit between Ren and me. In our education of her, we were one. She grew to be more than proficient in the classics, literature, and mathematics. Ren and I took pride in her growing knowledge and accomplishments.

But some skills still evaded her. Yi continued to hold her calligraphy brush awkwardly, causing her strokes to be shaky and unsure. Madame Wu stepped in, and through her I drilled Yi on all the lessons Fifth Aunt had taught me, using *Pictures of Battle Formations of the Brush;* Yi improved just as I had all those years ago. When she sometimes recited poems like a parrot with no sense of their deeper meanings, I knew my efforts still weren't enough. I remembered Ren's cousin. I went out and brought Li Shu home, and she became Yi's tutor. Now when Yi recited, she opened our hearts to the Seven Emotions and transported us to remembered and imagined places. Everyone in the household grew to love her even more.

Not once did I feel jealous, not once did I want to eat

Yi's heart or pull off her head and limbs for Ren to find, and not once did I try to reveal myself to her or visit her in her dreams. But by now I could do almost anything, so when they woke in the morning, I cooled the water they splashed on their faces. When Yi did her hair, I became the teeth in the comb, effortlessly separating each snarl, tangle, and strand. When Ren went out, I cleared his passage, pushed aside obstacles, eliminated dangers, and brought him home safely. During the dog days of summer, I enticed a servant to tie a watermelon in netting and lower it into the well. Then I went down into the darkness, seeped into the water, and chilled it even more. I loved watching Ren and Yi eat the melon after dinner, enjoying its refreshing qualities. In all these ways I thanked my sister-wife for being good to my husband and Ren for finding happiness and companionship after so many lonely years. But these were minor things.

I wanted to thank them in a way that would give them the deep-heart happiness I felt when I saw Yi sitting on Ren's lap or listened to him explain the hidden meaning of one of the Banana Garden Five's poems. What was the one thing they could want? What was the one thing every married couple wanted? A son. I wasn't an ancestor and I didn't think I could give this. But when spring came, something miraculous happened. The plum tree blossomed. I had come so far in my own learning that I made it happen. When the petals fell and fruit began to form, I knew I could make Yi pregnant.

Pearls in My Heart

I REMAINED TRUE TO THE PROMISE I'D MADE AND STAYED out of the bedchamber when they were making clouds and rain, but I kept track of the doings in that room in other ways. Certain nights are inauspicious and potentially dangerous for clouds and rain. On nights that were exceptionally windy, cloudy, rainy, foggy, or hot, I made sure that Yi sent Ren out to visit friends, gather with poets, or give a lecture. On nights threatened by lightning, thunder, eclipses, or earthquakes, I gave Yi a headache. But these nights were rare, so most evenings as soon as the rustling of the bed linens stilled, I slipped through a crack in the window and into the room.

I made myself very small, entered Yi's body, and got to work, looking for the right seed to bring to the egg. Making a baby isn't just about clouds and rain, although from the giggles and moans I heard as I waited outside the window, I knew Ren and Yi had fun and brought pleasure to each other. It is also about the union of two souls to bring another soul back from the afterworld to begin a new life in the earthly realm. I searched and searched in the sea of frantic swimming until, after several months, I finally found the seed I wanted. I guided it as it swam to Yi's egg and entered it. I made myself smaller still so I might comfort the new soul as he arrived in his temporary home. I stayed with him until he traveled to the wall of Yi's womb and embedded himself. Now that he was safe, I had other practical matters to attend to.

When Yi's monthly bleeding didn't come, great happiness infused the household. Just under that joy, though, was creeping worry. The last pregnant woman in the compound had died, suggesting evil spirits were after her. Everyone agreed that Yi, with her weak constitution, was particularly vulnerable to mischief committed by netherworld creatures.

"You can never be too careful about previous wives," Doctor Zhao said, when he and the diviner came for one of their regular consultations.

I agreed, but I comforted myself with the knowledge that Ze was in the Blood-Gathering Lake. However, what the diviner said next chilled me.

"Especially when one of them was not properly married in the first place," he mumbled ominously, just loud enough for everyone to hear.

But I loved Yi! I would never do anything to injure her!

Madame Wu wrung her hands. "I agree," she said. "I've been worried about that girl too. She took her vengeance on Ze and her baby. Rightfully, perhaps, but it was a hard loss for my son. Tell us what to do."

For the first time in many years, I burned with shame. I hadn't known my mother-in-law blamed me for what had happened to Ze. I had to win back her respect. The best way to do that was to protect Yi and her baby from the fears that infested the household. Unfortunately, my job was made more difficult by the instructions that the doctor and the diviner left and by a patient who was tenacious and uncooperative despite her frailty.

The servants made special charms and remedies, but Yi was too modest to accept things from those who had less than she did. Madame Wu tried to keep her daughter-in-law in bed, but Yi was too dedicated and respectful to give up making tea and meals for her mother-in-law, washing and repairing her garments, supervising the cleaning of her room, or bringing hot water when she bathed. Ren tried to coddle his wife by feeding her with his chopsticks, rubbing her back, and propping her pillows, but she wouldn't sit still for his goodness.

From my perspective—as a ghost who lived in the world of demons and other creatures who could cause harm—I could see that these things did nothing to help or protect her. They did, however, embarrass Yi, and make her anxious.

Then, one late spring afternoon during an unseasonable cold snap, I was so frustrated that after the diviner had pushed Yi from her bed to move furniture to build a barrier between her and me, had made her sick to her stomach by burning too many sticks of incense at one time in an effort to drive my spirit from the room, and had poked at her head with his fingers so hard to activate protective acupuncture points that would help guard against me that Yi was left with a throbbing headache, I shouted in disgust, "*Aiya!* Why don't you just order a ghost marriage and leave her alone?"

Yi started, blinked several times, and looked around the room. The diviner, who had never once intuited the truth of my presence, packed up his bag, bowed, and left. I stayed in the room by the window. I planned to hold my post all day and night to protect the two people I loved above all others. During the afternoon, Yi rested in bed. She nervously worried the quilt with her fingers, deep in thought. By the time a servant brought dinner, Yi seemed to have reached a conclusion of some sort.

When Ren finally came to the bedroom, Yi said, "If everyone is so concerned that Sister-wife Tong wishes to injure me, the two of you should be joined in a ghost marriage so she can be restored to her proper place as your first wife."

I was so taken aback that at first I didn't understand the implication of her words. I'd made the suggestion in a moment of supreme annoyance. It hadn't occurred to me that she would hear it or take it seriously.

"A ghost marriage?" Ren shook his head. "I'm not afraid of ghosts."

I stared hard at him, but I couldn't read what was inside his mind. Fourteen years ago when Ze was dying, he'd said he didn't believe in ghosts. At the time, I thought he was trying to keep Ze calm. But did he really not fear *or* believe in ghosts? What about when I'd visited him in his dreams? What about when I'd given him a good bed companion and an obedient wife with Ze? And how did he think his recent loneliness had been cured? Did he think the miracle of Yi was a matter of preordained fate?

I may have had doubts about Ren, but Yi didn't. She smiled at him indulgently.

"You say you're not afraid of ghosts," she said, "but I feel your apprehension. I look around and see fear everywhere."

Ren got up and crossed to the window.

"All this panic is not good for our son," Yi went on. "Arrange a ghost marriage. It will calm the others. If they are soothed, I will be able to grow our baby in tranquillity."

Hope overpowered my wounded feelings. Yi, my beautiful, kindhearted Yi. Was she really suggesting this not for herself but to bring peace to the household? Nothing was going to happen to this baby, of that I was sure. But a ghost marriage? Was it going to come at last?

Ren's hands gripped the windowsill. He looked wistful, optimistic even. Did he feel me at all? Did he know how much I loved him still?

"I think you are right," he said at last, his voice in the distant past. "Peony was meant to be my first wife." This was the first time he'd spoken my real name in twenty-three years. I was stunned, ecstatic. "After she died, we should have been married in the manner you've suggested. There were . . . problems, and this ceremony didn't happen. Peony . . . she was—" He took his fingers away from the sill, turned to face his wife, and said, "She would never harm you. I know that, and you should too. But you are right about the others. Let us have a ghost marriage and remove the impediment the others think surrounds you."

I covered my face and silently wept in gratitude. I had waited—*longed*—for a ghost marriage almost from the moment I died. If this came to pass, my ancestor tablet would be brought from its hiding place. Someone would see it wasn't dotted and finally fill in what was missing. When that happened, I would no longer be a hungry ghost. I would finish my journey to the afterworld and be transformed into an ancestor, the honorable and venerated first wife of the second son in the Wu clan. To have this be suggested by my sister-wife filled me with more happiness than I could have ever thought possible. To have Ren—my poet, my love, my life—agree was like having pearls poured into my heart.

I ATTACHED MYSELF to the matchmaker and went with her to the Chen Family Villa to observe the negotiation for my ghost bride-price. Baba had finally retired and come home to the one place he could enjoy his grandsons. He still looked proud and sure, but just under that I sensed that my death continued to haunt him. Although he couldn't see me, I knelt before him and performed obeisance, hoping that some part of him would accept my apologies for ever having doubted him. When I was done, I sat back and listened to him try to negotiate a new—and higher—bride-price than the one he had agreed to when I was alive, which at first I didn't understand. The matchmaker sought a lower one by appealing to his sense of *qing*.

"The Eight Characters were matched for your daughter and the second son of the Wu family. They were a match made in Heaven. You shouldn't ask for so much."

"My price stands."

"But your daughter is dead," the matchmaker reasoned.

"Consider the increase interest on time passed."

Naturally, negotiations failed and I was disappointed. Madame Wu did not like the matchmaker's report either.

"Order me a palanquin," she snapped. "We are going back there today."

When they reached the Chen Family Villa and stepped from their palanquins into the Sitting-Down Hall, servants hurriedly brought tea and cool cloths to refresh their faces from the journey around the lake. Then the two women were led through courtyard after courtyard to my father's library, where he lounged on his daybed with the youngest of his grandsons and nephews climbing over him like tiger cubs. He sent the children off with a servant, strode to his desk, and sat down.

Madame Wu sat in the same chair across from my father's desk that I used to occupy. The matchmaker took a spot just behind her right shoulder, while a servant came to stand by the door to await my father's commands. He smoothed his forehead and ran his hand down the length of his queue just as he had when I was a young girl.

"Madame Wu," he said. "It's been too many years."

"I don't go on excursions anymore," she replied. "The rules are changing, but even when I did, you knew that meeting with men was disagreeable to me."

"You have served your husband and my old friend well in this regard."

"Friendship and loyalty are what brought me here today. You seem to have forgotten that you promised my husband that our two families would be joined."

"I never forgot that. But what could I do? My daughter died."

"How could I not be aware of this, Master Chen? I've seen my son suffer from this loss every day for over twenty years." She leaned forward and tapped a finger on the desk as she spoke. "I send a go-between to you in good faith and you send her back to me with outlandish demands."

Baba negligently leaned back in his chair.

"You've known all along what needed to be done," she added. "I came to you many times before to negotiate."

She had? How had I missed that?

"My daughter is worth more than what you've offered," Baba said. "If you want her, you'll have to pay for her."

I sighed in understanding. My father still valued me.

"Fine," Madame Wu said. She pursed her lips and her eyes narrowed. I'd seen her irritated with Ze, but women weren't allowed to get angry at men. "Just know that this time I won't leave until you agree." She took a breath, and then said, "If you want a higher bride-price, I will need some additional items for her dowry."

This seemed to be exactly what my father wanted. They bartered. They traded. He made a higher demand for the bride-price; Madame Wu reciprocated with an even more outlandish one for the dowry. They both seemed very familiar with the offerings, which was shocking because it meant they had had this conversation many times before. But then the whole thing shocked me . . . and surprised and delighted me.

When it seemed they'd finally reached an agreement, my father suddenly threw in something new.

"Twenty live geese delivered ten days from now," he said, "or I won't agree to the marriage."

This was nothing, but Madame Wu wanted something more in exchange.

"I seem to remember that your daughter was meant to come with her own servant. Even now someone will have to care for her through her ancestor tablet when it comes to my home."

Baba allowed himself a smile. "I was waiting for you to ask."

He motioned to the servant standing by the door. The servant left the room and returned a few minutes later with a woman. She came forward, dropped to her knees, and kowtowed before Madame Wu. When she looked up, I saw a face worn by hard circumstances. It was Willow.

"This servant recently returned to our household. I made a mistake when I sold her many years ago. It's clear to me now that her destiny has always been to care for my daughter."

"She's old," Madame Wu said. "What am I going to do with her?"

"Willow is thirty-nine. She has three sons. They stayed with her previous owner. His wife wanted sons and this one gave them. Willow may not be much to look at," Baba said practically, "but she could serve as a concubine if you need one. I can guarantee she will produce grandsons for you."

"For twenty geese?"

My father nodded.

The matchmaker grinned. She would make a good profit from this. Willow crawled across the floor and put her forehead on Madame Wu's lily feet.

"I'll accept your offer on one condition," Madame Wu said. "I want you to answer a question. Why didn't you give your daughter a ghost marriage before this? One girl died because of your refusal to entertain my offers. Now the life of one who carries my grandson is threatened. This was something easy to mend. A ghost marriage is common. It alleviates so much trouble—"

"But it wouldn't help my heart," Baba confessed. "I couldn't let go of Peony. All this time I've longed for her company. By keeping the tablet in the Chen Family Villa, I felt I was still connected to her."

But I was never here with him!

My father's eyes clouded. "All these years, I hoped to feel her presence, but I never did. When you sent the matchmaker today, I decided it was finally time to let my daughter go. Peony was meant to be with your boy. And now . . . It's strange, but I feel her with me at last."

Madame Wu sniffed dismissively. "You needed to do the right thing for your daughter, but you didn't. Twenty-three years is a long time, Master Chen, a very long time."

With that, she stood and swayed out of the room. I stayed behind so I could prepare myself.

GHOST MARRIAGES ARE not as ornate, complicated, or time-consuming as a wedding when both parties are living. Baba arranged for the transfer of goods, money, and food for my dowry. Madame Wu reciprocated with everything that had been agreed upon for my bride-price. I brushed my hair and pinned it up and straightened my old and tattered clothes. I wanted to wrap my feet in clean bindings, but I hadn't had new ones since I'd left the Viewing Terrace. I was as ready as I could be.

The only real challenge was that my ancestor tablet needed to be found. Without it, the stand-in bride couldn't be made and I couldn't be married. But my tablet had been hidden away for so long that no one remembered what had happened to it. In fact, only one person knew where it was: Shao, the longtime amah and wet nurse to my family. Naturally, she was no longer a wet nurse; she was barely even an amah. She'd lost all her teeth, most of her hair, and a good part of her memory. She was too old to sell and too cheap to let retire. She was useless in locating my tablet.

"That ugly thing was thrown out years ago," she said. An hour later, she changed her mind. "It's in the ancestral hall next to her mother's tablet." Two hours after that, a different memory surfaced. "I put it under the plum tree just like in *The Peony Pavilion*. That's where Peony would have wanted to be." Three days later, after various servants, Bao, and even my father had begged, ordered, and demanded that Shao tell them where she'd hidden the tablet, she cried like the scared and frail old woman she was. "I don't know where it is," she warbled querulously. "Why do you keep asking about that ugly thing anyway?"

If she couldn't recollect where she'd hidden my tablet, she certainly wouldn't recall that she'd caused it not to be dotted. I'd come so far. I couldn't let everything fail because one old woman couldn't remember that she'd once hidden an ugly thing in a storage room on a high shelf behind a jar of pickled turnips.

I went to Shao's room. It was the middle of the afternoon and she was asleep. I stood next to her bed, staring down at her. I reached out to shake her awake, but my arms refused to touch her. Even now, when I was so close to having my ghostliness resolved, I couldn't do anything to help get my tablet dotted. I tried and tried, but I was powerless.

Then I felt a hand on my shoulder.

"Let us do it," a voice said.

I turned to see my mother and my grandmother.

"You came!" I exclaimed. "But how?"

"You are the flesh of my inmost heart," Mama answered. "How could I watch my daughter's wedding from afar?"

"We asked the netherworld bureaucrats and received one time return-to-earth permits," Grandmother explained.

More pearls filled my heart.

We waited for Shao to wake up. Then my grandmother and mother got on either side of her, held her by the elbows, and guided her through the compound to the storage room, where Shao found the ancestor tablet. Mama and Grandmother let go of her and stepped away. The old woman brushed it off. Although her eyesight was bad, I felt sure she would notice my missing dot and take the tablet straight to my father. When that didn't happen, I looked at Mama and Grandmother.

"Help me make her see it," I begged.

"We can't," Mama said regretfully. "We're only allowed to do so much."

Shao took the tablet to my old room. In the middle of the floor lay a dummy made from straw, paper, wood, and cloth that the servants had assembled to represent me at my wedding. It rested on its back with its stomach exposed. Willow painted two crude eyes, a nose, and lips on a piece of paper and fastened it to the bride's face with rice paste. Shao got on her knees and stuffed my ancestor tablet inside the dummy so quickly that Willow didn't have a chance to see it. My old servant threaded a needle and sewed the stomach shut. When she was done, she went to a trunk and opened it. Inside lay my wedding costume. It should have been thrown out with all my other belongings.

"You kept my wedding clothes?" I asked my mother.

"Of course I did. I had to believe things would be set right again someday."

"And we brought some gifts too," Grandmother added.

She reached into her gown and pulled out clean bindings and new shoes. Mama opened a satchel and brought out a skirt and tunic. The spirit clothes were beautiful, and as they dressed me, the servants mirrored our actions, placing the dummy in an underskirt followed by the red silk skirt with the tiny pleats stitched in the pattern of flowers, clouds, and interlocking good-luck symbols. They slipped on the tunic and closed all the braided frogs. They wrapped the muslin-covered straw feet in long binding cloths, tightening and tightening them until the feet were small enough to fit into my red wedding slippers. Then they propped the dummy against the wall, settled the headdress on its head, and covered the grotesque face with the red opaque veil. If my ancestor tablet had been dotted, I would have been able to inhabit the stand-in fully.

The servants left. I knelt by the dummy. I fingered the silk and touched the gold leaves on the headdress. I should have been happy, but I wasn't. I was so close to righting my path, but with my tablet undotted, the ceremony would be meaningless.

"I know everything now," Mama said, "and I'm sorry. I'm sorry I was too brokenhearted to dot your tablet. I'm sorry I let Shao take it from me. I'm sorry I never asked your father about it. I thought he'd taken your tablet with him—"

"He didn't take it—"

"He didn't tell me, I didn't ask, and you didn't tell me when I died. I found out when I reached the Viewing Terrace. Why didn't you tell me?"

"I didn't know how. You were confused. And it was Shao who—"

"You can't blame her," Mama said, waving away the idea as though it were insignificant. "Your father and I felt so guilty about your death that we abandoned our responsibilities. Your baba blamed himself for your lovesickness and your death. If he hadn't planted the idea of lovesickness in your mind with all his talk about Xiaoqing and Liniang . . . if he hadn't encouraged you to read, to think, to write—"

"But those things made me who I am," I cried.

"Exactly," Grandmother said.

"Be quiet," Mama ordered, and not very politely. "You've caused this girl enough heartbreak and confusion."

Grandmother set her jaw, looked away, and said, "And I'm sorry for that. I didn't know—"

Mama touched her mother-in-law's sleeve to keep her from saying any more.

"Peony," Mama went on, "if you'd listened only to me, you wouldn't be the daughter I'm so proud of today. Every mother is afraid for her daughter, but I was terrified. I could only think of all the terrible things that could happen. But what's the worst thing that could happen? What happened to me in Yangzhou? No. The worst thing was losing you. But look what you've done these past years. Look at what your love for Wu Ren has caused to flower in you. I wrote a poem on a wall in fear and sadness. When I did that, I closed myself away from all the things that had made me happy. Your grandmother and I, and so many other women, had wanted to be heard. We went out and it started to happen for us. Then the one time I was truly heard—the poem on the wall—I wanted to die. But you're different. In death, you've grown to be an admirable woman. And then there's your project."

I drew back instinctively. She'd burned my books and hated my love of *The Peony Pavilion.*

"So many things you didn't tell me, Peony." She sighed sadly. "We lost so much time."

We had, and there would never be a way to get it back. I blinked back tears of regret. Mama took my hand and patted it comfortingly.

"When I was still alive, I heard about Ren's commentary on *The Peony Pavilion,*" she said. "When I read it, I thought I heard your voice. I knew that couldn't be, so I told myself I was just a grieving mother. It wasn't until your grandmother met me on the Viewing Terrace that I learned the truth—all of it. And of course, she had to learn a few things from me too."

"Go ahead," Grandmother urged. "Tell her why we're really here."

Mama took a deep breath. "You need to finish your project," she said. "It won't be the scribble of a desperate woman on a wall. Your father and I, your grandmother, your whole family—those here in the earthly realm and all the generations of ancestors who watch out for you—will be proud of you."

I thought about what my mother said. My grandmother had wanted to be heard and appreciated by her husband, only to be relegated to false martyrdom. Mama had wanted to be heard, only to lose herself. I wanted to be heard, but only by one man. Ren had asked this of me in the Moon-Viewing Pavilion. He *wanted* this from me. He'd created the possibility for me, when the world, society, and even my mother and father would have preferred me to keep silent.

"But how can I possibly take it up again after everything—"

"I almost died to write my poem; you did die writing your commentary," Mama said. "I had to be cut to the bone and have my body invaded by many men to write the words on the wall. I saw you waste away as the words sapped your *qi*. For so long I thought, Maybe this sacrifice is what's needed from us. Only after watching you these last few years as you've been with Yi have I realized that maybe writing doesn't require sacrifice. Maybe it's a gift to experience emotions through our brushes, ink, and paper. I wrote out of sorrow, fear, and hate. You wrote out of desire, joy, and love. We each paid a heavy price for speaking our minds, for revealing our hearts, for trying to create, but it was worth it, wasn't it, daughter?"

I didn't have a chance to respond. I heard laughter in the corridor. The door swung open and my four aunts, Broom, Orchid, Lotus, and their daughters entered. They'd been brought together by my father to make sure I was treated like a real bride. They made adjustments to the dummy, setting right the pleats in the skirt, smoothing the silk of the tunic, and using a few kingfisher feather hairpins to help hold the headdress in place.

"Quick!" Grandmother said as cymbals clanged and drums banged. "You have to hurry."

"But my tablet—"

"Forget about it for now," Grandmother ordered. "Experience your wedding as best you can, because it will not happen again—at least not in the way you imagined when you were alone in your bed all those years ago." She closed her eyes for a moment and smiled knowingly to herself. Then she opened her eyes and clapped her hands crisply. "Now, hurry!"

I remembered everything I was supposed to do. I kowtowed to my mother three times and thanked her for all she'd done for me. I kowtowed three times to my grandmother and thanked her. Mama and Grandmother kissed me, and then they led me to the dummy. Since my tablet wasn't dotted, I couldn't step inside so I wrapped myself around it.

Grandmother was right. I had to enjoy this as best I could, and it wasn't hard. My aunts told me I was beautiful. My cousins apologized for their girlhood ways. Their daughters told me they regretted that they'd never known me. Second Aunt and Fourth Aunt picked me up, placed me on a chair, and carried me out of the room. Mama and Grandmother joined the procession of Chen family women through the corridors and past the pavilions, pond, and rockery to the ancestral hall. Above the altar table, next to the scrolls of my grandparents, hung an image of my mother. Her skin had been painted in a translucent style, her hair pinned up as a young bride, her lips full and happy. This must have been what she looked like when she and my father were first married. She might not scare anyone into conducting themselves well, but she would inspire them.

On the altar table everything had been grouped into uneven lots to signify that this wasn't a typical marriage. Seven sticks of incense stood in each of three braziers. Baba's hands trembled as he poured nine cups of wine for various gods and goddesses, and then three cups of wine for each of my ancestors. He set out five peaches and eleven melons.

Then my chair was lifted and I was carried to the wind-fire gate. For so long I'd wished to pass through this gate to go to my husband's home, and now it was happening. In a tradition unique to ghost marriages, Willow held a rice-winnowing basket over my head to screen me from heavenly sight. I was helped into a green rather than a red palanquin. Bearers carried me around the lake and up Wushan Mountain past the temple to my husband's home. The door to the palanquin opened and I was helped out and put on another chair. Mama and Grandmother stood on the steps next to Madame Wu, who greeted me in the customary way. Then she turned to welcome my father. In ghost marriages, parents are usually so happy to see the ugly thing leave their home that they stay behind to rejoice privately, but my father had come with me, trailing behind my green palanquin in one of his own, letting all Hangzhou know that his daughter—the daughter of one of the city's most respected and wealthy families—was finally marrying out. As I was carried over the Wu threshold, my heart was so full that the pearls overflowed and filled the Wu family's compound with my happiness.

The procession of the living and the dead went to the Wu family's ancestral hall, where the shadows of red candles dappled the walls. Ren waited there, and when I saw him I was overcome with emotion. He wore the wedding clothes I'd made for him. He was man-beautiful to my ghostly eyes. The only thing that set him apart from any other bridegroom were his black gloves, which reminded everyone present that this ceremony—as joyous as it was for me—was associated with darkness and secrecy.

The ceremony was performed. Servants picked up my chair and tilted it, so I could join my husband in bowing before my new ancestors. With that, I officially left my natal family and joined my husband's family. A full and very lavish banquet was served. No expense was spared. My aunts and uncles, their daughters and their husbands and children, arrived and filled table upon table. Bao—still fat, his eyes still beady—sat with his wife and their sons, who were also pudgy, with eyes set too close. Even the Chen family concubines had come, although they were relegated to a table at the back of the hall. They gossiped and twittered among themselves, happy to be out for an excursion. I had been given the position of prominence. My husband sat on one side of me and my father on the other.

"Once there were those in my family who thought I was marrying my daughter to someone of lower standing," my father told Ren as the last of thirteen dishes was set on the table. "And it's true that money and status were not equal, but I loved and respected your father. He was a good man. As I watched you and Peony grow up, I knew the two of you were perfectly matched. She would have been happy with you."

"I would have been happy with her too," Ren responded. He lifted his cup and took a sip before adding, "Now she will be with me forever."

"Take good care of her."

"I will, I will."

After the banquet, Ren and I were led to the bridal chamber. My dummy bride was placed on the bed, and then everyone left. Nervous, I lay down next to the dummy and watched as Ren undressed. For a long while, he stared down at the dummy's painted face, and then he joined us on the bed.

"I never stopped thinking about you," he whispered. "I never stopped loving you. You are the wife of my heart."

Then he draped his arm over the dummy and pulled it close.

IN THE MORNING, Willow knocked softly on the door. Ren, who was up and seated by the window, called for her to enter. She came in, followed by my mother and grandmother. Willow set down a tray with tea, cups, and a knife. She poured the tea for Ren, and then she went to the bed. She leaned over the dummy bride and began to unbutton the tunic.

Ren jumped up. "What are you doing?"

"I've come to cut out Little Miss's tablet," Willow said meekly, her head bowed down. "It needs to go on your family altar table."

Ren crossed the room, took the knife, and pocketed it.

"I don't want her cut." He gazed at the dummy bride. "I waited a long time to have Peony with me. I want to keep her as she is now. Prepare a room. We will honor her there."

I was touched by his idea, but this couldn't happen. I turned to my mother and grandmother.

"What about my tablet?" I asked.

They held up their hands helplessly and then faded away. And with that, my wedding and my moment of supreme happiness were over.

As Yi predicted, the ghost marriage soothed the household's fears. Everyone went back to their usual routines, leaving Yi to grow her baby in peace. Ren set up a nice room overlooking the garden for my dummy bride, and Willow cared for it there. He visited daily, sometimes staying for an hour or so to read or write. Yi followed all the customs and traditions by treating me as the official first wife by making offerings and reciting prayers, but inside I quietly mourned. I loved this family and they had fulfilled my desire to have a ghost wedding, but without my tablet—the ugly thing—dotted, I was still just a hungry ghost with some lovely new spirit clothes, shoes, and bindings given to me by my mother and grandmother. And I certainly didn't think about my mother and grandmother's request that I finish my project, not when Yi still had to give birth.

• • •

THE LAST MONTH of pregnancy arrived. Yi abstained from washing her hair for all twenty-eight days as recommended. I made sure she stayed relaxed, didn't climb stairs, and ate lightly. When her time approached, Madame Wu held a special ceremony to propitiate the goodwill of the demons who like to destroy a woman's life at childbirth. She placed plates of food, incense, candles, flowers, spirit money, and two live crabs on a table. She chanted protective spells. Once the ceremony was over, Madame Wu had Willow take the crabs and throw them out in the street, knowing that as they crawled away they would take the demons with them. The ash from the incense was wrapped in paper and hung above Yi's bed, where it would remain for thirty days after the baby was born to protect her from going to the Blood-Gathering Lake. Despite all this, Yi's labor was not easy.

"A no-good spirit is preventing the child from coming into the world," the midwife said. "This is a special class of demon—perhaps someone from a previous life, who has come back to seek payment for an unpaid debt."

I left the room for fear it might be me, but when Yi's screams worsened, I returned. She calmed as soon as I reentered the room. As the midwife wiped Yi's forehead, I looked everywhere. I found nothing and no one, but I felt something—evil and just outside my range.

Yi weakened. When she began calling for her mother, Ren went to find the diviner, who surveyed the scene— rumpled bedclothes, blood on Yi's thighs, and the midwife out of ideas—and ordered another altar to be set up. He brought out three charms on yellow paper, seven centimeters wide and nearly a meter long. One he hung on the door of the bedchamber to keep out bad spirits; one he hung around Yi's neck; the third he burned, mixed the ashes with water, and made Yi drink the concoction. Then he burned spirit money, chanted, and thumped the table for half an hour.

But still the baby suffered. He was being held back by something none of us could see or stop. I'd tried so hard to give this gift to my husband. I'd done everything possible, hadn't I?

When the diviner said, "The baby has grabbed hold of his mother's intestines. It is an evil spirit trying to take your wife's life"—the exact same words he'd spoken at Ze's bedside—I knew I had to try something drastic and dangerous. I ordered the diviner to renew his chants and incantations, Madame Wu to rub Yi's belly with hot water, Willow to sit behind Yi to prop her up, and the midwife to massage open the birth canal. Then I traveled up inside until I came face-to-face with Ren's son. The cord was wrapped around his neck. With each contraction, it pulled a little tighter. I took an end of the cord and pulled to loosen it from the hidden higher depths. Something pulled back and the baby's body jerked in response. It was cold in here, not warm or hospitable in any way. I slipped under the cord, relieving the pressure on the baby's neck, and then I grabbed the far end of the cord and pulled as hard as I could to free it from whatever was holding it. We began to move slowly toward the opening. I absorbed each new contraction, protecting Ren's son, until we slipped into the midwife's hands. But our joy was tempered.

Even after the baby took his first breath and was placed on his mother's chest, he was blue and lethargic. There was no question in my mind that the baby had been exposed to unpropitious elements and I was afraid he wouldn't survive. I was not the only one to worry about this. Madame Wu, Willow, and the matchmaker helped the diviner with four more protective rites. Madame Wu fetched a pair of her son's trousers and hung them over the end of the bed. Then she sat down at the table and wrote out four characters that meant *all unfavorable influences are to go into the trousers* on a piece of red paper and tucked it in the pants.

After this, Madame Wu and the midwife tied the baby's feet and hands with loose red string onto which a piece of *cash* had been looped. The *cash* served as a talisman against evil, while the tying prevented the baby from ever becoming naughty or disobedient in this and all future lives. Willow took the yellow sheet of paper from around Yi's neck and used it to fold into a hat, which she placed on the baby's head to continue the protection from mother to child. Meanwhile, the diviner took the paper from the door, burned it, and mixed the ashes in water. Three days later, that water was used to wash the baby for the first time. As he was purified, the deathly blue finally disappeared, but his breathing remained reedy. Ren's son needed even more charms, and I made sure they were gathered together, tied into a satchel, and hung outside the door: hair swept from dark corners to keep the sounds of dogs and cats from frightening him, coal to make him hardy, onions to make him quick-witted, orange pith to bring success and good fortune.

Mother and child survived the first four weeks, and a grand one-month party was given with great quantities of red eggs and sweet cakes. The women oohed and aahed over the infant. The men patted Ren on the back and drank cups of strong wine. A banquet was presented, and then the women retired to the inner chambers, where they huddled around Yi and the baby and whispered about Emperor Kangxi's first visit to Hangzhou.

"He wanted to impress everyone with his love of the arts, but every inch of his journey cost the people of the country an inch of silver," Li Shu complained. "The route on which he traveled was paved in imperial yellow. The walls and stone balustrades where he walked were carved with dragons."

"The emperor held a pageant," Hong Zhize added. I was pleased to see that Hong Sheng's daughter had grown into a beautiful and accomplished poet in her own right. "He galloped on horseback across the field, shooting arrows. Each one met its mark. Even when the horse bolted, the emperor still hit the target. This stirred something in my husband. That night, my husband's arrows met their target too."

This inspired other women to confide that the emperor's manly exploits had changed their husbands also.

"Don't be surprised if there isn't a flurry of one-month parties ten months from now," one of the women said, and the others agreed.

Li Shu held up her hands to stop the laughter. She leaned forward, lowered her voice, and confided, "The emperor says this is the beginning of a prosperous age, but I'm worried. He's very much against *The Peony Pavilion*. He says it's a debaucher of girls and puts too much emphasis on *qing*. The moralists have grabbed hold of this and are stinking up the streets with their added manure."

The women tried to cheer each other up with brave words, but their voices quavered with uncertainty. What had started as a comment here or there from one husband or another was now becoming imperial policy.

"I say no one can stop us from reading *The Peony Pavilion* or anything else," Li Shu said, with a conviction that no one believed.

"But for how long?" Yi asked plaintively. "I haven't even read it yet."

"You will." Ren stood at the door. He strode across the room, took his son from his wife, held him aloft for a moment, and then brought him back down to nestle in the crook of his arm. "You've worked long and hard to read and understand the things I love," he said, "and now you've given me a son. How could I not want to share with you something that means so much to me?".

The Clouds Hall

REN'S WORDS REAWAKENED MY DESIRE TO FINISH MY project, but I wasn't quite ready and neither was Yi. It had been fifteen years since I'd looked at the opera. During that time, I thought I'd harnessed my harmful qualities, but with the new baby in the house I had to be sure. Also, Yi needed to study more before she would understand *The Peony Pavilion*. I engaged Li Shu, Ren, and Madame Wu to help me prepare my sister-wife. Then, after another two years, during which I cared for the family without incident, I finally allowed my husband to give Yi the volume of *The Peony Pavilion* that Ze and I had worked on.

Every morning after Yi dressed, she went to the garden to pick a peony. Then she stopped by the kitchen for a fresh peach, a bowl of cherries, or a melon. After leaving instructions for the cook, she took her offerings to the ancestral hall. She first lit incense and made obeisance to the Wu ancestors, and then she laid her piece of fruit before Ze's ancestor tablet. Once these duties were done, she went to the room where my dummy bride resided and set the peony in a vase. She spoke to the ancestor tablet buried inside the dummy about her hopes for her son and her need for her husband and mother-in-law to remain healthy.

Then we'd go to the Moon-Viewing Pavilion, where Yi opened *The Peony Pavilion* and looked at all the notes about love that had been written in the margins. She read late into the afternoons—her hair hanging loose down her back, her gown flowing around her, her face set in a small frown as she contemplated this or that passage. At other times she'd pause on a line, close her eyes, and hold perfectly still as she transported herself deeper into the story. I remembered that when I'd seen the opera Liniang did the same thing, using stillness as a way for the people in the audience to reach inside themselves to find their deepest emotions. Dreaming, dreaming, dreaming—weren't our dreams what gave us strength, hope, and desire?

Sometimes I had Yi put aside her reading and wander until she found Ren, Li Shu, or Madame Wu. Then I'd have her ask them about the opera, knowing that the more she learned, the more her mind would open. I had her inquire about other commentaries written by women, but when she heard their writings had been lost or destroyed, she became pensive.

"Why is it," she asked Li Shu, "that so many women's thoughts have been like flowers in the wind, drifting off with the current and vanishing without a trace?"

Her question surprised me, showing, as it did, just how far she'd come.

Yi's curiosity never caused her to become overbearing, intrusive, or forgetful of her duties as a wife, daughter-in-law, and mother. She was passionate about the opera, but I watched to make sure she never tilted into obsession.

Through her, I learned a lot more about life and love than when I was alive or even when I guided my first sister-wife. Gone were my girlish ideas about romantic love and my later ideas about sexual love. From Yi, I learned to appreciate deep-heart love.

I'd seen it when Yi smiled indulgently at Ren when he said he wasn't afraid of ghosts as a way of soothing her fears when she was pregnant. I saw it in the way she looked at Ren when he held their son on his lap, built kites with him, and taught him to be the kind of man who would care for his mother when she became a widow. I saw it when Yi praised her husband for his accomplishments, minor though they were. He was not the great poet I'd imagined him to be as a girl, nor was he the mediocre man whom Ze had humiliated. He was just a man, with good and bad qualities. Through Yi, I saw that deep-heart love meant loving someone in spite of and because of his limitations.

One day, after months of reading and thinking, Yi came outside to the plum tree where I lived. She poured a libation on the roots, and said, "This tree is a symbol of Du Liniang and I give my heart to you. Please bring me closer to my two sister-wives."

Liniang had responded to this kindness with a shower of petals; I was too wary to try anything showy like that, but Yi's offering proved to me that she was ready to begin writing. I guided her along the corridor to the Clouds Hall. The room was small and lovely, with walls painted the color of the sky. The windows were filled with blue glass. White irises in a celadon vase stood on a simple desk. Yi sat down with our copy of *The Peony Pavilion,* mixed ink, and picked up her writing brush. I peered over her shoulder. She turned to the scene when Liniang's ghost seduces Mengmei and wrote:

Liniang's character shows through in the melancholy that inhabits her as she approaches the scholar. She may be a ghost, but she's chaste by nature.

I swear I did not plant these words. She wrote them herself, but they mirrored what I'd come to believe. What she wrote next, however, convinced me that her concerns were far different from the ones I'd pondered in my bed long ago:

A mother cannot be too careful when her daughter starts thinking about clouds and rain.

Then she swung back to her own girlhood dreams and the pressing realities of being a woman:

Liniang is shy and bashful when she says, "An insubstantial ghost may yield to passion; a woman must pay full attention to the rites." She is not wanton. She is a real woman who wants to be loved as a wife.

How these words echoed my own thoughts! I'd died young, but in my roaming I'd come to understand what it meant to be a wife and not just a girl dreaming alone in her room.

Tan Ze had styled her calligraphy after my own. How could she not when I'd guided her hand so often? I'd hoped that, seeing the writing came as if from a single hand, Ren would have understood that all the words were mine. I didn't worry about that now. I wanted Yi to feel pride in what she was doing.

She wrote some more and then she signed her name. Signed her name! I'd never done that. I'd never let Ze do that.

Over the coming months, Yi went daily to the Clouds Hall to add more comments to the margins. Slowly, something started to happen. I entered into a kind of dialogue with her. I whispered, and she wrote:

The mournful chants of birds and insects, the soughing of the rain-lashed wind. The ghostliness one feels in the words and between the lines is overwhelming.

Once my thought was complete, she dipped the brush in the ink, and then added her own words:

Reading this alone on an overcast night is frightening.

She called upon her own experience when she wrote:

Today, many fine marriages are delayed because people are picky on matters of family status and insist on amassing big dowries. When is this going to change?

How could she not understand that love—not money, status, or family connections—was what marriage should be about when she was living that herself?

Sometimes to me her words were like flowers flowing off her brush:

Mengmei changed his name because of a dream. Liniang fell sick because of her dream. Each had passion. Each had a dream. They both treated their dreams as real. A ghost is merely a dream and a dream is nothing but a ghost.

When I read this, I forgot my years of obsession and glowed with pride at Yi's insights and persistence.

Yi responded to things I'd written and sometimes to things that had come from Ze's brush. Along the way, I came to hear Ze in certain passages as clearly as if she were still with us. After all these years, I saw she'd contributed far more than I'd realized. Although Yi showed no inclination to join us in our lovesickness, it was as though she were summoning us. And we answered with our thoughts, which she read on the page.

I rejoiced in Yi's accomplishments and helped as best I could. At night, when Yi stayed up reading, I brightened the candle flame so she wouldn't strain her eyes. When her eyes got tired, I reminded her to pour a cup of green tea and hold it first over one eye and then the other, to refresh and soothe the redness. For every passage understood, every pastiche dismantled, every moment of affection deeply felt and written about, I rewarded my sister-wife. I kept her son safe when he wandered in the garden, preventing him from falling off the rockery, being bitten by insects, or escaping out the front gate. I warned the water spirits to make sure they didn't trick him into drowning in the pond and the tree spirits not to let him trip over their roots.

I also began to change and protect the compound as a whole. When Ze was alive, almost all I'd known was the bedchamber. Back then, I'd compared the house unfavorably to the Chen Family Villa. But what I'd thought was beautiful in my family home was actually the coldness and distance caused by wealth—too many fingers, no privacy, no quiet, and all that gossiping, angling, and strategizing for position. This, however, was the home of a true artist. It was also the home of a woman writer. Gradually, Yi made the Clouds Hall into a room where she could find sanctuary from the demands of the household, write in peace, and invite her husband for quiet evenings. I did what I could to make it even more pleasant by sending the fragrance of jasmine through the window, breathing on the blue windowpanes to make them seem even cooler, and running my fingers along the tips of the flowers that bloomed in the garden so their ruffling petals dappled the walls with quivering shadows.

I made the natural world open and bend to me. I made my feelings known in the prolific blooming of the peonies in spring, hoping the Wu family would remember me in their beauty and scent; in the snow that fell on the trees in winter, the time of year I'd died; in the subtle breeze through the willows, which should have reminded Ren that to me he would be forever like Liu Mengmei; and in the heavy fruit that hung from the plum tree, for surely they appreciated the miracle of that. These were my gifts to Ren, Yi, and their son. A libation poured had to be repaid and honored.

ONE DAY AS Yi was airing books in Ren's library, some sheets of bamboo paper fell out of one of the volumes. Yi picked up the brittle and cracked sheets, and read aloud, *"I have learned to use the pattern of butterflies and flowers in my embroidery...."*

I'd written the poem just before I died and had hidden it and the others in my father's library. Bao had sold them to Ren as Ze lay dying.

My sister-wife read the other sheets, all yellowed and fragile with age. She wept, and I thought about how long I'd been dead. The crumbling sheets reminded me that somewhere my body was decaying too.

She took the poems back to her writing table, where she read them again and again. That night she showed them to Ren.

"I think I understand Sister-wife Tong now. Oh,

Husband, I read her words and feel I know her, but so much is missing."

Ren, who'd had other concerns when he bought my poems from my adopted brother, read them now. They were girlish and immature, but his eyes filled and glistened as he remembered me.

"You would have liked her," he said, which was as close as he'd ever come to admitting to someone that we'd met. I floated with the joy of that.

The next day, Yi transcribed my poems onto fresh paper, adding a few lines of her own to those that had flaked away. In this way, we became one.

As she was doing this, a book fell from the shelf, surprising us both. It lay splayed on the floor with papers spilling from it. Yi picked them up. Here was the "real" story of the commentary that I'd forced Ze to write and that she'd torn out and hidden, only to be found and hidden again by Ren. These pieces of paper weren't old or disintegrating or in fragments. They still seemed new. When Yi gave them to Ren, my poems were forgotten as his grief swelled and spilled from his heart and eyes.

In that instant, I understood: I had to get my project published. The women writers who'd been collected two thousand years ago, the women writers my parents had gathered for our library, and the women of the Banana Garden Five were remembered and honored because their works had been published. I whispered my idea to Yi, and then I waited.

A few days later, she gathered up her wedding jewelry and folded it into a silk scarf. Then she went to Ren's library, laid the scarf on the table, and waited for him to look up. When he did, he saw her heavyhearted look. Concerned, he asked what the problem was and how he could help.

"Sister-wife Tong wrote a commentary about the first

half of the opera and Sister-wife Ze wrote about the second. You gained a reputation because of their words. I know you tried to deny responsibility, but their names have remained hidden and forgotten nevertheless. If we don't reveal the truth and make my sister-wives known to the public, won't they feel unfulfilled in the afterworld?"

"What would you like me to do?" Ren asked cautiously.

"Give me permission to publish the completed commentary."

Ren wasn't as positive as I'd hoped he'd be. "That's an expensive undertaking," he said.

"Which is why I'll use my bride-price jewelry to pay for the printing," Yi responded. She folded back the pieces of silk to reveal her rings, necklaces, earrings, and bangles.

"What will you do with those?" Ren asked.

"Take them to a pawnshop."

It wasn't proper for her to go to a place like that, but I'd be with her, guiding and protecting her.

Ren pinched his chin thoughtfully and then said, "It still won't be enough money."

"Then I'll pawn my wedding gifts too."

He tried to talk her out of such an undertaking. He tried to be a strict and forceful husband.

"I don't want you or any of my wives to be labeled a fame-seeker," Ren sputtered. "Female talent belongs in the inner chambers."

Comments like these were not like him, but Yi and I remained unfazed.

"I don't care if they call me a fame-seeker, because I'm not," she countered easily. "I'm doing this for my sister-wives. Shouldn't they be acknowledged?"

"But they never sought fame! Peony left nothing to suggest she wanted to have her words read by outsiders. And Ze absolutely didn't want to be recognized." He added, trying to compose himself, "She knew her place as a wife."

"And how they must regret it now."

Ren and Yi went back and forth. Yi listened to him patiently but didn't shift from her position. She was so determined that he finally revealed his real concern.

"The commentary brought Peony and Ze to no-good ends. If something happened to you—"

"You worry too much about me. By now you must see that I'm stronger than I look."

"But I do worry."

I understood that and I was concerned for Yi too, but I needed this. And so did Yi. In all the years I'd known her, she'd never asked for anything for herself.

"Please say yes, Husband."

Ren took Yi's hands and stared hard into her eyes. At last, he said, "I'll say yes on two conditions: that you eat properly and get enough sleep. If you start to ail, you must give it up that instant."

Yi agreed and immediately set to work, copying everything from the Shaoxi edition with Ze's and Yi's writing into a new volume of *The Peony Pavilion* to give to the woodblock printers. I insinuated myself into the ink and used my fingers as the hairs of her calligraphy brush as they flowed across the page.

WE FINISHED ONE evening at the beginning of winter. Yi invited Ren to join her in the Clouds Hall to celebrate. Even with a fire in the brazier, cold pervaded the room. Outside, bamboo snapped in the frozen air and a light sleet began to fall. Yi lit a candle and warmed wine. Then the two of them compared the new pages with the original. This was meticulous work, but I watched—awed and breathless—as

Ren turned the pages, stopping here and there to read my words. Several times he smiled. Was he remembering our conversation in the Moon-Viewing Pavilion? More than once his eyes misted. Was he thinking about me alone in my bed, desperate with longing?

He took a breath, lifted his chin, and expanded his chest. His fingers rested on the last words I'd written as a living girl—*When people are alive, they love. When they die, they keep loving*—and he said to Yi, "I'm proud of you for completing this." When his fingers caressed my words, I knew he'd finally heard me. Gratification at last. Euphoria, elation, ecstasy.

Looking at Ren and Yi, I saw they were as jubilant and blissful as I felt.

A few hours later, Yi said, "It must have started to snow." She walked to the window. Ren picked up the new copy and joined her. Together they opened the window. Heavy snow cloaked the branches with sparkling powder that looked like pure white jade. Ren whooped, then grabbed his wife and ran with her outside into the flurries, where they danced and laughed and fell into the drifts. I joined in their laughter, pleased to see them so carefree.

Something made me turn just in time to see sparks fly from a candle and fall on the Shaoxi edition.

No! I flew across the room, but I was too late. The pages ignited. Smoke billowed out of the room. Yi and Ren came running. He grabbed the wine jar and threw the contents on the fire, which only made things worse. I was frantic, horrified. I didn't know what to do. Yi grabbed a quilt and doused the flames.

The room went dark. Yi and Ren fell to the floor, panting from their exertions, crippled by dismay. Ren wrapped his arms around his sobbing wife. I sank down next to them and curled myself around Ren, needing his comfort and protection too. We stayed that way for several minutes. Then slowly, tentatively, Ren felt around the room, found the candle, and lit it. The lacquered desk was badly charred. Wine flowed in every direction onto the floor. The air was heavy with the odors of alcohol, burnt goosedown, and smoke.

"Could it be that my two sister-wives don't wish their writing to remain in the human world?" Yi asked, her voice shaking. "Did their spirits bring this about? Is there a demonic creature whose jealousy seeks to destroy this project?"

Husband and wife stared at each other in dismay. For the first time since their marriage, I retreated up to the rafters, where I hung on to a beam and shivered in misery and despair. I had allowed myself to hope, and now I was shattered.

Ren helped Yi to her feet and ushered her to a chair.

"Wait here," he said, and went back outside.

He returned a moment later with something in his hands. I slipped back down from the rafters to see what it was. He held the new copy of the commentary that Yi had prepared for the printers.

"I dropped this when we saw the fire," he said, showing it to Yi. She came to him and together we watched anxiously as he brushed the snow from the cover and opened it to make sure it hadn't been damaged. Yi and I sighed in relief. It was fine.

"Perhaps this fire was a blessing and not a bad omen," he said. "We lost Peony's original writings in a fire long ago. And now the volume I bought for Ze has been destroyed. Don't you see, Yi? Now all three of you will be together in only one book." He took a breath, and added, "You have all worked so hard. Nothing will stop this from being published now. I'll make sure of that."

A hungry ghost's tears of thanks mingled with those of her sister-wife.

The next morning, Yi ordered a servant to dig a hole under the plum tree. She gathered up the ashes and burnt fragments of the Shaoxi edition, wrapped them in raw silk damask, and buried them under the tree, where they joined with me and served as a reminder of what had happened and how carefully I—*we*—needed to proceed.

I THOUGHT IT would be a good idea for a few others to read what we'd written before it went out into the larger world. The readers I trusted most—and the only ones I knew—were in the Banana Garden Five. I left the compound, went down to the lake, and joined them for the first time in sixteen years. They were even more famous than when I'd clung to them during my exile. Their interest in the writings of other women had grown with their success. So it wasn't hard for me to whisper in their ears about a woman who lived on Wushan Mountain who had a unique project she was hoping to publish, or that they would respond with enthusiasm and curiosity. A few days later, an invitation arrived for Yi to join the Banana Garden Five on one of its boating trips.

Yi had never gone on an excursion or met women of such accomplishment or standing. She was apprehensive, Ren was optimistic, and I was anxious. I did my best to make sure Yi would be received positively. I helped her dress in a simple and modest manner, and then I hung on to her shoulders as she walked through the compound.

Just before we stepped into the palanquin to take us to the lake, Ren said, "Don't be nervous. They will find you charming."

And they did.

Yi told the women in the Banana Garden Five about her dedication and conviction, and then she read them the poems

I'd written and showed them the copy of *The Peony Pavilion* that held our writings in the margins.

"We feel as if we know Chen Tong," said Gu Yurei.

"As if we've heard her voice before," added Lin Yining.

The women on the boat even wept for me, the lovesick maiden who didn't know death was coming.

"Would you be willing to write something that I could include in the pages at the end of our project?" Yi asked.

Gu Yurei smiled, and said, "I would love to write a colophon for you."

"And so would I," chimed in Lin Yining.

I was delighted.

Yi and I visited several more times, so the women would have a chance to read and discuss what I'd written with my sister-wives. I didn't interfere in any way, wanting their interpretation to be purely their own. Finally, there came a day when the women pulled out brushes, ink, and paper.

Gu Yurei looked out across the lake to where the lotus were in bloom, and then she wrote:

Many readers in the women's quarters, such as Xiaoqing, have had true insight into *The Peony Pavilion*. I regret that none of their commentaries have been transmitted to the world. Now we have the combined commentary of three wives of the Wu household. They explain the play so fully that even the meanings hidden between the lines are understood. Isn't that a great good fortune? So many women hope to find a community—a sisterhood—of others like themselves. How lucky for these three wives that they found that in their writing.

I drifted over to Lin Yining and saw her write:

Even Tang Xianzu himself could not have commented on his play so well.

Responding to those who thought Liniang was improper and sent a bad message to young women, she added:

> Thanks to the work of the three wives, Liniang's name is vindicated. She is within all bounds of propriety, and her elegant legacy lingers.

To those who might not agree, she had harsh words:

> Those bumpkins will not be worth talking to.

Nor did she have much patience for those who wished to send women back to the inner chambers, where they couldn't be heard.

> Here we have three wives, all talented, who have succeeded one another in making this commentary, which is so monumental that, from now on, anyone in this vast world who wants to perceive wisdom or master literary theories has to begin with this book. This great enterprise will last to eternity.

Imagine how I felt when I read that!

IN THE COMING weeks, Yi and I took our copy of *The Peony Pavilion* with the notes in the margins to other women like Li Shu and Hong Zhize. They too decided to put brush to paper and record their thoughts. Li Shu wrote that she shed tears when she read it. Hong Zhize remembered as a small girl sitting on her father's lap and hearing Ren confess that he hadn't written the first version of the commentary but that he was trying to save his wives from criticism. She added:

> I regret that I was born too late to meet the first two wives.

Now that Yi and I were taking excursions, I saw just how brave and courageous these women writers were to acknowledge and defend our project. The world had changed. Most men had determined that writing was both a threat and an unladylike activity. These days, few families were proud to have their womenfolk publish. But Yi and I were not only pushing ahead, we were bringing in other women to support us.

We found an artist to do woodblock illustrations, and Yi asked Ren to write a preface and a question-and-answer piece about the project in which he told the truth as he saw it. With every word he wrote, I saw that he loved me still. Then Yi copied my poems into the margins of Ren's text:

> I am so touched by these stanzas that I enclose them here, hoping future collectors of women's writings will benefit from their remaining balm and fragrance.

In this way, Yi put me next to my husband forever, another gift that was so great I didn't know how I could ever repay her.

By this time, Ren had fully caught our passion for the project. He began to join us when we went to meet with different vendors. What a joy it was for the three of us to be together in this way, but truthfully we didn't need his help.

"I want finely wrought woodblocks for the text," Yi told the fifth merchant we visited.

These were shown to us, but I was uncomfortable with

the expense. I whispered in Yi's ear, she nodded, and then asked, "What do you have that's secondhand that I can use again?"

The merchant gave Yi an appraising look and took us to a back room. "These woodblocks are practically new," he stated.

"Good," Yi said, after she'd inspected them. "We'll save money without sacrificing quality." This is what I'd told her to say, but then she added something new. "I'm also thinking about durability. I want to make thousands of copies."

"Madame," the merchant said, not even trying to hide his condescension, "you probably won't sell *any* copies."

"I'm hoping for many editions with many readers," she shot back tartly.

The merchant appealed to our husband. "But, sir, there are other important projects that could use these blocks. Wouldn't it be wiser to save them for *your* work?"

But Ren wasn't concerned about his next volume of poetry or the criticism that was coming after that. "Do your job well and we'll come back for the next edition," he said. "If you don't, another firm on the street will help us."

The negotiation was intense, a good price was reached, and then we went to find a printer, select good inks, and decide on the layout. Everything that had been written in the margins or between the lines was moved to the top of the page, with the text of the opera below. When the setting of the woodblocks was complete, everyone—including Ren's young son—participated in checking for mistakes. Once everything was sent to the printer, all I had to do was wait.

The East Wind

"ON THE EAST WIND HEARTBREAK COMES AGAIN," Liniang had sung, and now it came to the Wu family compound. Yi had always been physically frail, and she'd worked hard for many months. Even though I'd watched out for her, and Ren had made sure she ate properly, illness overtook her. She retreated to her room. She accepted no visitors. She lost her appetite, which in turn caused her to lose weight and energy. Very quickly—too quickly—she no longer had the strength to sit in a chair; she now lay in her bed, looking emaciated, worn out, and exhausted. It was the middle of summer and very hot.

"Is it lovesickness?" Ren asked, after Doctor Zhao examined his new patient.

"She has a fever and a bad cough," the doctor intoned grimly. "It might be water-lung sickness. It could be blood-lung disease."

He cooked an infusion of dried mulberries, which Yi drank. When it did nothing to ease her lungs, he poured powdered sea sparrow down her throat to scare away the *yin* poisons that lurked there, but Yi continued to fade. I urged her to call on the inner strength that had kept her alive all these years, but the doctor grew increasingly bleak.

"Your wife is suffering from *qi* congestion," he said. "The oppression in her chest is causing her slowly to suffocate and lose her appetite. These things must be corrected immediately. If she grows angry, her *qi* will rise up and smash open the congestion."

Doctor Zhao had tried this with me many years ago and it hadn't worked, so I watched in dismay as they dragged Yi from the bed and yelled in her ears that she was a bad wife, an incompetent mother, and cruel to the servants. Her legs hung limp beneath her torso. Her feet slid along the floor behind her as they pushed and pulled her, trying to irritate her into barking at them to stop. She didn't oblige. She couldn't. She had too much goodness in her. When she started vomiting blood, they put her back in bed.

"I can't lose her," Ren said. "We were meant to grow old together, spend a hundred years together, and share the same grave."

"All that is very sentimental but not terribly practical," the doctor reasoned. "You must remember, Master Wu, that nothing in the world is permanent. The only permanent thing is impermanence."

"But she has lived only twenty-three years." Ren groaned in despair. "I had hoped we'd be like two birds soaring in flight for many years to come."

"I've heard that your wife has been indulging herself with *The Peony Pavilion*. Is this so?" Doctor Zhao asked. When told that, yes, it was, he sighed. "I've confronted problems caused by this opera for too many years. And for too many years I've lost women to the disease that oozes from its pages."

The whole family followed dietary restrictions. The diviner came to write charms and the like, which were burned. The ashes were gathered and given to Willow, who took them to the cook. Together they brewed a decoction made from boiled turnip and half the ashes to relieve Yi's cough. A second brew was made of weevil-eaten corn and the other half of the ashes to lower Yi's fever. Madame Wu lit incense, made offerings, and prayed. If it had been winter, Ren would have lain in the snow to freeze himself, come to the marital bed, and pressed his chilled body next to Yi's to cool her down. But it was summer, so he did the next best thing. He went out into the street to find a dog and put it in Yi's bed to suck out all the illness. None of these things worked.

Then strangely, over the next few days, the room turned cold, and then colder. Thin mists gathered along the walls and under the windows. Ren, Madame Wu, and the servants draped quilts over their shoulders to keep warm. The brazier roared, but Ren's breath came in great white clouds from his mouth, while only the lightest vapor escaped Yi's lips. She stopped moving. She stopped opening her eyes. She even stopped coughing. *Long were her slumbers, deep her stirrings.* Still, her skin burned.

But it was summer. How could it be so cold? At any deathwatch, ghosts are suspected, but I knew I wasn't causing any problems. I'd lived with Yi since she was six and, apart from her footbinding, had never caused her pain, sorrow, or discomfort. Rather, I'd protected her and given her strength. I lost all optimism and fell into heartsickness.

"I wish I could say that fox spirits were protecting your wife," Doctor Zhao said in resignation. "She needs their laughter, warmth, and wisdom. But already ghosts have gathered to take her. These spirits are filled with disease, melancholy, and too much *qing*. I hear their presence in your wife's erratic pulse. It's disordered like tangled threads. I feel their presence in her burning fever as they boil her blood as though she were in one of the hells already. Her heart fluctuations and flaming *qi* are sure signs of ghost attack." He bowed his head respectfully before adding, "All we can do is wait."

Mirrors and a sieve were hung in the room, limiting my movements. Willow and Madame Wu took turns sweeping the floor, while Ren swung a sword this way and that to scare away whatever vindictive ghosts were lurking, waiting to steal Yi from life. Their actions kept me up in the rafters, but when I looked around the room I didn't see any creatures. I lowered myself straight down to Yi's bed, avoiding the swinging sword, sweeping women, and refractions from the mirror. I put my hand on her forehead. It burned into me hotter than coals. I lay down next to her, let down the protective shields I'd built around myself these past years, and let all the coldness that I'd trapped inside myself come to the surface and seep into her in an effort to lower her fever.

I hugged her close. Spirit tears dripped from my eyes and cooled her face. I had raised her, bound her feet, cared for her when she was ill, married her out, and brought her son into the world, and she had honored me in so many ways. I was so proud of her—for being a devoted wife, a caring mother, a . . .

"I love you, Yi," I whispered in her ear. "You have not only been a wonderful sister-wife, but you saved me and made sure I was heard." I hesitated as my heart swelled and nearly burst from the pain of mother love, and then I spoke the truth of my heart. "You have been the joy of my life. I love you as though you were my daughter."

"*Ha!*"

The sound was cruel, triumphant, and definitely not human.

I swirled up, careful to avoid the swinging sword, and there was Tan Ze. Years in the Blood-Gathering Lake had left her hideous and deformed. Seeing my shocked look, she laughed, which caused Willow, Ren, and his mother to stop their actions and shiver with fright and Yi's body to heave and shake with a bout of brutal coughing.

I was too stunned to speak for a moment, too terrified for those I loved to think quickly. "How are you here?" Such a stupid question, but my mind was in turmoil, trying to figure out what to do.

She didn't answer, but she didn't have to. Her father knew the rites, and he was rich and powerful. He must have hired priests to pray for her and given them long strings of *cash,* which were then offered to the bureaucrats who supervise the Blood-Gathering Lake. Once released, she could have become an ancestor, but she'd obviously chosen a different path.

A swoosh of Ren's sword sliced away a piece of my gown. Yi moaned.

Anger roiled up inside me. "I've been burdened by you my whole life," I said. "Even after I died, you caused me trouble. Why did you do that? Why?"

"*I* caused *you* trouble?" Ze's voice grated like a rusty hinge.

"I'm sorry I frightened you," I confessed. "I'm sorry I killed you. I didn't know what I was doing, but I can't accept all the blame. You married Ren. What did you think would happen?"

"He was mine! I saw him on the night of the opera. I told you I'd chosen him." She pointed a finger at Yi. "Once this one is gone, I'll finally have him to myself."

With that, many of the events of the last few months became clear. Ze had been here for a while. After Yi found my poems, Ze must have caused the book holding the pages she'd torn out of the commentary to fall from the shelf, shifting Ren's attention back to her and stealing my poetry from his eyes. She must have drawn Yi to comment on what she'd written in the margins of the opera. The freezing temperatures on the day the Shaoxi edition burned also had to have been caused by Ze, but I hadn't understood what I was seeing because I was too entranced by Ren and Yi dancing in the snow. The cold in Yi's bedchamber . . . Yi's illness . . . and even farther back in time, when the boy had been born. Had Ze been inside Yi, trying to strangle the boy with his cord, yanking it tighter and tighter around his neck even as I tried to loosen it?

I took my eyes off Ze, trying to figure out where she'd been hiding all this time. In a vase, under the bed, in Yi's lungs, in her womb? In the doctor's pocket, in one of Willow's shoes, in the decoction of weevil-eaten corn and ashes used to bring down Yi's fever? Ze could have been in any or all of those places and I wouldn't have known, because I hadn't been looking for her.

Ze took advantage of my distraction by swooping down and sitting on Yi's chest.

"Remember when you did this to me?" she screeched.

"No!" I screamed. I reached down, grabbed Ze, and pulled her back into the air.

Willow dropped the broom and covered her ears. Ren swirled and caught Ze's leg with the sword. Spirit blood splattered the room.

"Ren loved you," Ze reproached me. "The two of you never met and yet he loved you."

Should I tell her the truth of that? Would it matter now?

"You were always in his mind," she went on mercilessly. "You were the dream of what could have been. So I had to be you. I remembered hearing about your lovesickness and how you turned away food—"

"But I shouldn't have stopped eating! That was a terrible mistake."

But even as I spoke, a memory of a completely different sort came to my mind. I'd always dismissed Doctor Zhao as stupid, but he had it right all along. Ze was jealous. He should have forced her to eat the jealousy-curing soup. And then I recalled a line from the opera: *Only women who are spiteful are jealous; only those who are jealous are spiteful.*

"I remember," Ze went on. "I remember it all. You taught me what the consequences of not eating would be. So I wasted away to become you—"

"But why?"

"He was *mine*!" She broke away from me, sank her black nails into the rafter, and hung there like a disgusting creature. She *was* a disgusting creature. "I saw him first!"

Ren dropped to his knees next to Yi's bed. He held her hand and wept. Soon she would be flying across the sky. At last, I fully understood my mother's sacrifice for my father. I would do anything to save the daughter of my heart.

"Don't punish this insignificant wife," I said. "Punish me."

I edged toward Ze, hoping she would forget about Yi and come after me. She loosened her grip on the rafter and breathed a noxious cloud of filth in my face.

"How best to do it?" In her voice I heard the little girl who was so selfish—no, insecure, I realized now, when it was too late—that she couldn't let anyone else speak for fear it would take attention away from her.

"I'm sorry I forgot to let you eat," I tried again, hopelessly, helplessly.

"You aren't hearing what I'm saying. You didn't kill me," she gloated. "You didn't crush me. You didn't steal my breath. I stopped eating, and for once I had total control over my destiny. I wanted to starve that thing you put in my belly."

I recoiled from the shock of her words. "You killed your baby?" When a satisfied smile came over her face, I said, "But he did nothing to you."

"I went to the Blood-Gathering Lake for what I did," she admitted, "but it was worth it. I hated you and told you what would hurt you the most. You believed it and look what you've become. Weak! Human!"

"I didn't kill you?"

She tried to laugh again at my ignorance, but sadness poured from her mouth. "You didn't kill me. You didn't know how."

Years of sorrow, guilt, and regret rolled off me, fell away, and disappeared into the cold air around us.

"I was never afraid of you," she went on, seemingly oblivious to how unburdened and light I suddenly was. "It was the *memory* of you. You were a ghost in my husband's heart."

From the first time I'd seen Ze, a part of me had felt sorry for her. She had everything and nothing. Her emptiness had left her unable to feel anything good—from her husband, her father, her mother, or me.

"But you've been a ghost in his heart too." Again I edged forward. If she hated me so much, she'd come for me eventually. "He couldn't abandon either of us, because he loved us both. His love for Yi is just a continuation of that. See how he stares at her. He's imagining how I must have looked all alone with my lovesickness and remembering how you looked when you were dying."

But Ze wasn't interested in reason, and she certainly didn't care for what she could see with her own eyes if she'd chosen to look. Both of us had been doomed because we'd been born girls. We'd both struggled on the precipice between being worthless or valuable as a commodity. We were both pathetic creatures. I hadn't killed Ze—the relief of that!—and I didn't believe she truly wanted to kill Yi.

"Look at him, Ze. Do you really want to hurt him again?"

Her shoulders slumped. "I let our husband take credit for what we did with *The Peony Pavilion*," she admitted, "because I wanted him to love me."

"He did love you. You should have seen the way he mourned."

But she wasn't listening to me. "I thought I could beat you in death. My husband and our new sister-wife made offerings to me, but you know this family has always been insignificant." I waited, knowing the word she would use next. "Mediocre. Fortunately, I had my father to buy me out of the Blood-Gathering Lake, but once I was free, what did I find?" She pulled at her hair. "A new wife!"

"And look what she did for you—for both of us. She heard our words. You were in the margins of *The Peony Pavilion* as much as I was. And you helped Yi with part two. Don't deny it." I moved closer to Ze. "Our sister-wife helped Ren to see he could love us all—differently but completely. Our project is going to be published. Isn't it a miracle? We're *all* going to be remembered and honored."

As Ze's tears began to flow, the ugliness of years spent in the Blood-Gathering Lake washed away, as did her anger, bitterness, spite, and selfishness. Those emotions—so persistent and strong—had followed her into death. They'd covered her terrible unhappiness. Now defeat, sadness, and loneliness oozed out of her like worms from the ground after a spring rain until Ze's true essence—the pretty girl who inhabited her dreams and longed to be loved—appeared. She was not a demon or a ghost at all. She was at once a brokenhearted ancestor and, at last, a true lovesick maiden.

I called on the inner strength of my mother and grandmother, reached out, and put my arm around Ze. I didn't let her argue. I just pulled her with me, skirting around Willow's sweeping, avoiding the mirrors, and slipping past the sieve. Ze and I went outside, and then I released her. She floated above me for a few seconds; then she turned her face skyward and slowly disappeared.

I went back inside and watched with great joy as Yi's lungs emptied of fluids, she gasped for breath, and Ren sobbed in gratitude.

Shimmering

THE THREE WIVES' COMMENTARY WAS PUBLISHED AT the end of winter in the thirty-second year of Emperor Kangxi's reign in what would have been my forty-fifth year in the earthly realm. It was an immediate and enormous success. To my amazement and unabashed delight, my name—and those of my sister-wives—became known across the country. Collectors like my father sought out my book as something unique and special. Libraries purchased it for their shelves. It went into elite homes, where women read it again and again. They cried at my loneliness and my insights. They wept over their own lost, burned, or forgotten words. They sighed for the things they wished they'd written, about spring love and autumn regrets.

Pretty soon their husbands, brothers, and sons picked up the book and read it too. Their interpretation and experience of it was completely different. What could make a man feel more like a man than the idea that another man's work had attracted and mesmerized women—not just the three of us, but all the lovesick maidens—to such an extent that we'd stopped eating, pined away, and died? It made them feel strong and superior and helped restore to them more of their lost manliness.

When New Year's Eve arrived, Yi joined the family to clean, make offerings, and pay debts, but I could see her mind was elsewhere. As soon as those duties were done, she scurried through the compound to the room where my dummy bride was kept. She entered the room, hesitated for a minute, and then she reached into her skirt, pulled out a knife—a forbidden object in the days leading up to the New Year—and knelt next to the dummy. I watched in shock as she cut off the dummy's face. She removed the clothes, put them in a neat pile, and then carefully sliced open the dummy's stomach.

My emotions were thrown into tumult: I had no idea why she wanted to harm my dummy, and Ren would be furious if he found out, but if she pulled out my ancestor tablet she would see what was missing. I hovered next to her, with hope surging through me. Yi reached into the body and extracted the tablet. She quickly brushed away the straw and left the room with my tablet and the painted face. But she hadn't really *looked* at the tablet.

She stepped down from the corridor and into the garden, and then made her way to the plum tree where I lived. She set the tablet on the ground and then went back to her room. She returned with a small table. She went away again. This time she came back with one of the commercially produced copies of *The Three Wives' Commentary*, a vase, and some other items. She put my tablet and portrait on the table, lit candles, and then made offerings of *The Commentary*, fruit, and wine. And then she worshipped me as an ancestor.

What I mean is, I *thought* she worshipped me as an ancestor.

Ren stepped out onto a balcony and saw his wife making supplication.

"What are you doing?" he called down to her.

"It's the New Year. We've made offerings to others in your family. I wanted to give thanks to Liniang. Think how she has inspired me . . . and your other wives."

He laughed at her simple ways. "You can't worship an imaginary character!"

She bristled. "The spirit of the cosmos dwells in everything. Even a stone may serve as the home of a creature; even a tree may serve as the dwelling of a spirit."

"But Tang Xianzu himself said Liniang never existed. So why do you make offerings to her?"

"How can you or I judge whether Liniang existed or not?"

It was New Year's Eve, a time when no arguing should occur for fear it will upset the ancestors, so he gave in. "You're right. I'm wrong. Now come up here and join me for tea. I'd like to read to you what I wrote today."

He was too far away to see the face painted on the piece of paper or what was inscribed on my tablet, and he didn't ask where she'd found these objects to substitute for Liniang.

Later, Yi returned to the plum tree to put away the things she'd brought out. I watched sadly as she carefully sewed my tablet back inside the dummy, dressed it, and arranged the paper face so it looked exactly as it had before the ceremony. I tried to fight my disappointment, but I was devastated . . . again.

It was time for her to know about me. I was the one who'd helped her, not Liniang. I remembered what Yi had written in the margins of the opera: *A ghost is merely a dream and a dream is nothing but a ghost.* This sentiment convinced me that the only way I was certain not to frighten her was to meet her in a dream.

That night, as soon as Yi fell asleep and began roaming, I stepped into her dream garden, which I instantly recognized as the one from Liniang's dream. Peonies bloomed all around me. I walked to the Peony Pavilion and waited. When Yi arrived and I revealed myself, she did not scream or run away. In her eyes, I was dazzlingly beautiful.

"Are you Liniang?" she asked.

I smiled at her, but before I could tell her who I was a new figure appeared. It was Ren. We had not met this way since I first died. We stared at each other, unable to speak, overcome by emotion. It was as if no time had passed. My love for him permeated the air around us, but Yi was there and I was afraid to speak. He glanced at my sister-wife and then back to me. He too was hesitant to say anything, but his eyes were filled with love.

I picked a sprig from the plum tree and handed it to him. Remembering how Liniang's dream had ended, I whirled away in a whoosh, scooping up all the petals from the garden and then letting them cascade on Ren and Yi. Tomorrow night, I would enter Yi's dream again. I'd be ready if and when Ren came. I would find my voice and tell him . . .

In the earthly realm, Ren woke up. Next to him, Yi's breathing caught and then caught again. He shook her shoulder.

"Wake up! Wake up!"

Yi opened her eyes, but before he could say anything she hurriedly told him of her dream.

"I told you Liniang existed," she said happily.

"I just had the same dream," he said. "But that wasn't Liniang." He grasped her hands and asked urgently, "Where did you get the tablet to use in your ceremony yesterday?"

She shook her head and tried to pull away her hands, but he held them tight.

"I won't be angry," he said. "Tell me."

"I didn't take it from your family altar," she admitted softly. "It wasn't one of your aunts or—"

"Yi, please! Tell me!"

"I wanted to use a tablet for someone whom I thought best represented Liniang and her lovesickness." Seeing his intensity, Yi bit her lip. Then finally she confessed. "I took the tablet from your Peony, but I put it back. Don't be angry with me."

"That was Peony in your dream," he said, quickly getting out of bed and grabbing a robe. "You called her to you."

"Husband—"

"I'm telling you it was her. She couldn't visit you like that if she were an ancestor. She has to be . . ."

Yi started to get up.

"Stay here," he ordered.

Without another word, he left the bedchamber and ran down the corridor to the room that housed my dummy. He knelt beside it and put his hand over where my heart would have been. He stayed that way for a long time and then slowly—as slowly as a groom on his wedding night—he unbuttoned the frogs that held closed my wedding tunic. Never once did he take his eyes away from the dummy's eyes, and never once did I look away from him. He was older now. Gray hair salted his temples and permanent creases etched the skin near his eyes, but to me he would always be man-beautiful. His hands were still long and thin. His movements were still languid and graceful. I loved him for the joy and happiness he'd brought me as a girl living in the Chen Family Villa and for the love and loyalty he'd shown Ze and Yi.

When the dummy's muslin body was exposed, he sat back on his heels, scanned the room, but didn't see what he needed.

He felt his pockets and found nothing. He took a breath, reached down, and ripped open the dummy's stomach. He pulled out my tablet, held it before him for a moment, and then wet his thumb with his tongue and used the moistness to wipe away the dirt. When he saw no dot, he clutched the tablet to his chest and hung his head. I knelt before him. I'd suffered twenty-nine years as a hungry ghost, and now looking up at him, I saw those years play out across his features in seconds as he guessed at the tortures of my existence.

He rose, took the tablet with him to his library, and called for Willow.

"Tell Cook to slaughter a rooster," he ordered brusquely. "When she's done, bring me the blood immediately."

Willow didn't question this. As she passed me on her way out of the room, I began to weep in relief and gratitude. I'd waited so long to have my ancestor tablet dotted, I'd given up believing that it would ever happen.

Willow returned ten minutes later with a bowl of warm blood. Ren took it from her and dismissed her, and then he went to the table, set the bowl down, and made obeisance to my tablet. As he did this, something began to stir in me and a heavenly fragrance infused the room. Tears filled his eyes as he stood and dipped his brush in the blood. His hand was steady as he reached out and dotted my tablet just as Mengmei had done to prove his love for Liniang.

Instantly, I was no longer a hungry ghost. The soul that had been harbored in my ghostly form split in two. One part found its proper place in the tablet. From there I would be able to watch over my family from close proximity. The other part was once again free to continue on to the afterworld. I'd been resurrected—not to life, but *finally* and *fully* to Ren's first wife. I'd returned to my rightful place in society, in my family, and in the cosmos.

I glowed—and with me the whole compound shimmered with happiness. And then I was floating away to complete my journey to become an ancestor. I looked back at Ren one last time. It would still be many years before my beautiful poet joined me in the plains of the afterworld. Until then, I would live for him in my writings.

Author's Note

IN 2000, I WROTE A SHORT PIECE FOR *VOGUE* MAGAZINE about Lincoln Center's full-length production of *The Peony Pavilion*. While doing research for that article, I came across the lovesick maidens. They intrigued me, and long after I wrote the article I kept thinking about them. We usually hear that in the past there were no women writers, no women artists, no women historians, no women chefs, but of course women did these things. It's just that too often what they did was lost, forgotten, or deliberately covered up. So when I had a moment here or there, I looked up whatever I could find about the lovesick maidens and came to learn that they were part of a much larger phenomenon.

In the mid-seventeenth century, more women writers were being published in China's Yangzi delta than in all the rest of the world at that time. By that I mean there were *thousands* of women—bound-footed, often living in seclusion, from wealthy families—who were being published. Some families published a single poem written by a mother or daughter whom they wanted to commemorate or honor, but there were other women—professional women writers—who not only wrote for large public audiences but also supported their families with their written words. How could so many women have done something so extraordinary and I didn't know about it? Why didn't we *all* know? Then I came across *The Three Wives' Commentary*—the first book of its kind to have been published anywhere in the world to have been written by women—three wives, no less. With that, my interest turned into an obsession.

There are several elements here—Tang Xianzu's opera, the lovesick maidens, the history of *The Three Wives' Commentary,* and the societal changes that allowed it to be written. I know they're rather complicated and overlap a bit, so please bear with me.

TANG XIANZU SET *The Peony Pavilion* in the Song dynasty (960–1127), but he was writing about the Ming dynasty (1368–1644), a time of artistic ferment as well as political turmoil and corruption.

In 1598, with the completion of the opera, Tang became one of the most important promoters of *qing*—deep emotions and sentimental love. Like all good writers, Tang wrote what he knew, but that didn't mean the government necessarily wanted to hear it. Almost immediately, different groups advocated for the opera's censorship, because it was considered too political and too lascivious. New versions appeared in quick succession, until eventually only a paltry eight out of the original fifty-five scenes were performed. The text suffered even worse treatment. Some versions were abridged, while others were revised or totally rewritten to fit society's changing mores.

In 1780, during the Qianlong reign, opposition to the opera escalated and it was blacklisted as "profane." But it wasn't until 1868 that the Tongzhi emperor issued the first official ban, labeling *The Peony Pavilion* debauched and ordering all copies burned and all productions forbidden.

Censorship of the opera has continued right up to today. The Lincoln Center production was temporarily delayed when the Chinese government discovered the content of the restored scenes and barred the actors, costumes, and sets from leaving the country, showing once again that the more things change, the more they remain the same.

Apart from sexual liaisons between two unmarried people and criticism of the government—both serious in their own ways, I suppose—why has the opera been so upsetting? *The Peony Pavilion* was the first piece of fiction in the history of China in which the heroine—a girl of sixteen—chose her own destiny, and that was both shocking and thrilling. It entranced and fascinated women, who, with rare exceptions, were allowed to read the opera but never see or hear it. The passion this work aroused has been compared to the fanaticism for Goethe's *Werther* in eighteenth-century Europe or more recently, in the United States, for *Gone With the Wind*. In China, young educated women from wealthy families— typically between the ages of thirteen and sixteen and with their marriages already arranged—were particularly susceptible to the story. Believing that life imitates art, they copied Liniang: They gave up food, wasted away, and died, all in hopes that somehow in death they might be able to choose their destinies, just as the ghost of Liniang had. (Every religion in the world has some elements that are hard for other cultures to understand, but for those in China today and for many Chinese around the world, the beliefs in the afterworld – from the annual honoring of ancestors at Chinese New

Year to the continued, but far more rare, practise of ghost marriages – are still very much a part of Chinese life, culture, and tradition, although many of them have been modified for contemporary times. As a parallel, many people in the West celebrate Valentine's Day, St. Patrick's Day, and even Christmas without giving much thought to the deeper religious meanings.)

No one knows for sure what killed the lovesick maidens, but it may have been self-starvation. We tend to think of anorexia as a modern problem, but it isn't. Whether it was female saints in the Middle Ages, lovesick maidens in seventeenth-century China, or adolescent girls today, women have had a need for some small measure of autonomy. As scholar Rudolph Bell has explained, by starving themselves young women are able to shift the contest from the outer world—in which they have no control over their fates and face seemingly sure defeat—to an inner struggle to achieve mastery over themselves and their bodily urges. As the lovesick maidens were dying, many of them—including Xiaoqing and Yu Niang, who appear in this story—wrote poems that were published after their deaths.

But these writing women—whether lovesick maidens or members of the Banana Garden Five—didn't just appear, and later disappear, in a vacuum. China underwent a dynastic change in the mid-seventeenth century, when the Ming dynasty fell and Manchu invaders from the north established the Qing dynasty. For about thirty years, the country was in chaos. The old regime had been corrupt. The war had been brutal. (In Yangzhou, where Peony's grandmother died, 80,000 people were reputed to have been killed.) Many people lost their homes. Men were humiliated and forced to shave their foreheads as a symbol of subservience to the new emperor. Under the new regime, the imperial scholar system faltered, so that the way men had traditionally gained prestige, riches, and power suddenly had no value. Men from the highest levels of society retreated from the government and from scholarly life to take up rock collecting, poetry writing, tea tasting, and incense burning.

Women, who were pretty low on the totem pole to begin with, suffered greater hardship. Some were traded and sold "by weight, like fish," and pound for pound had less value than salt. Many—like the real Xiaoqing or like Willow in the novel—became "thin horses" and were sold as concubines. But some women had very different and much better destinies. With so much else to worry about, men left the front gate open and women, who had long lived in seclusion, went out. They became professional writers, artists, archers, historians, and adventurers. Other women—in what might be considered an early form of the book group—gathered together to write poetry, read books, and discuss ideas. The members of the Banana Garden Five (and later Seven), for example, went on excursions, wrote what they saw and experienced, and were still considered fine, noble, proud, and upstanding women. Their success couldn't have happened without the growth in female literacy, a healthy economy, mass printing facilities, and a male populace that was, for the most part, distracted.

But not all this writing was happy or celebratory. Some women, like Peony's mother, left poems on walls that then became popular among the literati for their sadness and for the voyeuristic curiosity of reading someone's thoughts near the moment of death. These, along with the writings of the lovesick maidens, carried with them a kind of romanticism that combined the ideals of *qing* with the allure of a woman wasting away from disease or childbed fever, being martyred, or dying alone in an empty room longing for her lover.

Chen Tong, Tan Ze, and Qian Yi were real women. (Chen Tong's name was changed because it matched that of her future mother-in-law; their given name has not survived.) I have tried to remain as true to their story as possible—so true that often I was constrained by facts that seemed too fabulous and coincidental to be real. For example, Qian Yi used an ancestor tablet from the household to conduct a ceremony under a plum tree to honor the fictional character of Du Liniang, who then visited her and Wu Ren in a dream. But as far as I know, Chen Tong never met her husband-to-be, nor did she come back to earth as a hungry ghost.

Wu Ren wanted all three of his wives to be acknowledged, but he was also mindful of protecting them, so the cover of the book read *Wu Wushan's Three Wives' Collaborative Commentary of The Peony Pavilion*. Wushan was one of the style names he used when writing. The names Tan Ze, Qian Yi, and Chen Tong did not appear except on the title page and in the supplementary material.

The book was published to great acclaim and was widely read. In time, however, the tide turned and praise was replaced by bitter and often biting criticism. Wu Ren was accused of being a simpleton so eager to promote his wives that he lost sight of propriety. Moralists, who'd been against *The Peony Pavilion* for years, advocated for censorship of the opera through familial admonishment, religious tenets, and official bans. They proposed burning all copies of *The Peony Pavilion*—along with all complementary works such as *The Commentary*—as the most efficacious way of eliminating the offending words once and for all. Reading such books, they reasoned, could cause women—who were silly and unsophisticated by nature—to become dissolute and heart-dead. Mostly, though, they remembered that only an ignorant woman could be considered a good woman. The moralists told men to remind their mothers, wives, sisters, and daughters that there was no "writing" or "self" in the Four Virtues. The very things that had inspired women to write, paint, and go on excursions were turned against them. The return to ritual meant only one thing: a return to silence.

Then the arguments shifted again, zeroing back in on *The Three Wives' Commentary*. How could three women—*wives, no less*—have had such insights about love? How could they have endeavored to write something so learned? How was it that they'd gathered together all the editions of the opera for comparison? Why had the original manuscripts written by Chen Tong and Tan Ze been lost to fires? This seemed awfully convenient, since the three wives' calligraphic styles could not be compared. In the supplementary materials, Qian Yi wrote that she had made an offering to her two predecessors under a plum tree. She and her husband also described a dream where they'd encountered Du Liniang. Could these two not separate fact from fiction, the living from the dead, or waking from dreaming? People could come to only one conclusion: Wu Ren wrote the commentary himself. His response: "Let those who believe, believe. Let those who doubt, doubt."

In the meantime, order had to be restored across the realm. The emperor made several proclamations, all aimed at bringing society back under control. Clouds and rain, it was announced, should occur only between man and wife and the basis for it could come only from *li* and not *qing*. No more confidential women's books would be produced, so that when a girl went to her husband's home at marriage she would have no knowledge about what would happen on her wedding night. The emperor also awarded fathers complete control over their female offspring: If a daughter brought shame on her ancestors, he had the right to hack her to pieces. Very quickly, women were pushed back inside behind closed doors, and there they more or less remained until the Qing dynasty fell and the Republic of China was formed in 1912.

IN MAY 2005, ten days before I went to Hangzhou to research the three wives, I got a call from *More* magazine, asking if I would write a piece for them about China. The timing was perfect. In addition to going to Hangzhou, I visited small water towns in the Yangzi delta (many of which seem to have been frozen in time a hundred or more years ago), sites that are referred to in the novel (Longjing's tea farms and various temples), and to Suzhou (to be inspired by the great garden estates).

The thrust of that article had to do with finding my inner lovesick maiden. I have to admit it wasn't very hard, because I'm obsessed most of the time, but the assignment forced me to look inward and examine what I felt about writing and the desire women have to be heard—by their husbands, their children, their employers. At the same time, I thought a lot about love. All women on earth—and men too, for that matter—hope for the kind of love that transforms us, raises us up out of the everyday, and gives us the courage to survive our little deaths: the heartache of unfulfilled dreams, of career and personal disappointments, of broken love affairs.

Acknowledgments

THIS IS A HISTORICAL NOVEL, AND I WOULDN'T HAVE been able to write it without the wonderful research of many scholars. For place and time, I'd like to thank George E. Bird, Frederick Douglas Cloud, Sara Grimes, and George Kates for their memoirs and guides to Hangzhou and China. For information about Chinese funerary rites, beliefs about the afterworld, the three parts of the soul, the abilities and weaknesses of spirits, and ghost marriages (which are still performed today), I'd like to acknowledge Myron L. Cohen, David K. Jordan, Susan Naquin, Stuart E. Thompson, James L. Watson, Arthur P. Wolf, and Anthony C. Yu. Although sometimes Justus Doolittle and John Nevius—both nineteenth-century travelers to China—could be somewhat patronizing, they nevertheless did thorough jobs of documenting Chinese customs and beliefs. V. R. Burkhardt's *Chinese Creeds and Customs* is still a useful and practical guide to these subjects, while Matthew H. Sommer's book, *Sex, Law, and Society in Late Imperial China*, thoroughly delineates the regulation of sexual behavior and men's and women's rights in the Qing dynasty.

Lynn A. Struve has found, translated, and cataloged first-person accounts from the Ming–Qing transition. Two of these stories formed the Chen family's experience in *Peony in Love*. The first comes from an account given by Liu Sanxiu, who was taken captive, sold a few times, and eventually became a Manchu princess. The second is a hair-raising account given by Wang Xiuchu about the massacre in Yangzhou. His family's experience brutally explores the difference between volunteering to sacrifice yourself for your family and being volunteered because you're believed to have less value. (For the novel, I have reduced the ten-day massacre to five.)

In recent years, there has been some wonderful scholarship done on women in China. I'm indebted to the work of Patricia Buckley Ebrey (women's lives in the Song period), Susan Mann (women's lives and education in the eighteenth century), Maureen Robertson (women's lyric poetry in late imperial China), Ann Waltner (on the woman visionary T'An-Yang-Tzu), and Ellen Widmer (Xiaoqing's literary legacy). I was highly amused—and dismayed—by a list in a recent *Shanghai Tattler* of the twenty criteria for becoming a better wife. Although written in 2005, many of these suggestions found their way into the novel as advice for women to make their husbands happy in the seventeenth century. For those interested in reading more about footbinding, I highly suggest Beverley Jackson's classic *Splendid Slippers,* as well as Dorothy Ko's brilliant and illuminating *Cinderella's Slippers* and *Every Step a Lotus.* In addition, Dr. Ko's knowledge about Chinese women's lives in the seventeenth century, and the three wives in particular, is impressive and inspiring.

Cyril Birch's translation of *The Peony Pavilion* is a classic, and I am grateful to the University of Indiana Press for giving me permission to use his beautiful words. Just as I was writing the final pages of the novel, I was lucky to see a lovely nine-hour version of the opera, written and produced by Kenneth Pai, performed in California. For more scholarly approaches to the opera, I'm indebted to the work of Tina Lu and Catherine Swatek.

Judith Zeitlin of the University of Chicago has been like a fairy godmother to this project. We began with a lively e-mail correspondence about *The Three Wives' Commentary.* She recommended articles she'd written on Chinese female ghosts, spirit writing, self-portraits as reflections of the soul, and the three wives. I was extremely lucky to meet with Dr. Zeitlin in Chicago and spend an incredible evening talking about lovesickness, women's writing, and ghosts. Not long after that, a package arrived in the mail. She had sent me a photocopy of an original edition of *The Commentary,* owned by a private collector. Dr. Zeitlin never hesitated to share her expertise or assist me in getting help from others.

Translations vary tremendously. For Chen Tong's deathbed poems, what the three wives actually wrote, Wu Ren's account of events surrounding the commentary, Qian Yi's remembrances of her dream about Liniang, the words of praise written by the book's admirers, and all other supplementary material that was published with *The Three Wives' Commentary,* I have used translations by Dorothy Ko, Judith Zeitlin, Jingmei Chen (from her dissertation "The Dream World of Love-Sick Maidens"), and Wilt Idema and Beata Grant (from *The Red Brush,* their impressive and comprehensive 900-plus-page collection of women's writing in imperial China).

In addition to *The Peony Pavilion* material, I'm also grateful to the scholars listed above for their translations of the writings of so many other women writers of that period. I have tried to honor those women's voices by using words and phrases from their poems, much as Tang Xianzu created pastiches culled from many other writers in *The Peony Pavilion*. *Peony in Love* is a work of fiction—all mistakes and changes from the real adventures of the three wives are my own—but I hope I have captured the spirit of their story.

Thank you to the editors of *More* and *Vogue*, whose assignments bookended this project. Photographer Jessica Antola and her assistant, Jennifer Witcher, were wonderful traveling companions as they followed me almost everywhere I went on my research trip to China. Wang Jian and Tony Tong served as proficient guides and translators, and Paul Moore once again handled my complicated travel plans. I'd like to give special acknowledgment to author Anchee Min, who arranged for me to meet Mao Wei-tiao, one of the most famous Kunqu opera singers in the world. Ms. Mao showed me, through an interesting combination of movement and stillness, the depth and beauty of Chinese opera.

Thanks as well go to: Aimee Liu, for her knowledge about anorexia; Buf Meyer, for her provocative thoughts about ancestral emotions; Janet Baker, for her fine copyediting; Chris Chandler, for his unending and patient help with the mailing list; and Amanda Strick, for "man-beautiful," her love of Chinese literature, and for being such an inspiring young woman.

I'd like to thank Gina Centrello, Bob Loomis, Jane von Mehren, Benjamin Dreyer, Barbara Fillon, Karen Fink, Vincent La Scala, and, well, *everyone* at Random House for being so kind to me. I've been very lucky over the years to have Sandy Dijkstra as my agent. She's simply the best. In her office, Taryn Fagerness, Elise Capron, Elisabeth James, and Kelly Sonnack have all worked tirelessly on my behalf.

Final thanks go as always to my family: to my sons, Christopher and Alexander, for always cheering me on; to my mom, Carolyn See, for believing in me and encouraging me to persist and remember my worth; to my sister, Clara Sturak, for her good and kind heart; and to my husband, Richard Kendall, who asked thoughtful questions, had great ideas, and is very brave about my being away from him so much of the time. To him I say, This and all eternities.

A Conversation with Lisa See

Reader's Circle: In her commentary to the opera *The Peony Pavilion*, Peony writes: "Everything begins with love." In what ways did you intend for *Peony in Love* to be a commentary on the way women perceive and become aware of love?

Lisa See: I don't think of my writing as a commentary on anything. I wanted to explore different aspects of love: gratitude love, pity love, respectful love, romantic love, sexual love, sacrificing love, duty love, and finally mother love. Even though Peony dies at age sixteen, by the end of the novel she's experienced and explored what most women hope to have in their lifetimes—love.

RC: Doctor Zhao seems to be the voice of persistent doubt, always voicing his opposition to *The Peony Pavilion,* and to women's scholarship on the whole. Was Doctor Zhao based on a real person? How did you intend for him to function within the narrative?

LS: He's not based on anyone in particular, although the words that come out of his mouth come from things actual men said. Doctor Zhao functions on many levels. First and foremost, Peony needed a doctor and her family could afford one at a time when so many couldn't. I've always been interested in Chinese medicine. I love looking up old potions, cures, and remedies, knowing that many of them are still used today—some of them even on me! But Doctor Zhao also has to point out what others can't or refuse to see. Even today, parents of girls with eating disorders have a hard time acknowledging what's wrong with their daughters, finding treatment, let alone a cure. Finally, I needed someone—a man—to voice the belief that reading *The Peony Pavilion* was dangerous and that reading and writing could be fatal to women. Peony's father and Ren [her true love] believed women should be exposed to books, but I had to have someone who could say what half the men were thinking at the time—a view that eventually prevailed—that an educated woman was a worthless woman.

RC: Did you always know that Peony would die? How did you conceive of telling the story of *The Three Wives' Commentary* from her perspective?

LS: I thought about the three wives for five years before I began writing the book. At first I thought I would tell each wife's story, one right after the other, but I longed for one voice, who would have the strength to carry the whole story. One morning I woke up and knew that the first wife had to come back as a ghost. Not only would I have a single voice to carry me through, but Peony's experiences could parallel Liniang's in "The Peony Pavilion."

RC: The concept of the soul splitting into three parts upon death reads like a perfect way to give Peony life, functionality, and a concrete existence, even though her body was no longer active on earth. Why did you choose to express Peony's troubled existence through this transition?

LS: Spirits in the Chinese afterworld—whether beloved ancestors or ghosts—have the same wants, needs, and desires as living people. They need clothes, food, a place to live. They have emotions. Most important, in the Chinese tradition, spirits, ancestors, and even demons are very much a part of everyday life. This is why ancestor worship is so important. So for me the challenge was to create a believable situation (to Western readers, especially) for Peony. She can float, change form, and do many things that the living can't do, but she is also limited—as all Chinese ghosts are—by things like corners, mirrors, scissors, and fern fronds. In other words, she inhabits a very real parallel world to the living world; both have their own rules of what can and can't be done.

RC: Why was it important to place restrictions on Peony's knowledge and capabilities in the afterlife—namely not being able to turn corners, or still having to learn life lessons before obtaining greater understanding?

LS: I didn't place those restrictions. They're there by Chinese tradition. Let's take not being able to turn corners as an example. This belief permeates many facets of Chinese culture, including city planning, architecture, and landscape design. The first time I went to my family's home village, I was told I wouldn't be able to find it because I had to know the right set of tire tracks through the rice fields to get there. I thought my uncles were kidding, but they were right. I could see the village in the distance, but there were no straight roads to it or to any other village in China. Why? Because even today no one wants to give ghosts a straight line to a village. In wealthy homes and palaces, you see zigzag bridges, which are aesthetically beautiful but also have a practical purpose. How many zigzags you had depended on your rank. Only the emperor could have nine zigzags. Even in wealthy, elite, educated homes, people didn't want ghosts crossing their bridges. But obviously Chinese ghosts have found ways to get around these obstacles, otherwise there wouldn't be Chinese ghost stories. I took those things that are traditionally harmful to ghosts and then had to figure out how Peony would overcome or work around them.

RC: When did the Chinese stop believing in all this?

LS: They haven't. In mainland China, some of these traditions and beliefs disappeared during the Mao era, but a lot of them are returning now. In Taiwan, ghost marriages are still practiced, because even in death everyone needs to have a spouse. Around the world, even here in the U.S., Chinese still celebrate New Year by sending the Kitchen God to Heaven to report to the ancestors on the family's behavior during the past year.

My point here is that other countries and cultures have different belief systems. One isn't right and the other wrong, although certainly wars and even personal arguments are fought all the time over whose religion is right. But I hope readers who find these beliefs disturbing, unsettling, or unbelievable will consider for a moment what people on the other side of the world might think about the Christian belief in the father, the son, and the holy ghost. In China, I've been asked many times, "People in the West don't really believe in that stuff, do they?"

RC: You weave many secrets into this novel—secrets meant to protect but in the end only do harm, and harmful secrets that bring joy once revealed. What did you wish your readers to take away from this?

LS: People keep secrets from each other all the time. Wives keep secrets from their husbands; husbands keep secrets from their wives. We'll tell one friend something but not another. Secrets begin almost from birth. There are many things we choose *not* to tell our children. Of course, many wonderful things are passed from grandmother to mother to daughter down through the generations, and those things make us into the people we are. But there are other stories—secrets—that also have a ripple effect. We may not know what happened in the past—that's why they're secrets—but these things also help to turn us into the people we become as adults. I've found that many of these secrets have to do with how men and women treat each other, with the result that generations later you find women who are extremely fearful of men, or have a belief that men will somehow "save" them, or that they have a repeating pattern of choosing an alcoholic or abusive husband, and they don't know why.

RC: What was Wu Ren experiencing in the years between his weddings? Why did you choose not to express his experience during that time?

LS: At last, an easy question! Very little is known about Wu Ren and what's known I used. But your question reminds me of another one that I'm often asked: What parts of the story are true and what parts are fictional? I tried to stay as true as possible to the story of the three wives. This caused lots of problems, because truth is always stranger than fiction. One fire destroying a manuscript in a story is believable, but two fires? Yikes! And what about the dream that Ren and Yi share at the end? This dream is part of the historical record, but I had to try and make it believable. Finding the balance between fact and fiction was quite a challenge.

RC: What were your favorite scenes to write?

LS: My favorite scenes were the ones between Peony and her grandmother, Peony and her mother (once she arrived in the afterworld), and the three of them together. I got weepy when I wrote those scenes, particularly the one when Peony's mother and grandmother came back to earth for Peony's wedding. This goes back to the secrets you asked me about earlier. What we tell each other and what we know to be true are often completely different. Peony's grandmother is so sure she's right, but she isn't. Peony thinks she knows what's going on, but she doesn't. And Peony's mother is just incredible. She embodies all that's good and bad in mother love. She tries so hard to protect her daughter, but ends up failing in such a tragic way. But how can we protect our children, really? We can't. We can only do the best we can in the moment. Then, when Peony's mother turned out to have been the woman to write the poem on the wall . . . well, it nearly killed me. To me, these three women change in profound ways, but that's what women do. We change, we evolve, we make mistakes, we love, and we try to do the best we can.

RC: How did you prepare to write *Peony in Love*? Was extensive research needed, and if so, what were your sources?

LS: I'm a research fiend. I love it. I read everything I could on the three wives and I spoke with the top scholars in the field of Chinese women's history. I also found first-person accounts of what happened during the Manchu invasion of Yangzhou. These were true stories of terrible suffering, but I used them to tell what happened to Peony's mother and her family, because the truthful details were so much more wrenching and terrifying than anything I could have made up. A whole separate part of my research had to do with ghosts and the need for sons, which are closely related. And of course, I went to China. I went to every location that I wrote about. Even today, Hangzhou is considered China's most romantic city. So while that trip wasn't as hard or as dramatic as some I've done for other books, I know I couldn't have written the novel if I hadn't spent time in Hangzhou and its environs.

RC: Do you think *Peony in Love* has a broader message for its contemporary readers?

LS: Both *Peony in Love* and my previous novel, *Snow Flower and the Secret Fan*, tell part of a larger story about women and our lost history. Women today are very lucky, but we've only been able to get to where we are because of all the suffering, failures, tragedies, and triumphs of the women who came before us. We should rejoice in what they did. At the same time, I don't think our lives are so removed from theirs. We—and I'm speaking here of men and women—still long—*need*—to be heard. *Peony* is about what one person will endure to be heard.

RC: In the margins of *The Three Wives' Commentary*, Qian Yi asked: "Why is it that so many women's thoughts have been like flowers in the wind, drifting off with the current and vanishing without a trace?" How would you answer this question?

LS: We hear that in the past there were no women writers, no women artists, no women chefs— I could go on and on—but of course women did these things! It's just that so often what they did was lost, forgotten, or deliberately covered up. But even today, as far as women have come and as much as we've accomplished, women's words still can vanish without a trace, and it often happens at the most intimate, day-to-day level. Let's take a high-powered woman executive, as an example. During the day, she's accustomed to people listening to her, right? But when she comes home, she can say to her kids, "Clean your room, clean your room, CLEAN YOUR ROOM!" And they don't listen. They don't *hear* her, because she's just the mom. (This happens to stay-at-home moms too.) And you can tell your husband twenty times that the two of you will be meeting friends for dinner or that the cereal is on the second shelf, and he'll still ask, "Why didn't you tell me we were going out?" or "Where's the cereal?" because he hasn't been listening because you're just the wife. I'm not cranky about it or anything close to that. I'm just saying this is my experience and I know a lot of women share in this experience too. We laugh it off and call what our husband and kids do endearing, because we love them. But since this happens at the domestic level even now, it doesn't surprise me that in the past women's accomplishments—in particular their writings, their *words*—were lost and ignored. China was very lucky to have men who collected and preserved what women wrote, but where are women's writings from Europe and other parts of the world? Lost, and drifting on the wind. . .

RC: You do a lot of different things: you're a Los Angeles city commissioner, you curate museum exhibitions, you go out and speak, you're on several boards, you write books for which you sometimes go on quite adventurous (some might say scary) research expeditions, and you have a family too. How do you find time to do it all? And what's your day like?

LS: A lot of writers are shy by nature. That's part of the reason we become writers. We like to be alone in our rooms day after day. I know I do. But I've worked for years to force myself to go out and do things. When I was in my early twenties, I even challenged myself to do one "outrageous" thing a week. I have to admit I didn't do anything all that outrageous, but I did push the borders of what I could do and how brave I could be. Beyond that, how can you write if you have no experience of the world, of people, of emotions? E. M. Forster wrote, "Only connect." How can you write about the human experience if you don't connect? So I go out and I do stuff—lots of stuff—and I try to connect. Still, the writing comes first. I wake up early, get a cup of tea, and check my e-mail, because my husband exercises in the room off my office, so the music's blasting and he's thumping away on some machine or other. Once the room has quieted down, I write a thousand words. That's just four pages. Sometimes I write more but never less. Then I get dressed and start to think about the rest of the day.

RC: All your novels so far are set wholly or partly in China. Did the family background you discovered while writing *On Gold Mountain* inspire you to focus on this aspect of your genetic inheritance in your fiction?

LS: I've always been intrigued by lost stories and lost history. This was true with my own Chinese-American background, so yes, I'd say that my desire to find lost stories very much comes from writing *On Gold Mountain*. I mean, how crazy is it to look into your family history and find a great-grandfather who got his start in this country by selling crotchless underwear to brothels? So much of what my family did was either borderline illegal or full-on out-there illegal. At the same time, history was happening all around them. History was happening *to* them. I've stayed with this idea of history happening to individual people with all my novels, including *Peony in Love*.

But something else happened as a result of writing *On Gold Mountain*. I hadn't really thought too much about my identity. Who does, after all? All of a sudden people asked me—and still do—"What are you, Chinese or American?" I know that, because of how I look, I will always be seen as a bit of an outsider in Chinatown, but to me it's home. It's what I know. The same can be said for when I go to China. To me, it's just a bigger Chinatown—very familiar and comfortable, but again, because of how I look I'll always be considered an outsider. Then when I'm out in the larger white community in the United States, I look like I belong but sometimes I don't feel like I do. That world can seem strange and foreign to me. So in writing these books I'm also trying to figure out who I am. Where do I fit in? Here, there, anywhere, nowhere?

RC: Finally, what are you working on now?

LS: The new novel's tentatively called *Shanghai Girls*, and I've been having a lot of fun with it. It starts in 1937 with two sisters in Shanghai. They come to Los Angeles in arranged marriages. We often read about arranged marriages in other countries, but a lot of people don't know that we had and still have them here in the U.S. Back in the 1930s, my great-uncle took his sons back to China. A lot of dads would have said, "Here's some money, go find a souvenir," but he said, "As long as we're here, let's get you boys wives." And that's exactly what they did. The oldest was about twenty-five and the youngest was about fourteen. The women (and girls), who in China had had servants, came to Los Angeles and became the servants. They had very hard and often sad lives. *Shanghai Girls* is going to reveal a time and place that people know very little about, even though it happened right here in our country. Lastly, this is a story of two sisters. Every relationship between sisters, no matter how loving and close, is plagued by sibling rivalry: who's prettier, richer, more talented, happier, the better mother? Your sister is the one person who should stick by you and love you no matter what, but she's also the one who knows exactly where to stab the knife to hurt you the most. Every woman who has a sister will see the shared hopes, dreams, petty rivalries, and deep connections—for good and bad—that only sisters (and often best friends, who are like sisters) can have.

Reading Group
Questions and Topics for Discussion

1. On page 105, Lisa See quotes the poet Han Yun, who wrote, "All things not at peace will cry out." What do you think he meant by that? And in what ways does this inspire Peony and the other women writers in the novel?

2. What are the different kinds of love that Peony experiences? How does her love for Ren (as well as for her mother, father, grandmother, Yi, and even Willow) change through the years? Have you had similar experiences in your life?

3. Anticipating her first meeting with Ren in the Moon-Viewing Pavilion, Peony states: "Monthly bleeding doesn't turn a girl into a woman, nor does betrothal or new skills. Love had turned me into a woman" (page 67). Is Peony's statement true?

4. Peony is filled with doubt after meeting Ren—doubt about their relationship, doubt about ever finding love, and doubt about being a good mother. What is the source of this doubt and how does it grow within Peony?

5. In the nights of watching *The Peony Pavilion*, Peony has many visions of the man she will marry, and many visions of "her poet." Why isn't she able to make the connection that both men are one and the same? What signs does she overlook and why?

6. On page 131, Peony thinks she's being dressed for her wedding, but instead she's taken to the courtyard to die. Peony is certainly surprised by this turn of events. Were you? How does this moment affect Peony's future actions and her feelings about her family? How do you feel about this practice?

7. Many men have told Lisa See that they don't like the idea of the Chinese afterworld, where your relatives are still your relatives and your position remains the same as it was in life. Many women, on the other hand, have told her that they find the idea of the Chinese afterworld comforting. They want to be united with their families in the afterworld and *still* be able to interfere in the living world. What are the differences and similarities between the Chinese afterworld and Western religions' concept of heaven and hell? Which would you prefer—for yourself and for your loved ones—and why?

8. We see a difference in Peony's actions after Ze marries Ren and again after Ze dies. Do you see redemption here for Peony?

9. In what ways is mother love, from both a mother's perspective and a daughter's perspective, explored? What does Peony learn about mother love, and in what ways does she experience it herself? What aspects of mother love still hold true for mothers and daughters today?

10. How does what happened during the Cataclysm change depending on who's telling the story?

11. *Peony in Love* shows the strength of women and women's friendship, but in what ways does it also show the dark shadow side of women, whether in the women's chambers, between a mother and daughter, between wives, or even between friends?

12. *Peony in Love* is very much a tale of secrets and the power secrets can exercise over others. What are the secrets? Who is affected by the secrets and how do they change through the story?

13. You have read about three generations of women, and also about the people around them—both male and female. Of all the characters, which do you feel you are most like, and why? Are there any people like these characters in your life today?

14. Often what we hate most about ourselves—our weight, our tendency toward selfishness, our vanity, etc.— is what we are most critical

of in others. Trace the progress of Peony's relationship with Tan Ze—through life together in the Chen Family Villa and then in the afterlife. In what ways are Peony and Tan Ze alike, and in what ways are they different? Why do they need each other, and how do they serve one another? Do you have similar symbiotic relationships in your life, and in what ways would you expect those relationships to change in the afterlife?

15. How do Peony's experiences as a living girl and then as a hungry ghost parallel Liniang's experiences in *The Peony Pavilion*?

A Note on the Author

Lisa See is the author of the *New York Times* best-selling novel *Snow Flower and the Secret Fan*, *Flower Net* (an Edgar Award nominee), *The Interior,* and *Dragon Bones,* as well as the widely acclaimed memoir *On Gold Mountain.* The Organization of Chinese American Women named her the 2001 National Woman of the Year. She lives in Los Angeles. Visit the author's website at www.LisaSee.com.

A Note on the Type

This book was set in Bembo, a typeface based on an old-style Roman face that was used for Cardinal Bembo's tract *De Aetna* in 1495. Bembo was cut by Francisco Griffo in the early sixteenth century. The Lanston Monotype Machine Company of Philadelphia brought the well-proportioned letter forms of Bembo to the United States in the 1930s.